Curse of The Knight

The Untested Metal of The Knight

Pertunia Lehoka

Digital Edition published in 2025 by Tshibollo Group, South Africa.

Paperback Edition published in 2025 by Tshibollo Group, South Africa.

A catalogue record of this book is available at The National Library of South Africa – Pretoria Campus

Printed in Cape Town, South Africa.

For more information, or to book an event, contact: Pertunia Lehoka

maboemolehoka@gmail.com

www.pertunialehoka.co.za

www.amazon.com/stores/pertunia-lehoka/author

Book design and formatting by Pertunia Lehoka

Cover design by Khanyisile Lehoka of KKL Creative Solutions

ISBN: 978-0-620-92638-6 (e-book)
ISBN: 978-0-620-92637-9 (print)

First Edition: May 2025

C O N T E N T S

Dedication

To my family, without whom I'd be totally lost. Thank you for your patience during the time I was writing this book and had practically buried myself in it. Your support is what got me through all the difficult times. It's finally here now, in black and white – Curse of The Knight!

Curse of The Knight

Pertunia Lehoka

Prologue

Don't parents know that children tend to overhear the things that adults talk about? Well…, most of the time children do listen in. In the shadows of adulthood, secrets whispered among parents can shatter a child's world.

"We can't keep paying for her school fees," my father spat, his venomous tone piercing my soul. "She's too stupid for mainstream schooling. A corrective school is her only hope." His words hung in the air like a guillotine, waiting to sever my last thread of self-worth. "She is an embarrassment. This type of idiocy must run in your family, because there's definitely no failing in mine. This is a bloody waste of money, a disgrace!" he ended his rant.

I was that child, oblivious to the truth until the weight of my father's words crushed me.

My mother's quiet sobs and submissive replies fuelled my

father's rage. I felt his contempt like a slow-moving poison, infecting every cell of my being. The scar of his rejection ripped through my heart, leaving it dangling in tatters.

My father, my own father, angrily ended the conversation with my mother. I was terribly hurt, unable to fathom how my own father could speak such vile things about his own daughter, to his wife – my mother!

A phone call, I once overheard, now made sense. My father and his sister had discussed someone 'brain dead,' unable to do anything right. I realized, with a knot of nausea, that I was the subject of their ridicule.

Why didn't my mother defend me? Her silence was deafening, her tears a weak protest. I wondered if I was indeed 'brain dead,' or if my father's words were the poison that could kill.

With a deep breath, I gathered the shattered remnants of my heart and stepped into the unknown. The road ahead was long and uncertain, but I knew I had to escape the toxicity of my childhood. The question was, where would I find solace, and would I ever be able to heal?

Chapter 1

A Long Walk to Nowhere

A wondering mind, grime in my eyes, a hollow feeling in my gullet. I floated on air, unmindful of the dangers lurking around me. Walking on a long, fairly quiet road, I was accompanied by Blue Monarch Butterflies, as if they sensed my need for company that day, from any living creature.

One landed on my hair, as I slapped it, feeling remorseful only after the tiny creature tumbled off, its wing damaged. I considered ending its suffering, but its family hovered around me, and I hesitated, unsure of the consequences. They flew away, seemingly unconcerned, and I bet they knew their injured kin would soon re-grow its wing and join another family, perhaps in the nearby reforest.

"Sorry," I mumbled, continuing my journey to an unknown destination. Clouds gathered, threatening rain. I heard a car approaching, slowing down behind me. I stepped aside, assuming I was obstructing its path because I had not thumbed a lift. The car stopped, and I quickened my pace, afraid to face the driver. It was then that the reality of my actions hit me – leaving home in a huff, vulnerable and alone. I began sobbing, fearing the worst.

As a young woman, I was aware of the dangers that lurked in the shadows. The news had taught me that a woman walking alone was an easy target for predators. It was a harsh reality, one that I couldn't ignore. The car's engine roared to life, and I heard the sound of a German beast. I kept walking, though at a slower pace.

"Hello Sis," a baritone emanated from the car, startling me.

I turned around, trying to appear braver than I felt. "Hi," I responded, continuing my walk as the car kept pace with me.

"Are you alright? Can I give you a lift? Where are you going?" the man asked, his questions coming in rapid succession.

"Which question should I respond to first?" He smiled, as I faked bravery.

"Wow, for a moment there, I thought you weren't going to talk to me," he teased.

"Why would you think that?" I stopped walking, curious, as I became amazed at how I was beginning to feel at ease chatting to a stranger, while amply aware that my heart was still beating erratically and the possible danger I had placed myself in.

"Please get into the car; I'll take you to wherever you want to go. It's getting late and...," he paused, looking up to the sky, "it will soon rain and I won't really feel good about myself if I were to leave you out here by yourself, while unsure as to whether you will be safe or not."

The guy seemed like a guardian angel. *'He's concerned about my safety, yet he doesn't even know me?'* I wondered. *'Could he really be my saviour*?' He repeated his offer, breaking into my thoughts. "Sis, please get into the car; I'm one of the good ones, you know," he assured me. "I just want to see you safe and take you home or wherever you want to go. I swear, I won't try anything baleful," he added.

I hesitated, then opened up to him. "Fine, but just so you know, I'm nineteen years old and have run away from home. I don't know where I'm going at the moment. Perhaps I should go back home. But I'm hurting terribly right now and don't know what to do."

I looked at him warily, expecting him to react negatively or drive off. After all, I was unwanted baggage, the kind that nobody would want to take on. I could see pity written all over his face.

He turned off the engine, got out of the car, and walked around towards me. I shivered, noticing his gorgeous brown eyes. Okay, I admit it – he was strikingly handsome. His confident stride, expensive-looking faded blue jeans, navy blue and red striped shirt, and brown moccasins all screamed style and sophistication. I perused him quickly from head to toe and watched him do the same to me as well.

I, on the other hand, was dressed in my favorite sleeveless pink floral knee-length dress and tan sandals. I hadn't thought to grab a jacket or sweater, despite the ominous weather. The man's gaze swept over me, and I felt a flutter in my chest. When our eyes met, I felt a jolt of electricity.

"Please, don't be scared," he said, his voice deep and thrilling. "I'm not going to hurt you. What's wrong? You look very sad. Why are you crying?" His eyes seemed to bore into my soul, and I felt a lump form in my throat.

The man's medium dark chocolate and smooth skin tone was endearing; with patterned beard and a visibly new German hair cut.

He quickly invaded my space as I kept wrestling with my thoughts and pricked my eyes with his. "As I said, please relax, I'm not going to hurt you, I'm not that type of man."

"I'm scared; not only of you but I'm scared of being alone out here. I left home in a pant but now I realise that I shouldn't have done so," I muttered, demurely.

The man's aura was engulfing, but my feet couldn't stop wobbling and I truly was frightened. His scent was mesmerizing as well, and I found myself taking it in, closing my eyes, as if I was trying very hard not to allow the smell infusing my space to leave my person.

"My name is Martin," he greeted, extending his hand, and imploring me to shake his. I offered my hand in return. "What's your name?" he asked, but I hesitated, surprised that he wanted to know my name.

"You want to know my name?" I asked, feeling a sense of

wonder.

"Yes I do. I think that's only fair because I just told you mine." He smiled. "You seem hesitant to give me your name, why is that? Should I rather give you a name?" A smile played on my lips and I looked away.

"Oh My God, you have a very beautiful smile. In fact you are a very beautiful young woman," he breathed. His gaze remained intense, and I felt a blush rise to my cheeks.

"You don't mind me giving you a compliment do you, Lucia?" I chuckled.

"Oh, is that the name you've decided to give me? Lucia... really?" I rolled my eyes.

"You don't like the name? Well..., since you're refusing to tell me your name, we're gonna have to use Lucia until you decide to tell me your real name."

The guy was eccentric, as if he knew exactly what I needed at that moment. He made me smile, while I briefly forgot my afflictions, the kind that saw me leaving home – in fact running away from home, with nothing but the clothes on my body and shoes on my feet.

"So?" he raised his eyebrows.

"What do you mean so?"

"Are you coming with me or not?"

"I've already said it's okay Martin, I'll come with you even though I'm not sure I should," I responded impertinently, as I watched the man smile and opening the door to the SUV.

I climbed in and settled into the passenger seat. He hovered over me, his proximity making me feel uneasy. Perhaps he wanted me to notice his scent – it was a weird thought, but I couldn't shake it.

"I just want to help you fasten your seatbelt." He pulled the seatbelt, ran it across my chest and clicked it into its socket."

"Thank you," I whispered modestly, and as he fastened the seatbelt, his breath brushed against my chest, sending a shiver down my spine.

He closed the door and rounded the car. I took a deep breath, scanning the sleek interior of the SUV. The leather seats, gadgets, and luxurious trim all screamed sophistication. I'd never been inside an executive car like this before – a German Brute!

A nagging voice in my head warned me about getting into the car with a stranger. *'Are you sure you want to do this? You don't know him, but somehow, you trust him.'* I silenced the voice, telling myself this was a once-in-a-lifetime experience.

Martin interrupted my thoughts with my devout being, opened the door on his side and climbed in.

"Well, where am I taking you?"

"Your place," I mentioned hastily, and watched him widening his eyes and tilting his head.

"Are you sure? I mean, you told me that you were scared and now you want to go to my place?"

"You promised me that you are one of the good ones and that you won't hurt me. So, I choose to believe you. You were not lying to me, were you?"

Martin's expression turned serious. "No I was not lying to you but, are you sure about what you're saying…me taking you to my place?"

I felt a twinge of uncertainty. "Martin, is there any particular reason why I should be wary of going to your place? Now you're beginning to frighten me."

His eyes locked onto mine, and I sensed a hint of amusement. "No, Lucia don't be afraid. I just wanted to be sure that you know what you're getting yourself into."

The conversation was turning more and more bizarre.

"By the way, stop calling me Lucia, that's not my name. My name is Palesa. That's all you need to know for now. I'm serious…that's my name." He chuckled.

"So it didn't take long for me to break that wall you had erected around you, did it?"

"Which wall?" I shot back. "I just don't like that name you gave me. Anyway, why do you seem astonished that I'd like to go with you to your place? What do you think I want to do at your house? Please don't get any ideas; I simply want to go and sleep as I had a long and rough day. Then tomorrow, I will wake up and be on my way…please," I added, almost as an afterthought.

"Oh please…relax," he hastily replied. "I don't have any ideas, I promise you. Nice to meet you, Palesa. What's your surname?"

"I'd rather not say for now."

His eyebrows coiled and he simply said, "okay."

He started the engine and hit the accelerator. It was only at that time that I had a chance to look at the time – 18h00. I forced a cough.

"You feel a bit cold?" he asked.

"No, I'm fine; my throat is a bit scratchy, but I'm okay."

"Okay, Palesa, we are not going too far. I stay in a plot by myself, but there are other plots nearby so I'm not totally alone," he paused, perhaps awaiting input from me.

"Oh I see," I responded briefly.

The car fell silent, with only the sound of the engine and the occasional glance from Martin breaking the awkwardness. I could sense his eyes on me, but I didn't dare meet his gaze.

In about half an hour or so, I saw him signaling a right turn and I read the board on the side of the road..., 'LEBOYA HOMESTEAD'. Curiosity got the better of me and I had to ask.

"Are you Leboya? I mean, is your surname Leboya?" He chortled, a hint of smugness on his face.

"Right the first time," he responded, his tone haughty. It was as if he was saying, '*if you only knew who I am and what I really possess.*' I don't know why I got that feeling but I really felt it.

As we drove up to the house, a figure emerged from the shadows. He rushed to open the garage door using a remote control and greeted Martin with a high-pitched tone, "Good evening, Sir." I raised an eyebrow inwardly. 'Sir?' This must be a very important person.

"Good evening Mos, is all okay?"

“Yes Sir, everything is fine, no problem at all,” the man replied.

They continued to exchange a few words before Martin could drive the car into the garage. He switched off the engine and turned to me, his gawk lingering. It was as if he was savouring the moment. He took my right hand and kissed the upper part. "Martin, what was that for?" I shivered.

"Apologies, this is just to thank you that today I won't be sleeping alone... in the house, I mean. Amos has his own cottage a few meters from the house," he explained, pointing to a nearby cottage. I could see some light flickering at the direction he was pointing at.

“How many rooms have you got?” I had to ask. I must admit, his statement shook me a bit, even though I could see that the house was quite massive.

“I have five bedrooms; a kitchen…,” he paused. “Do you really want me to tell you about every room in the house? Let’s go in and I’ll take you on a tour and then you can count the amount of rooms yourself.”

I tried to unfasten the seatbelt but Martin beat me to it. He gazed at me, as if it was the first time he laid his eyes on me – or on a woman. He touched me on my hand and an eerie feeling shot my body in half.

“Your hands feel so soft; do you even do a bit of work at home?”

Home! Did he just mention home? I got slightly distressed

when he said that and hurriedly asked him to finish disengaging my seatbelt.

Somehow, I know he saw my expression because he paused, eyes wide. "Sorry… I didn't mean to upset you. I know you said you'll tell me later what happened…when you're ready that is."

"I already told you I ran away from home so please… no talk about home, at least not tonight. I'll see how I wake up tomorrow, then I'll let you in on what's happening in my life."

"Okay, that's fine." He asked me to remain in the car, while he got out and walked around it. He then came to my side of the seat and opened the door for me. '*What am I, a princess*?' I asked myself. '*Perhaps you are who knows*?' My inner person tapped me on my back, making me smile at least, after chastising me earlier.

"Thank you; I feel so important right now."

"Of course you are important, you are a very important guest - welcome home."

'*Did he just commit that offence again? Home*?' That nearly freaked me out again but I indulged him just one indiscretion. After all, that wasn't my home he was referring to, it was his home. So I guess he was simply referring to my home for the night. That wasn't so bad, was it?

When I eventually got out, I nearly fell as the model of that SUV wasn't making it easy for me to land easily on my feet. This led me to fall in his husky arms and for some reason, he felt the need to hug me or rather cling onto me as if I had indeed fallen.

"Okay… okay, thanks," I slightly rebuked him and smoothed

my dress down. “I’m fine,” I stated.

“Are you always this uptight?” he gurgled.

“Uptight? Me?” I looked away, as Bra Mos interrupted that soon to be awkward conversation. Not a moment too soon because that brought some reprieve to me.

“Good evening ma’m,” he greeted me. I was taken aback by the older man's warmth, and Martin's question still lingered in the air.

“Good evening Bra Mos…, I heard Martin mentioning your name.” He smiled.

“Mos, please take the stuff out of the boot. Where’s Lulama?”

I wondered who this one could be now. It looked like I would keep meeting his family one by one. Well…, Bra Mos was clearly a helper of some kind but who was Lulama?

“She has already gone to her cottage Sir. Should I call her?”

“No, I was just asking; just let her be. After all, she has knocked off. Just tell her not to come in tomorrow though, I have a guest and I’ll tend to her by myself. There was no one in the house the whole day except her, so I doubt the house will be dirty by tomorrow,” Martin asserted authoritatively.

“Yes Sir, I’ll tell her after I have put this stuff in the kitchen.” Bra Mos took one box full of food and some grocery bags out and got in the kitchen, through the door from the garage.

“Come let’s go in,” Martin motioned to me to follow him into the house.

He then held me by my hand and I let him, as I had no idea

why he did what he did. I saw Bra Mos looking at us censoriously, as if he wanted to say something but couldn't.

"Can I help with packing the stuff in the fridge Sir?"

"There's still some more in the boot Mos, please also take my medical bag out."

'*A medical bag? Who exactly is this guy? A doctor that stays alone in such a huge house*?' I wondered, as I allowed myself to be led into the house.

As I got in, I saw beautiful architecture right through, more like a cut out from some of the Top Luxury Magazines. Everything seemed like a huge thought went into it. From the glossy fawn marble tiles with gold patterns, to the wall, to the windows, up to and including high end furnishings, everything looked really pricey.

The kitchen was huge and it was fitted with modern appliances.

All I could do was to keep remarking, "mmm..."

"Do you like it?" He brought me back to the tour, while Bra Mos was coming in and out, packing food in the fridge and some grocery in the cupboards.

"Of course, what's there not to like about the house? This is massive and extremely beautiful. This makes me wonder why one would stay alone in a mansion like this one."

He slanted his head, as if to give me a sign that he didn't want to tell me his story then. Somehow I got it.

"Mos, when you're done, you can go. Have a good night. Oh…, don't forget to tell Lulama not to come in tomorrow; all is well here."

"I won't forget, Sir; Good night miss...," he paused.

"Palesa," I spoke up, taking the man out of his misery.

Eventually, Bra Mos left and I could see some kind of relief on Martin's face, as if there was something he never wanted the man to see or take heed of. I got a weird vibe that kept nagging me, refusing to leave. I didn't know what to make of it. I did get a sense that Martin was not really what he was presenting himself to be. Perhaps he was a good guy in a way; but a good guy with certain bloodcurdling flaws.

Martin held my hand while closing the kitchen door that Bra Mos had left open - probably deliberately. I then heard footsteps and I knew that it had to have been the man running away. I got the feeling that he wanted to listen in on our conversation. I could see that something was bothering the man – his expression was unsettled.

Martin then led me to the living room, a few feet away from the kitchen. The whole house boasted a well designed open plan setting with high ceilings. All I could do was to keep nodding and making agreeable sounds to acknowledge the ambience of the place and to also praise Martin for his house.

White sofas that made an L-shape in the huge living room, a shiny huge kiaat built-in TV unit, and a massive curved TV on it - about 200 inches, each side adorned by huge sound speakers, added to the grandeur of the living room.

As I was still admiring the gadgets, Martin took a remote

control from the decorated marble Italian Coffee Table in the middle of the room and switched the TV on. What a sound that TV or rather the speakers produced! He then directed me to sit down, eventually letting go of my hand.

"Thank you," I whispered, and then smoothed my hand on my dress. It had Martin's sweat and mine as he had been lacing our fingers together, ever since we got to the house.

"You must be hungry. What would you like to eat?"

"I don't know what you have. I can eat anything really. I am not picky," I stated.

"Come on, don't be afraid to tell me what you want, I can even cook something from scratch," he alleged.

"Oh no, please don't do that, not for me please don't. It's late anyway and I did say that I can eat anything."

"Okay, I hear you Palesa; I won't go all out. I'll check what's in the fridge. Do you want to come with me?"

"No, can I please rest in here. I'd like to watch TV if you don't mind."

"Okay, let me fix you something to drink in the meantime then. What would you like to drink? Please don't tell me that you can drink anything…," he smiled.

"If you've got some juice, I'd like some please."

"Coming right up." He immediately left to go to the kitchen to fix me something to drink, coming back in about five minutes or so.

He brought the juice he poured in a tall crystal glass with some ice cubes inside, placed on a beautiful white saucer.

"Here...," he handed it to me.

"Thank you very much." I carefully grabbed the saucer and touched the glass, noting that it was really cold.

I then took the first gulp, satisfied with the contents. I smirked as I watched him standing there, as if he was waiting for me to acknowledge that he made me the best juice ever!

"Delicious juice, thank you. I can't get the taste but there are remnants of some fruits inside. What is it?" I curiously asked.

"It's mixed fruits. I squeeze every fruit I can think of in the morning in one of the juice extracting machines in the kitchen. Then I put the concoction in the fridge so that when I come back from work, I would have something really healthy and cold to drink."

He gave me so much information I didn't ask about. However, I felt that it was okay as I was probably going to eventually ask whether the juice was freshly squeezed or not. '*Could it be he read my mind*?' I questioned myself.

"Oh, I see. Thank you," I said.

He reached for the sideboard at the foyer, opened a drawer and took out a small round placemat. He put it on the coffee table, motioning me to put the glass on it. '*Mmm... neat freak!*' I inwardly remarked.

I was amazed at the white leather sofas though, wondering if his helper ever gets into trouble should there be any stains that she might have missed or even battle to take out. I was and am still very afraid of white colour – of anything.

"Please be free, this is your home," he declared, staggering me with his proclamation.

"Come on Martin, my home really? I'm just here for the night and I'll be on my way tomorrow. Perhaps I should go back home tonight."

"How are you gonna get home at this time of the night? I'm certainly not taking you," he laughed. "Besides, wherever one lays their head, that's their home. Remember Paul Young once said that?"

"Who's Paul Young?" I revealed my age. But then again, I had already told him how old I was.

"Oh sorry, I forgot you did tell me how old you are. Paul Young is an old school musician; a very brilliant lyricist of note. Anyway, let me not bore you with the details. I'm not that old you know," he revealed.

"How old are you Martin?" I asked bluntly.

"Ah…, I knew you were going to ask that question. Like I said I'm not that old; I'm 35 years young," he responded without hesitation.

"Oh I see," I said, picking up my juice and gobbled it down, fully aware that the man had begun gaping at me again, this time even weirder than before.

"I trust you are content with my age huh?" What on earth did he mean by that? I opened my eyes wide, a bit dazed by that question.

"Why wouldn't I be content with your age? That's not a

problem; it is your age, unless I don't understand why you're asking me that question."

He sat down next to me and held my hand again, while I put the glass on the table.

"Martin, what is it you want to say to me exactly? I thought you were going to the kitchen to make food."

"Nothing is wrong but I just want to be honest with you Palesa. When I saw you earlier, there was a voice in my heart that told me not to leave you there, and that you were the one." He struggled to meet my gaze, his voice trembling.

"The one who does what Martin?"

"The one I should be with, as my girlfriend, as my wife eventually," he blurted, his eyes darting around the room.

I stood up from where I was sitting, squeezed my hand out of his and looked at him. How dare he say that!

"So this inner voice told you this in the two hours we have been together? That's uncanny. How many women have you done this to? Stop taking me for a fool. Were you driving around looking for your next conquest? So, you want me to believe that you are not married and don't even have a girlfriend?"

I was not only bemused but I felt some kind of rage emanating from deep within my belly, as I remembered what he said on the road; '*I promise... I will not try anything with you.*' The nerve of that man; he lied – bloody pervert!

"Don't get upset please, Palesa. I swear, I'm not trying to deceive you."

He stood up and walked towards me. He then tried to grab me by my shoulder. I shrugged and denied him the delight.

"LET GO OF ME!" I yelled, shivering incessantly. "Why did you lie to me? You said you were not going to try anything with me. So, are you gonna keep me here as your slave?" He took a step back, looking affronted by my outburst. But the bloody conceited bustard wouldn't let up!

"Oh my God, you're angry. The fire in your eyes makes me want to be with you even more. You definitely are the one – no doubt about it. There was only one other woman who could call me out…in fact there were two. It was my mother and my sister."

He took a few more steps back, as I saw his face becoming slightly morose. I calmed down a bit after noticing that.

"Martin, you said 'were', does it mean your mother and sister are no longer alive?" He looked at me, eyes glum.

"Do you really want me to tell you my story after yelling at me like that? Now I'm the one who is scared of you – I swear," he alleged.

"Come on, you told me on the road that you will not try anything with me, yet here you are, telling me that you think I'm the one and that you want me to be your girlfriend. Who wouldn't be upset about that? Besides, how do I know that since you feel this way now, you won't try anything else like forcing yourself on me?

"You have my word, Palesa. I know you don't know me but I swear on my mother's grave, I am not that type of man. All I want from you is love."

"Love? Isn't that a bit premature?"

"Oh, so you know about relationships, I see. Have you got a boyfriend?"

"No, Martin I don't have a boyfriend but that doesn't mean I'd like you to be one either. You are way older than me and I bet you have had quite a bit of life experience while I'm still finding my feet. Maybe you even have children."

"I don't have children and age ain't nothing but a number, Palesa, don't you know that?" He smiled as I shook my head, returning to my seat.

"About your mom and sister…have they passed away?"

"Yes…" he took a deep breath. "They are no longer alive. It's a long story though and very depressing. I cannot share that with you yet regarding how they died, as that hurts me terribly and I might just end up crying and won't even stop," he stated, while I watched his eyes becoming teary.

"I'm sorry Martin for your loss; I really am. Please don't cry." I then hugged him and patted him on his back. He welcomed the embrace fervently and began sobbing, literally like a little boy and hugging me tightly.

"Martin please, don't cry like this. I had no idea you have faced something this painful in your life." He eventually composed himself and apologized for falling apart like that in front of me.

"It's okay Martin, don't worry about it. What I'm faced with might be horrible but I doubt it comes close to what you're going through. Did they pass away recently?" I asked.

"No, it's been ten years now but I tell you now Palesa, it still feels like yesterday. Actually it happened on this day exactly ten years ago. My parents and my little sister had just dropped me off at the university after the holidays, as it was my second year at medical school. As my father reversed the car from the parking lot, after they all waved me goodbye, a drunk student came from nowhere, driving at the most horrible speed in that parking lot and hit them so hard, sending my little sister and my mom flying out of their windows. He also hit other cars that were parked there." He paused and began weeping, this time more than before. He continued sniffing, pulled out his handkerchief from his pocket and wiped his tears.

"My father survived, barely," he continued. "He spent a considerable amount of time in hospital as the collision had left him with a very bad concussion and they had to induce coma on him for about two months. When he came out of it, he was no longer the same and was in a catatonic state at an institution for a very long time, until a few years ago," he sighed as he continued. "He finally departed earth as well. So yeah…, I'm an orphan and that's my story in a nutshell," he concluded, looking at me as if to beg me not to leave him alone that night.

I felt really bad that I had earlier rebuked him. Did he just manipulate me? I had forgotten that the man had declared some discomfited love to me.

"Oh my God Martin, please stop; you don't have to tell me anymore, as I can see that this is weighing heavily on you; I'm really sorry. I didn't mean to yell at you. You just gave me a bit of a fright after you had earlier affirmed that you wouldn't try anything with me but suddenly turned around and did exactly the opposite," I mentioned remorsefully for some strange reason.

He wiped his tears again and pulled his breath. I was still very curious and wanted to ask him more questions about the accident and its aftermath, particularly where he was concerned but, I decided to shelve it for another time.

The information itself was too heavy for a teenager like me and I had no idea how to deal with it, let alone deal with him in that state. I offered to prepare food for us and he welcomed the gesture.

I then went to the kitchen and tried washing my hands, but the tap was too sophisticated and a bit difficult to operate. I had no choice but to call Martin to come and help me. He came at once still wiping his tears, while breathing heavily, pulling his breath and releasing it often.

"Whoa..., that was hectic!" he exhaled. "I don't know what it is about you, Palesa, but truly speaking, I have no idea how I managed to tell you that after such a long time of having kept it to myself. I haven't been able to release my pain like I just did to anyone, not even the psychotherapist that was trying to help me deal with the trauma." My eyeballs dilated from the shock.

I kept quiet and felt as if Martin was just trying to manipulate me to feel sorry for him, even though I did indeed feel sorry for the man. I felt him placing a very heavy responsibility on my shoulders already; that of helping him deal with his trauma. If therapists had failed, what was it about me that he felt I could do for him or that I managed to do for him, allowing him to fall apart like that and ultimately releasing a little bit of his pain?

No one should have to suffer such a horrible fate at once, losing both a mother and a sister and then a father who died in the condition he was in. That was horrible and something not to even wish on one's worst enemy.

"What's the problem?" he asked.

"I'm battling to open the tap; how does it work?"

"Let me show you. You put your hands underneath and just press either this red or blue button, depending on whether you want hot or cold water." He pointed at the upper part of the tap. "If however you simply want warm water, just press both buttons at the same time and then you release. See…piece of cake. Then you press them again when you want the tap to stop," he concluded the training, bearing a smirk.

"Wow," I remarked, "why did you elect to install such difficult to use furnishings?"

"Oh well…," he smiled and shrugged but ignored my question. "What are you making for us?" he asked.

"I was thinking that perhaps we can just have sandwiches. I'll check what you have in the fridge. On second thought, perhaps you can open the fridge in the meantime; I can see that all your fixtures need a manual of some kind. What have you got?"

"You'll get used to them, don't worry."

What was prompting Martin to keep speaking to me as if we

had an agreement that I would stay with him for a long time? I was just there for a day; in fact for the night. Because of his earlier display, I elected not to ask him as to why he kept talking like I was there to stay.

I was not aware that I had begun doing an injustice to myself and was likely to be sucked into whatever it was he was still to heal from. I was somehow drawn to him and on the other hand, I felt that I also needed to be around someone who didn't judge me; someone who saw the worth of having me around.

He opened the fridge and took out a container that had grated mozzarella and he asked me if I ate ham, to which I affirmed. He then took it out, all sliced and in a glass container as well, ready to be placed on slices of bread. I could see that he still wanted to take out more cold meat. I carefully asked him to just take out margarine so we can make simple sandwiches.

"Oh, you don't want something elaborate to eat?" he asked.

"No, I don't... this is enough for me."

He slanted his head and giggled. I have no idea what that chuckle was about. He then took out some plates, rinsed them and then wiped them.

We made sandwiches together while he kept stealing every moment to drool over me. I wondered then, what it was that was making it difficult for me to rebuke him like I did the last time. Could it have been the fact that he wept? Was I afraid to see him crying again or did I somehow feel responsible for him? Why would the universe place such a huge burden on my shoulders at my age? I was a child for Pete's sake!

"Give them to me." He extended both his hands so I could give him the sandwiches, while I took a few minutes to clean up the breadcrumbs from the surfaces and then deposited them in a dustbin next to the door. At least that was not difficult to operate. He then went to the dining room and came back again to fix us some drinks and to refill my juice.

"Come, let's go eat; you must be starving because I know I am," he instructed and I followed him to the dining room, which was also part of the open living area.

His furniture all around the house was impeccable and every colour scheme he used was in harmony; from the white couches to the fawn and brown dining chairs and the eight seater marble top table. Everything blended seamlessly.

"We can sit in here." He pulled out a chair for me.

"Thank you," I said, as I sat down, his hand brushing against my shoulders as he pushed it in. The touch sent shockwaves down my spine. He then leaned in, his lips grazing my neck, and I felt a rush of excitement mixed with fear.

I froze, unsure of how to react, as the sensation running through my veins felt weird. Martin, seemingly oblivious to my discomfort, took his seat and began eating his sandwich.

"Why did you kiss me on my neck Martin?" I asked, as I began eating my sandwich.

"I just wanted to thank you for helping me release my emotions today. You have a way of making me feel at ease." I smiled, even though I was feeling a sense of unease.

“I don’t know what exactly it is that you’re thanking me for honestly but whatever I did to make you this relaxed, you’re welcome, I guess.”

We continued eating and stealing glances at each other, as the sound of music drifted from the TV. The tension between us was palpable, and I couldn't shake the feeling that Martin's actions were more than just a simple thank you.

CHAPTER 2

Tacit Truths

"So, are you gonna tell me why you ran away from home?" Martin asked, catching me off-guard. I figured that I might as well tell him, as he had already allowed himself to be vulnerable to me. So, he was unlikely to judge me. I thought to myself.

"I haven't been happy at home for a long time. My father abuses my mother. I don't know why she doesn't leave him. All she does is to cry when he's becoming abusive with his words." I spoke quickly and Martin widened his eyes, looking shocked and nearly choked on his bread.

"And now you left her alone with him? Was that a wise move?" Now that was unexpected. I thought he didn't want me to leave his place?

"What do you mean, Martin? What could I have done?" I

shrugged. "He always does this but today was a different day; he was worse, tearing into me also." Tears ran down my cheeks.

"How so?" he asked, as inquisitive as ever. I had no choice but to indulge him, to also offload my demons onto him.

"He didn't only insult his wife but...," I recessed, watching as he listened to me attentively. I then related to him everything my father said to my mother, while I was listening and also everything that he had ever said to her and to me.

"I have never witnessed him hit my mother but, he is always yelling at her, calling her stupid and insulting her family. He is a very bad man and I don't even know that he truly is my father. He has also called me stupid more than once."

I sobbed and Martin got up, asking me to stop crying and not to tell him anymore. Did he just do what I did for him earlier? I guess he did.

"Okay, this is not a good day. Let's stop with all these depressing stories. I see why you left home. However, I am still worried about your mother though. Don't you think your father might hurt her if you don't go back? I know people like that; my father was one of them," he sighed.

"Martin, you did say we must stop talking about depressing stories. I feel a bit heavy right now."

"Sorry, but I was just mentioning how he sounds so much like my father. One moment he would be happy as a kid, the next he would start yelling at us without any real reason. That day of the accident, we travelled all the way from home to the university with him moaning about one thing or another. He was a monster and I say so because like you, I witnessed his bullying first hand. Perhaps the difference between him and your dad is that he did lay his hands on my mom."

Martin was visibly still distraught as he narrated the painful story of his upbringing.

"You know, I don't know if my dad has ever laid his hands on my mother or not because most of the time, I would be out, either at school or with some friends. What I do know though, is that my mother complains of her back all the time and that her body is always sore. Do you think he could deliberately be avoiding her face, knowing that no one would see her bruises?" I asked.

It was surprising how free both Martin and I were, when speaking about our unhappy childhood – well, I was still a teenager but boy, did I feel as if I had already lived a lifetime with that kind of horrible treatment both my mom and I were subjected to!

I have no idea why my father was always that angry. I asked myself everyday as to why my mother chose to live in that kind of environment.

I recall a time when I pleaded with her that we should pack our stuff and leave. She flatly refused; even chastised me for suggesting such a thing or even thinking it. She told me that there was no way she could leave my dad as he needed her.

I had no idea then, why my mother felt that a monster like that needed her, when it was vivid that he was doing everything in his power to get her to leave him instead.

I told Martin everything about my feelings for both my mother and my father and he kept quiet and really listened to me, while imploring me to not tell him anymore.

All these revelations took place while we were eating. Before we knew it we had finished our food and finished our drinks. Martin refilled my juice and his as well.

"Do you see what I was saying earlier about this being engineered by a higher power?" he stared at me and I shook my head, skeptical of his proclamation.

"Martin, this is a coincidence. I doubt it's that deep," I chuckled.

"Trust me, this is bigger than both of us, I promise you," he swiftly stated, as I watched him extend his hand towards me, entreating me to get up and go with him to the kitchen.

He stood up first and came to my chair as I was just getting up and helped pull the chair out. I felt his breath on my neck again and was well aware that he wanted to steal another kiss. I then coughed, prompting him to retreat and he did.

We then went to the kitchen and he asked me to just sit with him while he washed the dishes.

Although he had a dishwasher in the scullery, he told me that he hardly ever uses it because to him, it wastes water and time. He told me that he preferred to wash with his hands.

We spoke for a bit, while he also told me about the house and how he had always wanted to live in opulence.

"Martin, what do you do for a living? I heard you tell Bra Mos to take out your medical bag. Are you a doctor?" I asked candidly.

"Yes, I am a doctor; I'm a Specialist Physician, Palesa. I enjoy my work very much and although I consider myself successful, I just cannot seem to find a good woman to share my life with. I am truly hoping that you would give me a chance - give us a chance… I mean," he added.

"I cannot believe you are still on that subject, Martin. How many women have you dated since you started this dating journey? In fact, how many women have you picked up on the road and brought here? Have you been married before?"

He looked at me and gave me a half smile.

"No, I have never been married I swear," he responded, electing to answer the last question first. "I have been with a couple of women…but obviously not at the same time. It's clear that those relationships were not meant to be," he sighed, placing the last dish in the cupboard. We kept quiet and I watched him drain the water out and pour more water in to wash the dishcloths.

It was evident that he was doing something that he was used to doing and was not finding it difficult at all or considered it a big chore.

"What about you? Have you got a boyfriend? I did ask earlier."

"I don't know what to call him. He's just a guy I went to school with but, since he left me in grade 10 and is now in grade 12, I haven't seen much of him. That's all I can tell you about relationships if you consider that one.

"Okay, so do you still have feelings for him?"

I observed how he ignored what I told him about the guy leaving me in grade 10. He seemed not to have been bothered by the fact that I had been failing, if my peers could leave me in the grade I was in.

“No Martin, you first. Do you still miss all the women you were with?”

“Okay, if you insist, then the answer is no. I do not miss any of those girls. None of those relationships were real anyway. I bet you want to know why they ended?”

He rinsed the dishcloths and hung them on one of the rails in the kitchen.

“Come now; let’s go to the living room.”

“Before we go, where is the guest toilet?”

“Oh, let me show you because if I were to direct you, you might just get lost and start yelling again; ‘Martin, Martin, I need help!’” he teased me, making a squeaky sound.

“Oh, really now Martin, I didn’t say that,” I shook my head.

As he was about to respond by taunting me again, we reached the toilet.

“Here is the guest toilet. Must I show you how everything works?”

“Martin, I need to pee. Please leave before my bladder does the unthinkable,” I mentioned and watched him laugh at me. It looked like I had also become very relaxed around the man.

After finishing my business in the restroom, I told myself that there was no way I was going to call Martin to come and help with the flushing; I had to learn the system very fast. It wasn't so difficult to operate as there was a lever – a bit sophisticated, but not difficult to operate. So, I simply pulled it down. I then saw a basin whose tap mechanisms looked more or less similar to the ones in the kitchen. I recalled that I had earlier undergone a mini instruction regarding the mechanisms.

I managed to use everything in the bathroom unaided and somehow that pleased me. I then went back to Martin and found him dancing and singing along to Darion Frasier's '*That's All I'll Ever Ask.*' – speakers almost full blast now! Well, he was full of surprises.

"I love that song," I declared, while dancing slowly but his odd and deep gaze brought bashfulness from me. So I stopped dancing.

"Come now Palesa, why are you stopping?" I smiled.

"I can't really dance but I can move."

"Same thing; I can see you can dance though." I simply chuckled, even though I desperately wanted to dance.

"Oh, so you also know good music?" he continued. "Look here…"

He pressed one button on the built in cupboard, revealing a massive collection of CD's and DVD's. I might have been young then but I loved and appreciated grown up music. I guess I have always been an old soul. I was very impressed, even though I had thought that since he had such sophisticated appliances in his home, he wouldn't still be having CD's and DVD's in his house. He was still old school.

I walked closer towards him and checked his collection out and remarked at the incredible set. He was pleased and simply looked at me and continued singing along…

'*Tell me your dreams, so they can be mine too,*
Let me be there to help them come true
Tell me your fears when you feel afraid
Come to my arms, let me rock them away
That's all I'll ever ask
That's all I'll ever ask
That's all I'll ever ask
Of you……'

The man sure knew his music and sang pretty well. He was dancing, swinging his hips from side to side, while extending his hands towards me, imploring me to dance with him. Although I really wanted to, I elected not to show him my dancing prowess. His enticing moves and hazy eyes were suggestive though.

"Palesa, that's all I ask and will ever ask of you. Please give us a chance." His puppy eyes, almost suppliant, were not a pretty sight and a bit pitiable for a man of his stature.

"Martin, we will talk about this tomorrow if you are not going early to work. But right now I need to ask you for something please because it is very late."

"You can ask me anything, Palesa, anything at all," he held, looking at me intensely.

"Can you please lend me your old T-Shirt that you no longer

use so I can sleep in it?" I asked decorously.

"Of course I'll give you but tomorrow, we have to buy you some clothes. In fact, we can order some stuff online tonight that can be delivered tomorrow," he suggested.

"No, Martin, that won't be necessary. Besides, I'm leaving tomorrow aren't I? I'll wash my undergarments when I'm about to sleep and then I'll just wear your T-Shirt." *Oops, did I just say that*!

Martin virtually stood still, looking very pale for a man of his complexion. I could see his pupils dilating at an incredible momentum and his mouth trembled, as I also stood still after I had carelessly provided him with a picture of a bare Palesa. What on earth was I thinking?

"Do you see what you've just done, Palesa? Now you have made me picture you with nothing on. Are you teasing me? Did you do that on purpose?" He asked, seriously demanding an answer from me.

"No… no… no…, Martin, I swear I didn't do that on purpose; I'm sorry. That was my moment of foolishness I guess. Perhaps this is why my father liked calling me stupid. I sometimes don't think when I say something and just blurt it out. I truly apologise."

"If there is one thing you should never do, Palesa, is to ever apologise for the way God made you. Never ever call yourself stupid, please. You are a very unique person and you belong here with me. This is why I don't want you to leave. I can teach you a lot of things without ever judging you for struggling to understand much."

He walked closer towards me, and held both my hands. "What do you say?"

"Martin, I need to sleep... please. We can talk about the teachings tomorrow. Please show me where I'll be sleeping." I carefully asked, as I felt that bizarre feeling again. My legs quivered when he looked at me and a very bad headache ensued.

"Okay."

"Martin, I do not feel too good; I have a headache. Please just show me where I should sleep and bring that T-Shirt… please," I mentioned.

"Okay, let's go."

He switched off the theatre system and directed me to the passage, leading upstairs. We ascended the most gorgeous marble staircase there ever was, and fancy polished steel balustrades to go with.

We passed three bedrooms and he told me that they were guest bedrooms and we reached another one that was visibly bigger than the rest. It was grandly decorated and I asked him why it was different from the others. There were two huge portraits of an older woman on the wall and another one of what appeared to be a family picture.

"Is this your mom?" I pointed at one of the big portraits.

"Yes it's my mom. She was a very beautiful woman – inside and outside. This is my sister and this is me…," he pointed at the other picture (a family picture) and carefully neglected to say anything about the man who was with them in the photo. I assumed that was his dad.

He told me that he always felt as if his mother would somehow return and he would then accommodate her in that room, hence the big portraits he had in the room. That information freaked me out a bit. '*What if his mother's ghost does indeed visit and sleeps in here often*? Do ghosts even sleep?' I laughed at myself.

****

"This is where you will sleep, next to my bedroom. I'm giving you this room to sleep in so that I can hear you should you have a bad dream or something and start shouting again, 'Martin…Martin…Martin,'" he taunted again, this time laughing out loud.

'*This man is actually immature, I swear he is*.' I thought.

"Why would I have bad dreams Martin? Does your mom visit at night?" I asked brusquely. I mean, what on earth did he mean about bad dreams?

"Wow! Are you extrasensory? You know, I have always believed that my mom does visit at night whooo…," he chortled, lifting his hands up trying to scare me, while I made no attempt to join him in that bewildering laughter and that not so funny joke. I was freaked out and he saw my expression and stopped laughing.

"That's not funny, Martin. Please, I'd like to use one of the other rooms if this one is that sentimental to you. I don't mind."

"No, Palesa, you will use this one because it's right next to mine. Unless you'd like to come to my room if you're that apprehensive?" He grinned.

"In your dreams!" I said hastily.

"Okay then, you will sleep in here. Let me fetch your 'pyjama' for the evening."

He left me in the massive bedroom which to me, looked like it could be the main bedroom. It boasted a large fancy queen sized solid oak sleigh bed with a brown leather padded headboard and two huge pedestals.

The fawn and tan designer curtains were striking, patterned with gold shimmer and flowers, showing that they were made specifically for that particular bedroom. Material looked deliberately ruffled, but grandly woven. You could swear that the house was definitely not a man cave but a beautiful dwelling that had been touched by a woman's hands.

However, judging by how impeccably he had behaved earlier, I reasoned that it was probably all his doing.

I sat down on the chesterfield occupying a corner of the bedroom and continued to glance around. I then heard footsteps. Martin came back in, holding a couple of things in his hands including a vanity case.

"I remember being given these things as a gift by some company that was marketing its lingerie brand to me a while back, to give to a special person in my life. I didn't want to be rude but I just took these items and when I came back home, I simply put them in the closets till today. So I guess you are that person." He smiled and seemed to marvel at the timing.

I was not convinced and had to frankly ask, “Is that really the truth, Martin? Are these not the nighties you bought for a woman who later dumped you?”

“No!” he said hurriedly. “I assure you, these were gifts; in fact, marketing samples. Besides, no one dumps me!” What did that mean?

He sat with me on the divan and unzipped the plastic bag, revealing the most gorgeous black satin night dress and its mantle. He then took out some underwear which matched the two items and held out a small vanity case which had expensive looking skin products, judging by their packaging. The interesting part was that everything was my size, as if the items were bought for me.

“Martin, I wash with Cetaphil on my face and simply apply moisturising cream. Don’t you have aqueous cream? I don’t know what these things will do to my skin if I use them. I’d like to have a good night sleep, without having to worry about any allergic reactions etc.” There I was, a guest making special demands.

“Okay, I just brought them so you can have a wider choice. I doubt these products contain any suspect ingredients though. I have checked them, they have all natural products. But it’s up to you,” he concluded.

“Okay thank you Martin; I really appreciate this. I will take a shower and then go to sleep. Good night,” I said swiftly, keen to see him leave the room.

He invaded my space again as I was attempting to get up from the couch, held my hands and asked me to sit down a bit.

"Palesa, have a good night. Please think about what I said to you. What happened today was not a coincidence. I really want to be with you and I want you terribly right now. I know it is the first time we met but I swear, I feel differently and at peace with you here. We will talk about other things tomorrow."

I was petrified when Martin declared that he wanted me. That meant that he had wanted me ever since he saw me on the road. I felt powerless to say anything to thwart what he had declared to me, but simply nodded, letting out a single word, "Okay."

While he still held my hands after having practically forced me down the couch again, he gawked at me intensely. I felt my heart thrashing rapidly once more and I closed my eyes.

When I opened them, Martin's face had raided mine, his lips just a fraction away. He then cupped my cheeks with both his hands and gave me a lingering kiss on my lips. Afraid to say 'no,' I obliged.

Weirdly, I loved that kiss but didn't want it then, not at that time anyway. That doesn't even make sense to admit the two proclamations.

I had never been kissed by a man before. My stomach growled and that headache started pounding again. I stood up and wobbled on my feet, falling right into Martin's hands.

He wasted no time but to utilise that moment to consume my lips. This time, I tried to push him away but he wouldn't hear any of it. He was too strong, not at all allowing me the opportunity to disentangle myself from his clutches.

He pulled me towards him and pinned me against the wall, touching me all over, breathing heavily. I felt weak to say anything, shivering. I was terrified he was about to force himself on me.

"Come on, Palesa relax, all I want to do is to kiss you. You responded to my first kiss with vigour, so what's the problem now?"

Did he really say I responded? I never said no but that didn't mean I wanted him to kiss me again. Should I have shouted, or should I have yelled at him? I kept having mini bouts of fear each time I felt like telling him off.

"Martin, I'm uncomfortable about this. Please don't do this," I begged him.

"I won't do anything else I promise, unless you want me to. I just want to kiss you. Your mouth is so smooth and inviting."

I trembled and he kissed me again, forcing my lips open with his tongue, while he still had me pinned against the wall. I felt his hard groin against my front and jerked backwards. He pulled me close again, forcing my body to rub against his.

A man's tongue in my mouth – that was the first for me! I didn't know what to do with my tongue but I held on for as long as I could, as my fear intensified, worried that he might reveal his true colours and hurt me. He rubbed himself against me persistently as I stood there frozen, trying to take his tongue out of my mouth but failed dismally.

I felt very strange, petrified and quivering at the same time.

Something told me that he must have told himself that I owed him for having been a Good Samaritan, who saved me from myself or from possible danger on the road.

After a little while, he pulled his tongue out and gaped at me again, as I was about to cry from being troubled of what he intended to do to me. He saw my watery eyes and kissed me on my forehead.

“I'm not going to hurt you, Palesa, I swear. I told you I am not that kind of man that hurts women. Please just say you will be my girlfriend, please say it.”

He forced me to agree to be his girlfriend and I got a sense that he wouldn't react well if I were to decline. He had already force-kissed me; what else was he going to do?

“Fine,” I stated. I knew I didn't want to say that but I felt compelled to do so as I was scared stiff.

It was as if I had given him something he had been longing for, for a very long time. He lifted me up and kept kissing me, while I remained still, watching him do a roundabout with me in the air.

“Okay, okay put me down; I did say that I want to take a bath. So, please leave me for some time. Besides I have a massive headache as I told you.”

“I am so happy, oh my word, I am so happy! Thank you Palesa, for giving me a chance. I will not disappoint you, I promise. Just go take a bath and I'll bring you an aspirin later. You are not allergic to aspirin are you?”

“No I am not. Perhaps you can bring it now before I take a

bath."

"Okay."

He disappeared to his bedroom and I took that moment to reflect on what had just occurred, unbelievable as it was, it had happened. I had agreed to be an older man's girlfriend and that older man had just spent a couple of minutes French-kissing me.

I knew precisely what was on his mind when he was kissing me, as his gaze was too intense and after feeling his hardened groin against me, I wanted to psyche myself for what was to come, even though I was unwavering in my stance that I didn't want it, not at that time anyway.

I checked the setting in the bedroom Martin had accommodated me in. I acknowledged that at some point, I would have to flee that place but the challenge was going to be how I was going to achieve that.

Windows had the kind of burglar proofing I had never seen before - almost armoured, and doors were also made of re-inforced steel. It was more like a very sophisticated prison. I mean, the house had very complicated security system and I wondered if there were cameras in all the rooms.

Then again, if I were to flee, where would I go… back to my parents' house, where I was unhappy and have never been happy? There were a number of thoughts and feelings I beleaguered about in my spirit and each of those thoughts and feelings wanted to dominate others.

The man came in, as I was surveying the room and gave me a

glass with what seemed like a fizzy tablet inside. He told me that it was aspirin and that it would work fast to make me better.

"Please, take this; You will be fine in no time." He handed me the glass and watched me scrunch my face, in slight protest of the bitter pill.

"Come on, drink up… this is very good medicine and it will knock you out. You'll wake up tomorrow very refreshed."

I drank up as my headache was hammering. I then handed the glass back to Martin. He took it and bid me goodnight, taking that moment to steal another kiss. I obliged - I mean, he was now my boyfriend wasn't he? I did agree to that didn't I? Although I did so under cowed duress, as I was afraid of what he might do to me, I did eventually agree.

Perhaps I also needed to repay him for his mercy towards me. Was that really compassion, if it was laced with me paying him back with my body? I couldn't answer these questions I posed on my psyche.

When he did kiss me however, I had a strange movement in my intestines, as if they were knotting. I suppose that is what people mean when they call this sensation, "butterflies". Yeah, I felt that and Martin noticed what that kiss did to me. He seemed really pleased with himself.

"Please close the door on your way out," I pleaded.

"Of course I will… good night, Palesa. See you tomorrow."

After he closed the door, I was able to finally take a deep breath, hoping that I wouldn't have to see the man again. I then went to the en-suite bathroom and took a shower instead. Immediately when warm water hit my face, I began to feel woozy, as if I was going to collapse. The feeling didn't last long, so I figured that it could have been that tablet that Martin gave me. After all, he did say that the tablet would knock me out in no time.

So the next moments, I hurriedly scrubbed my back using the body brush he had hanging on the hook in the shower. I allowed a generous amount of water and shower gel to flow over my body.

I experienced that strange feeling again and the panting began. I rinsed myself quickly and then switched the water off. I took the towel off the rail and dried myself up, trembling.

I felt like I was going to faint. It took all the strength I had to help myself. I recall wiping myself with a towel and left the shower hurriedly. I then applied some lotion all over my body. At least the wheeze was getting better and the dizziness was slowly going away. I sat down on the settee for a few minutes, trying to compose myself.

After a while, I stood up and opened the vanity case, looking for some face creams brought by this enigma of a man. I read up a little bit on the label and realized that Martin was right about the all natural ingredients.

I applied the cream on my face and neck and felt it slide effortlessly on my skin, leaving it velvety. I didn't experience any tingling. I was happy that the odd feeling I had in the shower had finally subsided but, I was inwardly still uneasy, wondering when that might start again. I also wondered what that nameless tablet Martin gave me was exactly.

Sitting on the bedside stool, I took out the lingerie that Martin had brought for me and put it on. It fit me perfectly, as if tailor-made especially for me. I put the remaining items on one of the nightstands and took the vanity case to the cupboard in the bathroom.

I walked back to the bedroom and got inside the covers - satin sheets, pillows and comforter. I almost felt guilty for enjoying such opulence, while I had no idea how my mother was and what my dad might have done to her. I was troubled about her and frightened for her at the same time.

I decided that perhaps it would be a good idea for me to call her so that she could know where I was and to make sure that she didn't have to worry about my whereabouts and safety.

How could I have pronounced my safety not even knowing as to whether I was really safe? In a weird way, I convinced myself that I was going into the relationship with my eyes wide-open.

There was a phone on another pedestal and I was tempted to use it to call my mother. At least I knew her number off by heart.

I however thought that perhaps I should ask for permission to use the phone. I called out to Martin. He came instantly, launching himself into the room as if he was a man possessed, or he had been waiting for me to call him. That somehow amused me.

"What is it? What happened?" Clearly, I had alarmed him or did I?

"Sorry, I didn't mean to startle you." I slid back into the covers, revealing only my neck and head.

"I just wanted to check if I can use the phone. I know it's late but I now feel very bad for leaving my mother like that. She must be very worried about me. Perhaps she has even gone to the police to report me missing."

"Come on, Palesa, you scared me half to death." He held his right hand to his chest. "Don't scream like that again. Honestly, I thought you saw something scary." Like what really?

He sat at the foot of the bed breathless and I realized then that he was really fretful, frightened even. I wondered though, as to why a person like him would stay alone in such a huge mansion. I mean, he was typically a bird, which got startled by even the tiniest movement. I might be exaggerating, but that's what I deduced.

"Perhaps I should tug you in," he teased.

"No Martin, you don't have to do that. I'm fine honestly. Can I call my mom using this phone?"

"No, you won't be able to do that. These phones that are in the guest-bedrooms are for calling internally only. Well…except for the one in my bedroom of course," he added. "You can come and use that one if you feel that it is so urgent that you call your mother now at ten o'clock. I'm sorry, I can't give you my cell phone to use, because I do not want to be traced by your parents, lest they come rushing to fetch you or lay a charge of kidnapping against me." He laughed.

"Oh so you really don't want me to leave? What about your

landline, won't it be traced as well?"

"Of course I don't want you to leave. You and I are a couple now aren't we? You weren't just agreeing to be my girlfriend whereas you had no intention to follow through with it were you?" He asked keenly, not giving me a moment to say anything in response. "Besides, my landline can't be traced. It reveals some odd number on caller ID, so you can come and use it.

'*Why would Martin find it prudent to hide his telephone number*?' I marvelled.

"No, Martin, unlike you, I say what I mean and I mean what I say." He faced down in slight embarrassment.

"I didn't mean to embarrass you. Can we go to your room please so I can call my mom?"

"Of course, let's go," he said, grabbing my hand.

"Please face the other way, Martin; this nightdress is very short… please bring me that robe." I pointed at the chaise at the corner of the room, where I had thrown the robe. He begrudgingly took a few steps, grabbing the mantle and handing it to me, still facing the wall.

I put it on and wore the slippers he gave me. He took the moment to lead me again, this time to his bedroom. Immediately after getting out of the door, that strange feeling weighed me down again, and I felt awfully weak. He snaked his one arm around my waist leading me to his bedroom. I felt like vomitting and indicated my need to want to do so.

The man then lifted me up and rushed me to his bathroom,

lifting the toilet seat up. I vomitted, feeling the most excruciating pain in my stomach as well as pins and needles in my chest, while shaking hysterically.

Martin spent the entire time standing outside the bathroom door, asking me if I was alright and whether he should give me herbal tea. I was too sick to even respond to him.

I sat on the tiled floor and although the vomiting eventually eased up, my head was spinning out of control. Martin being impatient, stormed into the lavatory and sat down with me on the floor, rubbing my back in a few strokes, putting his head against my shoulder.

I laced my right hand's fingers with his left hand's and whispered to him carefully, "I'll be okay, Martin, I promise." He lifted his head and smiled.

"You promise? You're not going to get sick again?" He seemed worried and his actions were baffling. It was as if he had mistaken me for somebody else he loved dearly and never wanted to see ill or not doing okay generally. That would explain him clinging onto me and wanting me to be with him.

The realisation terrified me. I wondered as to whether I would escape his clutches, as I was obviously not who he thought I was, or who he was replacing with me. I wanted to give myself that chance to see how far he would take that, but I was unsure as to whether that would be a good move. I panicked at the thought.

"Martin, I want to get up; the dizziness has subsided," I said.

"Okay, let me help you." He got up and extended his hands

towards me, lifting me cautiously.

"Easy… easy," he cautioned sympathetically, flushed the toilet and took his facecloth from the rail and poured some cold water on it. He then put it on my forehead, seemingly to help ease the fever. I was not even aware I had a fever.

Finally, I managed to get up and that bad feeling had disappeared. I then opened the tap and rinsed my mouth.

'*What are the chances that what this man has given me earlier was some dangerous drug and not an aspirin as he had claimed?*' This unsettling thought crept into my mind, but I stood up anyway, allowing Martin to lead me to wherever he was directing me to.

"Do you still want to call your mother?" he asked, almost disapprovingly. "I'd prefer it if you just rest now, Palesa."

"Yes, I want to call her," I stated, as he drearily lifted the handset up, handing the cordless gadget to me and then sat on the foot of the bed. What was he trying to do, listen in on my conversation?

"Come on sit on the bed, you will be more comfortable. I doubt you are out of the woods yet," he advised.

"Can I have some privacy please, Martin?"

"Okay, I'll give you some privacy only if you promise not to tell your mom where you are."

"Martin, I don't even know where I am, so how am I going to direct my mother to a place I don't even know?"

"This place is easy to find. All you would do is to simply tell her which road you took when you left home and the plot I stay in. I mean, you saw the name of this plot didn't you?"

Did he want me to entangle myself? What would he do to me if I were to admit that I could do that? I felt that I should not even attempt to escape because there was no real danger I was in – not really anyway. Besides him force-kissing me and pinning me against the wall, he hadn't really hurt me. I reasoned inwardly, unmindful that I was doing great damage to my psyche, but also amply aware that I was afraid of something I couldn't even identify.

"No, Martin, I did say I won't leave. I just want privacy when I speak to my mother, that's all."

"Okay, I'm happy to hear that," he murmured, widening his grin, preparing to leave the bedroom and then closing the door.

I dialled my mother's number and my father answered instead, in an irate tone.

"WHO IS THIS? WHAT DO YOU WANT?"

That was not even his phone but there he was, answering it in a very rude manner!

"Papa, it's Palesa," I revealed.

"What do you want? Oh, let me guess; you suddenly realised how bad it is out there without shelter, food, clothing and everything else you get for free here at home didn't you?"

I was baffled… perhaps I chose to be. How could my father say that? How could a man speak that way to his daughter? I was hurt. I chastised myself for having taken that step to call my mom.

I should have listened to Martin when he demonstrated his disapproval. He clearly had extensive life experience and being a doctor, he must have known quite a few people who fit my father's profile. Once again, I elevated Martin to a very supreme status – he knew things!

I continued digging a hole for myself, where I may never escape from. I subconsciously held a yearning to learn from Martin regarding whatever he could teach me.

The question I asked myself was, was I truly ready for that and if I was, what would happen if I could not handle the methods of his teachings? Where would I go if I were to elect to run away? I asked myself that over and over. I was adamant however, to take the acid test. I wanted to know what lay beneath the riddle that the man was.

"Papa, can I speak to Mama please," I begged my father, choosing not to engage with him further, conscious of the fact that he might have either handed the phone over to my mother already or put it down.

"Where are you Palesa? Why did you leave home like that? Are you on your way back? We're worried sick about you!" My mother answered fervently, making me smile at least, after hearing that they were worried about me. I had no doubt that it was only her that was worried, judging by how my father spoke to me.

"NO, SHE SHOULD STAY WHEREVER SHE IS. SHE IS A WOMAN ISN'T SHE? WHY DID SHE LEAVE IN THE FIRST PLACE? I DON'T WANT HER BACK IN MY HOUSE!"

I heard my father growl in the background and my mother keeping the all too familiar short replies, electing to continue talking to me instead.

"Pale..., are you okay?"

"I'm okay Mama, don't worry about me. I just need a few of my things... if you would be able to take them to a place I'll direct you to," I implored.

"Palesa, why should I do that? This is your home. Don't take what your father has said to heart. You know how he is. He's just upset because of the way you left, that's all. You must come home please."

I don't know if my mother was naïve or as slow as my father used to claim she was. How could she say such a thing to me, knowing that I had lived with that man for 19 years of my life? In all those years, I got hurt and had cried at the sting of his words more times than I could count. I also witnessed him yell at her many times, calling her names and then she would pretend like nothing had happened. She made me mad sometimes.

"Mama, please don't say that. Can I have some of my clothes, shoes, my cell phone, my vanity case, my ID and a copy of my grade 10 mid-term results please? I'll sms all the items, just so you won't forget." I paused, as I heard my mom's rising wheeze on the other end, sounding as if she was about to cry. She was aware that she was indeed about to briefly lose her daughter to something she didn't know then.

"Palesa...," she gasped.

"Mama, please don't ask me any more questions about this. I'll call you often."

"Alright, but are you okay? Where exactly are you? Where are you going to sleep, Palesa?"

"I'm fine, Mama…very fine and safe too," I confirmed. How could I have affirmed such a thing, heedful that my inner voice wouldn't stop issuing counsel?

"I am at a friend's house Mama, I am not coming back home though… not now anyway. Papa never wanted me and I have just heard him affirm that. Please don't defend him Mama and please don't tell him what I've just requested from you. I really need my stuff."

"I won't," she responded succinctly.

I wondered after that response, if my father had somehow moved closer to her, so he could hear what the conversation was about. Quite frankly, I didn't care.

"Mama, please put everything in the black garbage bags so they won't be so easy to spot. Simply leave them outside, but towards the water meter that's occupying the corner of the house. That way, anyone who sees the bags, will assume that they are carrying dirt and they will not fiddle with them. Please do so very early in the morning, Mama. Perhaps around five o'clock," I added.

"Okay." That concise response again! My word, what was it about my mom that made her fear my father so much and never even defended me when I needed her to? I was certain that over and above the emotional and verbal abuse I had witnessed, he probably abused her physically as well.

I bid her goodbye and she wished me well. I then put the phone down and was satisfied that I had called because had I not done so,

I would have constantly worried about my mother or even my father, believing that he cared somewhat.

I called out to Martin to come in. He immediately opened the door after I called him, a clear sign that he had been listening at the door. That was not a very smart move.

“What did your mom say? Is she upset?”

I indulged him for that moment, taking him through my conversation with my mother and a brief non-conversation I had with my dad, up to and including what I heard him say in the background as I spoke to my mom.

“I’m sorry, Palesa, I really am. But this somehow doesn’t surprise me. I guess you are satisfied though, having made that phone call?”

“Yeah, I am,” I responded, inhaling and then exhaling. “I’d like to sleep now, Martin. We will talk tomorrow.”

“Good night, Palesa, we will indeed talk tomorrow. I am not going to work though, as I have checked my diary and there are no appointments at all. So I will be with you here to cheer you up.” I smiled, so did he.

“Good night Martin.”

I indicated my intention to leave his room but as I took a few steps, he pulled me by my left arm and brought me closer towards him.

“No more games, Palesa. We both know that we want each other badly. I want you and I want you tonight, I want you now. Trust me you will feel better after I have consoled you.”

He ran his palm up and down my face and kissed me on my right cheek once, repeating the process on my left cheek and then on my forehead. He then gaped at me with that unsettling stare and gave me a spun out kiss on my lips.

I felt numb and my stomach rumbled, while I felt a dash of heat flowing through my legs.

I relented, but felt my heart pounding. I was petrified of what he wanted to do and how that moment would feel. He had looked at me with lustful eyes, as if he was a man who hadn't been with a woman for a long time and wanted a release – a long release. I was alarmed and had to make him aware.

"Martin, I am not ready for this. Please don't force me to do this tonight. I am a virgin and I'm afraid because I don't know what to expect or how painful it's going to be. I have heard stories about the first time and none of them are flattering."

"Palesa, no woman is ever ready for their first time. But with the right person who cares about them, the apprehension is soon quashed. Allow me to make you happy, Palesa; I promise I will be gentle and if you feel pain, I will stop, I promise."

'*What did he just say? He made another promise which he intended breaking? He did promise me that he wouldn't try anything with me but here we are - he is insisting that he wants to have me right here and now.*' I bewailed within but kept still.

I felt powerless to keep resisting as I had no idea how forceful he might be and was panic-stricken that I'd make him angry. At that moment, he reminded me of my father, even though it was a faint mirror.

My father was a person who never took “no” for an answer and it looked like Martin was that kind of a person as well, particularly when it came to everything operating his way or the hi-way.

I acknowledged that much, and although I kept asking myself as to whether that was the type of man I wanted to be around or be with, or the type of life I sought to have, there was nothing I could do. It was very late in the evening and Martin was going to get what he wanted - one way or another.

I tried pulling away once more but he wouldn’t let me. I knew unerringly what he meant by “consoling” me.

I was not ready and I doubt I ever would have been. I tried to squeeze myself out of his tight grip again but he still wouldn’t let me. He was too sturdy. Eventually he released me and pulled his tongue out of my mouth, breathing heavily and affronted by my icy deportment. I could see it in his eyes.

“Palesa, you have been seducing me ever since you came here. You are the one who said you wanted to come to my place. What did you think was going to happen? I am a man and you are a woman and we are alone in this huge house.”

He stroked my cheeks, kissing me again on my lips and neck, while breathing heavily. What he said left me flabbergasted. Did it mean that, if a woman tells a man to take her to his place, she indirectly means that she wants to sleep with him? That gave me the chills.

“Baby, this was bound to happen. I have already told you that I want you as a girlfriend and I am well-off financially so you won't starve. Why are you being so difficult?"

"Martin, I'm not being difficult, it's just that I am tired and I'm not ready yet; please let me go. Have you forgotten that I am not well?"

"Oh Palesa, arghhh," he screamed, bearing signs of frustration. He then let go of me immediately after I reminded him of my being unwell and he walked towards the door, opening it and motioning me to get out. His eyes were scorching red and his face had contorted appallingly. "Get out!" he barked, startling me.

"Good night, Martin," I demurely mumbled.

"Close the door on your way out." He then turned his back on me, running his hand through his shaven head persistently.

I did as he instructed – closed the door. At least I was pleased with myself, having successfully avoided losing my virtue when I was not ready.

Was I ever going to be ready to lose my virginity to a man who had briefly reminded me of my father? Well, he visibly had some goodness in him, even though he acted like a douché.

He did stop pestering me about having sex after I had reminded him that I was not well. That was a very peculiar thing he did. I convinced myself that he must have some good traits in him, otherwise why did he stop?

I went to 'my' bedroom and locked the door, got under the sleek satin duvet cover and tried to catch some sleep, my heart beating erratically from fear. What had I done!

It took me quite a while before I could sleep, as I lay awake, pondering on the prior moment with Martin in his bedroom. Somehow, I did manage to sleep around midnight I believe.

CHAPTER 3

New Beginning

I was attending a dressmaking class and everyone was very happy for me, having just made a kaftan for my mother, as my teacher kept praising me for my skills and prowess. I was elated. Then out of the blue, the phone rang but I could not answer it, as my hand became too heavy to lift up. It stopped briefly and it rang again.

That was when I realised that I had been dreaming! I woke up quickly and checked the time on the phone screen – five o'clock. Did I really sleep for five hours flat out? I clearly did. I picked up the phone, knowing that it had to be Martin calling.

"Hello," I answered wryly.

"Hello Palesa, you are a deep sleeper I see. I think you should wake up and take a quick shower. You did ask your mother to put your stuff very early outside didn't you? So I figured that we can just park near your parents' house and watch your mom as she puts the stuff where you directed her. We can then quickly take them immediately afterwards. What do you think?" He was obviously used to telling people what to do. I wondered why he even bothered asking for my opinion.

"Oh, I see. So you woke me up so early to instruct me to take a shower? I'm still sleeping, Martin. Can't you go alone please? I don't want anyone to recognize me. I'll give you the directions."

"I thought you'd jump at the chance to see your mother at least, even if it is from afar."

"Okay, that's fine. I'll wake up but I'm still tired my God! Do you ever sleep?"

"Yes, I do sleep but this is the time I wake up every day so, my body is used to the trauma, if you'd like to put it that way. Besides, those who sleep a lot, never really achieve much. So, wake up and take a shower," he instructed, his tone dry and indifferent.

"Yes Sir," I responded. He put the phone down and didn't respond to my swipe. Was he still upset with me? If so, why would he care that I had to fetch my stuff? The man was eccentric.

I thought of going back to sleep but something told me that Mr Grumpy might not appreciate that. So I woke up, made the bed, took my nightdress off and went to the bathroom. I then recalled that I had no toothbrush or toothpaste. I wanted to call on Martin again but thought of checking in the vanity case first, as I hoped that there was probably some toothpaste among the stuff he brought.

I tiptoed out of the shower and quickly grabbed the vanity case. I checked inside and on the outside zipped pockets and found toothpaste of a brand I didn't know, with a miniature toothbrush and a mouthwash. I didn't care that it was an unfamiliar brand or how small that toothbrush was. It was actually more like a baby toothbrush. I was adamant not to call on Martin to come and help with a new toothbrush..., if he had one.

It seemed like he had a collection of everything that a person could ever need. I didn't mind as I was in as much of a fetid mood as I suspected he was. I had to pull myself together.

I used what I had found instead, and the toothbrush did do the trick. I then gargled and cleansed my entire mouth with the mouthwash and felt really fresh afterwards. I proceeded to take a shower and as I was still busy, I heard a knock.

I turned the tap off and responded, "I'm still in the shower, Martin. I'll come out just now."

"I brought you toothpaste and a new toothbrush," he said.

"It's okay... I'm sorted. I found toothpaste and toothbrush inside that vanity case you brought so, I am fine thank you," I answered.

"Okay, I'll see you later then."

I kept quiet and continued showering, enjoying the warm water running over my body. Strangely, I was beginning to love the feeling I had, the feeling of having a bedroom with an en-suite bathroom, so majestic and beautiful I thought it wouldn't hurt to live in there the whole day.

As I enjoyed the shower, my mind kept raising, making me re-think my hard stance towards Martin and what I believed he was giving me on a silver platter – opulence, shelter, food, possibility of money and hopefully education.

On the other hand, it sounded as if I wanted to allow myself to be used for sex, but then again, if he would use me for sex, then I could use him for everything else I wanted to have. Now where was the harm in that? Warped mentality of a young naïve girl at that time.

Different types of thoughts kept wrestling within my mind for either against or for the relationship with Martin. The domineering thought was that of agreeing to sleep with Martin as the fear of what could happen if I were to keep refusing beset my mind.

I was petrified at the possibility of being chased out of that home and landing on the street again. Perhaps this time, I would be unfortunate to land in the hands of someone who wouldn't be as pleasant as Martin had been to me. Another hard knock sounded as I took my time in the shower.

"Palesa, what's taking so long? It's getting late. Finish up so we can go. I want to come back before eight o'clock. I have a tele-conference at nine. So hurry up and get ready!" he howled.

Yes..., Martin used a harsh tone with me. It was only the first day with him and he was already roaring at me. Perhaps there was something wrong I did to warrant such behaviour from him – from men.

Why was I to blame for everything? Why was it expected of me, to constantly tread carefully and bend over backwards around the men I knew, instead of them doing the same?

I asked myself these questions but later justified Martin's annoyance. '*I think he is also apprehensive not to be seen by anybody from home or anyone who knew me. Perhaps he doesn't want the car to be identified, lest he be called a kidnapper or a prowler.*'

Yes, that made some distorted sense to me as to why he was so irritable that morning. I panicked and immediately rinsed off the shower gel that had been running over my body with warm water and wiped myself. I then got out of the shower and continued wiping myself. I opened the door to the bedroom slightly, as I wanted to let Martin know that I'd be done soon.

"Martin, I'll be done just now. Stop screaming at me."

I then closed the door but didn't hear him respond. I figured that he probably heard me but elected not to reply due to him being seriously goaded.

I applied the skin products on my face and my body, wearing one of the silky underwears that Martin gave me. I then put on my bra and my dress as well as sandals.

I eventually came out of the bedroom and was not aware that it was already approaching six thirty. It was a bit chilly and although I wasn't warmly clad, I didn't want to ask Martin for anything warm to wear – he'd be so lucky! Obstinate me again; it was more like cutting my nose to spite my face but oh well…

"Good morning Martin, I'm done," I greeted him as I reached the kitchen.

"Morning, I made you a sandwich, here…," he mumbled, handing me the sandwich which was in a rectangular glass container. He also gave me freshly squeezed juice, in a thermos mug. His tone was still dry and apathetic.

"We have to go; the sun is already out. You'll eat in the car. Did you switch off the lights in your bedroom?" he asked, as I looked up, wondering if I would be in trouble if I were to outright admit that I had forgotten to switch the lights off.

"Let me go and check." I watched him shake his head, as if he was about to call me an idiot for forgetting to do such a basic thing.

Once again, I saw my Father standing there in the form of Martin. I shivered inwardly and I ran to the bedroom and alas, I hadn't switched off!

I quickly switched off the lights and went back to Martin, who was already standing by the kitchen door with keys in his hand. He gestured at me to get out, maintaining a very serious facial expression, which I couldn't really read. Judging by the foul mood he seemed to be in, I could safely assume that he must have still been livid that I refused to sleep with him the previous night.

He was not the man I was with yesterday; the man who was gentle, even though he force-kissed me a couple of times, I still believed that he was a good guy. What I saw that morning however, was a mean streak, flashing through my eyes, as I felt like my father was admonishing me for disobeying him.

I did as he said, and waited next to the car. He locked the kitchen door and unlocked the car. I stood there waiting for him to open for me but he didn't. He instead rounded the SUV and got to his side, opening the door and getting in. He looked at me as if I was crazy.

"Aren't you getting in? What are you still waiting for?" he spoke unkindly again. I nearly lost it!

One thought came into my mind, petitioning me to tell him off and another imploring me to run home, as soon as he had dropped me off to fetch my stuff. However, there was this persistent thought that kept reminding me of the horrible situation at home. I had to quickly weigh the three as I opened the door and got into the car.

Martin immediately started the engine, telling me to fasten the seatbelt like he showed me the previous day. I did so but, I was now very annoyed but still slightly terrified of the man.

He reversed the car out of the garage and eventually closed the door using the remote control, waiting a bit while watching the door roll back down.

I took the moment to steal a glance at him. He was impassive, cold and brazen that morning. He eventually drove off, pressing the accelerator very hard, as if we were indeed late for something. At least it was warm in the car and my apprehension earlier about me feeling slightly chilly was quickly thwarted.

Why was Martin so upset and irritable with me? Was it

because I took too long to shower? Was it because I refused to sleep with him? It was not like that wasn't going to happen as I had agreed to be his girlfriend. So why would he be that ill-tempered?

'*Does this represent all men, meaning that if things do not go their way, then they believe that they are justified to react with anger; with withdrawal*?' I kept querying myself.

I wanted to call his bluff and also maintain my cheekiness but, I quickly remembered that I was the one who had no place to stay; the one who was practically fatherless as my father had disowned me. Now, if I were to react negatively to what Martin was doing, I would be placing my situation and perhaps my life in danger.

So, I had to carefully choose the next words I would say to him, in my bid to get him to be a bit nicer to me. I decided to make him a promise, a promise to give him my priced possession – my virtue.

"Martin, why are you so upset with me?"

"I'm not upset with you," he briefly responded.

'*Well, at least he was talking to me*,' I reflected.

"Yes, you do seem irritable and upset with me Martin; I'm not really a child you know." Did I just say that?

"Oh, you are not a child? What do you call what you did last night? It's only children who behave that way. If you indeed are not a child, you should not have behaved in the manner you did last night. If I am your boyfriend and you are my girlfriend, then there should not be a problem sleeping with me."

He took a jibe at me, not at all mincing his words. Twenty four hours hadn't even passed yet since we met, but there he was, making demands. What a blunder I had made!

"Martin, you are behaving this way because I refused to sleep with you yesterday? I can't believe this! Whose behaviour is childish between the two of us, mine or yours?" I went in on the offensive as well, protecting what was remaining of my dignity.

"I'm not really upset about that but you have to make a decision Palesa, whether you want to be with me or not. You cannot stay with me yet you refuse me what I am entitled to as your man. You did say you are okay with being my girlfriend so why won't you want to sleep with me?"

The question sounded really stupid, but I indulged him as he continued, "If you really meant what you said, you shouldn't refuse to be intimate with me. I told you yesterday that I would not hurt you, yet you continued to refuse. You are the one who kept touching me yesterday, hugging me and telling me that you were going to get naked. Was it your intention to toy with my feelings and then turn around and refuse me sex…huh?"

I could not believe what Martin had said to me. I felt a lump forming in my throat and I couldn't even respond to his verbal blitz. I looked outside the window, worried sick about my situation. How could so much happen in a day, leaving me fatigued as if I had been with the man for at least six months? He behaved as if we had been together for a long time.

As he continued driving, I felt a sensation on my thigh, making me jolt backwards. I was distressed by the shot of electricity that blew across my stomach, when I noticed that Martin was running his hand on my right thigh.

He pretended not to have seen how uncomfortable that move made me, but proceeded to put his hand inside my dress running it up and down and eventually touching my vulva. I couldn't move or breathe properly and my body trembled. What was he trying to do?

A reflection crept into my mind, entreating me to allow him to do what he wanted to do. I hated the thought. Should I have stopped him immediately? Was allowing him to continue caressing my thigh proof that I was not a child? Why then did that make me so uncomfortable?

He held onto the steering wheel with his other hand. I noticed then, that he was not changing any gears and figured that he was driving an automatic transmission car.

"Martin, please concentrate on the road. You will get what you want when we come back home, I promise," I assured him, eager for him to take his hand out and focus on the road. He smiled and removed his hand.

"Are you sure you won't start with your excuses again?"

"No I won't; as long as you promise not to hurt me."

"I made you that promise last night but you still refused, so what would be different this time?"

"Yesterday I was not well - you saw that. So why would you want to sleep with me in that condition anyway?" He tilted his head, nodding briefly.

"Was that the only reason? I could have sworn you didn't want to have sex with me."

"Martin, why are you in such a hurry? Everything is happening too fast anyway. We met yesterday, then you took me to your house, you then proposed love to me and you wanted me to sleep with you? Don't you think this love boat will crash soon if we rush so many things at once? I don't even know you."

"I'm a man Palesa and I don't see a reason for me to wait when I know what I want. You will get to know me in time. I also don't know you well enough but I'm willing to give myself to you because I feel deeply about you. This is why I want to know as soon as possible if you want me as well. If not, then this would be our last trip together. I will drop you off at your parents' house." His last statement bewildered me; scared me even.

I felt as if he was giving me an ultimatum, perhaps he was also daring me, knowing that I had lain bare, my fears of going home and the conditions I lived in at home.

"Before you answer Palesa, please think very carefully about your answer. I am the only chance you have at a great life. If you were to go back home, you will never get to experience the kind of life I have in mind for you, for us; the life that will see you immediately being the lady of the house; having a house helper; a personal helper; a bodyguard; a hairstylist; a personal trainer…," he paused. "Do you still want me to continue?"

He looked at me, expecting me to respond but I froze. The thought of such affluence made me feel good, even though the voice within kept warning me continuously. I was pleased but was wondering if he had just manipulated me into staying with him by showing me what I could miss if I went back home. He probably did that deliberately.

"Martin, let's concentrate on fetching my stuff. We will talk about other things when we get back."

"Did you just say when we get back? So you have made a decision already?"

"Martin, let's just make it snappy and like you said, the sun is already out." I smiled at him.

"Alright Mrs Leboya, let's do this your way. Aren't we close?" he chortled and I found no reason to call him out on how he had addressed me.

"Yes, we are," I affirmed.

The entrance of our township is marked by a prominent sign displaying the township name, "Mookodi", surrounded by colourful murals, depicting the rich history and culture of our community. This was the dwelling I was about to leave as I sullenly watched it standing tall and bold on the side of the road, as it would be the last time I ever do so.

Martin read the name out loud, "MOOKODI," and remarked, "So, this is where you come from? I see that we're about to transition from the tarred road to narrow and dusty streets. Please don't tell me that I'm gonna have to drive for too long through these streets that are lined with corrugated iron shacks." His tone was snobbish and full of pride but I still felt like I needed to go away with him, as I convinced myself that anything but having to stomach the situation at home, would be better for me.

There were already signs of life as people began their day. Fellow community members going about their daily routines – some heading off to work, some school mates walking in groups to go to school, while those who attended suburban schools were boarding either taxis or hired school buses. I quickly put my hands to my face to hide, as we passed some students that I knew. I could see that Martin saw me do so and he shook his head.

"Don't do that. Your life is about to change for the better. Don't feel guilty for choosing yourself over this trashy place!"

"Don't call my home trashy. Besides, I just don't want to be a subject of gossip at school; that I was seen in an SUV with an older man." He laughed.

"How will you even know if they gossiped about you or not? No matter what you do here on earth, people will always talk. Learn to live your life according to your own terms. The only person you should worry about is your mother. Anything else shouldn't matter," he counselled.

I showed him where he should turn; first right turn, immediately as one got into the Mookodi Township through the main road.

I spotted right away, the three big black plastic bags next to the fire hydrant that was next to my home. I pointed them to Martin and he stopped a few meters away. Once he stopped the car, I got out immediately and ran towards the plastic bags.

I opened them quickly to verify the contents. Indeed the stuff I had requested from my mother was all in there and a whole host of other items, including two of her favourite jerseys. I also found my lunch box, which I usually took to school.

My mother had made me sandwiches. She had spread margarine and added ham and grated mozzarella cheese. This might have seemed like something minor but when my mother made them, they would always taste like the best thing ever. My heart bled, thinking about the trouble my mother must have gone through to make sure that I got what I needed.

I opened another bigger container and found some grapes. There were a couple of other plastic bags that had peaches, apples, pears, dried fruits and four packets of potato chips. I decided not to check anymore as it appeared that my mother had thought of everything, mostly things I never even thought of.

She had also included one of her favourite handbags and when I lifted it up, it felt heavy and I didn't know at the time, what was inside.

****

I couldn't stop smiling but felt really bad for having had bad thoughts about her the previous night and for abandoning her. I had no idea that she really loved me that much even though I thought she didn't. I was still confused as to why she never wanted to leave my father, despite him subjecting her to such awful treatment. The strength and perseverance of the woman tore me inside.

I felt the chill on my body; a feeling that I was being watched by someone. I knew that it had to be her. I waved towards the house, just in case it was her watching me, probably through her bedroom window.

Martin got out of the car to help me, as he realised that my eyes were fixed towards my home, particularly my mom's bedroom and was bound to waste time as a result.

"You are not going to change your mind about coming with me are you?" Martin asked as he reached me.

"No, I am not changing my mind. But, I'd like my mother to come and visit me sometime at your place. Will that be okay?"

"If you think she will be able to do so and won't give me a hard time regarding staying with you, that's okay, she can come anytime. However, we have to make sure that we do not unwittingly put her life in danger as what you told me about your father did sound like the things my father used to do, even though you did mention not seeing him hit your mom. Let's go quickly before he comes out," he said, seemingly concerned.

"Alright, let's go," I whispered. There was no one on the street at that time but, I knew that a number of neighbours must have seen me from peeping through their windows. That was how they were.

Martin picked the two bags up and I picked the last one. We rushed to the car and he opened the boot, placing the two bags he had inside. He extended his one hand, indicating that I should give him the other bag. I gave it to him and got into my seat. My eyes remained glued to the bedroom window, as I had a feeling that my mother was still watching me. Tears nearly fell but I faced the heavens as I prevented them from swimming down.

As Martin climbed into the car, I saw curtain movement by my mom's bedroom window, affirming my suspicions that she was there, watching me. I smiled and waved again, pleased that she saw what she wanted to see and had indeed satisfied herself regarding me not being by myself. I just figured that I'd call her when I reached Martin's place.

Martin started the engine and drove off. It was already half past seven and the way he accelerating, it was lucid that he was rushing to reach home, so he could connect to whomever he said he was having a tele-conference with.

"I think my mom was watching us." Martin nodded in agreement.

"Yeah, I noticed some curtain movement as well. Do you think your father is home?"

"He has probably already left for work. My mother works from home. She is a baker and does catering as well. I just wonder how she managed to put the stuff out. I still cannot believe I asked her to do something so risky. But anyway, I'll talk to her later."

"I can see you're more relaxed and settled. In fact you look very happy. Perhaps we should have come yesterday already, then you and I wouldn't have fought."

"We fought? What fight are you talking about Martin? I don't remember us fighting. You love drama I see!"

He slanted his head and curved his eyebrows, continuing to

drive quite fast, as we left the township behind and all its woes.

As we approached the plots, Martin received a phone call and he ardently answered it, using his blue tooth receiver. I could hear from the conversation that the people he was expecting to have a tele-conference with, were postponing to a date still to be confirmed by them. Martin didn't seem too bothered by that phone call and simply switched off the call afterwards and produced a huge sigh of relief.

"You sound relieved," I remarked.

"Can you tell? Of course I am relieved. Nothing is going to stand in our way of spending the day together. I'm really glad you are so happy about your stuff."

"Yeah, me too."

Martin eventually indicated the car and turned into the road leading to his plot. Bra Mos was already working, going up and down, carrying a spade and a rake. He was wearing a blue overall. As we approached him, he raised his hand and spoke loudly, "Good morning Sir and Ms Palesa." I simply waved at him.

"Good morning Mos, Is Lulama awake? You still remember I mentioned that she shouldn't come in today?" Martin slowed the car down, opening his window as he spoke to Bra Mos.

"Yes Sir, I told her but she is inside the house. She mentioned that she has to fetch the laundry and she said she'll clean the kitchen and dust here and there," the man reverently responded.

Martin seemed peeved about that. "What is wrong with this woman? Why can't she take simple instructions?"

Instinct crept in and in some way, I knew why Martin didn't want Sis Lulama to come in. He probably didn't want her to see me or to start having something to gossip about, prior to him knowing unerringly whether I really wanted to be with him or not. I made that excuse for him in my mind.

I felt the need to justify why he reacted in the manner he did. Mind you, it had only been a day since I met the man but I already believed I knew what he was all about.

Finally, Martin pressed the remote control and garage doors rolled up. While waiting, he kept ranting about how he wanted to fire Sis Lulama because he didn't like to be disobeyed in his house and that he was the one paying the woman her salary, so his orders should be adhered to.

He was seriously piqued, worse than he was when we left earlier. His moods seemed to change in a whim and that unsettled me. I wondered if he might start behaving like that with me too, having taken such great offence when I refused to sleep with him the previous day. The journey was indeed going to be very long into figuring out the kind of man he was and to also decipher for myself, as to whether I truly wanted to be with him or not.

My choice was restricted and I acknowledged the fact but, I kept convincing myself that I was doing the right thing for myself as going back home was not an option anymore.

He drove into the garage and brought the car to a halt, rolling down the garage door with the remote control. He unfastened his seatbelt and I did the same. As I was trying to calm him down, he flatly ignored me and charged into the house, leaving his door ajar.

"LULAMA…LULAMA!" The man howled, as I remained seated after unfastening my seatbelt, unsure of what to do.

Eventually, I got out and entered the kitchen. I heard Martin screaming at the poor woman. I knew that if I didn't handle that situation then and showed him how wrong what he did was, he would never respect me going forward and he would be under the illusion that he could continue doing that to anyone - even me.

"Hello Sis Lulama," I greeted her, as I found her in the kitchen, very timid and facing down, taking Martin's abusive words.

"Did you hear what I said, Lulama?" he asked, in a harsh tone again.

"Yes Sir I did," the poor woman who seemed to be in her mid forties, responded.

"Fine, you can go," Martin instructed and got out of the kitchen door. I imagined then that he was fetching my stuff from the car.

As soon as he got out, I spoke briefly to Sis Lulama.

"Are you alright sis?"

"Yes Sis, I'm fine. Don't worry about me, I'm used to this."

"You shouldn't have to get used to this sis, this is wrong. I'll speak to him."

"Please… please… I'm begging you; don't do that. He will hurt you, he will hurt you sis please don't." Sis Lulama seemed truly terrified as she spoke to me, worried about me even. Martin came in and asked what she was still doing in the kitchen.

"I was just greeting Miss…"

"Palesa… my name is Palesa," I spoke up.

Sis Lulama left me baffled and I made a pact with my inner being then, to get to the bottom of Martin's uncanny behaviour. I knew that I didn't like it and there was no way I would leave an abusive father and walk straight into the hands of an abusive man and start a relationship with him with my eyes wide open.

"Martin…Martin," I called out to him.

"Yes…," he responded.

"I'd like us to talk please," I stated, noticing him seemingly confused.

"Okay, let me fetch the other plastic bag, then I'll lock the door and you and I can have a talk."

I went into the living room and noticed that sis Lulama had indeed tidied up as the smell of lavender from the furniture polish was permeating the house. All wood surfaces were clean and shiny.

Martin came in quietly after having locked the door and went upstairs with the other plastic bag. I followed him and found him still putting my stuff on the floor and others on the sofa.

"Oh, I didn't realize you followed me," he alleged.

"Yeah, I'd like us to talk now please."

"Sounds serious," he held, pretending to be nervous about the impending talk. He then sat down on the settee and I sat beside him. I held both his hands and indicated my desire to speak sincerely with him.

"Martin, I just want to mention that I feel very uncomfortable when you yell and you display an aggressive disposition. We have not even been together for two days, yet I am already unsure if we will make it."

He interjected…

"Palesa, what have I done to you? Have I done anything to upset you?" It was becoming lucid that the talk was going to be long and we were likely not to see eye to eye. He didn't see anything wrong with his earlier behaviour that morning and what he had done to Sis Lulama.

"I didn't like your behaviour this morning when you were cold towards me and I certainly didn't like how you spoke to Sis Lulama either. Why did you do that?"

"Palesa, are you calling me to order? You've got guts missy!" he responded to me in a cheeky tone. "What did Lulama say to you?"

"Don't call me missy, I'm your girlfriend remember? We are going to sort this out until you understand that I will also not be spoken to, the way you like. If I am going to stay here with you, we should both respect each other. I don't want to have to compare you to my father, nor do I want to remind you of how much you said you disliked your father's abusive behaviour." I couldn't believe my guts that day, but that had to be said.

He faced down like a naughty boy, not even maintaining eye contact with me. As he tried to interject or defend himself, I interrupted him.

"Martin, I am not done. Did you inwardly envy your father's

behaviour and now you wish to perpetuate it to others? If so, I will not stand for it. Remember that I left home because of such behaviour and will not go into another similar conduct with my eyes open. The onus is on you now Martin. I want peace and if I don't get it from you, I will leave and you will never see me again," I concluded and paused. "Now, you can speak."

"Ha! Ha! Ha!" he shook his head, laughing. "You are definitely the one I need in my life to constantly call me to order. Perhaps it was not right to treat you the way I did in the morning before we left. Although I didn't like what you did last night and was wounded when you refused to sleep with me, I do understand your anxiety yesterday."

"I'm glad we are on the same page. So why did you yell at Sis Lulama that way? Isn't she your elder?"

"She's my employee and once in a while, these people should know who the boss is. They cannot go against what the boss wants. You remember last night; I specifically told Mos to tell her not to come in today. What was she trying to do… see why I said she shouldn't come in? She is one of those gossip-mongers anyway. I might have spoken harshly to her but I do not regret it." His face grimaced.

"Why are you still keeping her then?" I asked keenly.

"Because I'm battling to find a replacement. A lot of potential helpers say this place is too far and there is no public transport around here."

"Okay, I hear you but please tone it down next time you feel it is necessary to reprimand her. Otherwise, I'll be more than happy to take over." Martin looked at me and smiled.

"I see you'll make a very good wife one day. You are already taking over employee management. Ha! Ha! Ha!," he laughed.

"I'm not taking over per sé, but I think I might realise quicker than you, what her gripe might be prior to anything spiraling out of control. So, what do you say?"

"Okay, let's see if you will be able to handle her. Remember that you are even younger so she might not even want to listen to you, let alone respect you."

"Leave her to me, I'll deal with her. If she starts disrespecting me, I'll set you on her so you can call her to order. But, enough with the shouting please. You're making me uncomfortable."

"I promise, I won't yell again," he giggled. "I cannot believe that in just a day and a few hours, you managed to do a lot for me than any woman has ever done. I don't mean to mention my past relationships but just for the sake of this conversation, I really thought it suitable to mention. You are a very wise young woman."

"It's fine, let's just not make a habit of mentioning exes while we are together alright?" Martin nodded.

I had never felt so good about myself the way I did that day. I managed to call a man who was sixteen years my senior to order and although he tried to justify his bad behaviour, eventually he did relent or did he? Perhaps he wanted to butter me up, so I could loosen up and eventually let him have all of me. I felt that I had no alternative but to allow Martin to break my virginity. I was still horrified at the thought because each time he came near me, I would just tremble and experience a strange feeling in my stomach.

"I noticed you didn't even eat the sandwich I made you this morning. When are you going to eat?"

"I'll eat just now. My mom made me sandwiches as well and also added some fruits, dried fruits and potato chips. I'll check what else she has included, so I can pack them in the fridge, if it's not too full, that is."

I looked at him, indirectly asking for consent to put my food inside his fridge. I knew that a person who had lived by himself for a long time, wouldn't just give up his space that easily, so I had to be sure.

"Of course you can but there's actually a fridge in here, so you can also put other things in here if you like."

He pointed at what I had believed to be a cupboard and stood up, beseeching me to do the same. He went to the "cupboard" and opened it, revealing a standard size fridge, not a bar fridge at all. I could literally put all the stuff I like in there.

"I had no idea that was a fridge. You love fancy stuff Martin, thank you; I'll see what can fit in here."

I opened the packages and Martin began showing signs of anxiety, as if he wanted to attend to something else. He was startled by a beeping sound. He removed his beeper from his pants checked it, letting out a sigh. He then took out his phone and made a brief call.

"I don't believe this; it's the hospital. I'm on call baby and have to go. One of my patients has just been brought in. So I do have to go. Are you going to be alright until I come back?" he asked, fidgeting with his hands.

"Of course, I'll be alright."

"I'll see you later then," he grinned.

He moved closer to me as I was busy with my packages, lifted me up, spreading my legs and forcing them to clasp his waist. I got that feeling again - my stomach was knotting and the current that went through my stomach at the time, was charging at high voltage. In fact, I could see that he was experiencing the same feeling as well.

He kissed me incessantly on my lips, and I snaked both my arms around his neck, allowing him to do as he pleased with me, without petitioning him to cease. I could not stop feeling apprehensive as my belly kept growling.

"Sounds like someone is very hungry."

He continued pressing his lips against mine, and I let go of my whole senses and surrendered, even though I was beginning to worry about the phone call he had made. He had to leave as there was an emergency at the hospital.

"Martin, shouldn't you get going? Aren't you going to be late for your patient?"

"I wanted to do this before I go. Look at how relaxed you are today. I better rush back home soon."

He disentangled my legs and put me down, while continuing to smooch me and took one of my hands, placing it against his groin. I shivered at the sight, more especially his hardened front.

"Feel that - this is how badly I want you, Palesa. I want you to make me happy."

I didn't understand what he meant and he had to be candid, telling me that he really wanted me to kiss him where it mattered the most. That got me perturbed. How was I going to do that? I was inexperienced and didn't know that one can even do such a thing. That sounded disgusting for a man his age to say that to me. The thought of it made me want to puke.

"You are going to be late, Martin. I'm not going anywhere; you'll find me here when you get back." He put his head on my shoulder, pulling his breath and bit my neck. He "rocked" me slowly, sensing my reserve. The pain caused by his bite was intense.

"Ouch!" I screamed. "I thought it's only boys who did this."

He laughed and drew me towards him with vigour, as if to make sure that his stiffness relaxed somewhat, while rubbing himself against me. That moment didn't feel too bad because in some way, I loved the feeling I had. I persuaded myself that I wanted it – that I was ready. The sensation of his fullness kept rubbing against me like a blistering cable against my nerve endings.

'*If it feels this intense on the outside, I shudder to think how I'm going to feel once he has entered me*,' I wondered.

I then initiated a kiss, which left him befuddled and he welcomed that with zeal.

"Whoa, I have to go before I find myself on this bed," he

sniggered. "I'll see you later."

"Okay, I will see you later."

He left the bedroom and I realised only after he had left, that I was feeling very excited about the experience I had just had. My body was soaking wet from the incident and I never thought that a few kisses could make a person sweat like that – from all the hidden places. He called out to me after fetching his medical bag from his office. I followed his voice, which led me to the kitchen.

"Please lock the door and do not open for anyone, until I come back. Do not even open for Lulama or Mos; or should I lock you in? Just kidding!" he giggled.

Did he really want to lock me in? What if he wasn't kidding like he claimed he was? I didn't like the on and off sporadic feelings I had where he was concerned. One moment I'd feel at ease with him and the next, I'd feel as if I was with someone who resembled my dad; someone I should fear. That's the feeling that made me uneasy. That was only the second day!

****

After he left, I locked the kitchen door, went to my room and locked myself in there. The house was too huge and spooky with Martin gone.

I resolved to remain in the bedroom but I quickly remembered that I had two sets of sandwiches still to gnaw on. I took Martin's sandwich and put it in the fridge and took out my mom's. I went to the bathroom to wash my hands and then ate two slices.

My poor mom had gone all out regarding how she packed everything. There was even my favourite grape and mango juice two litre bottles in the packages.

I took the entire foodstuff out, put some in the fridge and packed the dry items in the cupboard in my room. I did this while finishing my sandwiches. I made my way to the bathroom again and washed my hands, going back into the room to continue unpacking.

While unpacking my stuff, I found my mother's favourite handbag; a very beautiful and pricy tote. I marvelled though, as to why my mom could include that as one of the things to give me.

I opened it and found my wallet with some money, two of my debit cards, as well as other girly stuff in the bag. As I looked through one more time, I saw an envelope and it was clear that it was a letter from my mother to me. She had simply addressed it as "PALESA".

I opened the envelope and I flipped through the pages. There was an eight paged letter, beautifully handwritten by my mother. I sat down on the bed to read it but was very nervous regarding its contents.

"*My dearest Palesa.*

Ngwanaka, I cannot really say I am happy about the decision you took to leave home, particularly the way you went about doing this.

But, I understand. No one in their right mind can stomach the treatment that your father has subjected you to. Yes baby, I said 'in their right mind.' I say so because you are still in your right mind and I am not. I haven't been alright for a very long time and your father knows that. This is why he treats me the way he does, because somehow he feels justified because he saved me from myself at some point. He also knows that I can never leave him.

I know this might come as a shock to you my child and believe me, I never wanted you to know this but, Mama is not alright. I have suffered from depression before you were even born. My parents always felt that I was bewitched and did nothing constructive (well, according to me) to help me deal with my illness, but kept taking me to traditional healers who all said the same thing: 'This child has been bewitched.'

However, they clearly all failed to deal with this whole hex they claimed was put on me. Maybe I was hexed but they failed – they all failed anyway because at my age now, I am still on anti-depressants. Here's the story I have wanted to tell you for a very long time and I hope you will take it well:

There was a time when I felt something whispering in my ear, in the middle of the night while I slept, telling me to get out of the house. I could not resist the voice and got out of the bedroom and left the house at that ungodly hour. When I was finally able to comprehend that I was outside and walking barefoot and was already far from home, I began to weep.

That was when I decided to kill myself. I went to a bridge nearby and stood there for a couple of minutes. I prayed to whoever was listening to me at the time to accept my spirit as the physical me, was about to cease existing.

As I was about to let myself go, somebody grabbed me from behind and held me tight, pulling me down. The voice was very deep and clear. It was a man and although I couldn't see his face clearly at the time as it was dark, I could still see some glow emanating from the street lights here and there.

The man held me tight and forced me to face his way. His breath smelt like a brewery; an apparent sign that he was also heavily laden and dealing with something he might have believed then, could be eased by drinking the bitter juice.

"What on earth are you trying to do, girl? Things can't be that bad. Look at me. Although I am depressed, I can never kill myself. This is my friend." He pointed at the bottle he had in his hand.

He told me that he had made bad business decisions and very stupid investments, lost a lot of money and had since been humiliated. I looked at him and didn't care about his problems; I had mine and all I wanted was to die, whichever way that would come about.

"Come, let's go to my place so we can drown each other's sorrows," the man intimated to me.

I didn't know what to do because home was far away and it was also very evident that my parents hadn't noticed that I had left the house. I do not remember whether I had closed the door when I left or not as, I was like a zombie and only got to know later in life, that my condition also makes me sleep-walk.

The man was drunk but there he was, contemplating to drive with a person he didn't know to his house so we could drown our sorrows together. He gave me the bottle and told me to take a sip. I refused, as he had been drinking from it and at least sense told me that that would be a hygienic nightmare.

His car was nearby and his car-keys were in his pocket it had appeared, but trying to simply get them out of his pocket was a mission and a half, as he kept missing them and eventually he dropped them. Finally, he managed to pick them up from where they had fallen and opened the doors.

I got into the passenger seat and I watched him go over to his side, walking criss-cross. I was not worried about driving with a drunken man. I hoped that we would get into an accident and die anyway, because I wanted to die that night.

I do not recall anything that happened after I got into the man's car – nothing at all, at least until dawn.

I recall waking up in the morning exposed, in the man's bed, with him sleeping next to me naked and I saw blood all over me and on the sheets. I noticed then, that I had been sexually molested and the assailant was still sleeping next to me snoring like a sprite.

I was 22 years old when I lost my virginity to a stranger. The act which I do not even remember happening, save for excruciating pain I felt on my abdomen when I finally came to and the results of my lost purity on the bed and on me. The decision to give away my virtue was made for me by a depressed drunken man.

Perhaps he had drugged me or realised that I wasn't myself, hence he elected to violate me in that manner. I screamed after seeing blood all over me and he pulled me down, preventing me from leaving the bed. He was really strong.

He told me that I wanted to kill myself anyway so what he had given me was a new lease of life. He mentioned that we had sex and that I never said no to anything. He also said that I should not worry about the blood on me because it didn't mean that he had hurt me. It simply meant that I lost my virtue and that a lot of women go through that during their first encounter.

I was very hurt and it was then, that the pain inside my bladder became intense. I managed to disentangle myself from the man's clutches and looked around for my night dress that I had been wearing; I found it on the floor with my underwear next to it. I hurriedly put them on and looked for a door that I could open with ease. I ran outside that bedroom and hurried towards the front door. I then opened it, well aware that, that man was close by and putting his own pants on, trying to catch me and yelling that I should not run away.

I ran as fast as I could towards the main road and was thumbing lifts to any car that passed on that road. Each time a car passed me, I would keep running. It was still very early – around five o'clock.

As I ran, by sheer luck, I heard a hooter and a car stopped for me. It was an elderly couple that gave me a lift, asking me what happened, after seeing how I was. The woman in the car gave me one of her jerseys that was on the backseat of the car, telling me to wear it. I told the story and they drove with me to the police station. They in turn, related my story to the officers on duty and a doctor was called. I was then taken to a certain room to be examined and a statement was also taken down.

Before I knew it, my parents were called. The humiliation I suffered at the station was immense, as my parents had to tell the police that I left on my own accord in the middle of the night and they were surprised when the officers came knocking on their door, telling them that I was brought in by strangers, having just been sexually assaulted.

Once my father saw me, he unleashed an onslaught of vile words towards me, leaving me, my mother and even the police officers and the doctor baffled. He asked the name of the person I claimed had assaulted me and I couldn't do it because I had no idea who the man was. I however remembered his face, as I looked at him in the morning before I ran away.

A sketch artist was then called in. The man worked with what I gave him, as I described that man who assaulted me. It appeared that I had been accurate in my description because before long, a team of police officers had been despatched to pick the guy up. They found him.

Immediately when he was brought in, my father charged at him and had to be restrained by the police.

The man apologized right in front of many witnesses and told them that he wasn't himself that day. He told them that he saved me from trying to kill myself and all he did was to take me to his home to sleep as he didn't know where to take me. He concluded that he wasn't aware that I was a virgin and might have also missed my cries as he had been drunk. I could not believe what I was hearing. I was emotionally damaged that day.

My parents were then called into one separate room together with that man. He was released with a warning, right in front of me. My parents told me that they would speak to me at home.

We went home and although I kept asking my parents why the police let that guy go, they wouldn't tell me. Eventually, my father admitted that my case wouldn't hold water in court, as I had left on my own and the man's statement that he saved me trying to kill myself was damaging. The worst thing was that, I also could not remember the incident, besides having found blood on my person and on the sheets. That was the end of that case.

Three months after what happened to me, I started getting sick, so sick that I would vomit each time I tried to eat anything. My mother took me to the doctor who told us after examining me, that I was pregnant. I was carrying my rapist's child!

I'm sorry my girl to have to tell you this after so many years but, your father Phillip is the man I have been talking about since I began writing this letter.

When my family went to his family to tell them about my condition, he said he would marry me. My future was then decided there and then, by my parents, his parents and other elders.

That was his punishment, they alleged. Nobody ever thought to check with me at all whether I wanted to marry the man or not. They thought they were being gracious to me because somehow I would not have to shame the family name by being a single mother.

The rape case was also going to embarrass them in the community as well as at the church. I was blamed for what happened to me because I left on my own accord in the middle of the night. At that time, nobody saw it necessary to speak about my illness. Suddenly, I was responsible for going out in the middle of the night, even though they had maintained for years, that I had been under some spell.

Truth is my child, when I found out that I was pregnant, I immediately saw our life together, you and I only. However, other people made decisions for me and I had to follow the rules. I was already an adult but I was not financially self-sufficient. So I agreed to be married.

Ngwanaka, once again I apologise for giving you this information. I however think that it is vital that you know this so that you can have a full picture of why I am the way I am and why your father is the way he is.

We were both forced into this marriage and he was threatened with jail time should he refuse to marry me. So I have lived with chronic depression for years, so has he. He is unable to deal with life's issues correctly and as discomfited as our lives might seem, we have become each other's drug and nothing can separate us because we both need each other. I know too much about him and he knows too much about me. Should I leave him, I would have a lot of explaining to do as an agreement was signed and there is nothing I can do about that.

Once again my child, I am sorry but please know that as much as the circumstances you were born under were not ideal, I love you with all my heart because you are a part of me. I just hope that whoever you will be with, will treat you well and as a mother, I suspect that there is a man that saved you after you left home?

I pray that he doesn't abuse you and that you don't live your life fearful and with an aching heart. Remember that you can always come back home anytime, Palesa and we can talk to the elders so they can deal with your father somehow. That will be a mammoth task but I do think it can be done. If you'd rather stay away, at least keep in touch Palesa, so that I can know that you are still safe.

Mama has put a lot of goodies in the bags for you, as you might have seen already. Take care of this handbag, it's yours now.

I have transferred R50 000 into each of your two bank accounts. For as long as you are still happy with the man you are with, do not use this money. I know it's a man. Don't ask me how I know. Mothers know these things. You can use the money in the event that things do not go according to plan. Please use this money wisely my girl; R100 000, 00 is a lot of money and this is part of my savings over the years.

Once again, know that I love you and everything I do and every decision I have ever made, I did that for you, Palesa.

Please do keep in touch.

I love you.

Mama"

I realised after reading the last paragraph of my mother's letter, that my dress was soaking wet from crying. I had no appetite anymore. I wiped my eyes with tissue paper that was on the pedestal, took a deep breath and looked around. What was a girl to do now?

The information I had just consumed from my mother's letter was weighty and had left me sick to my stomach. I had so many questions and mixed feelings which made me wonder all sorts of things like, being an unwanted seed that only came to grow simply because some elders came together and decided that I should be allowed to live in a loveless marriage.

I was distraught and I needed Martin to comfort me but, he had already left to go to the hospital. I hoped that he would come back in a better mood than mine or rather in the same mood he was in when he left, so that I could cry on his broad shoulders and he would make me feel better.

I packed all the clothes in the closets, hanging those that needed to be hung. I then took the rest of the food out, also packing each item neatly inside the spacious fridge in the small kitchenette, which was inside my bedroom. I felt really heavy, weak and tired at the same time. I was hurt by my mother's letter, such that I wanted to even pretend I hadn't read it.

I wrestled with my spirit repeatedly, wondering if I should tell

Martin about the letter when he came back but, I figured that he might not be able to handle it, nor help in any way, seeing as he was also heavily weighed down.

Besides, that information simply meant that I was a product of rape and unlike many other people who were conceived the same way I had been, and didn't even know their fathers, I knew mine and my mother did marry that man. Now why did I feel as though I needed to release my pain through unconventional means?

CHAPTER 4
Lost Innocence

I comforted myself with scatter cushions, holding onto them and squeezing them against my belly. Although I still felt disgusted after reading that letter, somehow the hollow feeling I had, had eased up and I felt slightly better after some time.

I then dozed off for almost three to four hours, hugging cushions, crying and thinking long and hard about my life. I saw a vision of my life and it was not pretty.

I saw myself going back home, to confront both my mother and father about the news I had just read from my mother's letter. As I stood by the door, about to walk inside the lounge, I heard my father yelling at my mother, but she wasn't her usual quiet self. She was defending her honour, telling my father to stop yelling at her, explaining that they both needed each other. I jerked backwards and wondered if what I had heard was the truth or not.

Was it really a vision I saw or it was just my mind playing tricks on me? Perhaps it was. I could not stop thinking about my predicament and I suppose my subconscious mind had swallowed way too much from me, hence I thought I saw a vision of my not so pretty life, played for me by the cosmos, as if I was watching a movie. Seeing my mother defend herself to my dad had been my lifelong dream and it was good seeing her do that for a change – or did I even see that?

****

I was awoken by the sound of the SUV being revved hard and then the engine being turned off shortly thereafter. As I checked the time, it was clear that I had slept for about four hours and it was just after midday. I quickly got up from bed and rushed to the bathroom. I wanted to clean my face as I had been crying for a while.

I didn't want Martin to see me in that state. For some reason, my own feelings didn't matter as much. Instead, I wanted to protect my two day boyfriend's feelings, particularly since I had no idea what his day had been like.

"Palesa…Palesa…Palesa…," he called out to me as I listened to his footsteps ascending the stairs. I kept quiet. He knocked on my bedroom door.

“Come in,” I responded.

I had forgotten that I locked the door, and I got up quickly and unlocked it. I heard foot steps, as if he was checking something out.

He then came into my bedroom and found me in bed. He was too quiet, looking akin to a man whose whole world had just collapsed in front of him. He languidly put his medical bag down next to one side table, as I watched him, trying to read his indecipherable facial expression, which remained scrawled. He pulled his breath, letting it out again.

“Hello baby,” he forced the baritone out.

“Hi baby,” I responded.

I did learn quite quickly as to what he expected of me so, I told myself that I shouldn’t upset him as he was clearly not in the best of moods. I wondered if something had happened and felt the need to ask.

“Martin, you don’t look too good.”

I lifted my head up as he stood there in the middle of the room, looking unswervingly at me, bearing a gloomy expression. He then ran his one hand on his shaven head.

“No, Palesa, I am not alright; I lost a patient today. This doesn’t happen often and as I said, I am not doing okay. All I want is to rest for a bit.”

“Oh Martin, I am so sorry to hear that, I am truly sorry. What can I do to help relieve this pain you are experiencing?”

“I just want to lie down Palesa. Can I sleep in here with you for sometime? I don’t want to be alone in my bedroom.”

He opened the fridge, taking out a bottle of water, galloping the water as if he hadn't had it in a long time. "Nice and cold," he stated, after putting the empty bottle in the bin.

"It's okay, Martin, you can sleep in here. I was about to go make something to eat anyway."

"Palesa, I said I don't want to be alone. Did you miss that part?" he toughened his tone.

The question sounded like he was asking me if I was stupid or something, as he had already intimated that he didn't want to be alone. So why did I want to leave him to go to the kitchen?

Although I was getting sick and tired of his short fuse, I affirmed to myself, that it was not one of my brightest moments either.

"Sorry, I was just mentioning," I murmured demurely.

He didn't respond but shook his head, took off his shoes, pants and shirt, throwing them on the divan. He then retrieved his shoes from the sofa and placed them next to the bed. He left his sleeveless vest and boxers on. He sat on the edge of the bed and took off his socks.

I watched him quietly as he also kept still, but sighing constantly with every move he made. He really looked sad – distraught actually. I was unsure what to do as the battle was within his heart, even though I felt the sting from the energy he was exuding.

Knowing every corner of his house, he then got up, moved towards one of the cupboards and opened it, taking out two pillows.

Evidently, I hadn't thought of checking everything that was in that bedroom. I had no idea there were so many blankets, sheets, pillows and pillow cases in my room alone.

He then stared at me and gave me a smile. I smiled back as I was a bit edgy, worried that I'd make a mistake, leading to him yelling at me once again.

He then lay down on the bed with me and extended his hands towards me, lynching one of his arms around my waist. He then kissed me on my cheek.

"How was your day, baby?" he asked softly.

I never thought he'd ask me how my day was, but he did. That somehow pleased me because everything had seemed to revolve around him – even for only those few days.

"It was quiet and uneventful. I was resting most of the time and only woke up just now when you came in. I was clearly very exhausted," I mentioned.

He hauled his breath and muttered, "mmm."

He rubbed himself against me and then embraced me from behind as I faced the night stand on my side of the bed, my back away from him. He didn't seem to mind at first as he held me tightly, kissing my neck relentlessly.

I froze a bit but quickly remembered that I was set on not upsetting him, more so after he had told me that he had lost a patient.

Although it was not particularly chilly, it was not that warm either. I had a coverlet over me and Martin flipped it open and covered himself with it as well.

That was my duty to make him feel better; I held. I wondered though as to how I was going to handle that difficult task. I do think he knew exactly what he wanted that day; he wanted me, there and then, whether I was apprehensive, ready, frightened or not.

"Palesa...," he whispered in my ear while running his one hand up and down my whole body, reaching my left breast and squeezing it tenderly. I panicked and felt cold sweat shooting down my face.

"Yes Martin...," I garbled.

"I want you, I want you right now baby," he breathed, continuing to kiss me on my neck and eventually turning me around.

"Look at me Palesa; I want you to look at me." I did so, my heart beating sporadically.

He then pulled me really close to him and gave me a peck on my lips, looking at me intently, as if to check if I was going to pull another "stunt" like I did the previous night. Well...his words.

I was not only frightened regarding what was about to happen but, I was also worried about his temperament, which appeared to be sparked even by the simplest of things.

'*I have to make sure that Martin gets out of this mood he is in*,' I persuaded my inner person.

The man caressed me for a long time, running his hand all over my body, eventually reaching my underwear. As he was about to pull it down, I grabbed his hand. His face grimaced and he roughly removed my hand from his, continuing to undress me.

"Ouch!" I screamed. He was pretty staid about what he was doing. There was nothing I could do. He was a man, a very strong muscled man, albeit not too bulky.

"Palesa… relax, I am not going to hurt you." My cheeks tingled.

"Martin, are we doing this now while you are not doing alright emotionally?"

"I need this, Palesa. I know what's going to make me feel better. It's me making love to you. You did promise me, didn't you? So, please don't deny me this again," he begged, his eyes blistering. That concerned me, as I worried about his emotional and perhaps mental state.

"I'm not saying no to you Martin, but you do recall I'm a virgin right? Please don't hurt me." I tried to be brave, even though I was really terrified that day. I interrogated my inner person as to why she would worry about Martin's emotional state.

He kept quiet and puffed, eventually pulling down my underwear and I felt him touching my vulva with his one hand, running his fingers all over it, doing something I never thought I'd ever experience in my life, at the hands of a man, an older man I had only known for a few days.

There were so many things I was determined not to do in my life. I had my own time-line. The first one was to never be involved with an older man. The next was to never have sex until I had found the right man that I truly loved. I also wanted to get married first before I could experience that.

However, I broke my own vows and that proved to have been a dream, as circumstances forced me into the arms of a man whom, in a few days, had become my boyfriend. Yes, I left home in a pant and thought that I was doing the right thing for myself but the universe had other plans for me.

Martin then undressed me quietly while continuing to stroke me. I allowed him to have his way, not knowing whether I should do anything to him or not, as I had no clue what to do. He continued until all items I had worn were completely off, leaving me fully exposed. I felt really diffident as I watched him pore over my body.

He then took off his vest and boxers, frightening me some more as I watched his enormous and tight incline. I immediately shed a tear as he climbed on top of me, holding both my hands and bringing them above my head. He continued kissing me and then going down, kissing me all over my upper body and then my abdomen.

I felt as though I was going to die, as I felt a very sharp headache and my heart continued to beat unsteadily. I shivered and felt cold sweat all over me, his and mine. That electricity shock struck through my whole body again. '*Is this what death feels like*?' I asked myself.

The sensation I had inside my stomach was and still is arcane; it became even more intense than how I felt the previous day when Martin kept force-kissing me.

"Palesa, loosen up…, touch me…, hug me with both your

hands," he instructed. "Kiss my neck the same way I'm doing yours. Then kiss me behind my earlobes."

"How do I touch you when you're holding my hands like that?" He slackened his grip and let go of my hands.

I did as he asked and I felt his body tremble on top of mine.

"Yeah… I like that, please continue…," he whispered, breathing heavily and sliding his manhood down on me. I screamed and released my hands from him. He put his hand on my mouth and once again, held my hands with one hand above my head. I continued to screech.

"Shh… I haven't really done anything Palesa, why are you screaming?" His eyes frightened me; they were fire red.

"I'm not used to feeling this way, Martin. The feeling is outlandish and I feel as though my intestines are about to pop out." He laughed.

"No, nothing like that will happen. Just leave everything to me; you will be fine. Will you let me in now?"

I didn't know what he meant by that and assumed that he meant I should not worry as he got me.

"Yes Martin, I'm letting you in," I affirmed naïvely.

The next moment, I felt his hardened manhood all over my abdomen and him teasing me until I felt him slide himself inside of me. I could not tolerate the pain as it was excruciating. I squealed and asked him to stop.

"Come on Palesa, I am already in. You said you were letting me in, so what's the problem?"

"Martin, please stop, please stop. It's painful," I wailed. He ignored my cries, choosing to kiss me on my neck and then my lips, and then forcing his tongue inside my mouth.

He kept huffing and puffing, still holding my hands down above my head and with every move he made, he hurt me. I cried bitterly, asking him several times to stop as I was feeling a terrible twinge. He didn't stop and it was lucid that he was enjoying himself, making 'ah… ah' sounds while deflowering the nineteen year old me without even using protection. A whole doctor!

Martin took at least 20 minutes having sex with me, with no care in the world that I had asked him countless times to stop as I was feeling pain. He was clearly a person who made promises and broke them just as quickly as he had made them.

Even before he entered me, he had promised not to hurt me. The previous day, he had told me that I should let him know should I feel pain and he would stop; he didn't.

When he finally pulled out, he looked at me and kissed me again, letting go of my hands but totally ignoring my sobs and tears and the fact that I had been weeping the whole time.

"You're so beautiful you know, especially when you snivel like that. You are beautiful and you are mine now, my woman," he declared and climbed off.

I wept, feeling a burning sensation on my passage and felt the need to go to the bathroom.

"Martin, I need to go to the bathroom."

"Really, or you just want to run away?"

"I really need to go to the bathroom, Martin."

"Okay…stop crying now. What has happened here is natural. The first time is always painful and every woman goes through this. You are a woman now… my woman," once again he avowed proudly.

I couldn't believe how flippant the man was with me. I had expected him to have apologized each time I cried out or at least comforted me. I looked for evidence of my broken hymen on the sheets but there was nothing. I was evidently one of those few who didn't bleed after the first time of losing their virtue.

I went to the bathroom and got in the shower, feeling terribly sore. I was upset and was glad that it was over.

My relief was short-lived because as I closed the shower curtains, I saw them being flung open. I thought that perhaps the system was malfunctioning. To my surprise, Martin had opened them and came into the shower with me, his manhood erect so much that he had turned pale. He then closed the curtains.

"Martin, I am tired and in pain," I sternly warned.

"I want to help wash your back and you do mine as well." He ignored my plea.

I got irritated and wondered if I would ever enjoy sex, particularly with him. I felt powerless to rebuke him and gave him my face cloth; he poured shower gel all over my body, rubbing it in a few strokes using my face cloth. He took the moment to keep touching me everywhere, holding my breasts and spreading my legs apart.

"There is no set place where a couple can make love, Palesa. At some point, we will do it in here; at other times we will be on the stairs; on the couch; on the floor; on the balcony, in fact everywhere," he whispered in my ear and chuckled, as I felt his warm breath on my neck.

"Can't we rest please Martin?" He ignored me.

"Now that's your lesson for today. Remember that I shouldn't be the only one to initiate sex. If you want me, you should verbalise it and show me that you want me." I nodded.

What could I do? How could I have fought him should he have decided to be brutal with me? The way I was feeling then, I was certain that there was no way I would want Martin again, seeing as he hurt me earlier and didn't even apologise for doing so. I inclined, holding onto the shower wall with both my hands, afraid to slip and fall.

While I was debating with my subconscious, the man chafed himself against me and pinned me against the shower wall, switching the shower tap off. My hands slipped and he snaked his one hand around my waist and caressed me again, stroking me all over and kissing me.

"Don't fall Palesa, I got you," he assured as I closed my eyes.

'*I hope this man is not a sex addict*,' I prayed.

"Palesa, do to me what I'm busy doing to you."

"What do you want me to do to you, Martin? I am tired," I mumbled gallingly.

It was as if I hadn't mentioned that because he entered me

forcefully. I told him to stop doing that as I didn't like what he was doing but he ignored my pleas. He was having a good time. Why did I run away from home? I could have just retreated to the bedroom as I always used to do. I began chastising myself.

Although I didn't really feel as much pain as I did earlier, I didn't appreciate what he did. I felt him literally stirring my pelvis, coiling himself inside of me, wheezing and panting like a man possessed. He then lifted me up, forcing me to do what he wanted to make him happy. Not once did he ask me if I was okay or if I was enjoying myself.

I told him persistently that I wanted him to stop and he never did. I thought that perhaps I had a duty to make him happy as he had lost a patient and he needed somebody to console him, So, I was the obvious choice, seeing as I was his girlfriend and there with him. I had put myself in that situation didn't I? How twisted my thinking had become in just a couple of hours!

Within an hour I had lost my virtue to a man I wasn't sure I really liked but, I had to succumb to him because I held that I had no choice.

He rough sexed me in the shower, remarking about how happy he was that I had finally agreed to sleep with him and that I was giving him what he needed. Eventually he hauled himself out, while continuing to run his tongue inside my mouth. He then bit my neck – a love bite again? I got really annoyed.

"Let me wipe you so we can take this party back to bed." What did he just say? The man wanted to have a third round? I knew then that I was in trouble and had landed in the hands of a sex pervert.

He didn't seem tired but my whole body was tired but somehow the itchiness had subsided. Perhaps it was the warm water I had no idea. However, my hip joints were aching as if they had been dislocated from being pulled apart doggedly.

Martin wiped me as I kept quiet, not at all saying anything. I was worried that the house was like a prison of sorts with a security system that was too urbane. So, even if I were to run away, he was probably going to find me before I even left the compound.

Martin then lifted me up again as I clung my legs around his waist. We left the shower and went to the bedroom. He literally flung me onto the bed and lay next to me, as the bed springs objected to the abuse – pzzing! He was huffing and out of breath.

"You'll hurt me!" I protested. He chose not to respond to my protestation.

"This is beautiful lovemaking we just made, Palesa. You just need to know what I love. If you make me happy, then I will make you happy. That way you will enjoy it as well. This is how it should go, not the other way round. It's important that you learn how to arouse me so that I can make love to you anytime and satisfy you. I cannot believe I finally broke that wall! I am going to make you very happy."

I forced a smirk and lay faced up, listening and taking heed of everything the man was saying to me. It was my duty to make him happy he said; if I played my part, he would then play his. What an arrogant thing to say!

"Do you know why you didn't bleed?" he asked, running his hand up and down my abdomen.

"No, I don't know," I answered curtly.

"Do you do any sport?"

"Yes, I play netball. Why do you ask?"

"Sometimes the hymen does break during some rigorous sporting activities, even if it's not fully, at least until full penetration. Perhaps that was the case with you, even though you still felt some pain." The man gave me a mini lesson about my body; bloody swine!

"Oh, so you were aware that I was feeling pain? I thought you didn't care."

"Come on Palesa, how can I not care about my girlfriend? I couldn't apologise because in my opinion, I was not really hurting you. I wanted you to relax and what I was doing was simply to break your virginity, something everyone goes through in their lives. I couldn't stop either because I was really enjoying myself, making love to you for the first time," he declared, bearing a wide grin.

Martin's declaration made me sick, because it sounded like he didn't care about me and everything was all about him; how happy he was; how much he was enjoying himself and that sort of thing. However, he had called me his girlfriend; so soon? Suddenly, I had no words to say to the man I had chided earlier. I feared responding to him.

"I am hungry, Martin; I didn't cook anything."

"Don't worry, I brought us takeaways. I wasn't expecting you to cook, given that you were still going to unpack your stuff."

"Martin, why didn't you use protection?" I asked brusquely.

"Did you want me to use protection, Palesa? Why didn't you say anything? More to the point, you were a virgin weren't you and that plastic would have hurt you terribly."

What did the man think I was… an idiot?

"Besides…," he paused. "I know I'm HIV negative and being a virgin, to me, that meant that you haven't slept with anyone else and as such are HIV negative. So, we are going to be loyal and faithful to each other, aren't we?"

I could not believe what I was hearing; a whole Specialist Physician reasoning like an uneducated person. Even I knew that there were other diseases that are communicable via intercourse; not HIV only. What about pregnancy? What if either him or I had been victims of blood transfusion gone wrong?

As I was about to bring that subject up, he instructed me to stop talking and to make him happy again, as he was battling to get over the fact that he had lost a patient earlier. Now he was emotionally blackmailing me by using me to get over the loss of his patient – such a perverse thing to say!

"Come on top… let me show you what to do," he instructed.

He flipped me over and brought me up to his groin, slithering himself inside of me, as I felt his manhood hitting my cervix. Again, I had to play along; I was trapped.

That time however, I felt the weirdest sensation ever! I twisted and swivelled, crafting my own techniques and moves until I saw his wide smirk. I think I enjoyed myself on top of the man, so much that I eventually felt like fire was burning inside my stomach.

I could swear I saw the heavens open that day. I felt like weeping but it was not from pain, it was an orgasm… I think. I felt as though there were diminutive horses running amok inside my belly and my bladder. Then blood roared through my veins, as if it had just been injected forcefully. My legs felt warm and my whole face trembled.

We both screamed as he tossed me over one more time and dominated me again until I couldn't take it anymore. My legs wobbled, shaking frenziedly. Hearing him roar like a lion, I could tell that I must have done something really good for him, as he was now clearly worn-out and content. It was the first time since we began having sex, that he had let out that kind of sound – a roar of some kind.

He nearly ruined the moment of contentment by releasing himself inside of me before he pulled out. I felt some warm movement inside of me. At that time though, I was still on cloud nine, with no pain in sight. I got worried about the possibility of getting pregnant when he released himself inside of me.

"Before one of us dies, let's rest," he jokingly cautioned, throwing himself on the side and kissing me, while panting as if he had just run a marathon. I was breathing heavily as well. I felt like I had just died and rose again.

"Is that why you have been pestering me since yesterday about sex? You wanted to feel this way?"

"Now you know, Palesa. The attraction between us is too powerful and we couldn't just be together without making love. That would have been a travesty of nature," he giggled, as we hugged and rested bare next to each other.

I had a man and he had, within two days and a few hours, taught me so many things I never thought I'd ever want to learn, at least not at that stage. That was the beginning of our whirlwind romance.

CHAPTER 5

Dreadful Wake Up Call

Six months had passed since I stayed with Martin. I hadn't seen my mother as I had promised. I did call her often and from time to time, she would ask me when I would invite her over and I would tell her that I would do so in no time. I never did. I could tell though, her apprehension about my safety had somehow ebbed.

I was now sharing Martin's huge bedroom with him, while some of my stuff still remained in the bedroom I had occupied first. He had bought me a fancy laptop and the house had unlimited fibre Internet access. That meant that I did not have to worry about data bundles, something that was always a big issue for me, when I stayed at my parents' house.

This awakened me somewhat and I utilised my new toy to its

fullest capability during the day when he wasn't home. I would read as much as I could about life and did a lot of research on vocational colleges that would accept me so that I could complete my grade 10 schooling.

We were already in August and I had missed a lot of months of schooling. However, I was growing mentally and maturing but I kept this to myself. I was learning new things and that pleased me. I enjoyed my company and while I had not seen or heard from my friends in a while, I was not particularly lonely.

I communicated often with my two friends, Luzuko and Dineo via facebook. At least time had not passed me by. They were already in Grade 12 and although they were two classes ahead of me, we had kept very close up until I left school.

They were very concerned that I was not in school but, I promised them that I would still continue with some studies and that I was alright and I was happy. I had a man. I however didn't know what to post on the platform, so I spent the next few weeks studying it so I wouldn't make a mockery of myself the next time I decided to post.

All I did was to simply send my friends direct messages and they would always ask me to post on my timeline. I would refuse every time they asked me to do that. They wanted to see the house I was staying in and who the man I was involved with was. It was evident that the rumour mill had already spread the news about me and what my life had turned into. I suspected my mother or my father in his fit of rage, might have told whoever cared to listen that

I was a scoundrel that left home to be with some man. Obviously he would have omitted his role in that matter.

My hesitation to post about my then current life on my facebook timeline, was not met with gusto by my two friends. They then unfriended me and as much as I convinced myself that I didn't care that they did that, I wasn't being honest with myself because I cared enough to worry about their move. Now I was not only alone during the day but, I became lonely too.

That platform was not to my liking anyway and I felt like one would expose oneself to public scrutiny way too much, some of whom didn't even know me, risking my man's wrath. My loneliness did get the better of me. I ceased being active on the podium and never told Martin that I had opened an account. I shuddered to think how he would react since he was such a very private man, the kind that would give one a sense that he might have a lot to hide.

The helpers, Sis Lulama and Bra Mos seemed happy to have me in the house because Martin had also stopped yelling at them for some strange reason.

He demanded sex anytime he felt like it. At night, I would be awoken by his weight over me, ready to pounce on me. During this time, he would be like a different person altogether and it felt as if I was sleeping with someone else – a monster. He would also be particularly rough with me. I would sometimes wake up in the middle of the night and find him starring at me. This frightened me because I never really knew what he was thinking at the time he had been staring. I never consented to that kind of lovemaking. I was terrified to admonish him, even though I protested somewhat. Evidently, my complaints had not been punchy enough.

I figured that it must have been my fault he was continuing with that bad treatment; otherwise why would he keep doing that, even though I had told him that I didn't like it? He would just climb on top of me, entering me cogently and gyrating until I was fully awake while I pretended to be fine with what he did.

This then led to me taking sex as a chore and retribution for something I might have done and never knew what it was. Unfortunately for me, that made him want it even more once he got a sense that I had relented. I didn't know whether to call what was happening rape or not. He knew I didn't like what he did but he would roughly force himself on me at midnight, leaving me bruised and worried about the next day. Still, I saw no reason to go back home – I was no longer welcome.

He seemed to want it more every time I cited fatigue. He would ask me what I was doing during the day, which made me tired as we had helpers to do house chores. I wouldn't know how to respond to his questions about my fatigue, but resolved to stop complaining about being tired. I was also not sure why I was always tired. Perhaps it was those midnight escapades, so the sleeping cycle had become abnormal.

Martin would only stop sleeping with me when it was that time of the month, which gave me some time to myself. He would be so irritable during those three to four days and I would feel guilty, as if

I had stolen something valuable from him or done something seriously wrong to upset him. I would intentionally avoid him altogether and allow him his space to do whatever he wanted to do by himself.

I initially got worried, wondering if he would be cheating on me during those days. I didn't want to ask him what he did to ease his longing, lest I came across as accusatory or even jealous because I wasn't.

We never used protection, something he convinced me not to do. He told me that if I were to fall pregnant, that would be fine because that would mean that it was meant to happen. I was very uncomfortable about that. I guess the universe must have been on my side because I never wanted to fall pregnant, not at that time anyway, perhaps not even by him.

Although we were together, my feelings alternated between being happy and content, particularly regarding how other things worked in the house, to being extremely unhappy and frightened. I brought myself to this place – my own fault. Perhaps having been condemned to fend for myself by my own parents.

I never wanted to think of myself as a victim of abuse because everything else worked well, didn't it? Still, the fact that I would wake up in the middle of sex at midnight, being pushed and persuaded beyond rebuff and being told in no uncertain terms that my boundaries were irrelevant, frightened me and constantly plagued my mind, leaving me crestfallen. I had lost my body autonomy to my man's exploitation within a mere six months.

I had to think long and hard about my future, whether it would be with him or I'd be by myself. I wanted to give myself a chance to finalise my high school studies and to later register for a course in Fashion Designing. I was very good at making patterns and then sewing clothes, even without formal training.

I continued feeding my mind off the articles and free books I found on the Internet. I kept quiet about my new found knowledge. Besides, the knowledge I had accumulated at the time, was not enough for me to help myself, or to leave. It was mere information about human behaviour, some sales books and about lovers and relationships.

As much as I was maturing, I had no other resources but the ones Martin had afforded me. I somehow still believed that I was being ungrateful but then again, why was my inner voice warning me constantly about the life I had chosen?

I battled to even articulate my yearning to study to Martin and I was worried that he might not like the idea of me studying, as he seemed to want me at home all the time. I was resolute however, to obtain a good education, suitable for my abilities and talents. I had to find a way to break the news to him. I had to keep buttering him up until a suitable moment could present itself.

At some point, I contemplated utilising the money my mother gave me to register at a Vocational College. But, I remembered her stern words that I should not use it for as long as Martin and I were happy.

Why did she think that there would come a time when I would

not be happy with him? She had to have be projecting, I deduced – no two relationships can ever be the same.

I had no idea whether I was happy or not though. I didn't even know what being happy constituted in. Can one be happy for a couple of days and then become miserable for a month? Does that amount to happiness of some kind? Is there anyone who is totally happy with every aspect of his/her life, particularly in a relationship?

All I knew was that I stayed at a place where there was no constant yelling or bickering; where I ate anything I wanted anytime, without being made to feel guilty that money didn't grow on trees. Martin had a short fuse as well but, to me it was nothing compared to my dad's.

I was a child then but from what I could gather, it did seem like my father was paid well where he worked as a Financial Consultant even though he was really hard with his money. Now that I had read my mother's letter, I figured that perhaps it was due to those bad investments he had made in his early adulthood, that made him to be so tightfisted.

Although we didn't really lack at home, my stay at Martin's place introduced me to a whole new world of magnificence and opulence. So, that made all the thoughts of missing home go away, remembering how badly my father had treated my mother and I.

I swayed myself that I had to grin and bear the hard treatment in the evening, because I was enjoying all of life's comforts. There was that thing that Martin held over me and I couldn't put my finger on it. I constantly defeated myself with my thoughts, alternating between my home life and my new found “freedom”.

I felt responsible for Martin somehow, as if I had been brought to his house to look after him. I noticed also, that he didn’t really like seeing me talk to either Sis Lulama or Bra Mos. I therefore made certain that all our chitchats ended before he came back from work. He would at times, chase Sis Lulama out of the house should he find her making even an innocent small talk with me. He would candidly tell her to leave the house and stop talking to me as if I was her pal. The woman would just leave head down without any protest whatsoever.

Most of the time, he would demand to know every little detail about my daily activities with the helpers, particularly regarding what we spoke about and what each of them said to me.

His mean and jealous streak seemed very endearing, something that should excite me instead of leaving me apprehensive. That did excite me in a way. My man wanted to protect me from being corrupted by the help!

It was lucid though, that Sis Lulama and Bra Mos were afraid to tell me anything damaging about Martin in any case. I did ask them a couple of times to divulge some information regarding the kind of person their boss was. They flatly refused to let drop any information.

As much as they had, to some extent warmed up to me, I could tell that they didn’t fully trust me. Perhaps it was my youth? They probably thought that I would tell on them and then they would lose their jobs. Martin paid them really well. Every time the man came back home and found me in the kitchen cooking or busy with something, he would literally order me to the bedroom, before he could sit down or do anything meaningful.

I made excuses for him in my head and labelled myself a pacifier. I did so because it appeared that each time he was not feeling too good emotionally, he would covet sex from me and he would cling to me with vitality, compelling me to make many promises not to leave him. That left me uneasy but I continued protecting this bizarre behaviour from my soul, who kept issuing counsel I did not ask for.

I never really wanted to push the talk about Martin with the helpers further and resolved to subtly do my own investigations, while letting the man do whatever he wanted to with me.

He took a day off one day, something he had craftily neglected to tell me the previous day. I woke up early as usual and took a shower, eager to prepare breakfast. I wondered why he wasn't making a move to wake up. After my shower, I tried to wake him up as I figured that he must have been tired after all his hard work the previous day, coupled with his over the top gyratory moves at night.

While I was still busy applying my lotion, I heard him cough, slowly waking up.

"Good morning, baby," he greeted me.

"Good morning baby, did you sleep well?" I greeted back.

"Yes I did, can you tell? I'm not going to work today by the way; I want to see what exactly it is you do with Lulama and Mos the whole day."

That sounded like a joke, but I sensed a shrewd note in his voice when he said that. I paused and gave him a half smile. "So you took a day off just so you can spy on me and the helpers?"

"No…, obviously I took this day off to be with you. I don't want those two feeding your mind with all sorts of twaddle about me," he hastily alleged, while getting up from bed, heading to the bathroom. I thought he would tell me that he was joking about the helpers remark but he didn't. He swiftly took a shower, mumbling something unclear from the bathroom and called me out to him.

"You can prepare something for us to eat. Today we are having breakfast together; I want us to talk about something really serious. If you see Lulama, tell her not to come in today as I'm home. I don't want her going up and down when we're trying to talk. Besides, it is not really dirty in the house."

"Okay, I'll prepare breakfast," I mumbled.

I went to the kitchen after getting dressed to prepare breakfast and set the table. It didn't take Martin long to shower and I hadn't even expected him to finish that quickly. He came to join me in the kitchen, and as soon as he reached me, he hurled questions at me regarding Sis Lulama.

"Did you tell Lulama that I said she shouldn't come in?" he asked.

"I haven't told her because I haven't seen her yet." That day,

Sis Lulama had unfortunately thought of coming in later than usual.

"I see that people do as they please in my house in my absence. Does she do this often?"

"When you say people, does that include me?" I really needed to know what he meant, as he was acting really weird, as if he had a lot to say but was beleaguered to do so.

"Come on baby, I'm talking about Lulama and Mos. Let's finalise the table setting. What did you make?"

I didn't respond. He took various items from the kitchen and helped me to place some food on the dining table. He remarked about how good of a cook I was.

I was surprised to hear him praise me that much and thought that perhaps he was trying to soften me up for whatever it was, he wanted us to talk about.

"Thank you," I responded politely.

As we sat down, I prayed for the food as usual and he held my hand, bearing a very queer grin. We then began eating.

"Palesa, I love you," he avowed. I stared at him, startled by the declaration.

"I want to be with you forever and I hope you don't harbour thoughts of leaving me at some point," he curiously mentioned.

"Martin, what is it that makes you strongly believe that you love me so much?"

"The six months we have been together has made me certain that I really want to be with you Palesa. You now do everything I tell you to do without any trouble."

I wasn't sure how I felt about that last statement, as it felt insulting to me. It was clear that he wanted a woman that didn't have her own opinion or ideas; a woman that just did as she was told; a woman whose duty it was to serve him, never seeking any bliss or fulfillment for herself. So, obviously I had become that subservient woman and he liked it. Even so, I was determined to amass myself with a qualification.

"You are quiet, Palesa; don't you feel this way too?"

"I'm not sure what to say, Martin, especially about love. If you believe that what is happening between us is love, then love it is."

He raised his eyebrows, his brow grimacing.

"Ouch! This hurts," he alleged, putting his hand on his chest. "Are you saying you don't know how you feel about me?"

"No, I'm not saying that. You do need me to be honest don't you? All I'm saying is that I do have very strong feelings for you but, I'm not sure if I can equate those feelings to love. I truly do not know what love is."

Martin wasn't quiet chuffed with my response, particularly after praising me earlier, telling me how I did everything he wanted me to do. I had obviously said something he wasn't expecting.

"Okay, I see. Are you planning to leave me at some point, Palesa?"

"No Martin, I'm not planning anything. Why would I leave you?"

"Only people who love each other stay together. So, if you are here, yet you don't love me, what is your reason for being here?"

I had to think fast as I could sense his rising pant. At this stage, save for his bedroom tomfoolery, I had become accustomed to the life I was living and knew that should Martin get a sense that I wasn't really as happy about my life as he believed I was, he could chase me away as he had threatened to do so a couple of times. Would I return to my parents? Certainly not!

"Martin, everything has been overwhelming ever since I got here. I feel useless being here as there is nothing stimulating for me that I do. I need to study."

He ogled me, listening attentively.

"Remember that I am not in school now. So, I keep asking myself why you would want to be with me, an uneducated young woman. Now you have declared your love for me and that to me doesn't make sense."

"Oh, is that the reason you don't know whether you love me or not, because you are worried that my feelings for you might not be genuine?"

What could I say, I had to affirm what he had assumed to me, "Yes, that's the reason and like I said; I want to study."

He ignored my sentiments about needing to study.

"Oh, you gave me a fright there for a bit. I thought you have simply been leading me on and were planning an exit. Now I know you actually do love me. Please don't scare me like that again. Thank you for loving me; at least you will not leave me like my mother and my sister left me. I have you forever now." That shook me to the core and my stomach nearly turned.

I noted that he might not have dealt with the death of his mother and sister at all and was expecting me to heal him.

Was that perhaps the reason he would cling onto me so much, particularly in the evening? What about the long strange sex sessions at night? I was unyielding in establishing what it was, that he was longing for in his life, which he hadn't gotten over and that had since created that void in his heart; the very thing that made him seek succor in sex.

I reasoned that if I could help him deal with his fiend, then I would also live a lot happier because I had begun to feel like a sex slave, even though living with him was not so bad for the six months I had been with him.

The problem I faced was that, I did not know how I would go about doing research on the man. But my computer was going to be the best gadget to use. I also had a smart-phone but it wasn't going to be easy to work through it as there were a number of features it didn't possess. One way or another, I had to know what Martin's issue was.

There were times when I would look at him pitifully and see a little boy starring at me; a little boy who constantly needed to be called out and hugged afterwards. He would sometimes tease me deliberately, knowing that I would not be happy with what he was doing. But, he would continue anyway, until I would perhaps remove myself from the situation or chide him. That would then be followed by him apologizing by taking me to bed to show me how remorseful he was!

I decided to finally relent, surrendering fully to Martin, with no intention to ever leave him or run away.

A huge responsibility was placed on my shoulders by the Cosmos, I presumed. As much as I made that decision to be Martin's real girlfriend, I was steadfast in my stance of working really hard to get help for him – for us.

My worry about what I was planning was that, should I succeed in finding some kind of cure or treatment for his weird conduct, what would happen if he really became well to the point that he didn't need me anymore? I had become accustomed to him needing me and wanting me, even though that really tired me out. A messed up situation I was in!

I had to play my cards right and also make sure that I secured my future with him. If he thought he was using me, then I could also use him to better my life.

****

"Palesa, we have been invited to a wedding this coming Saturday," Martin stated, staggering me from my thoughts. "It is short notice I know, but I wasn't sure whether you would want to come with me or not. I have known about this wedding for a while now. That's another reason I decided to take this Thursday off. I want us to go to Rainbow Mall, so we can get you something very beautiful to wear. You should also change your hair; perhaps get a wig or something. You have worn your hair natural for a while now. It's time you changed it. I want you to look superb."

The man spoke and I listened, affirming a nasty feeling that I had about him and his calculating tendencies. I didn't take kindly to what he had said. I mean, that was my hair and I loved it like that. In fact, I preferred wearing my hair natural as opposed to constantly having to wear other people's hair.

"Martin, I love my hair. Why would I want to change it?" His brow frowned.

"You will change it because I want you to change it, Palesa. The natural hair is fine for when you are in the house and I don't really mind it. But when we go to events, I want you to look extra beautiful for me and style it at least. So, we are getting either a wig or you must have a weave installed; you can choose," he concluded.

I couldn't believe Martin's hard and unrelenting tone. Evidently, he was slowly but surely attempting to change me. '*Should I let him do that? Perhaps I should – he did say that it will just be for when we go to events*,' I reassured myself.

I persuaded myself that doing something for Martin wasn't really a bad idea. I wanted to keep him as being in a relationship had begun exciting me, in spite of all other intricacies that it came with. Besides, it was just a wig and I would take it off when we got home, so where would the harm be in that? I could still be in my cornrows when I was at home.

"Alright, I'll get a wig or wigs so that I can change as and when we go to events or I go out. Maybe I might even enjoy the transformation."

There I was, wanting to appease him as I realized that he got worked up by my natural hair stance. “Are you sure though that you are ready to be seen with me in public?” I asked.

“What kind of question is that? Of course I am. I have told my friends about you so everyone is eager to meet you. This is why you haven’t seen any of them here at the house because, I wanted to be certain that you and I are indeed on the same page. I didn’t want to be embarrassed,” he added.

“Embarrassed by what?”

“You have pulled many funny stunts before, Palesa; like now when you said you don’t even know whether you loved me or not.”

He brought that up again, while I did all I could to maintain composure. His on and off mood was honestly now getting on my nerves.

The cost of carrying an emotionally heavily burdened man on my shoulders was beginning to really weigh me down. Still, as I made a resolution earlier to go in the relationship with everything I got, I had to calm myself down and convince myself that the relationship would work and I would somehow find a way to deal with everything that the universe had thrown my way. I was still worried about the broken man that Martin was, and the possibility of cutting myself in the process of trying to “heal” him.

He held a grudge no doubt and he was obviously not going to let me get away with my uncertainty about my feelings for him, while he had made declarations of love to me constantly. He wanted me to finally say the word ‘love’ and to make it convincing that I truly meant what I said.

"Come on Martin, hasn't what I said to you landed credence to the fact that I feel the way you feel?" I asked.

"See, you cannot even say the word. How can I bravely introduce you to my friends not even sure that you really love me? You have to make me believe that you really do love me and that you want to be with me forever."

"Martin, why would you say such a statement about us being together forever, while you and I have only been together for six months and are not married? It's only people who are about to be married that can really speak about 'forever'," I cunningly chided him.

"Oh, I know what you want. In fact, I have known for a while what you want. This is actually the main reason I didn't go to work to be here with you."

He looked at me anxiously as I witnessed the spectacle of his trembling hands, which left me baffled. I wondered what the problem was. He then stood up, imploring me to keep seated.

He hurriedly ran to the bedroom, leaving me wondering what was going on. When he came down panting the same way as the time he left, he went to the kitchen and I could hear him locking the door from inside and pulling the bolt to make certain that the door wouldn't open.

I deduced he didn't want Sis Lulama to come in and since she still hadn't come in at that time, he saw no reason to open the door for her. He came back and asked me to close my eyes.

"Why should I close my eyes? I'm still eating."

"Please do so and stop second guessing everything I say… please," he added, as an afterthought.

"Okay then." I drank my juice and closed my eyes.

I had closed my eyes for about three to four seconds and as he asked me to open them, I saw him bending on one knee, having an open navy blue velvet box housing a ring with a huge shimmering emerald stone inside; too striking to even contemplate wearing it.

"This was my mother's ring, Palesa. It's very precious to me and I am here asking you to marry me. I love you baby and please never doubt that and I'd like to honour her by giving this to you," he declared swiftly and pouted. "Please say you'll marry me…please please…please," he pleaded. He was really weird when I was still getting to know him.

"Yes, I'll marry you Martin... I'll marry you."

I was afraid to turn him down, even though I knew that I was not ready for marriage. I had begun to feel worn-out having to tend to his needs, living like his wife anyway; a wife that was trapped in a marriage she didn't know she still wanted.

He smiled and asked, "Are you serious? Oh my God, I thought I'd have to convince you. Thank you…thank you very much Palesa. You have no idea what you have done for me just by saying yes. My love… my baby… my friend. I really love you." His elation was palpable and that frightened me.

He pulled my left hand and slid the ring on my finger. That seemingly innocent move gave me goose-bumps. I felt an eerie presence in the house after Martin slipped that ring on my finger. I experienced some heaviness on my shoulders, as if someone was hugging me from behind but, there was no one there. I felt it though but pretended there was nothing going on. That sensation however, spooked me.

The ring was indeed gorgeous and visibly very expensive. It fit my finger perfectly, as if it was made especially for me. I wasn't sure however that I wanted to wear a ring that belonged to his mother; the woman who was abused by the very same man who probably bought that expensive ring. I kept quiet, tussling with my feelings constantly. There was no turning back; I was now someone's fiancé.

He implored me to get up from the chair. He wasted no time and literally consumed my lips, as I stopped him, pleading with him to let me gobble down my juice before I choked.

He could not stop declaring how happy he was about the fact that I didn't give him a hard time when he proposed and simply agreed without any hassles.

What had I done? After wearing that ring, reality finally set in. I was ensnared and had landed in the hands of a man sixteen years my senior; a man who still longed for his mother and sister. What were the odds that the reason he gave me that ring was so he could continue feeling closer to his mother? Was I supposed to be like his mother or be his mother?

My decree earlier of finding out certain things about him and how he truly felt about the absence of his loved ones, intensified. I had to find out, not only for him but for my peace of mind. For the time being though, I had to live in the moment, giving him my full attention.

"You need to finish and go change your clothes as I want us to go to the mall as early as possible. You can buy anything you want; shoes; jewellery; many dresses, skirts, lingerie, pants or blouses. I will not interfere at all, I promise. Money is no object. You have truly made me the happiest man alive. We will go to the Rainbow Mall, where there are many boutiques for only those with serious cash," he proudly stated.

"It's really not necessary to buy expensive stuff, Martin. I'm not that fussy." He ignored me.

I could see by how he was beaming, that the man was on cloud nine. I wasn't going to spoil his mood as that would have been a seriously dangerous move!

CHAPTER 6

The Girl Is Maturing

It took me quite some time to prepare myself to my satisfaction to go to the mall. I had briefly put the ring down on one of the pedestals in the bedroom. Martin came in as I was trying to figure out what I would wear and saw the ring.

"Why did you take the ring off?" he asked, slighted.

"Come on, Martin. I am busy with water and lotions, so I don't want to ruin it. Please don't tell me that you're going to police me everytime to see whether I'm wearing the ring or not." I had to speak up. The man was really frustrating.

"No, of course not. As long as you don't forget to wear it after you have taken it off, like when we go out now, you have to make sure that you do not forget to wear it. Everyone at the mall has to see that you are spoken for, by me." He cupped my cheeks and gave me a peck on my lips.

"Why are you so worried that people would not realise that I am spoken for? It doesn't take a ring for people to respect a relationship. I believe that they will see by how we carry ourselves, that we are a couple."

"Okay I see...," he looked at me critically, perusing me as I got dressed. I had just put on my sleeveless knee-length blue pencil denim dress which had a collar.

"That dress doesn't flatter you. You look like...a child," he said shaking his head, seriously showing his disapproval about the dress. He stood in the middle of the room, his eyes piercing mine.

"Martin, I am a child or have you forgotten? Besides, there is nothing in the closet that will suddenly make me look older than I really am. Why should I dress like an older person anyway? I'm only turning 20 in January."

"Yeah... but I don't really like that dress on you. Let me look at what else you got in here." He stood up from where he was seating.

I was amazed, as I watched him in dread, opening the closet. I wondered what on earth the man was really up to and what he would be looking for anyway. He kept flipping my clothes, checking and scrutinizing everything.

"Martin, I love this dress and I am going to wear it. So, stop trying to determine my wardrobe," I asserted myself.

"Fine, I wasn't trying to determine your wardrobe but I just thought you would want to look extra beautiful for me." There he went again, doing something for him and not for me!

"According to me, this is beautiful enough and I will not wear anything else. Let's go," I said, his expression staggered, even thought he was trying hard to conceal it.

I could see that he wasn't thrilled with what I had intimated to him. Honestly, I didn't care; one way or another, the man had to know that there were things I was not prepared to surrender to him, and changing my wardrobe was one of those things. If I were to do it, it would be my own decision and not his.

"Damnit, you are so stubborn! Anyway, if you're fine with that, we can go," he surrendered, flicking his hand impertinently.

There he was, trying to make me feel awful about my choice of attire that day; it didn't work. I took out my Moto-X multi-pink high heeled platform sandals and wore them, finishing my outfit with equally beautiful rose-pink chandelier earrings made of cubic zirconia. These were two of my mother's gifts to me. I took my crimson velveteen handbag and put some essentials in it.

I then took one final look in the mirror and felt really beautiful. In fact, I knew I looked splendid. I noted that Martin had already left the bedroom and I chortled by myself, pleased that I won the minor scuffle.

As I descended the stairs, I saw him standing in the foyer, clad in a different shirt and blue jeans than the one he had worn earlier.

It was as if we had planned it or perhaps he did that on purpose as he realized that I wasn't going to change my outfit. The shirt matched my sandals and earrings perfectly. It was also multi-coloured, the main colour being lilac.

"Wow, wow, wow!" Martin remarked. "I withdraw what I said earlier about the dress. I have never seen those shoes before and those earrings! You look gorgeous, Palesa. I am sorry I said the wrong thing to you. I guess I am truly a man," he admitted.

"Yes you are indeed a man, a typical man who wants to decide a woman's wardrobe, without knowing what it is that actually suits her. I trust that it was the first and the last time you try to interfere with my sense of dressing again?"

He lifted his hands up in mock surrender and forced a cough out, while I was still descending. He then hurried towards me once I had reached the foot of the stairs, looked deep into my eyes and declared once more, "I love you Palesa. You are very beautiful."

"I love you too, Martin. Let's go please."

"You said you loved me…you said it!"

"Yes I said it, Martin and I mean it."

The man couldn't stop smiling. We hugged and he ended the brief romantic moment with a kiss to my forehead. I must admit, that move melted my heart.

It was only at that time, that we realized that sis Lulama didn't even knock, neither did Bra Mos. I got concerned.

As we got out of the kitchen door into the garage, Martin

decided that we were going to use his metallic blue BMW 5 series sedan for that trip. Ever since I moved in with the man I had never been inside that BMW before. That was the first time I did. He sometimes used it to go to work but not often. The sleekness in that car! It still smelt new and the leather seats smelt pure. You could tell that it was still fairly new.

"Martin, let me call sis Lulama; I'm worried about her. Perhaps she's not feeling well, hence she didn't come in," I said.

"Are you forgetting that I locked her out?"

"No, I haven't forgotten but this is atypical of her, so I'd like to see what the problem is."

I took out my cellphone from my handbag and as I was about to dial her number, I saw Bra Mos coming towards us in a puff.

"Mos, what's the matter?" Martin asked.

"It's Lulama Sir. She's not feeling well. She says she has been having a terrible headache since last night and she would like to rest it off."

Before Martin could even respond, I spoke up, "It's okay Bra Mos, please tell her to rest. The house is not really dirty anyway and there is no dirty laundry. If she has taken headache tablets, she must make sure that she eats well; otherwise the tablets will scour her intestines. Isn't that right, Doc?" I looked at Martin to verify.

"Yes… yes, that's true. Mos, is she not too bad though? Should I come and examine her?"

"I don't think that will be necessary, Sir. She said she is not too bad but she's still feeling the headache, even though it's not as bad as yesterday."

Bra Mos was adamant in his response, not to let us see Sis Lulama.

"Okay, I'll come and see her when we get back. Please wish her a speedy recovery," I stated.

"Thank you Miss Palesa, I will tell her."

Martin opened the car door for me, careful not to close it before I could fully settle on the seat. He was particularly chivalrous that day and that delighted me, although I remained guarded.

As we drove out of the compound, the man grabbed my left hand and remarked, "Oh, you haven't forgotten your ring…just checking…don't bite my head off." I smiled and allowed him to have his moment.

"I'm worried about sis Lulama," I said. "Perhaps I should call her, just to hear from the horse's mouth, that she is indeed alright."

"Well, if you feel that you must, then you can call her. But you heard what Mos said." Martin brushed my arm with his hand as he drove out.

I took out my cellphone and dialled sis Lulama's number. She answered.

"Miss Palesa…," she whispered.

"Sis, are you alright? I heard that you have had a headache since yesterday? Have you taken anything for that?" I asked, truly concerned about her.

"I have had it since yesterday, it's true Miss Palesa, but I'm not too bad today. I took headache tablets but I just ask that I don't come in so that I can rest. Will that be okay?"

"Of course it's okay, please take your time. I just wanted to check that you are not in too bad a state, warranting us to come back so that Doc can look at you. We have just left the house."

"No… no… no…, I'm fine Miss Palesa. I'm really not doing too bad at all. Please… please, that will not be necessary. I will be fine tomorrow," she assured.

Well…that was really odd how eager she was to get off the phone with me. I wondered as I spoke to the woman, as to whether she was really ill as she claimed, seeing how resolute she became about not being examined. Besides, how would she know that she would be fine the following day? I elected not to tell Martin about my instinct regarding the woman's illness. I was determined to go and see her when we got back, to try and help her with any problem she was possibly having that day. I was almost certain it was not physical.

We drove for about forty five minutes into town, with not much traffic as one was used to, while I enjoyed the ride in the lustrous BMW 5 series, whose idling was not even perceptible. I enjoyed every minute of that ride, while I chose not to ask Martin why he hadn't been using it often.

As we saw the big billboards showing the entrance to the Rainbow Mall, Martin indicated the car and we drove into the undercover parking lot. I realized then, that he had arranged for reserved parking space at the mall. I was flabbergasted by what I witnessed, as the security guard removed the rails, allowing him to park there.

He parked the car and took out his wallet out of the cubbyhole and stole a kiss from me. He bowled me over again, briefly making me forget about my reservations about some of the things he had subjected me to.

As I was about to open the door, he chastised me. "What are you doing? Do you want people here to say that I don't treat my woman well?"

"It's not that at all, I'll stay and wait for you then," I rolled my eyes.

He got out of the car and greeted the guard standing close to other cars. After closing his door, he rounded the car until he reached my side, opening the door for me. He extended his hand to help me out and snaked his right arm around my waist, while I smoothed my dress down.

"You look incredible baby," he whispered in my ear and kissed me on my cheek.

"Thank you; you look really good too." He locked the car, stopping for a moment, making sure that there were no funnies happening to the car, like someone trying to jam the mechanism. When he was satisfied, he laced his fingers with mine as we walked towards the mall entrance.

I felt good that day and I swung my hips from side to side –

catwalk affinity!

We entered the mall from the upper floor where all the high end boutiques were located. We walked hand in hand, as Martin spoke about how he wanted to see me look exceptionally good on Saturday and that he wanted all eyes to be on me.

I marvelled at the statement, wondering how a person like him, who was visibly jealous and somewhat domineering, would not have a problem with all eyes fixed on his fiancé. I deduced that it was probably a figure of speech and thought nothing of it afterwards.

We entered 'Delilah's Boutique', a high end fashion boutique with serious price tags on the items. There was nothing I liked in that shop. The cheapest item cost about R1500 and that was some T-shirt. It appeared as though some people loved the items being sold there. The power of a brand, I suppose.

The way the sales assistants looked at me specifically as I entered, made me feel really superior about myself. One lady came to me and asked me where I got my shoes. I told her that my mother bought them for me from some overseas store.

They remarked about how beautifully I had co-ordinated my items. That pleased Martin to the point where he could not even hide it.

"That's my girl!" he affirmed proudly.

"Thank you ladies, I'll come and check your clothes some other time," I held.

"Were you looking for something specific?" Margaret, the

sales manager standing behind the till asked me. Her name tag was visible.

"Yes, I'm looking for something to wear for a wedding this coming Saturday. However, I cannot even describe to you what it is I want. When I do see it though, I will know immediately because it will call me and it will just grab me. You know what I mean?"

I even surprised myself by how bold and to the point I was. I was a doctor's fiancé after all, so when I spoke, people had to take notice. Was I beginning to change? Of course I was.

"Wow, the lady knows exactly what she wants. We hope to see you again sometime, when you are not looking for something in particular," the woman said.

"Thank you, let's go baby," I motioned to Martin, who also thanked the ladies. They couldn't stop salivating on us.

We left the shop and Martin couldn't keep his hands off me. One moment he would steal a kiss on my cheeks, the next he would just walk behind me, grabbing me by my waist, while kissing me on my neck. That move itself brought attention to us and everyone around us gave us peculiar glances. I felt loved beyond measure.

His magnetism had also begun engulfing me and I inwardly rebuked myself, wondering as to why I had been dramatic the previous days, in an attempt to see the negative in an otherwise not too bad a situation. I began to question myself, my actions as well as some of my convictions. Martin was my man and I had to make the most of the relationship and give him whatever he wanted, when he wanted it.

Besides, I also got everything I wanted and desired didn't I? I concluded in my mind that I would stop nit-picking on superfluous things and be a good fiancé and ultimately a good wife to my man.

We got into another shop and pretty much a similar thing happened, as in the boutique a few stores away. This time, the staff hovered around us like bees. I wondered then, what it was that they thought about us.

Martin left me briefly to go to the men's side. One of the sales assistants approached me, asking to help me choose what I wanted. I politely declined the gesture as I had no idea what I wanted. I gave her the same speech I gave Margaret from Delilah's Boutique, the fact that I would know what I wanted when I saw it. She understood precisely what I meant and left me alone.

"Okay, please shout when you need some help," she appealed.

"I will thanks."

Yet again, there was nothing that tickled my fancy at the store and I called Martin so we could go. I could see that he was beginning to get irritated with the fact that I couldn't find anything I liked. According to him, both stores were full of clothes and all I could do was to just pick or choose; then have a fitting after-which we would pay and then go home.

"Baby, you still haven't found what you're looking for?"

"You make as if this is the hundredth store we have been to. I do not find anything I like. So until I do, we will just have to keep walking and going from store to store."

"I wasn't fighting, baby; I just wanted to know exactly what you're looking for. Perhaps I can help you pick." I laughed.

"No baby, you will not be able to pick anything I like. Just let me be."

"Okay," he admitted defeat.

We left the second boutique with our fingers still lacing together and as we were about to go into the third one, I just scanned all the items quickly while still at the door and nothing popped up that demanded that I go in and check it out. So, I told Martin that we should not go in. Naturally, he was perplexed to see me do that and felt the need to ask candidly.

"Baby, we didn't even go inside. How can you tell, just by looking from the door, whether the items are beautiful or not?"

"Martin, I can tell so don't even go there. We are not going to fight here at the mall, are we?"

"Who's fighting? I just wanted to understand that's all."

"It's a female thing; you wouldn't understand even if you tried, trust me."

We went from store to store, as I battled to find something to wear for the wedding. I was even beginning to get irritated as well. When I was about to give up and looking at my fiancé's dreary face, there it was, "Boutique Mornadette" calling my name as I was about to pass it, totally dejected.

I hurried inside, disentangling my hands from Martin's. When I got in, my face lit up at once and I knew that I had reached the right place.

"You're smiling. Does it mean we have arrived at a boutique you wanted?" Martin asked.

"I believe so baby… I strongly believe so," I responded, beaming from ear to ear.

"Thank you God!" he exclaimed, lifting his hands up high. I laughed as he joined me in that laughter too.

Like in the other shops, everyone wanted to help me. This time however, I didn't mind the attention because for some reason, I could sense that I was going to find everything I wanted from that store.

"Baby, I suggest you leave me in here and go check your stuff. I have a feeling I will be in here for at least an hour or two."

"Really?" he remarked. "Are you sure you won't need to go anywhere else?"

"I'm certain; I will call you when I'm done here. I think we will save time if we split up so that you can also go and get whatever you want. Seeing as we never planned to co-ordinate what we were wearing today, yet we matched, perhaps your spirit will tell you what to buy," I sniggered a bit and watched him join me in mirth as well.

He cupped my cheeks and kissed me on my lips, took out his wallet from his pocket and flipped his debit and credit cards inside. He then took out a black card and gave it to me.

"Baby, you can use this when you're done."

I noticed the sales assistants giving each other uncharacteristic peeks after Martin gave me the card. I grabbed him by his arm imploring him to move from where we were standing.

"Is everything okay?" he asked.

"Yes, everything is okay but are you sure you want to leave me with your card; this card – thee black card?"

"Of course; why shouldn't I leave you with my card? You're my fiancé, so you deserve only the best. If I don't spend my money on you, who should I spend it on?"

"Okay then… thank you."

"You're welcome."

I felt a bit sheepish after what he said. "You're not worried that I might go overboard and blow out all the money in here?" he laughed out loud.

"You clearly have no idea who you're marrying do you? Trust me; you can never finish all the money in this card, unless you're preparing to buy the whole mall. That's not your intention, is it?" he grinned.

"Of course not. If you're sure about this though, then that's fine. I am truly grateful."

"I am certain; stop worrying so much. Come here...," he hugged me tightly and gave me a forehead kiss. "Let me go then and see what I can find. I get the feeling I'll finish before you anyway," he chuckled.

"Yeah, that's highly likely."

"I love you," he stated.

“I love you too,” I affirmed, as I watched him leave the store. When I turned around, all eyes were on me and that made me self conscious.

I put the card in my wallet and then threw the wallet in my handbag. The women remarked about us as a couple, mentioning how good we looked together and another remarked that the love we seemed to share was extraordinary, referring to a man who would leave his woman with his black card. I mean seriously now, is that how love is measured, by a black card?

Anyway, I went through the rails, checking the many clothes that they had. I loved everything in that boutique and with the help of the sales assistants, I got a lot of clothes that were not even my style. However, they made me look really good and so grown up. The heels I had on, made it easier to fit the dresses, as most of them required one to wear high heels for the outfit to really make a statement.

I eventually found the dress that I would wear for the wedding. I also found high heeled 4 inch platform sandals to match and a clutch. I didn’t think it would be necessary to purchase jewellery as my mother gave me most of her jewellery; very beautiful stuff. I figured that I’d mix and match everything until I find the correct ones to go with my outfit on Saturday.

When I was content that I had bought everything I wanted, I pulled out the black card to pay. I wondered about the amount that I had spent, but as my man had said, I let go of my apprehension.

The woman scanned all the items, recording them in the till.

She then tilted the machine, showing me the monitor. All items cost R22 500, 65. I was mystified, shocked even.

"Should I run the card ma'm?" she asked.

"Yes, here…," I handed her the black card.

As the sales assistant slid the card through the speed-point, my heart beat really fast. Before I knew it, the slip came out and everything had gone well. She then handed me the card and the slip, advising me to keep it safe, just in case I might need to return some items.

Martin came in as I was still speaking to the sales assistant, wide eyed but smiling.

"So you bought the whole shop?" he teased, as I lifted my eyebrows. "I just go the notification," he mentioned, showing me the cellphone message.

"Come on…you did say I shouldn't worry about money didn't you? Don't fret, I didn't buy the whole shop. Things in here are very expensive though. I just bought 15 items only and two pairs of shoes, that's all." I covered my eyes with my hands and the sales ladies laughed, inviting my fiancé to share a giggle as well.

"As long as you're happy with what you got, I'm happy as well."

That caught me off-guard as I thought that he would scold me. That made me very happy and my inner child resurfaced – inwardly, I was jumping up and down.

I was now a "grown up" and had to behave as such. So I hard-edged my whole face and smiled like an adult. In my heart though, I wanted to scream my lungs out to show the man how happy I was about my acquisitions, which he had paid for freely and as it seemed that day, he did so gleefully.

Martin helped me carry the shopping bags as we prepared to leave the boutique, bidding the sales assistants farewell. We left the boutique to go to a hair and beauty store to purchase wigs to go with my “grown up” outfits as well as some make up. I was now hell-bent on making a good impression; on making Martin happy, particularly after he had purchased so many things for me with no gripe at all. I wanted him to be proud to show me off to his buddies and everyone else he hobnobbed with.

We found Glamour Hair Studio situated towards the end of the floor we were in, en-route to the parking bays on the eastern side of the mall. As I kept talking to the shop assistants and hair dressers about what I wanted, they took out a couple of wigs and helped me fit them on my head, to see which ones would look good on me. I eventually bought five of them after all the hair modelling I did. I also got them to match a suitable foundation for me. They helped me choose the correct brand and colour suitable to my skin, giving me a few pointers. The wigs and makeup were very expensive and at some point that got me worried.

Throughout the whole shopping spree, Martin was exceptionally well-behaved and had also mentioned that he got the items he wanted. He furthermore told me that he didn’t really have to buy a lot of stuff as he had a number of clothes that were suitable for an event of that nature and he hadn't worn some of the shirts, suits and even shoes.

All he wanted to do was to purchase some stuff to go with what he already had at home. For me though, I didn't only buy a dress to wear at the wedding but, I bought some other clothes, which would help me change my girly look to a lady look. I believed that it was time for me to change my look. In fact, I was convinced that it was time for me to act all grown up, particularly since I was involved with an older man. So, it looked like Martin was right after all. Some clothes did make me look like a child or was I trying to convince myself?

"Aren't you hungry? Shouldn't we find a restaurant to have some late lunch?" Martin asked.

"I am hungry but I'd rather we eat at home; I'm very tired and these shoes are now beginning to kill me," I laughed.

"Really? It seems like you handle pain really well though," he mentioned.

What did he just say? Was he still talking about pain caused by the shoes or something else? Why did I immediately think he was not referring to the shoes I was moaning about anymore? My hunch could have been misleading me but it got me slightly tense. There was a knowing feeling inside of me and I couldn't shake it – the man was truly uncanny.

We left the mall with heavy shopping bags, laughing nonetheless and with no issues. I was so excited that day and I truly believed that nothing would spoil my mood. I quickly removed my uneasiness about what Martin said to me being able to carry pain well and rebuked myself for allowing my imagination to always think the worst.

I stood next to him as he was paying for parking at the parking machine. 'He pays for parking yet he has reserved parking? What was up with that?' I didn't ask. I just stood there until he had finished.

At the time though, I was famished and wanted nothing more than to go home and have a light meal. The queue was quite long at the parking bay machine but Martin was patient, awaiting his turn. When he was done, he called out to me, as I had moved away from him a bit, having leaned against the wall.

I rushed towards him as I watched him closely, noticing his sudden contorted forehead. He was not saying a word. I assumed he must have been as fatigued as I was, particularly since he had to stand for some time at the queue. I made attempts of some small talk but the man wouldn't engage, giving me succinct responses. I wondered as to whether he was as happy as he had claimed he was, about the amount of money I had spent at the stores. Still, I didn't ask about what had suddenly stolen his bliss.

'*Oh well..., he should say if he is not happy about something. I'm not going to read his mind – this man is such an irritation!*'

My inner person resurfaced simply to dismiss the man as well as my concern for him. What was I supposed to have said? It was clear that Martin wanted to play a game and I was not interested –

not at that time anyway.

We reached the car and he pressed the remote control to open the boot. He put the shopping bags inside, extending his hand towards me so I could give him the ones I had. He then put them inside quietly like he had a lot on his mind.

I waited for him to open the door for me, lest he rebuke me for denying him the chance to be chivalrous again. He gave me one look, "Palesa, get in the car," he instructed, in an eccentric and dry tone.

'*What on earth is going on now*?' I got aggravated and then I opened the door, fastened my seatbelt like the good girl I was and awaited my man to get in as well.

Martin's creepy mood had resurfaced again. I knew that I had done nothing wrong that time and I convinced myself that his sudden weird frame of mind had absolutely nothing to do with me because I behaved in accordance with what he had expected of me. Again, he hadn't shown me that he was unhappy with my purchases, irrespective of how much money I spent. So, what was the issue?

I figured that he would let me know once we reached home, as I was in the dark and was not about to crack my skull thinking about what it was, that had suddenly distressed him.

We drove out of the mall quietly and I decided to play music in the car and watched him smile faintly.

'*Okay, he's smiling at me. So, I'm not the reason for his*

crabbiness.' My inner person convinced me.

We eventually reached home and once the car came to a halt, I wanted nothing more than to jump out and not even wait for him to open the door for me. He was behaving weirdly so to keep up with him, I would probably have gone insane.

He said nothing and after closing the door, I waited for him to hand the items I bought to me but, he just spoke in a hush tone, "I'll bring them in."

"Okay, I'll see you inside."

"Mmm," he responded.

There clearly was something going on with the man, which I was finding difficult to put my finger on.

When I reached the bedroom, I was eager to take off all the items of clothing I had on, so I could wear something that was free flowing.

Martin came in and placed the shopping bags on the settee towards the corner.

"Do a cat-walk for me and wear each item you bought," he demanded, his tone parched and indifferent.

"Martin, we have just arrived home. My feet are killing me!" I said, bearing a soft smirk for him. "Can't we just have something to eat, rest and then later I will play dress up for you?" I added, totally oblivious of what was to come next. I had thought my fiancé was teasing me but I soon realised that he wasn't, when his face grimaced and he hardened his tone.

"Palesa, I said wear the clothes you've just bought and everything else. I want to see that they really suit you as you claimed."

"If in your eyes they don't suit me and then what?" I retorted.

"Then you will return them; it's as simple as that," he responded in a callous tenor. I could see that he wanted a fight and I had no idea as to why he would do that.

I could not believe my eyes and ears. The charmer I went to a shopping spree with had disappeared and making demands. I thought that I'd plead with him to let me have a rest first, but he wouldn't hear any of that.

"Baby, please...," I pouted. "I'm hungry and I want to rest. These shoes are killing me."

"Palesa, I'm hungry and I want to rest too. This is why you should do this now and then you can do whatever you want afterwards."

Martin was serious and unrelenting in his tone. He wanted me to do exactly what he wanted at the time he wanted or else!

I realized then, that he was not about to concede and I gave up trying to convince him otherwise. I first took my shoes off to try to relax my feet a bit, as I was still going to wear more high heels when fitting the clothes – actually when modelling the items I bought. I then took off my dress and left the lingerie on, which he insisted I take off and wear new ones that I bought.

It took me some time to get him to understand that, it wouldn't be necessary but he insisted. I had to do as he instructed. I undressed everything, parading naked near Martin and he couldn't stop drooling.

A voice inside me consoled me, telling me that I should consider myself lucky because I had a man who still enjoyed seeing me stripped, because other women weren't so fortunate. I tried all I could to concur with the voice, but I couldn't understand why the whole thing felt so inept and perverse.

Nonetheless, I tolerated the exercise for as long as I could, beginning with lingerie that I had bought, while I had scattered all other items on the bed to enable me to pick them up with ease.

As I was about to put on the dress that I had picked up for the wedding, Martin stopped me.

"Just leave that one and come here. We don't want to make your dress dirty now do we? I can see that it's very beautiful and I have no doubt that it fits you well and that you look beautiful in it."

'*Bloody hell... What is wrong with this man!*?' I got annoyed and barked inwardly, frowned even. As I was about to ask him why he did that, he stood up from the bed-chair he had been occupying and walked towards me standing in the middle of the room.

"Come on, don't look so goaded; I wanted to see how far you would go with your back-chatting. I noticed that you tried but somersaulted for some reason. This means that you are now beginning to know your place. You nearly failed my test."

I couldn't believe the man's bravado; admitting that he was testing me? In other words, if I were to air my qualms about whatever it was that he was instructing me to do, then that would have meant that I was a bad girlfriend or fiancé; or I was disrespecting him?

According to what I could gather, respect in his book meant that I was supposed to do everything he told me to do. That rattled me because now, I held that I was trapped. I had spent almost R35 000 of his money buying clothes, lingerie, hair, cosmetics and shoes. He had fed me, gave me shelter and practically took care of me for six months. I was also wearing a very costly engagement ring, which belonged to his late mother!

As he reached me, he slapped me hard across my face and I froze, unbelieving of what just happened. He then held me roughly, grabbing me by my waist and threw me on the bed. Bed springs protested, sounding seriously miffed.

"Martin, what are you doing? Why are you beating me and rough handling me like this? What did I do?"

He didn't answer but simply took the items I had spread on the bed, throwing them on the divan, one by one.

I repeated, "Martin, why are you upset? What did I do?"

"I'm not upset or you reckon there is something I should be upset about?" His tone was definitely that of a man about to seriously hurt me, and I knew then, that I was in trouble for something I didn't even know.

"If you are not upset, then why did you slap me?" I asked.

I tried getting up but he pinned me down using his knee on my back and I felt a clack. He forced me to face down and climbed on top of me. I could feel his hardened front on my behind and his full weight on my rear.

He then breathed on my neck like he wanted to whisper something in my ear. That terrified me.

The man pinned me down and then held my neck with both his hands, as if he wanted to choke me from behind. I screamed and my heart pounded. I could tell that what was about to happen, wasn't going to be pleasant for me at all. I was going to endure the most excruciating pain ever.

"Martin, why are you behaving like this? Did you try to choke me just now?" I cried.

I wasn't really asking and I honestly had no idea what I was hoping he would say in response. Of course he had choked me, having exerted all his might to threaten me.

"If you think what I'm doing right now is bad, you're mistaken. I will definitely strangle you and hurt you terribly if I ever see you smiling at another man ever again, DO YOU HEAR ME!?" he howled.

"What man was I smiling at?" I sobbed, squeezing my whole body from his clutches but he was too strong. He allowed all his weight to fall on my back, gyrating on top of me but not even doing anything else. I thought he wanted to have his perverse sex but he clearly had his own sinister things in mind. He kept rubbing himself against my behind until I asked again, that time trying to plead with him to stop hurting me.

"Baby, do you really want to hurt me over something I don't even know? What exactly are you accusing me of?"

"When we left the mall, as I was paying for the parking ticket at the parking machine, I saw a man winking at you and you winked back…smiling even. I SAW YOU PALESA…I SAW YOU AND I KNOW WHAT I SAW; DON'T EVEN ARGUE WITH ME. YOU THOUGHT I DIDN'T SEE THAT?" he kept his hands on my neck and all his weight rested on me as he kept barking at me like a dog with rabies.

I was too frightened to continue speaking and was finding it difficult to respond because my mouth was touching the bed. The man I had earlier convinced myself that I loved, had slapped me and even threatening me with more serious harm. Was this the first of many?

I do not even recall any man who passed me or winked at me, while I was waiting for Martin to finalise paying for parking as my whole focus was on him. So what was he on about?

He held me down and my back was aching dreadfully while my fear and panic produced a massive headache. I hadn't expected that kind of behaviour or treatment after what I believed was such a beautiful and very romantic day I had with my fiancé. I cried bitterly, begging him to stop.

"Martin, you are hurting me; please get off. I never winked at any man and if I was smiling, even though I don't think I was, it wasn't to whomever you claim I was smiling at. Please get off," I continued weeping.

"Fine, I'll leave you. I wanted to give you a warning to never betray me. I have invested a lot in you emotionally and now financially, Palesa. I am not saying I do not want to spend on you but, if I do so, my woman has to be faithful and loyal. Is that understood?"

He frightened me once more and I wept uncontrollably, my heart unable to take the strain anymore. He climbed off and sat next to me on the bed, as I turned around slowly, trying to get up and coughed, tears continuing to run down my cheeks. I felt some heat rushing round my neck and as I ran my hand around it, it felt rutted.

"I really don't understand why you would want to hurt me when I haven't done anything wrong. I can never betray you Martin, please believe me," my voice trembled while I continued to make promises.

I shivered and as he was about to touch me on my face, I moved my cheek away and he apologized for hurting me.

"I'm sorry for hurting you baby. But I was just letting you know how I feel about unfaithfulness, especially from my woman. I am not the kind of man to be cheated on. Keep that in mind," he added.

An apology and a threat at the same time – the nerve of the man! I kept quiet but couldn't stop sobbing. I felt a throbbing pain emanating from my chest and I was certain that my heart had bled, unable to take the physical and emotional pain I had just endured.

Why did I allow that to happen to me? I thought I was really strong. I mean, I was able to assert myself to Martin now and then. Now why did I become so helpless and not even try to also throw a punch or two?

Would you have dared? Of course not – he was a man; a very burly man, so fit he was that at times, it looked as if his biceps were in danger of getting ripped in the middle.

Emotional strength cannot be faked at all. You either possess it or you don't. At some point, amidst my superficial sobs, I felt as if blood had stopped flowing and a hollow feeling I had felt the day I ran away from home resurfaced. This was the kind of feeling that left my legs wobbly and my mouth dry as if I was dehydrated. My heart was continuing to beat in erratic beats.

I looked around the room, closed my eyes, disallowing my inner person from giving me counsel yet again. I wanted to flee but I knew that I couldn't and it would be dangerous for me to do so. After all, my father had made it lucid that he didn't want me to come back home.

What Martin had done to me had left me horrified and in complete panic mode. As much as I had seen his erratic moods in the six months I had been with him, that was the first time, he ever got seriously physical with me.

I couldn't comprehend how I was going to continue living with him, knowing that he got upset in a whim and about something that I might not even have been aware had happened at all.

Chances were that it was all in his head, particularly about the man who supposedly winked at me. I wondered as to what would happen should he see me having an innocent chat with any man at all.

This realisation of his perverted unpredictability didn't sit well with me. I resolved to live carefully, making sure that I did not make him angry and making certain that I did not allow myself to be in a situation that would warrant me talking to men, such that Martin would feel offended as a result.

I was still not prepared to run away and go back home. What kind of life was waiting for me at home anyway? Another abuse from my father of all people? What sort of life was I preparing myself to live at Martin's? I kept asking myself these questions often as I continued to cough, trying to clear my throat, while my headache was pounding. My back hurt from the weight of the knee he had used to pin me down.

As I was about to get up from the bed to take off the lingerie that I had on, Martin grabbed me by my hand, tightening his grip, practically barring my movement.

"Baby, I'm sorry. In the few months we have been together, I have grown really fond of you and I love you immensely. The thought of you being taken away from me by any man, can send me straight to prison, as I might just kill for you. I swear, I can kill for you, baby."

I was appalled to hear him make such a declaration. Did he mean it? I think he did. I got even more restless of the knot that was beginning to form in my gullet. Should he dare go ahead and kill someone because of me, that would be pre-meditated murder!

Was I still prepared to stay with such a man? Of course I was. My father had disowned me and my mother had allowed herself to be manipulated by him and to be helpless and unable to stand up for herself and for me.

"Martin, you do not have to speak such vile and dangerous words like kill and prison please. I can never cheat on you and I trust you can never cheat on me either."

"I'm not the cheating type but I have been cheated on before…twice, by previous women I have been with. I know that you are not like them; this is why I wanted to tell you what I like and not like, just so you can always bear that in mind."

"So, you had to hurt me in order to get through to me and let me know what your deal-breakers are?" He kept silent and my inner person resurfaced after a very long time of her not speaking keenly to me.

'*Palesa, this is the time for you to make your move. Leave now before you find yourself in a worse off situation than this.*'

I ignored her and refused to listen to this very wise mortal. I told myself that I would be able to change Martin because he was simply a victim of unfaithful women, who abused his kindness. Since I was not that type of girl who could cheat on her man, he would never hurt me again and I wouldn't have to worry from that day onwards.

He stood up and hugged me, as I tried unsuccessfully to

disentangle myself from his grip. He wouldn't hear any of it. He kissed me incessantly, asking for forgiveness. I relented; after all, I had no choice but to do so.

The eerie day went away as if it never happened. I once again swayed myself into believing that lovers do treat each other that way sometimes, particularly when one is seriously distressed or offended by the other and it shouldn't be such a big deal.

I spent the late afternoon wondering all kinds of things - thoughts like: Why would a man harm his woman that he has professed to love? Why did it feel as if I was being punished for sins of women who preceded me?

I toughened up and took the armour of a strong woman. Really? A strong woman? Why is it that a woman's strength is measured by how much pain she can endure at the hands of her man? Was this the reason we were created? It certainly seemed so to me, as I utilised that brief moment of thought to think about my mother, particularly her deportment towards my father. Was she regarded as a strong woman for staying in an abusive marriage?

I was slowly turning into her, even though I would, from time to time, assert myself to Martin. I was however still consumed by my fear of him, which would come and go, depending on what the disagreement was about.

There were some issues he handled better than others. That then made me learn his pressure points and I made sure that I never pressed those. I had begun walking on hot burning coal each time I was with him.

“Baby, I’m going to make us something to eat okay,” he mentioned.

“Fine,” I responded briefly.

He came back after about an hour, having made sandwiches.

I looked at the food and felt nauseous, unable to even touch the sandwich. His face crumpled when he saw me do that. He tilted his head, trying very hard to compose himself.

“Palesa, please eat. You did say you were hungry didn’t you?” he tried hard to not harden his tone but, I sensed it being obstructed in his throat.

“Yes I did say so, but now I am not feeling too good. I will eat when I feel better.”

“What is the matter?” The man was not letting up. How he would ask me what was wrong really beat me. I mean, as a doctor, surely a person who had just endured pain hardly ever wants to eat, particularly food prepared by her assailant.

“Martin, I will eat some crackers. I’ll eat this sandwich later as I feel nauseous at the moment.”

“Okay then. I’ll put this in the fridge and you will eat when you are feeling better.” I nodded.

I walked to the bathroom slowly and washed my face, noticing that my eye had become red from the slap. My right cheek was also slightly swollen. I poured warm water in the basin, placed the facecloth in the water, squeezed a bit of water out. I then pressed it against my face. I did that a couple of times and then finally applied tissue oil on my face.

I went back into the bedroom and flipped through my clothes, taking out my sleeveless, free flowing knee length dress. I actually didn't want to eat the meal he prepared that late afternoon. The thought of him acting as if nothing had happened was exasperating to say the least.

I took some crackers and dried peaches from the cupboard and put them in a small bowl. I then took my very chilled mango juice from the fridge and retreated to the balcony, while he watched me closely, trying to help me walk. His mere touch however, produced an impenetrable sensation on my body, leaving me dazed and weak.

I then later retired.

Even as we slept at night, Martin tried not to touch me and I could sense that he wasn't enjoying his sleep at all. Each time I made a move or turned on my side, he would ask me if I was in pain. I would just keep quiet and not respond.

CHAPTER 7

It never rains, but it pours

I could not check on Sis Lulama when we came back home the previous day, as my afternoon had soon turned into a nightmare. I was determined to see how she was doing though, as my brief chat with her the previous day had left me concerned. Martin didn't even wonder about his employee as all he wanted to do at the time, was to assert his authority on me.

Morning felt acerbic for me as I was unhappy and very panicky. I checked the time – 06h30! I then propped myself up slowly attempting to lean against the leather headboard. It took me an age to do that simple thing. I now needed to get up from bed and go about my day but I couldn't move with ease. What on earth was going on?

I got such a fright when my feet wouldn't touch the floor when I tried to stand up. My ankles were swollen. I could feel pain travelling from my tailbone, encircling my hips and bum, then landing firmly on my legs and feet. This produced a hellish amount of pain on my bones and I wailed.

As Martin had already woken up, he came rushing to the bedroom, huffing and wheezing.

"Baby, what's the matter?" he asked, wide eyed.

"My ankles are painful and my back is very sore, Martin; it's really bad," I wept, clasping both his hands as he tried to see if I could still battle to stand up if he held my hands.

"Oh my God, what have I done?" he cried out, shaking hysterically. "Baby, please let me examine you. I beg you please, let me undo the wrong I did," he pleaded.

In his bid to correct his wrongs of the previous day, he tiptoed around me like a lost puppy. He couldn't keep his hands off me, apologising constantly for scaring me and for hurting me. I would snub him every time he touched me.

He pleaded with me persistently to let him examine me and to rub some ointment on my back, as I had been in pain since he climbed on top of me the previous day, kneeling on my tailbone. I was steadfast in not allowing him to lay a hand on me.

At this time however, I didn't even care about what he did to me anymore. All I wanted was for pain on my back and everywhere else to ease up and for the man to do whatever he could to make me better.

"I think you broke my tailbone, Martin. Why can't I even stand up?" I had to shove guilt into the man. After all, he did hurt me. However, seeing him weep that much, as if he was the one who had been badly injured, melted my heart and I felt sorry for him. I quickly forgot or chose to forget that I had made a resolution earlier, that I wanted to make him squirm before I could allow my emotions to take over or forgive him for what he did to me.

Eventually, I managed to get up and I allowed him to lead me to the bathroom, walking slowly and feeling the most excruciating pain on my tailbone. In fact, my whole back was aching as well as my legs and ankles.

"Please baby, hold onto me tight," he directed, snaking his one hand around my waist, while holding me with another and helping me to walk. He continued to snivel, beseeching me to be strong and to stop crying. Typical!

It became a big struggle for him to get me to do what I needed to do in the bathroom. It also took all the strength I didn't know I had, to sort myself out, while he stood outside the door, sniffing as if he had just had an onslaught of sinusitis.

I slowly left the restroom and got into the shower, holding onto the shower wall. When Martin heard the shower door opening, he launched himself into the bathroom.

"Baby, why didn't you call me for help?"

"Because I don't need it!" I responded cheekily.

"Baby come on, I am trying here; I need to help you. This is my mess and I need to sort it out, one way or another."

"Whatever!" I snapped, stripping off my nightdress and as I was struggling to elevate my leg to step onto the shower stair so I could enter the shower, Martin held me.

"Baby please…, you could have taken a shower later after I had examined you. As matters stand, I don't know how much damage is on your back."

I gave him a homicidal look and he jerked backwards, seemingly spooked. I don't know if I had truly frightened him or that was simply an involuntary jolt.

He begged again, "Baby, please allow me to help you shower so that you can go and rest quickly."

"Fine, do whatever you must," I muttered.

Martin hurriedly released warm water and let it flow, as I stood underneath the shower-head bare, waiting for water to run on my back. I held onto the shower wall and the move reminded me of what he sometimes does to me when I go into the shower. I got upset and closed my eyes, waiting for that memory to wane.

He took my face cloth and poured my aloe based shower gel on it and then ran his hands up and down my back gently and slowly with the cloth, as well as my front upper body.

"I can't believe that I hurt my fiancé like this. Your back has reddened. Oh my God… baby believe me, I love you. I have never loved anyone the way I love you. I'm so sorry for hurting you. This will never happen again, I promise."

Did it really look like I gave a damn? Of course not! How many promises had he broken? Plenty! However, I was still not prepared to leave him; I was certain I could change him to be the man I wanted him to be; the man I needed him to be.

I kept still as he continued to sponge me down. Warm water felt delightful on my back and it did the trick to soothe the pain, albeit slightly. I enjoyed being pampered by my batterer – twisted I know.

After what seemed like an elongated amount of time, he wiped my back and my arms.

"Thanks, I'll finish up here. You can fetch your medical bag as well as whatever ointment you want to apply on my back. I still have to wash my face and there are certain body parts I'd rather clean by myself. I'm not yet an invalid," I scoffed.

Martin smiled and I kept my grin to myself. He then kissed me on my forehead.

"Okay baby, please shout when you need to get out and I'll take you to bed. Be careful please," he added.

"I will do that, thanks," I said, smiling.

Was I calmer now? Of course I was. Martin was pampering me wasn't he? I felt sorry for him even though he was the one in the wrong. He was my man, my fiancé and what happened the previous day was simply a lovers' tiff. I again persuaded myself, failing to reason that a lovers' quarrel doesn't take place when it's one-sided, which was the case in my situation.

I took my time in the bathroom, while finishing up and eventually when I was done, I wiped myself, took slow and careful steps out of the shower, towards my beauty corner in the bathroom, where Martin had already placed my creams and lotions.

The leather ottoman welcomed me with vigour, even though it felt like an epoch to settle on it. I then dolled myself up warily and when I was done, I took a towel gown hanging on the lingerie line and wore it, finishing that by wearing my bathroom slippers. I then stood up slowly, holding onto the marble stand onto where the basins were mounted and then later the corner of the wall in the bathroom. I then took short steps back to the bedroom.

I walked around it at a snail's pace until I reached the bedroom wall, which did a good job in helping me straighten up, enabling me to reach the room without any incident.

It was at that time when I was busy pondering on how I was gonna get to the bed, that Martin appeared with his medical bag and what seemed like a hot water bottle.

"Let me…," he said in a high pitched tone, quickly put down the bag and other stuff he had on the side table and rushed towards me.

"You managed fine?" he asked with concern.

"Yes I did," I responded succinctly.

"Okay…easy easy… there you go," he whispered, as he helped me to the bed, motioning me to lie down. The man sure was trying to make amends. His eyes had dried up and he had stopped crying.

After helpeing me to lie down, he took a deep breath, "Baby, please take off the gown and lie face down. I need to examine you thoroughly. I will put this cushion underneath your belly as I need to inspect your coccyx properly," he pleaded, holding up the blood red satin cushion.

I arched on my stomach and he quickly put the cushion underneath my belly as I relaxed my arms on one pillow, faced down.

"Baby… I truly hurt you, oh my God! What on earth has gotten into me? I truly am the son of Satan aren't I?" he sighed, after making such a terrifying declaration.

Did he really mean Satan… Satan, contrasting his father's character with that of Satan – Lucifer? I didn't respond and gave him that moment to continue rebuking himself.

He ran his fingers up and down my spine in stages and then brought them down to my coccyx and on my sides. I could feel by how he touched me, that he was very cautious not to touch too solidly. Whatever he was doing, it did feel like a serious examination of my frame to establish as to whether I had any broken or cracked bones, particularly on my tailbone.

After a while, he let out a sigh.

"Oh…thank God nothing is broken. I was already freaking out!" he paused, "Baby, I want to give you an injection to speed up the healing process. Will that be okay?"

"Go ahead, I want to rest anyway."

He reached into his medical bag and took out a syringe. Then he took out a needle from its package, inserting it into the syringe. He then took out a small bottle, inserting the syringe inside - about 10 milliliters of some white substance. When he was done, he placed the empty bottle on the side table. He noticed my apprehension as I watched every move he made.

"Baby, relax please and face the other way. You're not scared of needles are you?"

"Needles I can handle. A lover's hands around my neck and knee on my back though…? I can't handle."

I might have said that hurriedly and on impulse but I definitely said it on purpose. I never wanted him to think that I was or would ever be okay with him abusing me. Deep down in my heart I knew what I had just done was a bad move but I did it anyway.

"How many times must I apologise? Are you going to keep reminding me of what I did to you?" He lost his temper!

I hang about my guard as I now knew that he was still as capricious as he was the few days into our relationship. As much as I was trying not to upset him, I was steadfast in not allowing him to do what he did to me the previous day ever again, but was I going to be able to see the maltreatment coming? Probably not.

"See, you don't deserve my forgiveness. Look at how vexed you are already that I am hurting – something you did yourself without any provocation," I paused, waiting for him to respond but he instead sighed.

"Baby, it hurts me that I hurt you this badly but I promise

never to do this again. I swear on my mother's grave." He put both his hands on his head.

What did he just say?

"We'll see what happens. Please do what you need to do; the chilliness in this room is bringing back the pain with vigour," I mumbled, as I turned my face away from him and involuntarily exhaled.

He touched my back with both his palms and gave me a lingering kiss on the core of my spine. I shivered, irked by the move as it sent some bizarre vibrations down my legs.

"This is a promise, Palesa. From today onwards, you will always be safe in my arms, believe me."

I closed my eyes and shook my head, taking in what sounded like a sincere pronouncement, forcing myself to believe him. He had to have been sincere didn't he?

He then said nothing further but the next moment, I felt a tingling sensation on my tailbone and I could literally feel medication being injected inside my frame, flowing as if propelled mechanically and then it settled down. I squealed.

"Sorry…sorry…sorry. Does it hurt?" he asked

"Yes it does hurt but if it's going to help numb this pain, it's okay, do what you must," I responded.

"It will numb the pain and make you better, I promise. Let's not use the water bottle for now though. We will use it later if there is a need. It might interfere with the medication I have just injected in you."

"You are the doctor," I shrugged, "you know better, I suppose. All I want is to get better," I mumbled.

"That's true; I am the doctor. I know what's good for you and right now, it's you resting and listening to your doctor fiancé's every instruction," he sternly stated, while his hands were still firmly covering a better part of my lower back.

The man's engorged ego resurfaced once more. Well, what could I say as he really was a specialist physician and I had no reason to dispute the fact that he knew better.

"Okay…we're done now. Just arch a bit so I can take out the cushion," he whispered, "slowly, slowly…don't move too quickly; I've got you," he affirmed.

Was that the same man who almost choked me to death the previous day? Of course it was and he probably would do it again but, I could tell that he wanted to make amends and I let him. I inwardly prayed and forced my inner being to be in accord with my thoughts, and trust that Martin would never dupe me into believing that he will change. He was my man and he wanted us to have a good marriage; a good life together.

My love and respect for him as my man wouldn't just disappear like that simply because of that incident. I lessened the severity of his assault on me. I wanted the matter to rest because my man was trying; he really was trying.

Nevertheless, I obliged and he took the cushion out carefully, helping me to settle down on my side, something which took longer than it should have, considering I was anxious not to hurt myself. I propped myself up and leaned against the cushy leather headboard.

"Let me try to sit up for a bit. I'll sleep on my side when I feel pain again. Please pass me my robe," I pleaded, extending my hand to Martin.

"Sure; let me help you. Get up slowly please don't hurt yourself."

He handed the gown to me. I tried lifting my hand up to put the gown on. That move took long and I got irritated and took it off hastily and drew my breath.

"What's the matter?" he asked.

"Nothing!" I responded cheekily. I mean, he could see that I was struggling to help myself and my back was still sore, so why was he asking me such a dim question?

As I had already taken a bath, I quickly discarded the idea of wearing the robe, electing to wear my silky flowery kaftan instead. It was warmer and its material would be soothing to my skin.

"On second thought, just hand me that floral pinkish kaftan from the closet. It's the only one on the hanger, others are just packed away; you won't miss it."

"Okay," he paused, after taking a few steps towards the closet. "By the way, what's a kaftan?" he asked and I could see that he was becoming seriously chagrined.

He threw the gown on the bed while opening the closet.

"Open it… I'll tell you," I smirked. At least I still found a moment to amuse myself.

He impatiently flipped through my clothes, as I gave him a callous look, trying to establish as to whether he was really willing to make amends as he promised he would.

"It's silky and loose-fitting," I responded. "It's more like a summer body throw. I wear it often when it's pretty hot." I could not finish describing the garment to him because the next moment, he had found it.

"Phew! Finally, I found it," he exhaled, as he handed the kaftan to me while I was still sitting up, leaning bare against the headboard on the bed.

"Thank you." I grabbed the garb and put it on, careful not to hurt myself. I then leaned back against the headboard and brought a throw on my legs for coverage.

I could not believe how gentle the man was that morning. I inwardly prayed that the fiend in his heart would ebb. But then again, I had seen that horrendous side to him very early in the relationship, so I wasn't going to hold my breath. I was simply happy that he was trying.

He helped me pack away all the stuff I bought in the cupboards. The stuff he had scattered all over the room the previous day. He then went to the kitchen, seemingly to make us food. I noticed that the medication was making me feel drowsy and I had to allow it to work on me. I slid down while still on the bed and spread the fluffy grey throw, allowing it to cover my entire body.

CHAPTER 8

Things will never be the same!

It did seem like almost an hour or two had elapsed since the examination as well as my subsequent sleep. When I opened my eyes and moved my body, I realized that I felt better. That pleased me.

The savor of grilled chicken strips emanating from the kitchen permeated the whole house. Although I inwardly salivated on the food I couldn't even see, I was determined to teach Martin a lesson that day.

The thought alarmed me as much as it gratified me. Martin, being at my mercy, begging me to eat and forgive him absolutely. A bit inept of me, I know. However, I was eager to take back control of my life and my power, irrespective of the kind of situation I had found myself in.

I stretched my hands and attempted to get up from the bed. I was chuffed that I was able to do that without much effort.

I then took a few steps, reaching for one of the cabinets towards the corner of the room and retrieved one of the novels I had always wanted to finish. I then walked slowly and retreated to the balcony, sitting on the patio sofa, leaning back, preparing to read the book.

It was only at the time that I remembered that I never spoke to Sis Lulama the previous day as I had promised to check on her. Martin hadn't even mentioned her at all and it was palpable that he didn't really care or perhaps it was because he was pre-occupied with helping me heal.

After settling down on the patio sofa, I reached for my cellphone and called Sis Lulama.

"Hi Ms Palesa," she answered ardently.

"Sis Lulama, are you in the house?"

"No, I'm in my room now but I will come in shortly. I was just drinking some morning tea."

As to why she chose to have her morning tea in her room, while she usually had her breakfast in the house, beat me. Besides, it was already late and she at least should have begun working an hour prior.

"Sis, do you still have a headache?"

"No, I don't, it has subsided. I will be there shortly… sorry for being late. I overslept I guess, and it was also due to the tablets I took yesterday," she babbled.

Sis Lulama sounded odd when I spoke to her. I could sense that she wasn't being completely truthful but I couldn't fathom what it was she was on about or what she had chosen to do in her room, which made her to be that late.

I could kick myself for doing what I did but since I was worried about her, I had no choice but to call Martin, asking him to check on Sis Lulama. I scrolled down my cellphone again and called him.

"Baby...," I said after he answered the phone. "Please check on Sis Lulama. I called her just now and I can tell that she is not herself. She doesn't sound too good at all."

"What do you mean she doesn't sound too good? Does she still have a headache?" he asked.

"I'm not really sure. She told me that she is doing better but she was just having morning tea."

"Baby, she's probably just slacking as usual but it's okay, I'll go check on her now. I've already finished with the chicken strips and I'll come and finish up here after seeing Lulama. I'm doing this for you since you are worried about her. Otherwise I wouldn't even bother. I have told you before that you will see how they sometimes try to take chances once you can show them your wisdom tooth." I chuckled.

"Thank you baby; if she is still not feeling well though, please let her know that she doesn't have to come in. She can continue nursing herself."

I was happy after Martin told me that he would check on Sis Lulama. At least I wouldn't have to worry about her, I thought.

The next few minutes as I prepared myself to now read my book, I heard a lot of shouting outside and apologies flying around, coupled with a screeching sound of a man's voice.

"Whoooo, whooo, whoooo, please forgive me Sir…. I'll never disrespect your compound again. Please don't kill me!"

What on earth was going on? I got up slowly from the chair, and moved towards the balcony banisters, trying to see what the commotion was about.

There was a man in his forties, I presumed, leaving Sis Lulama's room…attempting to run towards the main gate which was far by the way. He was in his underpants and a white vest; his hair unkempt, with his shoes, trousers and shirt firmly tucked under his arm as he ran out.

I then realized that Martin was chasing him while one shoe kept falling from his hands. As he tried picking it up, Martin gave him a strong kick on his butt. Bra Mos was just standing there, looking very stupid and placing his hands on his head.

"WHO IS THIS MAN, MOS AND WHAT THE HELL IS HE DOING IN MY LAND? SPEAK NOW OR I SWEAR I'LL…!" Martin barked at Bra Mos, who was shivering like a child about to mess himself.

"Sir, I…I…I…"

"MOS! I'M NOT IN THE MOOD. I ASKED YOU A QUESTION. WHO THE HELL IS THIS MAN?! CAN'T YOU SPEAK NOW?"

"Sir, I'm sorry. Lulama…eh…eh…Lulama…"

"WHAT ABOUT LULAMA? IS SHE THE ONE WHO BROUGHT THIS MAN HERE?"

"Yes Sir. She asked me not to say anything and I also didn't want to get her into trouble. He's her boyfriend, Sir. His name is Alpheus." Bra Mos sang like a canary – where was his loyalty?

At that moment, all I wanted to do was to prevent Martin from yelling and to not cause anymore harm to the man or do worse things which he might regret later.

"Baby… Baby…," I called out to him and he looked up to the balcony where I was standing. "Please come inside, I'm starving," I moaned, as he pulled his breath, forcing himself to calm down.

"You two must thank Palesa because if it wasn't for her, I swear I would chase you both out of my compound. You are very disrespectful. This is my place and I decide who comes in. Next time, you will both regret this. LULAMA…!" he hardened his tone again as he called out to Sis Lulama.

"Sir…," she responded in a shaky voice as she appeared from her room, hair all messed up and wearing her night gown. One could see that there was no morning tea that she had been drinking – perhaps tea of a different kind?

"This ought to be the first and the last time this happens. If you want to see that man, you have to ask for a day off and go to him. I don't want strange men in my yard; is that understood? What if he's a thief?"

"He's not a thief Sir, he's my…," Martin interjected before the woman could even finish her statement, trying to defend her boyfriend's honour.

"LULAMA, DON'T MAKE ME ANGRY… PLEASE DON'T! HE MIGHT NOT STEAL FROM YOU BUT WE CANNOT BE SURE THAT HE WON'T STEAL FROM US NOW, CAN WE?"

"No Sir, we cannot be sure. I'm very sorry Sir…, please don't fire me." She had no choice but to apologise and agree with Martin, whose eyes were blistering with anger.

I looked towards the main gate where Alpheus had been running towards, but I could not see him anymore; he had disappeared! I wondered as to how he was able to put his pants on so quickly, including his shirt and shoes, seeing as he was being kicked around. Perhaps he ran out in his boxers.

"Baby...," I called out to Martin again.

"I'm coming baby, please rest; I'll see you now," he responded affectionately in a calmer tone.

I turned around and went back to the patio sofa I had occupied prior to having been so rudely interrupted by that strange man's wail or rather that circus!

As much as that incident was terrifying because it was palpable that Martin had given that man a few blows and perhaps some kicks before I saw them, it was somehow amusing. His violent streak gave me a fright though, a serious fright, but I resolved to continue watching him closely.

I never thought I'd see Sis Lulama in trouble like that. What was I thinking though? The estate was very lonesome and for a woman her age, she clearly needed some form of entertainment in her life.

I wondered how Bra Mos was doing in that department, as I also hardly recalled him asking for a day off so he could go and entertain a woman or himself. I figured that it was time that they took a weekend off, leaving Martin and I alone in the massive house. I was not sure if I would be safe or not with him for the whole weekend but I was determined to take back what Martin stole from me – my sanity and power. Perhaps being left alone with him was my moment to assert myself.

Should he agree to my suggestion to let the helpers go away for the weekend, in particular on Saturday, the same day we were supposed to go to a wedding, then that would please me because that would have meant that he was truly beginning to take me seriously and acknowledging my role in his life as well as in the household. After all, we were now engaged and had to make decisions together weren't we?

****

When I sat down, that pain on my back had indeed subsided. In fact, it seemed to have disappeared altogether. I touched my coccyx, trying to exert some pressure on it but, I got no feeling at all, save for the force of my hand. It was as if the medicine Martin had injected in me had totally numbed the area and that sent my mind raising and I panicked, not knowing the danger and long term effects that medicine would have on my back going forward.

I leaned back slowly against the patio recliner. I wasn't aware that the Lulama incident and the turbulent flurry of emotions I experienced the previous day had truly drained me, so much that I wasn't even able to comprehend when I fell asleep, while I awaited Martin who took his time to finish preparing food for us.

****

I was awoken by a spine-chilling sensation of something crawling all over my thighs and it was about to creep inside my kimono. I didn't want to open my eyes just yet, but peeped slightly first, before I could carefully decide to whack it as hard as I could.

Even though I couldn't identify what that creepy-crawly might have been, I thought of drawing strength inwardly to remove it from my body and jump off.

I thumped my thigh so hard, giving myself an enormous sting. It was only after that move, that I felt myself touching what felt like a firm substance, that I knew that there was no bug at all. I opened my eyes and realized that Martin's hands were the ones creepy-crawling all over my thighs.

“What do you think you’re doing?” I asked, irate and annoyed with him. How dare he scare me like that!

“Sorry babe, I didn’t mean to startle you. That was quiet a beating you just gave me; revenge for yesterday perhaps?” I kept quiet.

“Why did you wake me up Martin?”

“Baby, please forgive me for yesterday. I can see that you’re still very upset with me. I’m sorry my baby, I’m a crazy man sometimes; you’ll get used to me in no time. I love you and didn’t really mean to hurt you.” So, he was expecting me to accept and get used to the fact that he was crazy sometimes? The nerve!

“Martin, just because you’re begging me to forgive you doesn’t mean I should do it now and you cannot force me to get over what you did just like that. You did what you did and that will stay with me for the rest of my life and it will also stay with you as well. This is what you did, Martin. You hurt me, slapped me, held me down with your knee and chocked me.”

His jaw dropped down, as if to plead with me again to forgive him. He kept quiet, jerking backwards while exhaling. “What was that commotion about? Why did you beat that man up?” I asked.

“I had to beat him up and you saw how I kicked his dirty behind?” he laughed, mouth wide open like a child who had just messed up the creativity of his buddy’s mud house. “The bastard was huffing and puffing on top of Lulama when I got into her room and I saw red. She is not even ashamed of what she has done. I cannot believe this!"

The response indicated to me that Martin's reaction was too personal and that had absolutely nothing to do with him feeling disrespected in his compound by that man and Sis Lulama.

"Martin, why did this work you up like this? Surely Sis Lulama is not a child. Did you even knock first? Did you not have a talk regarding visitors, girlfriends and boyfriends when you first employed them?" I launched a couple of questions at him.

"Baby, I told them in no uncertain terms that I didn't want anyone I don't know in my land. If she wanted to have a guest, why didn't she ask me? Did you know that this was going to happen?"

"Of course not baby, why would you even ask me something like that? Perhaps she was embarrassed to ask. I think we should let them go away this weekend. Besides, we are going to a wedding, so they can go home I suppose and come back on Monday."

"This is their home; the only home they have. I saved them when no one wanted to take them in and I gave them jobs and a roof over their heads. Now they're repaying me with disrespect!" Martin howled like a man possessed, revealing something I was certain he didn't really want me to know, at least not at that time. I didn't want to push for information regarding what he had intimated to me but elected to keep it at the back of my mind and only when I would feel I was ready, would I then ask him about it or ask the helpers about Martin's assertions.

"I'm not going to speak to them because I'm too angry with them right now," he paused. "You know for a moment, I thought you would surely cancel attending the wedding." I ignored the jibe.

"Okay… thanks. I'll speak to them later," I stated.

He at least noticed my disinterest in his swipe about the possibility of me cancelling our trip to the wedding. I didn't care. He was being childish – again!

"How are you feeling?"

"I'm fine. I don't feel any pain and I hope it will stay this way." He smiled, as I returned the smirk. "I hope I will be fine to go to the wedding tomorrow. There's a lot I still need to do. I also have to do a test makeup later or at least very early tomorrow morning."

"Whatever you want, you can ask. I will make it happen for you. Don't you want me to call a make-up artist and possibly a hair stylist for you?"

"Would you do that?" I was baffled, as I thought he loved the idea of me not meeting anyone, at least until the wedding day. Maybe he was toning down his possessiveness - I presumed.

"Of course my love, I will do anything for you. Perhaps they can come tomorrow as we should be leaving around 10 o'clock. Let me call them now so I won't forget."

He reached for his cellphone from the bedside table and scrolled down.

"How come you have details of the stylist and makeup artist?" I queried.

"Their salon is not far from my workplace. So I once took their details with the plan to give them to you. Now you don't really like wearing make-up so I figured that when you do want to wear it at some point, I will give the details to you and this day is fitting right?"

I couldn't believe how thoughtful my man was and to think of me when he was at work, was something else altogether.

"Thank you baby, I really appreciate it."

He smiled and placed his index finger on his mouth, a move imploring me to stop talking, while pointing at the mouthpiece and indicating that someone was now answering the phone.

I could hear him speaking to a guy…Sibusiso, who sounded like he was giving Martin a hard time, citing short notice of the request. Martin promised to double or triple their call out fee as his fiancé needed their services urgently.

They agreed, albeit begrudgingly or so they pretended. That was a lot of money they were going to make and Martin also promised to give them money for petrol. He had one stern warning for them before he dropped the phone. They must not dare be late. They had to be by our place at 7 o'clock or else.

"Baby, we agreed...," he paused, putting the phone back on the pedestal, "they will be here first thing in the morning."

"Seven o'clock is too early though. I thought you would tell them to arrive at least around 08h30. But then again…it's probably for the best so that I can have enough time to prepare myself."

"Yes of course it's a good idea; your man is always right haven't you noticed?" I faked a leer. The haughtiness!

"Okay, 7 o'clock it is then. They should however start to do my hair and makeup around 08h30. That way, it will still be fresh when we leave. On second thought, perhaps Sis Lulama and Bra Mos shouldn't go anywhere this weekend. I think I'll need help."

"Yeah, my thoughts exactly. But she must make sure that I don't see her. She has disrespected me for the last time."

"Oh, come-on baby, forgive the poor woman, I'm certain she is very sorry for bringing that guy to her room without checking with you first," I pleaded on her behalf.

"I'm doing this for you and not for them," he giggled.

"I asked you a question earlier. Why did you creep up on me as I was napping and resting? I mean, you took some time to come up, hence I slept."

"I thought you'd forgotten about that? I just wanted to let you know that food is ready. I grilled some chicken strips and mutton chops and made some Greek salad full of feta cheese and mashed potatoes. I know you'll love it," he responded.

"I'm indeed starving. What exactly are we having here… brunch?"

"Yes, it is brunch indeed," he stated, "You have forgiven me haven't you?" he asked again, his eyes full of what I perceived to be love and deep regret. He was trying hard to make amends, even hiring a hair stylist and make-up artist - all for me.

Even at that moment when my internal antenna kept alternating at a speed of lightning, I still wanted to forgive my man completely, as I could see that he was remorseful and I also didn't want to stay mad at him for a long time because that was weighing heavily on me anyway. Couples do fight don't they?

All I wanted to do at that stage when he kept begging me for forgiveness, was to punish him for a bit but resolved to forgive him in the end.

Was I becoming a walk-over? Of course not; I was a woman in love. Was I afraid to continue with my hard resolve of not forgiving him just yet for fear of being hurt once again, perhaps seriously this time? Of course I was.

"Babe," he grinned at the address, arching his eyebrows.

"Yes baby…"

"I will eventually forgive you but my heart is just too bruised and heavy right now. Please don't rush me to forgive you, Martin and you cannot tell me when I should do that either. Look at you…, you're still walking around internally bruised and wounded due to everything your father ever did to your mother, your sister and even you. Now tell me, do you want to be like him?" I asked this hurriedly, eager to protect my dignity from the man I strongly believed I loved.

He faced down, mouth hanging very low and about to touch his chin. As he had knelt down next to me again after the phone call, touching me constantly, he slowly removed his hand from my thigh, jolted backwards while still genuflecting and stood up, his eyes watery, craftily beseeching me to feel sorry for him.

"Baby, I understand. As long as we are talking, I'm happy

about that. I love you so much and tomorrow we are going to the wedding and I would love nothing more than to see you happy, mingling with people and enjoying yourself. It's our time now Palesa, to showcase our love."

I kept quiet, while wondering as to why Martin was suddenly so eager to show me off to whoever was going to attend the wedding. I had always thought of him as a recluse as I had never seen his friends before. So, I wondered if he was really serious about his desire to see me mingle.

"That's fine," I responded concisely.

He leaned down on me and gave me a peck on my lips. I responded eagerly, astounding myself even.

He stopped briefly, gazing into my eyes, as I dropped mine in unexpected coyness. He seemed astounded by my response to the kiss. He then gave me a cavernous enduring kiss as I felt heat rushing through my veins. I now wanted my man badly, forgetting my hard stance of earlier.

He cupped both my cheeks and made his way on top of me. My heart was beating terribly, as if I had suddenly run a marathon. I fervently removed his Polo T-Shirt and he smiled at me with what seemed like ease, contentment and satisfaction of the moment.

He ran his hands through every part of my body while he continued smooching me and kissing me on my neck, then my earlobes. He then unfastened my kaftan, leaving me exposed as I whispered into his ears softly; my legs wobbly like jelly.

"Martin, make love to me, right here, right now." I stunned myself once more. He responded fervently, removing his khaki shorts and everything he had on, while he continued to caress me.

I ran my hands on his now bare back, clasping my legs around his waist. I could see by the look on his face that he was in awe of how I was responding to him, recalling how adamant I had been in not forgiving him for his "indiscretion" the previous day. That was just sex right?

Martin gripped my breasts with both hands as if they were about to fall off, then lowering his head and sucking them both. He then let his tongue play around my nipples. I froze but was very thrilled, particularly at the vibration I was feeling in my belly. He then stopped to give me another enduring look, eyes full of regret and pain, evidenced by the sudden watery sight I was now witnessing from him.

His whole weight fell on me, as he breathed down my neck, kissing me once then whispering in my ear, "Baby, I'm truly sorry about yesterday; I really am. I love you so much future Mrs Leboya," he declared, drawing his breath, while I could feel his front hardening.

"Baby, I forgive you," I murmured in his ear. "It was an unfortunate incident but I can see how remorseful you are. So yes baby, I forgive you. Now are you just gonna keep still on top of me or are we gonna make love?" We both gurgled.

"Thank you, thank you, thank you baby. I promise to spend the rest of my life making you happy, loving you and never hurting you," he affirmed.

At that moment, heat had engulfed me and I was no longer interested in my man's apologies. I brought his head forward as he had been leaning against my chest. I kissed him, all thoughts about the previous day fading away from my mind.

I could see how appreciative Martin was of that move and he responded ardently, slowly sliding himself into me as I arched backwards, allowing him to consume all of me. We became lost in the moment as we made love, beautiful lovemaking or make-up sex; I didn't care.

All I knew was that, that instant made me content and satisfied. I wanted my man and I had him. He gave me what I wanted, more than satisfying my horniness.

I could not get enough of him and I insisted that we stay in that state till we became drained. That gave rise to a second round, as he obliged; I mean, that was exactly what he wanted. His fiancé had forgiven him for assaulting her and contrary to the norm, she initiated a mind-blowing sex session and was holding onto him for dear life. Of course he also didn't want that moment to end.

I felt myself slide deeper and deeper into what felt like a bottomless cushy fissure and I almost blacked out. He used all the strength he had to pull me back to the moment.

"Baby, where did you go just now? Are you alright?" he asked.

"Yes, baby I'm alright… I'm alright," I mumbled softly.

"Are you happy?"

As I was about to respond to him in attestation of my "happiness", I saw his face adjusting, turning slightly pale and he changed his rhythm, proof that he was about to let go. He gave me a mother of all painful orgasms; the first I had ever had, since we got together. I felt like weeping but only for a second.

My voice trembled as I tried to speak but he barred me from saying anything by pressing his lips against mine.

"Sh…sh…sh…, don't say anything my love…allow your whole body to get lost in this."

I opened my eyes and smiled at him, now wanting to thank him.

He didn't want me to say anything still, as to whether I was blissful or not but I guess the expression on my face had said it all. I felt weak and my legs kept vibrating. It felt miniature creatures playing and running amok inside my belly again. The chilling second orgasm I felt was too intense for me, so much that I shed some tears, as Martin used that moment to kiss me all over my body, declaring his feelings for me constantly and kissing my tears away.

He indicated his desire to go again and I let him have his way with me one more time. I allowed him to gyrate as deeply as he felt he needed to, while I ran my fingers all over his back, elated and I held him tightly, not wanting him to withdraw. As much as I was now feeling fatigued, it didn't matter to me.

I squeezed him in further and further as he began showing signs of exhaustion; his pant now gaining momentum as he kept a straight face. My bladder felt chock-full with all the exhilaration.

His sweat dropped on me. We exchanged fluids; soaking wet from our sweat, as if we had just come out of a swimming pool. I held Martin tight, preventing him from giving in. I made him work as he relished my tenacity. I felt him go deeper and deeper inside of me again. I could have sworn I felt his manhood touch my womb. Did I imagine it? It was a very strange feeling, something I will never forget for as long as I live.

The lion roared, really performing and liberating himself. Where had I seen the king of the jungle mating with his lioness? He then rested on top of me as I also allowed myself to respite, both our hearts continuing to beat intermittently. The session had been spontaneous, totally unexpected but very overwhelming and we cherished every minute of it.

We had never made love at any other place except our bedroom, which included the shower. I had never been that comfortable and pleased like I was that day. The events of the previous day were forgiven, all because the man brought his A plus game and made love to me as if we had just met, so he was eager to make a huge impression.

"I love you, Palesa," he declared, after catching his breath.

"I love you too, Martin," I whispered.

"Woman, are you trying to kill me today?" he jokingly asked, resting his whole body on top of me.

"Oh don't tell me you're tired old man!" I teased.

"Who are you calling old man? Are you sure you can handle the fourth round?" He tickled me, as I laughed my lungs out, so did he.

"I'm now getting worried we might hurt your back."

He had to spoil the moment and speak about my back! I never wanted to think about it, as I tried very hard to forget that episode.

He shouldn't have said that as he spoilt the whole mood. He noticed my hassled demeanour and apologised. I shook my head in amazement.

"I'm very sorry baby. I didn't mean to bring that up."

"That's fine; don't worry about it; just keep holding me and don't get off just yet," I implored.

Nothing was going to destroy that instant as the unremitting sensations I felt inside my body became severe, adhering to the deep connection I had with my fiancé.

He pressed his lips against mine incessantly, bringing his whole body on top of me again, utterly gratified by my tenderness that mid morning, as well as my eagerness to make love to him.

After a brief moment of silence, he lifted his head up and looked into my eyes.

"Baby, this has just reminded me of the very first day we made love. Boy was that moment intense!"

I took what he said in, taking my mind back to that day, but continuing to relieve the sessions we had just had. To me, it was nothing like the day we first made love. I was a novice then and sex had been foreign to me and very painful at that.

We lay stripped on the recliner as we rubbed our bodies against one another's.

"Baby… now I'm starving. Let me go fetch our food, which I'm sure is now very cold. I'll bring the dishes in here so we can eat by the balcony. I'm certain we have worked up quite huge appetites and will definitely enjoy our meal."

"No baby, don't worry; we can eat downstairs. Let me just freshen up and I'll come downstairs while you warm the food."

I felt lost as Martin climbed off, finishing the move with a peck on my cheek. He then went to the bathroom and cleaned himself up. After sorting himself out, he went to the kitchen.

I pulled my kimono from the other chair where he had thrown it and covered just my front with it, while I continued to rest on the reclined patio chair, taking the moment in.

'*What on earth was in that syringe*?' A very disturbing thought crept in but I quickly dismissed it, preventing it from occupying space in my mind and disrupting the beautiful mid-morning lovemaking sessions. Why did I wonder about the medicine in the syringe? '*Let it go Palesa, let it go*,' my inner person advised.

I pulled the lever of the chair up, so I could stand up effortlessly. I was careful not to hurt myself, just in case the whole shebang had left me with a twisted coccyx.

I managed to get up slowly, nursing myself and I noticed that I was indeed able to stand up with no pain in sight. I got up with my mantle in my hand and wore it. I then slid my feet inside my slippers and walked to the bedroom.

I closed the sliding door that separated the bedroom and the balcony and then pulled the curtains. I undressed the kimono, throwing it on the bed and retrieved my morning gown from the cupboard. I headed to the bathroom and got into the shower, figuring that it wouldn't hurt to run some warm water on my back again, just in case.

When I was satisfied with myself having freshened up, I dried myself up with a towel and went to my beauty corner, retrieving my skin products. I applied both my velvety creams and lotion. The way I felt good about myself that mid morning, I was certain that nothing would spoil my mood.

I heard, once I silenced my thoughts that Martin was calling out to me. "Baby, food is ready. Are you coming?" he asked lovingly.

"Coming!" I responded.

As I was about to get out of the bedroom after wearing my knee length kimono again, my man had already arrived to escort me downstairs.

"Should I carry you downstairs? I mean, to warm the food again would just turn everything dry."

"Yeah, I know. But you don't have to carry me," I sniggered and he did too. "I was about to come downstairs anyway as you can see. I had to freshen up." He kissed me on my forehead.

"Did you manage fine in the bathroom? How's your back

feeling?" Although I was irked earlier by his mentioning of the injury on my back, I was pleased somehow to see that he cared about my feelings and he wanted nothing more than to see me well and up and about.

"It feels a bit better," I replied, as he grabbed my arm, leading me out of the bedroom.

As we descended the stairs, the kitchen door opened and closed. From my peripheral view, I could see Sis Lulama coming in with cleaning products in a basket.

"Good day, Miss Palesa," she greeted me.

"Good day Sis; you can start upstairs as we are about to eat right now." I had to keep the pleasantries very short as I felt Martin's hand tightening inside of mine, especially when we reached the foot of the stairs. Perhaps he was trying to get me to cut my chat with Sis Lulama short. Well, whatever his reasons were, I got the message.

"Yes, I will," she succinctly responded.

She ascended the stairs, stealing a look or two at Martin, who was uninterested in her at that moment. He had the best time and he intended to keep it that way. Besides, we were starving.

We reached the dining room swiftly and I realized that Martin had indeed gone all out, finishing the laid out food with some décor – a couple of red roses in a crystal vase; all for me, I presumed.

"Baby… this looks really good," I praised.

"I'm glad you like it, baby."

He pulled a chair for me, allowing me to sit first. He then brought it forward.

"Let us pray baby," he whispered.

I gave him a puzzled look and nodded.

"*Dear God, thank you for always being kind to us even though we hardly ever appreciate your kindness. I thank you for the food that we are about to eat and I ask you for the blessings so the food can nourish our bodies. Please help me to always do what's right for my fiancé and I. God, I love her very much and I do not want to keep hurting her. Please God, I pray for your intervention into my life. Thank you Father. Amen.*"

Martin's prayer left me flabbergasted. Who would have thought the man could pray? I knew then, that my man would soon change and be exactly what I wanted and needed him to be. I was very happy as I extended my hand to him and held his, "I love you baby; that was a beautiful prayer," I stated.

"Thank you baby; I love you too," he avowed. "Let's eat."

As we began eating, my cellphone vibrated and on checking the caller ID, I realized that it was my mother calling. I briefly acknowledged in my mind that had she called me the previous day, I probably would have told her what happened to me. But now that Martin and I had sorted out our issues, I was determined not to breathe a word to her.

I had no idea why she was calling as I was always the one calling her and not the other way round. I punctured the device with my eyes, uncertain as to whether to answer it or not.

"Aren't you going to get that?" Martin probed.

"It's Mama. I don't know if I should answer it now. I'm getting a distressing feeling just realizing that she's calling me. She never calls. I think we should just eat and finish. I will call her when we're done."

"Okay then. It's worrisome though as to why she could be calling. What if she's in some kind of trouble and needs our help urgently? I think you should answer it now baby." Martin widened his eyes and tilted his head.

"Baby please, let's not let our imaginations run too wild. I would like to enjoy this delectable food first and I'll call her once we're done." The phone stopped ringing.

As I was about to resume eating, the phone rang again and it was at that moment that my heart started beating dreadfully. I took a sip of the juice Martin had already placed on the table, took a serviette and wiped my hands. I then answered the phone.

"Mama…"

"Palesa…, how are you doing? I haven't heard from you in a long time. How are things going?"

This was truly unexpected; my mother called me just to say hello simply because I hadn't called her in two weeks? That couldn't have been the real reason for her call. That much I could tell.

"I'm fine Mama, nothing is the matter. Are you alright? You never call. What happened?" I had to be direct, otherwise my mom would not have found the courage to tell me the real reason for her call. It was evident from the tone of her voice that she wanted to tell me something important, now she was just commencing the conversation with small talk.

“Palesa, why should anything be wrong for me to call my daughter? Has it ever occurred to you that I miss you?”

“No Mama, it hasn’t occurred to me that you miss me,” I laughed, as she shared a quiet mirth with me.

“Okay baby, you got me. Your father is very ill, Palesa. As I speak to you now, I am at the hospital. I left the doctors with him in the ward.”

I felt nothing move me when my mother told me that my father was in hospital. I didn’t even care what was wrong with him. However, that comprehension of my frosty stance flustered me. I became aware of how hurt I still was and evidently, the emotional wounds the man had inflicted on me were still raw and very much wide open. I detested him.

I said nothing to my mother after she had told me that my father had been admitted to the hospital. Why would she tell me anyway? What did she want me to say or do?

“Palesa, did you hear what I said? Your father is in hospital and he is asking for you.”

“I heard what you said Mama. What’s wrong with him?”

“He had a stroke and his speech has been affected. His right side is not functioning well at the moment and I don’t know whether it’s permanent or not.”

"Mama, why is he asking for me? He is with the doctors isn't he? So what does he think I will do for him? Why must I come and see him?"

Martin widened his eyes as if to admonish me for my careless words to my mother. I shrugged and twisted my mouth, standing my ground. I was unyielding in my stance of not wanting to see my dad. The man abused my mom and I so why was I expected to be nice?

"Palesa, this is not like you. You are a good person. Please don't allow the past to change the kind of person you are. I also don't know why your father would like to see you but I think you should come… please my baby."

"Mama, this is still very much the present; it is not the past. Papa should start by first asking God to forgive him for ill-treating us for years. I don't know Mama, what you want me to say to you right now. I also blame you for telling me that I was a product of rape. I cannot get that out of my mind and now I really don't want to see that man!"

As I had never told Martin about the letter my mother had written to me, offloading the secret she had lived with for years, I noticed that he got distressed by my revelation and almost choked on his food. He swallowed what was still in his mouth, gulping it down hastily with some juice while coughing briefly.

"Palesa, I thought you forgave me for that. We have spoken many times since you read that letter but now, I realize that you are still hurting. I'm really sorry for telling you how you came about. I didn't mean to hurt you."

"Mama, how did you envisage me reacting to the news? It was not the right way of doing things Mama but you did it anyway. So, pardon me if I feel nothing for the man who raped you, resulting in me being born."

"Palesa, when did you become so disrespectful? How dare you speak to me like that! I'm still your mother. That man you stay with is listening to you disrespecting me and is taking notes. Do you think he will respect me after this…?"

I interjected before my mother could guilt trip me or pretend to know what Martin was thinking.

"Mama, this has nothing to do with anyone but the man who's now sleeping on the hospital bed, having suffered a stroke. I'm still hurting and I'm not sure whether I'll ever heal. He disowned me and now he wants to see me? Hell no, I'm not coming!"

I ended my rant to my mother, panting, as she held on taking my rude remarks to her. It was only when I heard her sigh and feeling Martin's hand squeezing mine, that it dawned on me that I had been utterly discourteous with my words to my mom. It was too late – my vile words could never be returned.

"Palesa, it sounds like you are not only angry at your father but at me also. What exactly is it that has gotten you so angry? Is it really me or your situation where you are is not ideal?"

"Mama, you cannot shift the blame to somebody else. It's been six months since I left home, but not even once, have you ever spoken to the elders to speak to dad about his attitude towards me, nor have you personally tried to persuade him to do right by me. So Mama, how can you even think that I am not upset with you? Of course I'm angry at you; I'm angry at both of you!"

As I was still bellowing at my mother, Martin thumped the table hard, reprimanding me with his eyes and then spoke up, his pitch high and hard.

"THAT'S ENOUGH PALESA, STOP IT!" he howled, getting up from his chair and snatching my cellphone from my hand.

"What are you doing?" I asked, irritated but inwardly pleased and proud that my man stepped in. Where did that sudden pride emanate from? I just know that I loved the idea of him taking charge of the situation, without him necessarily doing anything bad to me.

"Good afternoon, Mama," he said to my mom.

What the hell gave him that idea to call my mom 'Mama' – very presumptuous of him!

He put the speaker on, possibly wanting me to listen in as he tried to score some cheap points with my mom.

"Good afternoon, Martin. Thank you for what you have just done now. It does show that Palesa is in good hands and is involved with a good man."

"As much as I might not know what you and Palesa were talking about right now that has gotten her so vexed, I am quite privy to the situation at home, as you might be aware. This is however the first time I learn of how she came about as she has never shared the information with me."

"I hear you, Martin and I'm sorry that you had to find out this way and have to be involved in this. All I'm asking her to do now is to please come and see her dad as he is asking for her. I don't know how long he still has to live and why he would like to see her. I do think though that she must put aside her anger for a bit and come see him..., please," my mom pleaded as I coiled my eyes in amazement.

"I'll speak to her, Mama but I'm not promising anything. Which hospital has Papa been admitted to?"

"West Side Medi Clinic."

"Okay. I'll tell her, thank you for calling."

The call ended and I marvelled at how at ease Martin was while speaking to my mother, as if they had spoken before or they had known each other for years.

The odd conversation between the two of them went by quickly and I could see by how Martin gazed at me, that he was not as disappointed as I thought he would be. I suppose he understood my pain and why I was behaving in the manner I was.

He reached for me behind my chair, snaking his arms around my chest. He kissed me on my neck, as I moved my head away.

"Are you alright, baby?" he asked.

"I'm alright baby, I'm alright," I affirmed.

"Look at me," he entreated.

I lifted my head up and our eyes met, as his face was very

close to mine, since he snaked his arms around my torso.

"I'm fine baby; I'm sorry you had to hear that."

"It's okay; I'm glad I did. I suppose when you are ready you will talk to me about that letter?"

"No, I don't think it will be necessary. Everything you heard is what's in that letter so, there's nothing further to discuss."

The nerve of the man! Imagine discussing my mother's letter with him and divulging all the contents, which included the fact that my mother gave me R100 000 and it's in my savings accounts. There was no way I was going to do that. In fact, I immediately wanted to find the right time so I could burn the letter. Who knew what he could get up to at some point? That wouldn't be far-fetched of him. He still had controlling issues.

"Okay baby if you're sure." He then let go of me, finishing his smooching with a kiss on my lips.

"I'm certain," I sternly stated.

Martin went back to his seat and we continued eating, while the atmosphere had now changed due to the phone call I had with my mother.

As we finished eating, I heard sis Lulama's footsteps on the stairs and I was glad that she finished working upstairs as I wanted to leave the table as soon as possible.

"Sis Lulama," I called out. "We're done here thank you."

"It's okay, Miss Palesa, I'll clear the table."

She concluded her cleaning by spraying some lavender

household cleaner on the rails and on reaching the foot of the stairs, Martin implored me to get up so we can retreat to the bedroom.

Sis Lulama did all she could to avoid eye contact with Martin and he attempted to intimidate her with his callous look. I elbowed him on seeing that and he sniggered.

We climbed the stairs and on reaching our bedroom, Martin pulled me towards him, holding me tightly, trying to comfort me. Mama's phone call to me and my subsequent responses to her had visibly flustered him. He gave me a forehead kiss again, beseeching me to sit down on the divan as he joined me.

"Baby, I know you are upset with your dad. Believe me, I understand. If there is anyone in the world who understands what you are feeling right now, it's me – you know that."

"Baby, please do not try to convince me to go see that man. He spoke many vile things to me; things one can never ever think they would hear being spoken by a father to his daughter.

"My love, as I said, I understand. I however think that you must rethink your stance of not going to see him. Remember that we don't know why he would like you to go see him. Perhaps he thinks he's dying or something and would like to make amends before he does so."

I listened to my man as he went on and on, in his attempt to convince me to go see Papa. '*What if he was right though*?'

"Baby…," I sighed.

"Yes baby," he held both my hands.

"I know there's a likelihood that you could be right about this.

I don't know how I'll feel seeing him though, more so after having gotten angry just hearing my mother pleading his case to me like that."

"I know baby, believe me I know. I will be with you every step of the way and if at any time you feel uncomfortable being there, you will let me know and we will leave right away. Besides, we have to prepare for the wedding tomorrow. So, we cannot stay for too long."

"You think we should go today?"

"Yes baby, I think we should go today – now actually. That way, we get this out of the way and we can come back on time to prepare for tomorrow."

"Okay, we can go." My hard standpoint faded away, as quickly as it had appeared.

"Thank you baby for taking your man's advice," he proudly said, as I sat there, chortling at the grandiosity.

We both got up from the chaise, still hand in hand as I squeezed my hand out of Martin's. I sought to change my outfit and to wear what would somehow affirm that I was now a grown up woman and was indeed happy where I stayed, in spite of my parents not taking care of me.

I took out my leopard print figure hugging dress with quarter sleeves and wore it, finishing the outfit with red stilettos I bought at Boutique Mornadette.

"Wow, you look incredible my love," Martin extolled me.

As he was about to smooch me again, I jerked backwards, "we'll be late," I cautioned.

"Oh…, all I wanted to do was to just kiss you – nothing else I promise," he smiled.

I moved closer to him and initiated a kiss and he responded with great fervor.

"It's gonna be okay, you'll see," he assured.

We hurriedly prepared ourselves and I took my red clutch bag, while making sure that I did not forget my engagement ring. For some reason, I felt proud to wear that ring as my intention was to show it off to whoever would be at the hospital, particularly my dad's sister, aunt Thoko. That woman was one piece of work! She was exactly like his brother. It was lucid that they carried bad genes as they were sick in the head; rude and evil as hell! Well…, I assumed that she would be at the hospital because she and my father were as thick as thieves.

We went downstairs and I called out to Sis Lulama, informing her that we would be leaving, even though we didn't intend coming late as we had a lot to do in the evening.

It was already mid afternoon and West Side Medi Clinic was about an hour away from where we were. So, we had to leave when we did to avoid coming back too late. I had no idea what awaited us at the hospital.

Before we could get into the BMW, Bra Mos came running towards us, asking if everything was alright. I guess he must have observed our solemn mood as we prepared ourselves to leave.

He regretted asking that question because he didn't even finish the next thing he wanted to ask, as Martin scolded him, clearly still upset about what had happened in the morning.

"WHY DO YOU CARE MOS? THIS IS NONE OF YOUR BUSINESS!" Martin barked.

"Baby, come on now, please let him be." I held Martin's hand to calm him down.

"Just get in, we will be late," Martin held, his tone suddenly hard and unmoved towards me, not even opening the door for me. His moods changed in a whim – no "baby" this time? Just a few minutes ago he was smooching me and "babying" me like crazy but now?

I told myself that I should stop being so sensitive and so needy of reassurance of Martin's love, as he hadn't really done anything wrong to me on that day, save for not calling me baby. I said I forgave him for his indiscretion didn't I? So why was I offended by that mundane error? I had to have been crazy wasn't I? A woman knows though… I knew that the road ahead, was never going to be easy but I was determined to hang on.

"Bra Mos, we'll see you when we come back," I confirmed and then got into the car.

"Okay… Miss Palesa."

The man left us with his tail between his legs after Martin's rebuke. There wasn't much I could have said to Martin in persuasion of him handling the situation better because Bra Mos and Sis Lulama had erred in judgment. He should never have helped her bring that man into the compound, knowing how particular Martin was in having only people he knew in his yard.

We drove out as Bra Mos closed the garage door with the remote control.

"Baby, I'm getting an uneasy feeling and I don't know where that's emanating from now all of a sudden," I revealed.

"Don't worry, we will see when we get there as to what is going on," he sort of comforted me, his expression still hard and unreadable. After what seemed like a moment of thought by him, he held my hand with his free hand.

Martin did all he could to calm me down as I felt my whole body threatening to give in, my heart continuing to beat rapidly. There wasn't much more he could do as I felt what I felt and I suppose it was important that I go through all those flurry of emotions, in preparation of what I had assumed would be terrible news awaiting me at the hospital.

There were a lot of cars at the parking lot at the hospital, as Martin drove leisurely, looking for an empty parking bay. Scores of people were milling about, some bowing the heads, others bearing solemn expressions. While he continued driving restfully, we saw one of the parking attendants motioning us towards him and then lifting his hand up so Martin could stop.

We noticed then, that there was a car leaving the parking bay our liberator was about to direct us into. Once the car had driven out, Martin made his way into the open bay, while the attendant made a point to earn every cent he would be given once we got back to the car.

I glanced at my wrist – 15h30! That meant that the sun would soon set in a few hours and we still had a lot to do, in preparation of the wedding we would be attending the following day.

"Don't even think of opening that door!" Martin admonished me.

I lifted my hands in surrender, "I won't even dream of it."

After getting out, Martin rounded the car, wanting to display his chivalry. This time, I believed that he wanted to show everyone who was coming and going that I was spoken for - by him. He opened the door, held my hand as I got out, retrieving my clutch bag. I then fell into his brawny arms as I utilised that moment to smooth down my dress.

"You're very beautiful," he praised.

"Thanks baby; you're a very handsome man too. So yeah, we're perfectly matched I guess."

Martin locked the car and we laced our fingers together as we made our way out of the parking lot. The parking attendant spoke in a high pitched tone, "I'll take care of the machine, Boss."

"Sure man," Martin succinctly replied, giving the guy thumbs up.

We strolled hand in hand towards the rotating doors of the hospital and on getting inside, we saw three ladies and one gentleman sitting towards our right side as we walked in. On reading the notice above, we realized that they were admission clerks. We then went to the one who had no one to help at that stage.

"Good afternoon," I greeted her."

"Afternoon," she responded sluggishly, looking akin to a person who was not interested in being there; perhaps she was tired or had just been upset by something else.

"I'm here to see a patient that has been admitted here. I'm not quite sure when he was admitted – today or yesterday," I ended.

"What's the patient's name?"

"Phillip Ditheko."

She searched the name from the computer system in front of her and then told me, "He's in ICU – 3rd Floor. Have you been here before?" she asked, while I inwardly wondered what the relevance of the question was.

"No I haven't been here before."

"Actually, this is not visiting hours. You might have to wait until 19h00. How are you related?" I couldn't imagine having to wait for almost four hours just to see the man I despised. My head began spinning.

"He's my father and my mom called me about two hours ago saying that my dad was asking for me. So I don't know what's going on. Please let us go in."

"Okay, let me call the nurses' station on that floor and hear what they say."

The woman picked up the phone and dialled nurses' station on the 3rd floor. We moved slightly away from her and sat down on the chairs next to her cubicle, while we watched her closely as she tried to explain our request.

After a few minutes, she called out to us, "Ma'm…"

We got up from our chairs and went up to her.

"You can go; just take the elevators towards the corner and go to the third floor. When you get off, follow the arrows that will take you straight to the nurses' station on the floor. When you get there, they will direct you to the ward where your father is," she advised.

"Thank you…," both Martin and I chorused.

We left her and went to where she had directed us, then going to the elevators, while we awaited one to come down. It wasn't long till it opened and some people got out. We then got in and I pressed third floor on the wall.

We kept still in the elevator as it was not only us in there, so we figured that it wouldn't be proper to talk about us or where we were going at the time.

Finally doors opened and we landed on the 3rd floor. When we got out, we looked around and quickly saw the nurses' station on the far end of the floor. The stench of medicine, sanitizers and cleaning products permeated the very quiet floor. My heart began beating irregularly again and I mentioned that to Martin, "Baby, I'm scared. I don't know what awaits us in there."

He held my hand tighter than before as we moved towards the

nurses' station. "Don't worry baby, I've got you," he guaranteed.

There were three nurses at their station, going about their day, as one was indicating signs of leaving to do her rounds.

"Good afternoon," we greeted.

"Good afternoon, can we help you?" One stout brunette, with a network of wrinkles around her eyes, attesting to her advanced age, greeted us back.

"We're looking for Mr Phillip Ditheko. I'm his daughter."

"Oh…yeah, we were waiting for you. Your father just woke up. Please wash your hands by using that soap on the wall which is next to that tap and then apply the sanitizer afterwards." She showed us the tap as well as the sanitizer she spoke of, which was also attached to the wall.

We did as advised and then she motioned us to follow her. We followed her for a few steps and then arrived at the private ward my father was in.

"There he is; I will check on him later," the nurse affirmed, pointing at where my father was sleeping. It was only my father and my mother in the ward and somehow that pleased me as I was not in the mood of explaining myself or my life to anyone other than the two of them.

"Oh…Palesa, thank you for coming," my mother happily greeted me and attempted to hug me. I jerked backwards and noted her disappointed face turning slightly pale. It was at that time that my father, on hearing my name being called, moved slowly, struggling to open his eyes. I saw his mouth and right cheek tremulous, as the lips even slanted when he tried talking.

"Hi Mama," I greeted her and decided to give her half a hug after having let her down a few seconds ago.

"Good afternoon Mama," Martin reverently greeted her.

"Good afternoon, Martin. Thank you for bringing Palesa. I appreciate it. The last time I briefly "met" you was when I saw you from my window when you came to fetch her stuff." Martin lowered his head in mortification.

"Pa…Pa…Paalesa…," my dad stuttered, as we all now faced his way to hear what he had to say. His voice kept trembling.

"Tha…than….tha…thaaank you for coming ngwa ngwa ngwanaka." (Thank… you… for… coming… my… child).

Tears scuttled down his face as his voice trailed off, battling to release full speech. I realized then, that in spite of what the old man had subjected my mother and I to, there was and would always be that unbroken bond between us as we had the same blood running through our veins. I felt sorry for him, particularly when I looked at his very emaciated frame, not knowing how long he had been that way.

"Mama told me you wanted to see me," I said, eager to liberate him so he could deal with whatever he wanted to deal with as soon as possible – just in case he was about to die.

"Yes…, I'm so so sorry…Pa…Pa….le…Paleee…sa."

The nurse who brought us to the ward came in and advised us that there were instances when my dad's speech was more audible and in spite of the stroke he had, according to the tests the doctors had conducted, that was not really permanent as it was a mild stroke, even though his health would still be monitored. His right cheek and lips however, were probably going to remain slanted.

"How are you again Mrs Ditheko?" the nurse greeted my mother.

"I'm fine Sister, how are you?"

"I'm fine too. I'm here to check on the patient and to help him with his speech."

Without awaiting any input from us, she put a cushy spiked ball inside my dad's hand and implored him to talk. There's a likelihood that she wanted to listen in as well. People always find an opportunity to gather gossip so they can have something to talk about when they have tea – we all know that. I didn't really care that much what her motives were as all I wanted, was to hear exactly why my father had summoned me. He started speaking while the nurse held his hand.

"Palesa, I'm sorry for everything I've ever done to you. I hope you can forgive me one day. I nearly died and now I realize that you and your mother are all I have," he glaringly declared. "your uncles are out of the country and your aunt couldn't even be bothered," he moaned.

"Okay…," I mumbled, shrugging. Honestly, my father and I had never had a civil conversation and I had no idea how to even hold a brief chat with him, even in his sick state. I didn't know how I was supposed to react or what to say to him after that declaration.

What he said was totally unexpected. Unfortunately, it made no difference to how I was feeling towards him. Did he want me to say that I forgave him? I did feel sorry for him but not enough to warrant me to suddenly cling to him in embrace.

"It took this stroke to make me realize that I had been unkind to the only two people that always had my back; the two people who would probably bury me. I brought my sister into my home and into our lives and allowed her to influence me against you and your mother. I'm sorry Palesa. You are my child and I love you," he added.

Did he say love? That was a lie. He didn't even know the meaning of the word - how dare he use that word! I was an unwanted child, a product of rape, so how could he make such proclamations of love, in front of Martin and the nurse?

"It's fine," I concisely garbled, as Martin kept quiet, keeping check of what would be said next by either me, my mother or my father.

"For how long will he still be here sister?" I directed my question at the nurse.

"He was very lucky indeed. There doesn't seem to be too much damage on any nerves but it was a stroke, albeit a mild one. The doctor insisted that he stay here until we can see real progress. We will discharge him once his speech returns unaided," the nurse pledged.

"Who is this?" My father pointed at Martin with his eyes.

"This is Martin, Papa," I tersely replied, craftily omitting our relationship status.

"Nurse…could you please give us a moment. My wife can put the ball inside my hand. I'm sure she can manage."

My dad probably sensed that the nurse certainly wanted to leave that ward with tittle-tattle for days, so he had to chase her out. That somehow amused me.

"Okay, do you need me to show you what to do, Mrs Ditheko?" she asked my mom.

"No sister, I think I saw what you did. I'll manage, thank you."

After the nurse left, my father continued with his interest in Martin. "You're the one who took my daughter and are staying with her in your home without permission? What are your intentions towards her?"

I nearly told my dad that it was a little bit too late to start playing a dedicated and loving father to me. I however elected to keep still, while Mama and Martin exchanged glances.

"Yes, it's me Sir. I'm not sure if I should start by revealing where I found her after you chased her out of your home, should I?" Martin went on a trivial offensive revealing his claws, while thwarting what he believed was an attack on his person and deeds by my dad.

I stood there, awaiting my father to respond but he just widened his lips, plummeting his eyes.

"What's that on your finger, Palesa?" My mother asked me.

"It's an engagement ring, Mama. We got engaged yesterday. I

was actually going to call you today to tell you. However, you called first with the news that Papa was ill so yes…here we are."

"You're engaged!?" My father exclaimed, releasing a strained cough as my mother tried in vain to calm him down, so he would desist coughing.

"Easy… easy, do you want some water?" My mother asked him, while he shook his head.

"Yes Papa, I am engaged."

"Young man, you know that this is not how Africans do things. You were supposed to have asked permission from me to marry my daughter first and then get my blessing. It would only then be proper for you to put that ring on her finger," he concluded. "You have even taken her as your wife without permission and have been staying with her with no shame at all."

My mother was chagrined to hear papa say that, particularly as it was due to the situation he created. How could he have expected that of Martin when he was the one who practically chased me out of home? He did say I should not come back home, didn't he?

"I know that's not how Africans do things, Sir but… I heard that Palesa had no home to go to anymore as her father has disowned her," Martin mocked, bearing a silly grin while looking at me, as if he wanted me to affirm the information he had. "What you told me is the truth isn't it baby?" he directed his question at me.

"Yes baby, it is the truth," I giggled and my mother gave me a scornful look.

"I guess I deserve that. She is my daughter nonetheless and you really do need to do things the right way," he commanded as he continued, "When I get better, I would like the two of you to come home so we can talk about a way forward in the family relationship."

I elected to release Martin from my father's verbal clutches, as I spoke up.

"Papa, when we find time, we will come and see you. Right now though, we have to go as we are attending a wedding tomorrow. We still have a lot of things to do."

"Okay Palesa. Am I forgiven?"

"I heard what you said Papa; I don't think my forgiveness matters that much right now. You have to get better so that we can see whether you really are remorseful. Chances are that you could be asking for forgiveness because you are dreadfully ill and are afraid to go to the other side, not knowing whether ancestors will welcome you or not," I snapped.

"PALESA!" my mother chided me in a harsh tone, pinching me on my arm.

"Sorry, I don't mean to be disrespectful but why are you quiet Mama…again? Don't you see what's going on here? You have never defended me to Papa in the years I have lived with both of you and now you rebuke me for saying what's in my heart? No Mama…, this is wrong and we cannot allow it to continue."

"I understand my child. I was never a good father to you; I admit that. I would like you to give me a chance please, for us to talk in earnest about our relationship. I want to fix things between us. Please give me a chance," my father pleaded.

"That's fine. Right now though, Martin and I have to go. I will come and see you some other time."

"Okay, thank you for coming to see me and thank you Martin for bringing her. I never got to ask – what do you do for a living?"

"I'm a Specialist Physician Sir," he proudly stated.

I saw my mother widen her eyes, as if she forgot that I once mentioned that to her.

"That's impressive; I bet you're always busy."

"Yes I am and right now, we really do have to go, Sir. It was nice meeting you," Martin affirmed.

"Thank you again for coming," my dad reiterated. "Palesa, I will get your new number from your mother. I am serious; I want to make amends."

"Okay Papa, it's fine, no problem. We have to go baby," I motioned to Martin.

"Goodbye Palesa...," my mom and dad chorused.

As we left the ward, I could feel my parents' eyes stabbing my behind. I knew that they must have been watching us as we leave. I pulled my feet as fast as I needed to, while Martin held my hand, well aware of my intention to disappear as quickly as possible.

On reaching the door, we noticed nurses at their station giving each other peculiar glances. Only then did it become apparent that they were recognizing who Martin was. It was the first time I ever felt a slight amount of jealousy when I saw other women ogling my man. I had no idea where that stemmed from but I didn't like it.

Martin on the other hand, made it known that he was spoken for as he held me tight, snaking his arm around my waist. That pleased me somewhat. He was mine; how dare those nurses check my man out!

"Thank you Sister Jessica for allowing us to see my dad outside of visiting hours," I said, only then acknowledging her name after glancing at her name tag.

"You're welcome Palesa. Yes…I heard your mom and dad calling your name," she chortled, after noticing my astounded expression, reacting to her knowing my name.

"Dr Martin Leboya!" a man's voice originating from down the corridor, called out to Martin. It looked like it was another doctor. '*Who is this one now*?' I wondered. The man moved with a leopard-like grace and waltzed towards us. He was as tall as Martin was and had a very light complexion. He had a military cut on his head and had the most beautiful big brown eyes I had ever seen. Martin's eyes were very striking and deep brown as well but this guy's were something else. They told a story, just by glancing at him.

As I kept perusing the man even before he could finally reach us, I noticed that his right side on his face was patterned with a map-like segmented vitiligo. It occupied a better part of his forehead and his elevated cheekbone, extending to the side of his upper lip. His nose and ear were spared the 'art'. He had a shiny goatee as if he spent his mornings trimming it to perfection.

He had to have been a doctor because he had a white coat on and a stethoscope hanging around his neck.

On hearing his name being called, Martin turned around at once and I discerned his face lighting up instantly on seeing the man. The doctor seemed equally elated to see him. They shook hands and hugged tightly, beating each other with their chests, while exchanging pleasantries. They laughed and displayed how much they really cared about one other and were happy to see one other. That piqued my curiosity.

"So, what are you doing in this part of town?" the man asked.

"Man, I brought my fiancé to see her father. He has been admitted here," Martin disclosed proudly.

That caught me completely off-guard as I thought he might hide the fact that he was engaged – to me.

"Your fiancé! When did this happen?" the doctor turned his attention towards me. "Is this the girlfriend you've been hiding away from us? Now fiancé?" He extended his hand to me and I offered mine. He then balanced my hand with his left one, as if to prevent me from disentangling mine out of his.

"Hi, I'm Lucas, Martin's best friend." His eyes perforated mine deeply, while his smile made me slightly bashful.

I noted Martin's sudden ineptness after Lucas introduced himself to me, albeit full of pride still.

"Lucas, I'm the one who has to introduce you. It's so typical of you to…" Martin couldn't finish his sentence as Lucas interjected, his hand still holding mine firmly. That felt really weird for me and I felt the need to disentangle my hand out of his. I however tolerated that move for as long as I could as I didn't want to seem rude. His eyes were still locked on mine, making me very uncomfortable.

"What did you expect me to do, seeing as you have been hiding this beautiful miracle of creation from us and refusing us to even come and see her?"

'*What did he just say? What am I, an ornament?*'

Martin, looking furtive, laughed as Lucas joined him in that bewildering laughter. Although that moment felt awkward and indeed warranted some glee from me as well, I elected to withhold my reaction, but simply smiled. I didn't want to be too open to Lucas, lest I get myself into trouble for laughing too much with a man I had just met. I didn't want to inadvertently upset my fiancé.

I released my hand from Lucas' and then laced my fingers together with Martin's. He seemed to have 'forgotten' that he held my hand for longer than it was necessary.

Lucas did seem like a really polite man and I wanted to speak to him a bit, just to see if there was something he might 'carelessly' divulge about Martin. However, I wasn't going to be responsible for starting a fight, as Martin was watching every move I made. He thought I paid no attention to how he had behaved when Lucas joined us, especially after having greeted me. He was edgy and fidgeting with the car keys, even though he tried to hide it.

"Yeah, this is my fiancé Palesa. Baby, this is one of my best friends, Lucas. He's a Gynecologist and works at this hospital. We will be together at the wedding tomorrow," he added.

"Oh, that's nice. I look forward to seeing you tomorrow Lucas," I swiftly said and then kept quiet.

"Oh, you're finally letting her out of the house! Whoever thought huh!" Lucas teased.

I felt insulted by Lucas' tongue slip, as it sounded like I was some entity that had been hidden away from people. What could I have said? I knew that Martin had another life outside of the one the two of us shared. I was inwardly happy nonetheless that I would be mingling with other people.

"I'm very pleased to meet you Lucas," I garbled again. I felt tense around the man, taking in his inscrutable energy as if he was one of those people that could see beyond that which one was presenting at the time. Could he also sense as well? Maybe he did. His eyes were mysterious and very intense; not at all the type of man who simply gave a person a measly one look. There was something about him but at that moment, I was not able to put my finger on it.

During that brief moment when he had held my hand for at least five seconds, Lucas and I connected on a level I couldn't and cannot articulate. There was something there but it was not romantic. It was deep and I know he felt it too.

"Same here," Lucas responded, smiling and still intensely

stabbing his eyes with mine.

"Okay…Okay… I'm still here you know!" Martin interpolated. The man's jealousy knew no bounds. That was a meager greeting but he felt left out of a few seconds conversation. I don't blame him though; I would also have butted in if my fiancé and my friend had a strange connection as Lucas and I did. Did Martin notice that though?

"Jealousy makes you nasty, Martin," Lucas chided, as Martin made an attempt at dismissing him and laughing the whole thing off.

"We've got to go man as my baby has got to rest. The day hasn't been kind to her as you can imagine. We're also worried about her dad."

"Shame man, I can imagine. I have no doubt he's in good hands though. Isn't that right Sister Jessica?" he directed his question at the nurses, in particular the eminent Sister Jessica, who was pretending to have not been listening in on our conversation.

"That's true Doctor, that's true indeed," she affirmed proudly.

At that stage, all I wanted was to leave that suddenly gauche area and be alone with Martin so I could gauge whether he was upset that I made small talk with Lucas or not. I was walking on egg-shells where he was concerned.

Inwardly, I was pleased that my father was coming around and was seriously willing to make amends with me. That meant that there was nothing Martin could hold over my head anymore, should I elect to go home at some point. I sometimes had thoughts of leaving him. However, when I thought of my father and the fact that he sternly warned me not to think of going back home, I wanted to do all I could to make things work with Martin, in spite of the earlier declaration of my dad. That knee on my coccyx episode however, had rattled me.

As much as I loved the man, I figured that my love for him was ill at ease because he had rescued me from myself and possible kidnappings by criminals or at worst death. I had placed myself in danger when I left home in a huff but Martin saved me… the damsel in distress.

"Sure man, see you tomorrow," Martin promised.

"Sharp my man, I'll see you guys tomorrow," Lucas affirmed.

They hugged, beating their chests together again, while Lucas' stethoscope nearly fell as a result. He had to grab it quickly, chuckling like a little boy.

Martin and I left the hospital still hand in hand, as we leisurely walked towards the elevator. We were both quiet. I knew that I was taking in Lucas' aura, which was very bizarre and overwhelming. I couldn't comprehend why I felt the need to know more about him. If a situation was to present itself, would I talk to him and about what exactly? I thought of the wedding, '*perhaps I'll speak to him there.*'

On reaching the elevator, we stood silently next to it, while awaiting it to come to our level. Before we knew it, its doors had opened and a few people got out and went about their business on the third floor.

It was only after we entered the elevator, still lacing our fingers together, that Martin finally breathed in heavily and out again. I was certain he was scrutinizing me.

"Baby, you're awfully quiet; are you alright?" he asked me.

I wondered as to why he was asking me that question because we were both quiet. Perhaps he wanted me to mention something about Lucas or cite what I thought of him. By that time, I was no longer that naïve little girl he found on the side of the road. I was maturing at an alarming rate and dealing with his manipulative tactics was becoming one of my specialties. I had become very sharp and my man had no idea that his jealousy and erratic moods had made me street smart and with insight into his psyche. The mind of a little boy who jealously guarded his toys and never wanted even his friends to admire them!

"Baby...," I sighed, "I'm actually thinking about Papa and what happened in there. I can't believe he can't speak coherently. He must be feeling seriously piqued about that. The man sure loves the sound of his voice you know."

"For a moment there, I thought you were taken in by Lucas. He seemed very keen to talk to you," he ridiculed, looking at me intensely, while noticing that I wasn't sharing any smirk. "I'm just teasing you," he claimed afterwards.

"I know you're teasing. I'm thinking about my parents," I mentioned again.

Of course he wasn't kidding. He wanted to see how I would

react when he mentioned his friend's name. I had become witty. I elected not to indulge him, dismissing the talk further by mentioning my mother instead.

"I think I was a bit harsh on my mom earlier. She did all she could to be what she believed was a good mother to me. I feel really bad about what I did. I do hope that my father's illness has given him a wake-up call and he would start treating my mother with a little more respect. That would make me really happy. What do you think about him wanting us to go home at some point?" I promptly demonstrated to Martin what I would rather talk about, as he joined me, briefly forgetting about Lucas.

"I think he wants me to admit to what he believes I did wrong; you know having taken you to live with me. Who know? Maybe when we do eventually go to your home, there would be aunts and uncles there, who would all be bombarding me with cultural tirade." I laughed.

"Of course they are going to do that. They say it's a huge cultural transgression to live with a woman without marrying her. I hate this whole thing of having to keep following the masses, simply because we're told 'that's culture'."

Doors opened while still talking about my parents and we got out, heading towards the hospital's main rotating door. As we passed reception desk, we waved at the lady that helped us initially and she waved back, finishing the wave with a question, "Is all okay?" she asked.

I disentangled my hand from Martin's clutches and lifted both my hands, showing the receptionist both my thumbs up. She was pleased, so was I.

We hurried towards the car parking lot while the parking attendant rushed towards us after spotting us. He had been on the other side earning another rand or two. I thought he said he'd watch the car! But then again, we do know that it was an impossible ask for one to watch a car like a hawk, while the intention for being there was to make money by 'guarding' as many cars as possible.

We got into the car and as Martin reversed out of the car park, the guy kept gesturing and mumbling something muffled, seemingly working hard for his money. As we were about to leave that car parking lot, Martin slowed down and gave him R20, 00.

"Thank you… thank you Ngamla (rich man)," he said, visibly excited about what Martin gave him.

****

We stopped by the Pizzeria at Rainbow Mall and bought two meaty pizzas with lots of cheese. There was no intention to cook as we had to prepare our stuff for the next day – the wedding that was awaited with baited breath. It was billed to be a grand affair.

We arrived home at around 19h00 and found some of the lights in the house well lit. That was nice of Sis Lulama to have done that. She was a good employee, even though Martin didn't really appreciate that.

"Baby, I can't believe I'm starving. Should I take plates out now?" Martin asked me.

"Yes please," I responded and I went upstairs. "I'll come down just now. Pizza is quite sumptuous when eaten hot with cheese hiding away in the middle of the teeth," I remarked and then heard Martin laugh out loud.

'*At least it appears as though he has forgotten about Lucas and what you thought of him. So you can relax Palesa. Just make certain your tongue doesn't slip up again. Perhaps I should have a conversation with your heart – it's threatening to betray you, I can tell.*'

That was a one-sided conversation I had with my inner person, having just appeared only to taunt me about my interest in Lucas. Hopefully, that was not a romantic interest. I persuaded myself to think about anything but Lucas. The wedding was the next best thing to think about. So yeah, thoughts of the wedding and how I was going to feel overwhelmed, had to be the only ones that occupied my mind. I wasn't complaining though. I couldn't wait to be seen out there with my man, all dressed up and grown up.

After carefully getting out of my tight dress, I felt a slight twinge on my spine. It emerged quickly and then disappeared just as rapidly as it had appeared, scaring me to no end. I sat down, my legs and hands trembling. I then felt heat on my tailbone, similar to how I felt after having endured pain exerted by Martin's knee. Then it was followed by a sharp headache. I got frightened and called out to Martin, crying.

He came upstairs running and as soon as he saw me, I could tell by how he had suddenly become pale, that he knew something was horribly wrong.

"Baby, you don't look too good. What happened? Did you fall?"

"No, I didn't fall. After taking off my clothes, my spine became sore and my feet and hands began trembling." I showed him my hands, as he touched them, finishing the move with a thumb touch on both of my wrists.

My hands had rapidly turned purple-blue and that distressed me. That frightened Martin too. The concern in his eyes was evident and difficult to ignore. I cried as the spasm on my back had reappeared, making it impossible for me to move, even slightly. I also experienced a very unusual headache, which left my eyes blurry. I could still see but barely. I couldn't fathom what was happening to me but, it was clear then, that something was amiss.

"Baby, lie down please. I have to examine you. If you are not better in an hour or two, I will have to take you to the hospital so that they can take some x-rays and run some tests. This is not looking good."

"What do you think happened when you exerted pressure on my coccyx? Did you pinch a nerve?" I had to ask; the pain was unbearable. I was not necessarily shoving guilt into his heart but I needed to know, truly.

"Oh baby, I am trying very hard not to think about what happened. But now, it appears that it could actually be the reason you're struggling like this. I cannot tell you just how sorry I am. What would I do if this is really serious or if I have caused permanent damage on your back?"

Why on the earth was he asking me that stupid question? Did I care that he was worried? I didn't care; I was the injured one, not him.

He helped me to lie down on the bed as my quivering legs became slightly better. My headache however, kept pounding like a drum, particularly with each move I made. However, I had to work hard as Martin helped me to settle down.

"Should I give you an injection? It did help you the last time?"

"You cannot keep dealing with the symptoms while I don't even know what's going on with me. Martin, what was in that syringe?"

"It was just an anti-inflammatory mixture but it looks like its effect has ebbed. I can't take your screech baby, please let me give you the injection again. If you're not better in an hour, we should definitely go to the hospital."

"Fine; just make this pain go away Martin, I'm terrified," I sobbed.

He went to his office, briefly leaving me on the bed. He swiftly came back with another dose of medicine to inject into my body.

"Baby, please arch like the last time. Will you be able to first turn on your side?"

"Yes, I will manage," I whined.

I slowly turned on my side, eager to sleep on my stomach. I arched for Martin to place a cushion underneath my belly. After that exercise that took longer than it should have, he ran his hands up and down my spine, a move that gave me the chills. It was as if he was counting my bones. With every move he made, he hurt me.

"I don't think I will be able to go to the wedding tomorrow," I mentioned hurriedly, noticing Martin's face grimacing.

I didn't care how he felt about the revelation. How was I going to enjoy myself at the wedding when I was that ill? Even if that medicine could make me better like it did the last time, none of us was sure as to whether it would stay that way or not. What if I start experiencing pain again as was the case again that time?

I would have to tell whoever would enquire about the pain on my back as to how I got injured. I was certain Martin didn't want that. Although I really wanted to attend that wedding, it didn't seem like I was going to manage with such an enormous sting on my back.

Martin injected me again. This time though, the dosage felt like it was a lot more than the last time. That concerned me. How could he do that? He did seem worried but did that really warrant me receiving an overdose of whatever it was he was giving me – the anti-inflammatory mixture whose name he was trying hard to conceal?

My whole back felt warm and then a tingling sensation followed, after-which I felt ferocious heat that got me weeping so hard, I thought I was dying. Martin began crying as well, pleading with me to hold on and not cry so much as I was making him cry as well. I felt like my body was no longer mine as I experienced chills, then heat, then weird vibrations around my waist and pins and needles underneath my feet.

The experience was unbearable and for the first time, it appeared as though Martin was clueless as to what to do to me and for me. Perhaps it was because he was too close to the situation and personally involved with the patient.

CHAPTER 9

Scarred for Life!

Something was not right. I couldn't feel my legs, nor could I feel my back. I was numb from my neck to the tip of my toes. There were too many people hovering over me with lights piercing me as I attempted to open my eyes. I then heard a man's wail and I was able to make out seconds later, that it was Martin and figured that he must have been informed about my prognosis. '*Perhaps I have died and this is my soul that's hearing all the commotion. Is this a dream?'* I wondered.

"Martin please, you cannot come in here; you know protocol. She is in good hands. Let us do our job and attend to her as soon as possible."

I realized only then, that I was in theatre at the hospital and I could not recall how and when I got there. The last thing I remembered was ferocious pains on my back, particularly my coccyx and the numbness from my neck to my toes. I slipped back into deep sleep and was unable to wake up and couldn't move.

I saw myself on the bed, surrounded by people I didn't recognize. I also stood next to them, but they were oblivious of my presence as they rough handled my body, while I remained powerless to protest.

The room was gravely arctic; it felt more like a huge cold room but the men and women in white and blue were not bothered. There I was, stepping closer to the bed attempting to figure out why I was powerless and practically at the mercy of the doctors and nurses. I was about to undergo an operation but my spirit was already ready to give up. I wanted to wake up but I couldn't, as one of the men in white coats pushed me down, using his might to do as he pleased with me.

****

'*Well, my soul has the power here'*. It might have been mystical as they couldn't see me but we had the power – the frail me and my soul. Weird experience I was undergoing. My late grandfather suddenly appeared, walking through the wall. He stood next to my stronger self, not my vulnerable self at the mercy of the many doctors that were hovering over me.

"Go back into your body at once!" he yelled at me. How could my grandfather do that to me when I was still having so much fun, taking notes of what the doctors were doing to me? I pretended as if I didn't hear him.

"Do you want me to call your great grandfather or are you tired of living? Do you want to come with me?"

"No!" I screamed - both versions of me screeched. I experienced a hollow feeling and sadness as I looked at my emaciated frame, in total reliance of the medics. "Papakie, why would you want to take me away with you? I'm happy in this part of the world," I stated.

"Are you really happy? Do you think we don't see how you live your life and whose fault it is that you ended up being here?" his eyes widened.

"Am I dead, Papakie?"

"Not yet but you will be soon, unless you get back into your body right now. If you don't do as I say, I'm taking you with me. Now got back I say!"

"I don't have the strength Papakie; I don't think I will be able to do that. Look at me; there is so much blood oozing from my back. What if I will be paralyzed after this? Isn't it better for me to rather come with you?" I faced down.

"No… my grandchild, it's not yet time; not yet time. I was just fooling around with you when I told you that I wanted to take you with me. Now hold my hand, I will help you to quickly enter your body. Your heart is about to stop and then you will no longer be able to enter your body after that. That would mean I will have to take you with me, even though your time hasn't arrived yet.

I extended my right hand to Papakie, as I used to call him when I was just a little girl. He then held me tight, pulling me towards my body. I watched the doctors' faces frowning and I asked them what the matter was. They obviously didn't hear me.

"Her heart is taking strain, please let's bring her back. Come on now Palesa, come on, you can't leave us now!" one doctor Duvenhage muttered. I heard the nurse call him as such.

Papakie didn't seem to have the strength anymore, as he attempted to carry me, thinking I was still that little girl he once knew. He couldn't do that with ease. I was tired, ready to give up.

Another elderly man, whose features mirrored Papakie's, walked right through the doctors and they didn't flinch. He looked at me and smiled.

"Let me…," he motioned to Papakie to let him help him. He then carried me, as Papakie moved backwards, giving him space. He literally threw me inside my body and then he smiled.

"You have to revive your strength now child, we are the Ditheko clan and we are very strong. You will not die now, do you hear me? There is a lot you still have to do. Now pull yourself together and never ever leave your body ever again."

"Eya Ntatemoholo (yes grandpa)," I responded pitifully, watching both these strong old men disappear before my eyes and then reappearing again as they prepared themselves to walk through the wall they came through. They waved at me bearing wide grins.

I literally felt myself connecting with my essence again, although I felt as if my eyesight had left me. I was positioned on my right side, as if they knew that, that was the side I struggled to sleep by.

'*Should I protest*?' I asked my inner self.

'*Oh just pack it in, will you – pack it in and take it! Weren't you listening just now? We are the strongest clan and nothing daunts us*.' Who was scolding me now? I felt a sharp object cutting me open on my lower back. I squealed but nobody heard me.

****

"I can't see! I can't see! Who are all these people? Where am I? Where's Martin?" I wept, frightened and my head felt like it had cotton wool inside. Perhaps it did or my brain had swollen! I couldn't see; it was as if I was using wrong eyes to see what was happening around me, even though that eyesight was quickly fading.

"Doctor, she's waking up! Has she been awake this whole time? Should we give her another dosage?" Some woman - a nurse I presumed, asked.

"This is very sore you know! Aren't you supposed to put me under anaesth...?" I have no recollection of what happened after attempting to ask that question.

I was awoken by the stench of medicine and a feeling of being in motion, while I was not walking by myself. I still couldn't see properly and whatever I landed my eyes on was blurry. I looked up and noticed the ceiling and big down lighters – moving with me. It took time for me to realize that I was on a stretcher and men and women in powdered blue scrubs were wheeling me to God knows where!

"Look who's with us! How're you feeling?"

Seriously now, did that doctor expect me to speak? I was stiff and it was like there was wood tightening my waist and I still couldn't feel my legs. My lower back to my toes were numb and I cried, not knowing whether I was going to be able to walk again.

We entered the ward, still being wheeled by the men and women in blue. They then positioned me to an empty space towards the window.

"The operation went really well," a Doctor Duvenhage revealed to a man preparing to get up. I couldn't see who it was at first, but as I prompted myself to look, I noticed that it was Martin, looking lost and sighing often.

"Ngwanaka, bophelo bo bokgutshwanyane (My child, life is very short)," my mother stated, holding both my hands and kissing them. Yes, my mother was there too.

"Mama...," I struggled to speak.

"Sh sh sh sh…," she beseeched. "Don't try to speak. Martin told us that you were here. I had to come and sign some papers so that you could be operated on."

I was happy about what my mother had intimated to me, even though I was still very weak to respond to her. Mama then extended her hand towards Martin, who was behaving strangely the way I could gather.

"Martin, I'll leave you with her for a while. I cannot believe you left us just a few hours ago and now Palesa and her dad are both admitted at the same hospital," Mama paused. "I guess I will have to keep going back and forth between wards."

"Mama, you do not have to do that. I will keep checking on Palesa," Martin held.

"Martin, I was not complaining. Palesa is my daughter and I should look after her. I was simply mentioning and amazed by the weirdness of what has happened today…the mystery of life!" Martin groaned.

"Baby, how're you feeling?" I didn't want to respond to Martin. How did he expect a person who had just been operated on to feel? Tears rolled down my cheeks as I attempted to turn on my side but found it very difficult to do so with ease."

"Please don't try to move."

"I can't feel my legs…and my waist," I wept.

"Oh my God…please… please doctor, what's happening now?" Martin asked.

Doctor Duvenhage joined us after completing my file,

instructing everyone to leave him with his patient. Two nurses joined him.

"Martin, what's happening?" I heard my mother ask.

"At the moment Mama, I honestly have no idea what is happening." I stopped listening to the conversation as the doctor and nurses wanted to examine me and to also ask me a few questions as they were doing so.

"Palesa, I'm going to run this under your feet, so if you feel any sensation, please just wiggle your toes," Doctor Duvenhage showed me some steel object.

"Okay," I nodded.

He indeed ran that underneath both my feet and although I was still feeling slightly numb, I had some sensation and I could feel the coldness that came with that steel object. I wiggled my toes.

"You just moved your toes…you will be fine. How did it feel?"

"It felt a bit cold but I still feel a bit numb."

"Don't worry, you will soon regain all your senses more so after the anesthetic has waned. It's normal."

"Okay…I see." I slid back into deep sleep again.

CHAPTER 10

Cryptic Revelations

'*These hands feel familiar. Whose are they*?' I was trapped, suspended in a nightmare from which I couldn't awaken. My eyes were open, but I was paralyzed, unable to move, unable to scream. I saw myself lying in the hospital bed, my chest rising and falling with each laboured breath, but my body felt like lead, unresponsive to my desperate commands.

I tried to wiggle my toes, to shake my head, to twitch a single muscle, but I was frozen, a statue of fear. My heart kept racing, pounding in my chest like a drum, threatening to burst free. I was convinced I was dying, that this was the end.

Darkness closed in around me, a suffocating shroud. I felt myself being pulled down… down… down into a deep, dark hole, with no escape. The air grew thick, heavy with malevolent presence. I sensed dark forces lurking, watching, waiting, laughing in evil tones.

A demon…that's what it felt like! A presence that fed on my fear, growing stronger with each passing moment. I was helpless, unable to defend myself, unable to flee. My mind screamed, but my voice was trapped, silenced by some unseen forces.

I was aware of my surroundings, the beeping machines, the sterile hospital smell, but it was all distant, muffled. The only thing that was real was the terror, the crushing weight of it, pressing down on me, squeezing the life out of me.

I was desperate to wake up, to break free from the living hell, but my body refused to obey. I was locked in, alone, and terrified, with no escape in sight. The darkness was again closing in, and I was running out of time.

****

I had no choice but to relent to my fate, but I was spared. Alas! I was finally able to pull my willpower from deep within. I breathed hard, my eyes widening as the hands that were touching me tightened.

"Easy… easy… easy," a proverbial male voice consoled me, as

nurses approached.

"Did you have a nightmare?" The man asked.

"I think I just did. I wanted to wake up but I found it difficult to do so. That frightened me. I thought I was dying. It was painful to watch myself awake but not fully awake and struggling to really wake up. The feeling was weird," I declared.

That was the second time I felt as though I had or was about to die and there was absolutely nothing I could do about that feeling. I was helpless and at the mercy of the medics. They had no idea how to help me through the passage. Was it the anaesthetic that made me hallucinate or there was something sinister attacking me? A demon? Why did I think it was a demon that attacked me? It felt evil as I had never experienced that before, but whatever it was that was pulling me down as I attempted to wake up, I was certain it was not of this world.

"We might have to sedate her again or induce coma. We need to call Doctor Duvenhage. Her body needs to recover without the agitation that she's causing in her body and mind right now," one of the nurses mentioned.

"Please, please…," I mumbled. "Don't sedate me… I'm begging you. I'm afraid to sleep again. There's something that doesn't want me to wake up – I can feel it. So, I cannot sleep," I wept.

I felt their strength holding me down and the hands that were holding me got disentangled and the owner of those hands stood up, mumbling a few words to me.

"Palesa, please calm down. Try not to fight this. It's important that you not overexert yourself, otherwise they might have to put you under. You're probably having a very bad reaction to the medicines, especially the anaesthetic," the man advised.

"Who are you?" I asked.

"It's me…Lucas."

"Lucas! What are you doing here? Where is Martin?"

"Doctor, should we leave you with her for a bit?" nurse Moipolai Motloung asked. I glanced briefly at her name.

"Yeah..., please don't call Doctor Duvenhage yet. Give me 10 minutes to talk to her. Besides, we are still waiting for Martin. I'm wondering why he hasn't arrived yet."

"Okay Doctor, but this is atypical. You are not her doctor and we don't want to get into trouble so please, it should be exactly ten minutes." Both sister Moipolai and another one whose name was undecipherable from the name tag left me with Lucas. However, they seemed troubled as they exchanged ephemeral looks.

Lucas sat down on a chair next to the bed and grabbed my hands again. What was it with the man always holding my hands? This time, I felt uncomfortable about the move, and I disentangled my hands from him. It bordered on being inappropriate. I was Martin's fiancé and not his and besides them being friends, I didn't know him well enough to merit him being in my space. Furthermore, we had a brief chat which lasted for a few minutes only when I was with Martin. So, what was it about him that made me so apprehensive? What did he want? Who exactly was he really? Where was Martin? Was he the demon I dreamt about?

"Please stop doing that. Where is Martin?" I was stern in my question.

"I apologise; I didn't mean to upset you. I was just trying to comfort you seeing as you were so edgy earlier. Can you tell me about that nightmare you had?"

"No, why should I tell you about my nightmare? You're not my doctor. Another thing, I was told you're a gynecologist. So why should I divulge my innermost feelings and illness to you? Where is Martin?" I ended the seethe with a question again.

"I have no idea where he is. I was just doing my own rounds and realised that you were in here. That's when I elected to come and be with you, so that you can have a familiar face when you wake up."

The revelation crept me out. Didn't Lucas realize that he was being indecent with his declaration of 'concern'? I felt that he was totally out of order. That was not his place to show that much concern and affection. What did he want to do… beat Martin to it?

"You're not exactly a familiar face Lucas. I only met you for a few minutes and you cannot exactly call that 'me knowing you'. Please call Martin and let him know I'm awake."

"I'll call him just now. Firstly though, I would like you to please not be offended by the question I'm about to ask you." Offended? What on earth was he on about? He wouldn't let up even after I had told him that he was being inappropriate. Bloody cheek!

"Nurses gave me only ten minutes with you, so I might as well ask you this question: How did your back get injured?"

"You're a doctor Lucas, yet you seem to not be too bright. I told you that I don't want to discuss my life with you. But you are hell-bent on asking me personal questions which are and should be reserved only for my personal doctors and nurses working on my case," I defiantly responded.

"I don't mean to distress you any further, Palesa but it's important that I know how you got injured."

"Why is it so important? What's it to you?"

"I just want to piece certain information together, which I have had for years, with what you'd tell me. That is, if what you're suffering from is the same as what my late wife experienced, just a few months before she passed away – before she was murdered actually."

'*Did he just tell me that his wife was murdered? By whom? No one attempted to kill me? I'm certainly not a victim of attempted murder*,' I inwardly remarked.

"Come on, Lucas. Why would you want to contrast my ailment with that of your late wife? Please be honest with me. What's going on here?"

"Did Martin hit you?" he asked hurriedly as my whole body shivered and froze, unsure what to say or do.

"Martin is your friend, yet here you are asking me inept questions and insinuating that he hit me. Why would you ask me something like that? Are you mad?"

"Please… please don't get agitated by my questions, Palesa. I know the signs of abuse. I can tell that something is amiss here. My late wife……"

"Hey… hey… hey…STOP IT!" I howled. "I don't want to hear anymore, let alone anything about your late wife. Sorry to hear that you lost her. I hope her murderer or murderers were arrested and that you find closure. But for now, please leave me alone. I don't feel comfortable discussing my fiancé or talking to you at all. I thought you were a good friend to Martin. But here you are, making some unfounded stories about him. Please leave!"

"Like I said Palesa, I'm sorry. My aim was not to offend you but to get to the truth."

What truth was that? I didn't even feel like hearing that truth because I was upset and felt sick to my stomach due to those odd and very offensive questions and insinuations Lucas was levelling against Martin. I still cannot fathom why I felt the need to protect Martin, because he really did hurt me and perhaps he was on his way to subject me to abuse. '*Should I tell him when he gets here*? *If I do tell him what his friend has been up to, what if he goes to fight him? Then I would be responsible for causing a rift between two seemingly good friends – at least from what I saw the other day.*'

Nurses approached us on hearing me roar at Lucas, mystified by the upheaval and wondering what it was about, since they left me with a person who appeared to be a really good man and a high ranking Obstetrician.

"Doctor Lucas, what's going on? Is she having another episode? Is that why she was making such a noise?" Nurses asked as soon as they reached my bed.

"I think she is having another episode, but my professional opinion is that she might need to be sedated. It looks like she is not herself still. Perhaps you can call Duvenhage and let him know," he cunningly stated and winked at me. '*How the hell could Lucas do this to me?*' He might not be as good a man as I thought he was. He clearly didn't want me to blurt out what he had intimated to me.

Tears immediately rolled down my cheeks, as I realised what he was trying to do. I felt helpless because if I were to go ballistic or hysterical, I would definitely be sedated. Nurses asked him to leave and he obliged without protesting, while giving me a pithy look.

"Palesa, are you okay?" nurse Moipolai asked.

"Not really. Why did you allow that man to come in here? He is not my family and he is also not my doctor. I'm feeling very uncomfortable around him. He was busy asking me strange questions which left me reeling with distress. Please… I'm begging you, I don't want to see his face again," I pleaded.

"This is startling Palesa, because we saw you yesterday with him and Doctor Leboya, chatting and laughing together. So we assumed that you were all good friends. That's why we didn't refuse when he asked to be with you. What did he do to you?"

"Nothing! Just find out where Martin is or my mother at least.

I'm begging you," I implored, turning my face away from the nurses.

"Okay we will no longer allow him to see you. We called Doctor Duvenhage about your situation and he advised that we give you a sedative so that you can rest. Right now, we have just filled the drip with vitamins and antibiotics so that you can get better as you might not be able to eat normally."

"You know what, I don't care. Just do what you have to do but please don't let that man come and see me ever again."

"Okay… okay, we hear you," sister Moipolai affirmed, while exchanging weird glimpses with Sister Nozimanga. Yes, I was finally able to read her name tag.

"Sister Nozi will inject the sedative inside this drip," she pointed at the drip hanging, as the woman did what she had to do. They had earlier ignored my request of not being sedated. They all probably thought I was still hallucinating, otherwise why would they flatly ignore my stern wishes of not wanting to sleep again?

****

I woke up calmer and it seemed like I had slept for hours. My throat was dry and there was a burning sensation inside my nose and my ears had a hollow feeling. What happened to me when I was sedated? I didn't know what the nurses or doctors had subjected me to.

"Welcome back!" I opened my eyes slowly, unable to fathom

whose voice that was. It was a male voice though. My sense of smell however was still as sharp as ever. The man smelt like a brewery and I almost puked.

"Please stand back. You don't smell too good." Yes, I was blunt and didn't even care that I was that frank. How dare the man hover over me with such a dreadful smell emitting from inside his mouth!

"Ouch! That hurts. Do I really smell bad, baby?"

'*Did he just say, 'Baby'? What on earth is going on here*?' I forced my eyes to open a bit wider and then realized that it was Martin next to me. He was clad in a navy suit, a white shirt and a red tie. This was how he had planned to dress for the wedding. The tie however, was hanging lower and the shirt had a few top buttons undone – very unkempt.

"Baby, what has happened to you? You've been drinking? What time is it? What day is it?" I mumbled, hurling questions at him and he coughed, covering his mouth with his hand.

"Hello baby. It's Saturday and it's 18h47. I went to the wedding. I had to make an appearance as you were clearly not going to be there. The reception is still in full swing, but I had to leave to come and be with you." It was as if he felt that he needed to explain himself in earnest. That was the first!

"Oh really! I needed to see you when I woke up this morning but you were not here. You could have at least informed everyone that you weren't going to be here when I wake up. Instead, when I opened my eyes, Lucas was here." He raised his eyebrows, imploring me to repeat what I said.

"What did you just say? LUCAS!" his mood changed instantly and his brow creased. I quickly regretted telling him that his friend had been to see me. I had no choice but to continue telling him that Lucas claimed to have visited me simply to see how I was doing, while he did his rounds at the hospital.

"Yes, he said he had some rounds to make but somehow realized that I was in here. I found that odd since this is not the maternity ward. I guess he was being nice, seeing as you were not here to hold my hand."

As much as Martin's reaction rattled me briefly, I found it amusing; I know that's a bit warped, but how dare he attend the wedding without me!

"So the bustard came late to the wedding because he was trying to replace me! He said nothing about having been to see you when he arrived. He greeted me as if nothing has happened. He's got some explaining to do, BLOODY PERVERT!" he ended his rant, as I tried all I could to help him compose himself as I was not the only one in the ward.

Once again, I had to calm a grown man down because he couldn't handle his emotions. It didn't matter that I was the one lying in a hospital bed but somehow, I still had to play mom to my fiancé. Was I responsible for his change in mood? Why did I tell him about Lucas even though I knew that, that would rub him up the wrong way?

"Martin, don't get so worked up. Maybe his visit was truly harmless, and he found no reason to tell you that he has been here. He knew you are going to see me anyway and that I would tell you," I emphasized, slightly pleading Lucas's case.

I don't even know why I did that. Somehow deep down, I knew that at some point, I might need to have a candid conversation with Lucas because he seemed to have a lot on his mind. Perhaps the connection we had when we first met, meant that we were supposed to talk about something deep and that it might involve Martin.

"Oh no, don't even think of speaking for him. You have no idea what Lucas is capable of. He might be my friend but I'm not oblivious to the things he has done or what he is capable of." The statement baffled me even more. There were the two men, both slyly accusing one another of something sinister and speaking in riddles. What was I supposed to do or think – guess what they were both talking about?

"Baby, I've only just woken up as nurses had to sedate me again after I had a very bad nightmare. I really wish you were here, Martin. Was it really that important for you attend the wedding? Surely your friend would have understood?"

"Baby, don't worry about that; it has passed. I'm here now and not leaving your side again. I still cannot believe that dog came to see you! What exactly did he say to you?" he asked cunningly.

"Nothing much, save for what I have already told you. I guess he felt sorry for me. But what I still don't understand is why he had to be in these wards. I presume that will always remain a mystery," I coughed.

"I know why he was here - believe me I know why he was here. He probably wanted to make an impression on you and score some cheap points; bloody dog!" Martin continued with his tirade, calling Lucas a dog.

"Why would he want to score points with me? There is no comparison between any of these two relationships is there? You are my fiancé and he is your friend, your best friend as you both told me. I don't even know him and I'm relying on that brief introduction of yesterday. So, I still don't understand why you would speak like this about your friend. What exactly is he capable of?"

I had to ask, as Martin was acting more and more bizarre. His temple scowled and I sensed his heavy breath, albeit still muddled with alcohol reek.

"Don't worry about it, baby. I will deal with it myself. Right now though, tell me how you're feeling. Can you feel your legs? What did Doctor Duvenhage say?"

"My legs are fine. I haven't seen the doctor since I woke up. I have only seen the nurses, who kept poking me and turning me and causing so much discomfort to me. Maybe that's how you doctors work – leaving everything in the hands of nurses after having cut patients open and putting them back together again," I chortled and he did too.

“Yeah, pretty much!” he smiled, nodding in agreement.

At least he was calming down and sharing a smile or two. There was still that distressing feeling inside of me that, whatever it was the two men held over each other’s heads, must have been huge, likely to be scandalous even. That much was evident. How does one explain what Lucas briefly told me about his wife having been murdered and his comparison of my condition to that of his wife? Now there was Martin, telling me that I have no idea what Lucas was capable of? What on earth was I supposed to think?

Whatever it was, my detective cap sprung out from out of space and landed right on top of my head. ‘*When I leave here, I will be visiting Google and will not rest until I find out exactly what went down between these two.*’ I was still saddened by the fact that I was not able to attend the wedding though, particularly since I went through all the trouble of buying the best clothes and shoes. I knew that I was going to look superb but my fate had been sealed by my fiancé, after kneeling hard on my coccyx.

“Baby, what kind of operation did I just have exactly? Will I be able to walk again?” I asked. Martin faced down and shook his head, holding my hand with both of his.

“Baby, I’m so ashamed of myself, you know. I’m the reason you are here and the reason you had the operation.”

“I have already determined that, Martin. Just tell me what happened to my coccyx after you knelt hard on it.”

He widened his eyes. “Please keep your voice down,” he

whispered, "I know that it is my fault but please… please baby, can we not air our dirty linen? You didn't mention this to Lucas did you?" he queried.

"Is that all you're worried about, losing face to your buddies? What about me? What if I won't be able to walk again, Martin? What do you say about that? So yes, this is your fault, all your fault!" I shrieked.

"Baby, please calm down. I'm begging you."

"Why? Are you going to tell me how badly you injured me? If not, I am going to sing like a canary. So tell me!" I barked.

He shook his head, eyes dropping and his cheeks became pale. He rested his head on my chest and then kissed me. Yuck! That awful breath again. What did he drink exactly? He was an occasional drinker at home but he had never smelt that awful. I wondered as to what he had taken at the wedding. Whatever it was, it couldn't have been anything he was used to taking and possibly not good for him either. Yeah, I diagnosed him and was getting really good at it too.

He nearly removed the drip from my arm when he lay on my chest, as I quickly moved it out of the way. "Baby, it's okay, I'm not going to tell anyone, but you also have to tell me exactly what's going on and why I had to be operated on," I prompted.

"Okay baby, I'll tell you," he whispered and then kissed me again, lifting his head up. He looked around and saw a chair nearby, and then pulled it towards the bed, sitting on it. He held my right hand. "Baby, it looks like I pinched one of your nerves when I did what I did. So, they had to correct the disfigurement," he mumbled demurely.

"Did you just say disfigurement?"

"It's just a bad choice of words my love. They had to straighten what got out of alignment but you are going to be fine now and I promise that nothing like that will ever happen again. I swear on my mother's grave. You will be able to walk."

I simply kept silent, as I felt my eyes becoming watery. I tried to change my sleeping position just so I wouldn't have to keep looking at Martin's face, but I couldn't do that with ease and he tried to help me as I snapped at him, "stop it! I'll manage." He quickly removed his hands and sat back on the chair, while the two patients in the ward began showing signs of discomfort from my outburst and the constant war of words I had with Martin. I had to apologise.

"I'm sorry, I'm sorry," I whispered. They smiled, indicating their eagerness to rest.

"Baby, I just want to go home and freshen up. Perhaps when I come back I won't smell of booze so much," he chuckled.

"No, don't come back tonight. I need to rest. It's already late anyway. You can come back tomorrow. Just go and sleep it off, I'll see you tomorrow."

"Have you forgiven me?" he asked.

"I said I forgave you already, so why would you ask me that again? The operation scar will always be a reminder of what you did to me and there is no way you can erase that from my memory."

"I know baby, I know. I'll work very hard to regain your trust. I want you to feel safe with me. I want you to let go of all inhibitions when I touch you because you are my life. I don't know what I'd do if I were to lose you. I doubt I'd survive very long if you were to leave me," he alleged, shedding a tear.

"Baby, please go home. I'll see you tomorrow." His mouth widened. I bet he thought that his sudden morose expression would somehow make me declare love and pat him on his back, as if he were some little boy. All I wanted was for him to leave me in peace so I could rest.

"Baby, do you still feel like sleeping even after you have been sleeping for such a long time?" he asked.

"What exactly do you want me to say to you? I'm at the hospital and constantly feeling sleepy. I'll probably tell you about my stay here and how I felt once I have been discharged. So like I said, please go home," I beseeched again.

"Okay baby, I'll go. I love you." He gave me a lingering peck on my lips. This time however, I felt some gag threatening to come up.

"Mmm…," I murmured restlessly. "Get me that bucket," I mumbled, pointing at the bucket next to the bed.

He quickly picked it up, as I hurriedly propped myself up, feeling the most excruciating pain there ever was on my lower back! He put the bucket underneath my chin as I threw up inside. I trembled and asked him to call the nurses for me. He called out to them, while I noticed that they were coming in anyway, probably about to chase him out as visiting hours were over, I presumed.

On reaching me, I noticed that it was a different nurse that was about to attend to me. Perhaps Sister Moipolai's shift was over. Sister Margaret, a middle aged brunette with an arrangement of lines spread across her forehead and spectacles adorning her eyes, spoke in a high pitched tone, "Doctor Leboya, please let go of the bucket. I'm here now. You are aware that visiting hours are over aren't you?" she frowned.

It appeared as though everyone knew who Martin was. So, the next best thing was for me to listen in on conversations or gossips the nurses would have among themselves. Whether that would be a good move or not, was another story. I was determined to understand unerringly who I was marrying.

"Yes, I'm aware, sister. Apologies, I just wanted to see how my fiancé was doing."

Sister Margaret gave Martin a scornful look, reacting to the booze smell emitting from his mouth, no doubt. She pinched her nose and brushed it, while shaking her head. She held the bucket underneath my jaw so I could continue depositing the toxins from my stomach.

After a while, I stopped and Sister Margaret quickly wiped my mouth with a tissue paper and took the bucket to the designated toilet near my bed. I could hear her rinse it and swiftly brought it back.

Meanwhile, Martin was still standing next to the bed, looking daft as if he was a little boy who had just been caught with his hand in the cookie jar. I could tell he was troubled.

“Can I have water please, Sister?” I asked, coughing incessantly.

She took the water bottle from the nightstand and poured a bit in the glass that had been covered by paper towel and put a straw inside.

“Here you go…,” she helped me to drink, while holding the back of my head. “Easy… easy,” she cautioned.

“Thank you, Sister,” I thanked her after having gulped down the water. She aided me to settle down again and asked to see my wound as she needed to check stitches and establish how the wound was fairing since the operation.

“Palesa, I’m gonna have to turn you on the side because I want to check your wound. This may aggravate the pain a bit. I just want to call another nurse to come and help me, okay. Don’t try to move on your own.” Before she could leave to call for help, she stopped briefly midway, staring at Martin. He knew precisely what that expression meant, as he lifted his hands up in ‘total surrender’.

“Okay… okay Sister, I’m leaving. Baby, I will see you tomorrow. I love you.”

“Bye,” I stated, unwilling to return the declaration of love.

He left disgraced, as I inwardly scolded him because he was the reason I was there in the first place. All I wanted to do was to simply shove guilt into him so that he could feel as much pain as I was feeling, albeit different types of pain.

Nurses Margaret and Ntombi arrived and they carefully lifted me up and turned me on my side. The wound was still painful to the touch. I held on for as long as I had to, giving the nurses their space to work on me.

"The dressing is still intact and it doesn't seem like there is any blood coming out. Doctor Duvenhage is not messy; he's a really good surgeon," they both affirmed as they worked. Eventually they turned me back on another side and put cushions under my belly and another small one on the other side, to support my upper back.

"Just press here please, when you need to turn. Don't try to do it by yourself." Sister Margaret pointed at the bell hanging on the side of the bed.

"Okay Sister, I will do so. Thank you."

CHAPTER 11

All the beans are spilt!

I was hospitalized for two weeks and a couple of days, something that left me puzzled. I had thought I wouldn't stay that long at the hospital. I was beginning to see the hospital as my second home, much to the chagrin of Martin who always made a point to tell the nurses that he was paying very good money to have me taken care of at that hospital. I had always wondered as to why he didn't choose to take me to the hospital he worked at, Libertas Private Hospital. I never got a chance to ask.

I wasn't sure as to whether I wanted to go home to him when I was going to be discharged. Each time he came to check on me, he would upset me, leaving me emotionally drained. '*Perhaps he is taking strain*'; I would convince myself.

There were times when he would send both Bra Mos and Sis Lulama to come and check up on me. That was not too bad a decision because that meant that we would have chats without the risk of our conversations being listened to. Bra Mos drove the van he utilised to buy his garden supplies and other things that were reserved for him to purchase, which included his and sis Lulama's groceries.

On one odd visit to me while still at the hospital, both him and Sis Lulama were acting inexplicably, prompting me to even ask frankly. "What's going on? Why are you two fidgeting with your fingers and keys? Is there something wrong? Is Martin alright?"

"Tell her, Mos," sis Lulama elbowed Bra Mos.

"Tell me what?" I asked impatiently.

"Miss Palesa, please don't tell Mr Martin that we told you this. He can fire us instantly. Please promise us that you won't tell him."

"This sounds serious, just tell me already," I prompted anxiously, as I reached for the bed, Sis Lulama helping me to settle down. I had just come out of the bathroom when they arrived.

"Okay ma'am, ever since you got admitted here, Doc has been drinking a lot. One day he slept in the car with a hartes (whisky) bottle in his hand and it was at a time he came back from work." I was bemused to hear Bra Mos tell me the unsettling news, as Sis

Lulama took over.

"Two weeks ago, he fought with one of his best friends, Doctor Lucas. I don't think you know him, but Mr Martin was accusing him of wanting to have you for himself. Mos had to intervene as they were both going to seriously hurt each other."

"Wow, is that why he hasn't been coming often lately? I thought it was because he didn't want to see me in this state I'm in. I even thought that he lost a patient or something. This is absurd. I don't even know that man. Did this doctor come to the house to fight?" I asked, pretending not to have an idea of what the fight could have been about or who that "Dr Lucas" was.

"Yes ma'am. It was actually on Sunday after they went to the wedding on Saturday. I'm certain something must have happened at the wedding, otherwise why would they fight the following day?" Sis Lulama was spilling beans, as if she was about to feed the pigeons, making unfounded statements, presenting them as facts. I listened attentively, as I was hoping there would be certain information that could help me decipher the depth of Martin and Lucas' feud, which seemed to have re-emerged due to my hospitalization.

"This doesn't really make sense because as much as Martin is pretty scarce here, wouldn't he have told me about the fight?"

"Not if you were at the centre of the fight ma'am," Bra Amos declared, blinking often and avoiding eye contact with me.

"This still doesn't make sense, Bra Mos. I refuse to believe that those two were fighting over me. For what reason? I don't even know Lucas. So why would he start a fight with Martin?"

"Ma'am, they had one of the most horrible fights about six years ago. I think Doc had an affair with Dr Lucas' wife and when..." The poor man was coming on nicely with the tidbits and Sis Lulama had to spoil the fun and entreated him to stop talking, elbowing him.

"Mos, you are talking rubbish now! Why would you tell Miss Palesa such a thing? Mr Martin is not that kind of man and you know that. He doesn't cheat but I think his friends sometimes tend to be jealous of him. Miss Palesa, don't take what Mos said seriously because I don't think what they accused Mr Martin of was the truth," she stated firmly, as Bra Mos gaped at her, mouth hanging low and his face brazen out.

"Okay, I need the truth please. Sis Lulama, please don't hide anything from me. Did Martin have an affair with that woman or not?" She blinked incessantly, now embarrassed by my probe. She stared at Bra Mos, as if to request him to take over the narration. It was evident that they had both bitten off more than they could chew.

"Miss Palesa, we don't know for sure that Mr Martin had an affair with that woman or not. But Dr Lucas accused him of beating up his wife when she wanted to end things with him. She denied everything but Dr Lucas was unwavering in his stance of believing what he wanted to believe at that time. Two years later, Dr Lucas' wife passed away and he and Mr Martin reconciled after the funeral. I don't know what exactly happened now that triggered a similar fight ma'am – about you this time," Bra Mos recounted.

Bra Mos was adamant that I was the cause of the fresh brawl between my man and his best friend.

"Wow, I think I've heard enough. Doctors have advised me to take it easy and to not allow myself to be stressed at all. So, I wonder if I shouldn't just go home to my parents when I get discharged. We sorted out our differences. It sounds like there's a lot of stress awaiting me at the Leboya Homestead and that's the last thing I want. You have actually just missed my mom. She left a couple of minutes ago, just before you guys came in. You probably passed her on the way without knowing who she was."

"It would have been nice to meet her, Miss Palesa, really. But I don't think Mr Martin will allow you to go home as he is already not doing well as we speak. Perhaps when you come back to the compound he will stop drinking. Please don't go home," sis Lulama begged.

"I can see that the reason you don't want me to go home has absolutely nothing to do with your concern for your Mr Martin but you are worried about yourselves. Has he been impossible lately?"

They both shared a sneer, covering their mouths with their hands. I had hit it on the nail it appeared.

"Yes, he is back to yelling again. He is constantly shouting at us and he hasn't been going to work like he used to. So we don't know if he took leave or not. But, his drinking is getting out of control, Miss Palesa, so please don't go home."

"What do you think I can do for him in the state I'm in now, Sis Lulama? He's a grown man and he should be able to handle his alcohol."

"I think he'll stop drinking ma'am. He really misses you; we can tell. I think he genuinely does love you, Miss Palesa," she concluded.

"Well, I think it's time for you to leave now. I need to rest. They might discharge me tomorrow from what I heard the doctors say. I have already told Martin. I pray that he doesn't come here drunk."

"Miss Palesa, please don't tell him we told you about his drinking," Bra Mos breathed heavily. "Lulama, we should get going now."

"Yes ma'am, we are going now. I hope you really get better Miss Palesa. A back operation is very scary. Good bye Ma'am." Sis Lulama covered my legs with the very thin hospital blanket, as we shared a tender moment.

"Thanks Sis Lulama. Goodbye and please drive safely Bra Mos. By the way, what are you going to tell your boss we spoke about? You know how he is. He's going to question you till you bleed the truth," the three of us laughed.

"No ma'am, we cannot tell him anything otherwise he will chase us out," Bra Mos continued chortling, covering his mouth with his hand. They then left, waving at me still.

As they left the ward, they kept fleeting looks at me, possibly feeling my eyes gawking at them as well. We shared a smile until they reached the door and all I could see were their shadows.

****

"I'm very happy you are being discharged ngwanaka (my child). You are coming home with me aren't you? You need your mother to look after you. I still don't know what kind of operation you had and nobody is telling me anything." She widened her eyes.

My mother did all she could to assert herself as my primary caregiver. However, in my heart I felt that the ship had already sailed. I was just somewhat happy that when I did need them, I could go home without worrying that I would be chased away.

"No mama, I cannot come home with you; Martin needs me. I will come and see Papa when I feel better. Remember that Martin is a doctor so if there's any medical emergency, he will be on hand to attend to me." My mother wasn't pleased to hear me say that and her gloomy face and shaking head were evidence of that.

"Oh well…, as you wish Palesa. I'm just happy that you will come home at some point. I think you should stay at least for a weekend when you do eventually come."

"I will do so Mama, I promise," I held her hand in assurance.

Martin came in as my mother and I were still talking, looking spruce in dark blue jeans and a navy and white print shirt. He was flashing his car keys and holding his leather man bag. He had a fresh hair cut and just by glancing at him and how much he had elevated his shoulders and walked with purpose, I felt proud that,

that was my man, my fiancé and that he had been waiting for the day he would fetch me from the hospital. So how could I go home with my mom when my man had made such a great effort and also vowed to take good care of me? I wasn't going to disappoint him and risk him drinking even more than he had been already.

As he reached us, he greeted my mom reverently but she wasn't too keen this time around to exchange pleasantries with him. I could see that she somehow blamed him for my decision of not wanting to go home to be tended to by her. She was also not too chuffed by the load of problems he had placed on my shoulders as I mentioned candidly that he needed me.

Time was 11h45 and I was eager to leave the hospital and be pampered, perhaps if not by Martin, by both Sis Lulama and Bra Mos.

"Good morning, Mama," he greeted my mom again, pretending not to have been aware that my mom ignored him earlier.

"Good morning, Martin," she briefly greeted back and then kept quiet, folding her arms. Her tone was stiff and unfeeling. I noted Martin's brief leer, as if he knew what my mother's gripe was. I chose to ignore that as I continued packing my stuff in my bag with the help of my mother. I was still sitting on the bed while doing so.

The tension between the two, which could be cut with a blunt knife, made me very uneasy and although I initially elected to pay it no mind, I felt the sting somehow because it appeared that I was at the centre of that impasse.

Nurse Moipolai came in just as the two important people in my life kept “scolding” each other with their eyes.

“Palesa, I can’t say I’m excited to see you go as you have been a very pleasant patient to nurse. However, I am very happy that you are doing well. Please take care of yourself and don’t overexert yourself unnecessarily. Please also do not carry any heavy stuff; you will hurt your back terribly,” she added.

“I promise to take good care of her,” Martin commented, giving me a wide grin and patting me on my shoulder. Sister Moipolai then helped me out of bed as I took my time, not wanting to hurt my back. Once my feet reached the floor, Martin perused me from head to toe, as if there was something he didn’t approve of, making me feel uncomfortable. This prompted my mother to ask frankly.

“Why are you checking my daughter out like this? Is she not dressed to your satisfaction?” My mother asked, leaving me flabbergasted, as I inwardly wondered what that emanated from. What was that look from Martin for anyway?

“No mama, I just want my fiancé to look good, irrespective of whether she is leaving the hospital or not,” he responded, turning his attention towards me. “Baby, are you going to comb your hair or you’re going to wear a doek (turban)?”

I couldn’t quite figure out that dark note from his tone but as I had sung his praises to my mother, I chose to not make a big deal of it. However, I wasn't oblivious to the uncharacteristic looks both my mother and Sister Moipolai gave one another. Again, I ignored them, as I reached for my bag wanting to take my doek out. Martin helped me to look for it, pretty chuffed with himself that I was doing what he wanted.

He took out my pink silky doek and helped me to wear it, while I felt the sharp eyes of our audience standing in the middle of the room, watching every move we made.

"I think people love our movie." Martin whispered.

"Movie? What do you mean?" I asked.

"This movie that we're already in right now. Don't you realize that their eyes are just fixed on us and none of them is moving?" We laughed briefly as I tried my best to not even look at my mother.

"Am I fine with my satin night dress and gown?" I asked my fiancé.

"Yes, you're fine, baby. This is the one I bought you and it just screams perfection on you and you ooze grandeur." Martin's words made me feel good about myself and about us. He then kissed me on my forehead as I felt slightly sheepish. My mother rolled her eyes.

"Oh… for Pete's sake, you're going to be together! Can't we leave already? By the way, I'm coming with you guys to your place, Martin. I want to help Palesa settle in." My mother mentioned, hurriedly.

"Mama, you say you're coming with us?" I asked, amazed that she hadn't mentioned this before.

"Yes, I'm coming with you, Palesa, Is that a problem?" my mother responded with a question, almost insolently. Martin widened his eyes and then looked at me. I bet he thought I'd say something to sway my mother from her resolve that she was coming with us. However, I kept quiet.

"What about Papa? Who's going to look after him Mama if you're coming with us?" Martin asked, pretending to care or did he really? My mother elected to not respond to him directly, directing any response to me instead.

"Palesa, your father is fine and he's home. He has even started working even though he's doing so at home, consulting from his home office. Remember we were told that the stroke was minor but even then, your aunt will be with him for a few days." Did my mother just say a few days?

"Mama, did you bring your clothes? I did everything in my power to try to dissuade her from coming with us, while Sister Moipolai was losing patience with us.

"I hate to break this party, but we need the bed please. Palesa, here is your medication," she handed a bulged paper bag to me full of medicines as she continued. "Please adhere to all instructions and as mentioned, do not engage in anything that will cause your back to take strain for at least a month, sex included," sister Moipolai mentioned hastily, patting me on my shoulder and raising her eyebrows as I noticed her pupils dilating.

"Thanks Sister," I chuckled. "I promise I will not do anything that will cause strain to my back."

"One last thing before you leave Palesa," she paused. "Please never forget to take periodic walks; the same way you were doing daily here. You must keep that routine please. That way, you encourage blood to keep flowing and you will heal quicker. Just don't overdo it but walk a few steps initially and increase as the days go by. I trust you will adhere to this, Palesa."

"I will do so, I promise."

"Don't worry Sister, I will be with her all the way and will certainly make sure that she doesn't go beyond what's stipulated," my mother affirmed.

"Sister Moipolai, why don't you just write a booklet that explains all these things you've just told my fiancé. I'm here and I know what to do to help her but here you are speaking as if you know far more than I do. Write a book already!" Martin mocked the poor nurse callously, leaving us mortified. She on the other hand, gave him a disdainful look, showing us that she didn't really care about what he had intimated to her.

"I'll pretend I didn't hear that, Dr Leboya. You're still some piece of work, I see! I wonder if Palesa knows what she has gotten herself into."

Martin directed a lethal look at Sister Moipolai, who was not deterred and remained defiant in her stance. My mother's face wrinkles became thinner as they formed a complex gathering instantly on her face. I could see that she was unsettled by what Sister Moipolai had proclaimed.

Martin tried to wave the moment as bad jokes between colleagues by laughing hard, but Sister Moipolai didn't even flinch, nor did she even share a brief smirk.

"Palesa, let's get out of here. I think you can travel with me in my car. I came in your father's Merc," Mama said, asserting her authority.

"Okay Mama," I nodded.

"Mama, it's okay, we don't want to bother you. Palesa will come with me in my car. I think the Beemer is smoother anyway. No offence," Martin held, almost contemptuously.

"I cannot believe you want us to fight about who will be travelling with Palesa and which car is smoother. You do not have any authority over her; she is my daughter and if you keep this up, I will drive with her straight home and you will not see her ever again. You're so full of yourself and I cannot believe that I actually thought you were a respectful man."

Mama snatched my bag from Sister Moipolai's hand, who was so chuffed with the somewhat intense exchange between my mom and Martin. I had no strength to engage in their power games. I let them be. I felt that it wasn't my circus to be part of.

Martin gave me an enduring cold and intent look, trying to force me to intervene and be on his side. That look gave me shivers down my spine and I felt the pain and I relented, forgetting my earlier stance of not participating in the mini brawl.

"Mama, please stop fighting. Have you two forgotten that I'm ill so please don't do this to me," I paused and faced Martin. "Babe, it's okay, I'll travel with Mama. Once we get home, we will be together so let's give this one to her, okay."

"Fine let's go," Martin said in a strained tone, indicating his uneasiness and motioning us to leave. Other patients were now watching us, as were the other nurses who had come in to help Sister Moipolai prepare the bed to get it ready for the next patient.

Sister Moipolai then brought a wheelchair and advised me to sit on it. She had already placed a round cushion that had a hole in the middle. I sat down and didn't feel any strain on my back. She then leaned down on me and whispered in my ear. "Be very careful of this man… please. I inserted my number on your phone when you were sleeping. So please use it should you find yourself in danger of any kind. I will know what to do and who to call."

I looked at her and kept quiet as my mom thanked the nurses and wheeled me out. Martin was already at the door but he did notice that Sister Moipolai was murmuring something in my ear and I was almost certain that he would ask me about it when we got home. My mom then veered me out of the ward as we left the nurses.

"You've got quite a lot of stuff. Should we ask one of the potters to accompany you to the car?" Sister Moipolai asked.

"I thought you couldn't wait to get rid of us. I'll find the potter; just continue making the bed as you were about to. Your work here is done, thank you very much," Martin cheekily responded.

I couldn't quite understand Martin's insolence towards the poor woman but she didn't even care. It was as if she was used to that kind of behaviour from him. She simply flipped her hand and murmured, "Goodbye Palesa."

As my mom was wheeling me out, Martin had a phone against his ear and I heard him contacting someone to come and take my flowers. He specifically asked whoever he was talking to, to bring a trolley of some kind so that the flowers can be loaded onto it properly.

We left him at the door of the ward and my mom continued veering me slowly. We passed the porter on the foyer, who was clearly rushing to get the flowers, knowing that he would be handsomely rewarded, I gathered.

Arriving at the elevator, my mother pressed the ground floor button on the wall and I asked her to wait for Martin, who swiftly arrived with the porter.

"Mama, please don't push Palesa so quickly. She's still very fragile," Martin derided my mother. She on the other hand, was not even interested in participating in such clear impertinence.

"Martin, please leave mama alone. I would complain if she was wheeling me too quickly to the point that I was uncomfortable," I chided him firmly.

I looked at him and quickly realised aggravation perched on his face. I winked at him, craftily asking him to relax. Although I knew that I wasn't really joking, I was trying to prevent him from getting distressed after I had chastised him about him speaking the way he liked with my mom and practically giving her orders regarding my health and condition.

We got inside after elevator doors opened and suddenly without any warning, Martin snatched the wheelchair from my mother's hands, leaving my mom staggered and unable to utter any protest as that move came as not only a surprise but, it was apparent that what Martin wanted was a fight and to assert his clout to my mom, subtly indicating to her that she was on his cabbage patch.

"I've got this, thank you," he whispered. "This is my canoe to paddle mama, so please let me do this."

My mother, utterly frustrated with what had just transpired, breathed heavily, in an attempt to compose herself. She gazed at me and I looked away. I was not going to get in between the two people who were both trying to prove how much they cared and loved me.

Besides, if I were to rebuke Martin again, he would have gotten upset and my mother would have been pleased but that would have left me in a worse off position as I stayed with Martin, the person who took me in after I ran away from home. My family never bothered to search for me up until I told my mother where I was. Even then, she simply let the whole thing slide, while I was expecting them to come and fetch me. I was hoping that they would prove their love to me I suppose, but I was left with egg on my face instead.

The tension in the elevator could be cut with a blunt knife as I closed my eyes, trying very hard to not make eye contact with either my mom or Martin. One way or another, they both had to know that I was under a lot of strain and I needed to rest and not be bothered by minor squabbles between the two of them.

We eventually reached the ground floor and Martin carefully pushed me out, with my mother holding my bags and on the other elevator, the potter also came out, pushing a trolley that had many flowers and some left over dried fruits that Martin had bought me while I was still admitted at the hospital.

I realised then, that there was nothing really that my mother ever brought me while I was in the hospital, save for her visits once in a while. Why was she trying to upstage Martin now that I was out of the hospital?

Reaching the parking lot, our self-appointed parking attendant rushed towards us, mumbling unclear utterances to my mother, who was walking ahead of us and had parked a few metres from us. As Martin and I arrived at our car, the guy asked why I was on the wheelchair when I was just fine a few weeks prior. As usual, my man snapped but composed himself just in time before my mom could catch him in that not so pleasant mood.

"Man, not today please, not today!" He raised his hand, his tone hard, callous and not at all apologetic to the young man. "Just concentrate on making sure that we do not bump into other cars when we get out of here. Now earn your penny for once!" he flippantly ended the rant.

"Anything for you, Ngamla," the man sheepishly responded.

I felt sorry for the poor guy but I also couldn't have said anything in consolation, even if I might have wanted to. Martin would probably have scolded me for speaking to just anyone or telling my stuff to strangers, even though this one was somewhat a familiar face.

There is always some kind of friendship motorists form with parking attendants and an implicit agreement that they have with them – that is, they should find parking bay for you and look after your car once you have parked it, until you come back to retrieve it. After that, you will then pay them. So, the young man must have gotten a shock at Martin's insolence but he took it in his strides. I bet all he wanted was the money he would have 'worked' hard for in both finding an open parking bay and then helping us to direct traffic out of the parking lot.

I got in the car slowly, Martin helping me out of the wheelchair. My mother was not even coming to help us. It looked like she was really offended so I was wondering if she was still going to follow us or was just going to go home to look after dad who was recovering well I understood. I was hoping that she would somewhat calm down.

After I got in, my mother walked towards the car, huffing and puffing. As soon as she reached us, she yelled, "Palesa, bula fenstere ena!" ("Palesa, open this window!").

I slid it down and she yelled at me again, right there and then. "Didn't you say you're travelling with me? What's wrong with you,

Palesa?" Should I respond? I nonetheless plucked up some courage, after pulling my breath.

"Mama, please let this go. I cannot do this here at this time. How can you want to fight with me in my condition? I have just come out of the hospital. This is not right, Mama, it's not right." I felt a tear run down my cheek and I wiped it out of the way. Martin was silent for a bit and I could tell that he was bothered, particularly when he saw my mother yelling at me like that. He had also taken heed of the tear I had quickly wiped away.

I felt a sudden twinge on the upper part of my spine and I asked Martin to close the door so we could go.

"Mama, please stop doing this. You did say that you are here to help Palesa and to look after her. What you're doing however is anything but that. We're adults here and I am not going to just keep quiet and allow you to upset her, knowing that she is not well. Do you see why she'd rather stay with me and not with you?" Martin poked my mother intentionally, leaving her standing there staggered.

I didn't care that Martin had given my mother a tongue lashing, even though she was an elder. Her behaviour was wanting and someone had to cut her down to size. Yes, that tirade ignited certain feelings from me; feelings I had thought I was well on my way to bury.

Martin walked over to his side of the door, got in and started the engine. My mother then paced herself, rushing to her car, anxious that we might leave her behind.

"Man, please take the wheelchair back to casualty," he motioned to the parking attendant.

"Yes, Ngamla, I will," the young man responded.

Martin reversed the car out of the parking bay as the parking attendant 'helped' to watch oncoming cars. My man displayed a very wide sneer of satisfaction on his face, a vivid sign that he was really chuffed with the turn of events, despite him chastising my mom earlier about their affray.

"Baby, please do not drive too far ahead of Mama. Remember she doesn't know where we stay. You can see that she's already in a fetid mood."

"I won't do that, baby. She is the one who seems to have issues though, not me. So, I'll drive out and wait for her just after we have gone through the boomed gate."

I was pleased to hear Martin respond to me calmly which made me certain that what he had subjected me to, leading to my subsequent hospitalization was the wakeup call he needed. I believed he would do everything in his power to make sure that he took care of me better than he ever did and was not going to scold me or be unkind in any way.

He took out a R50 note and gave the parking attendant, who seemed bemused by the gesture, what with Martin having rudely berated him earlier, leaving his heart broken.

"Thank you, thank you, thank you Ngamla," he fervently expressed, thanking Martin constantly.

"It's my way of apologising about being unkind to you earlier. I'm sorry for the way I spoke to you. I'm not having a good day as you can tell. So yeah, I guess this is your lucky day, man." Did he just apologise? I was taken aback by his act of contrition.

"Don't worry Ngamla, Modimo o teng ebile o a phela ('God is there and he is alive')." They both smiled and I shared a sneer too.

Martin drove off and when we got to the boomed gate, I noticed as I turned my head to check where my mother was, that she was only then reversing the car out of the parking bay, with our guy doing what he usually did the most to earn some money. I couldn't see whether she gave him money or not.

We left the hospital and as I thought that Martin had forgotten his resolve of waiting for Mama somewhere on the road and was about to remind him, I felt the car slowing down and he brought it to a complete halt and then pressed the 'hazard' button.

"Baby, are you still fine the way you're sitting? How's that cushion feeling now that you're in the car?"

"I'm fine, baby. Please just drive slowly. I'm a bit worried about what's going to happen when we get to the speed humps. So please take it easy."

"I promise, I'll take it easy baby," he assured.

Martin had his moments and that day, he was the ever charming and chivalrous man I got introduced to briefly by the universe and the man I was going to marry. He was trying his utmost best to be really sweet and I appreciated the effort with open arms.

While we were still chatting, my mother appeared from my peripheral view and Martin switched the 'hazard' button off and drove away, with my mother in tow.

Almost out of nowhere, Martin played Freddie Jackson's '*All I'll ever Ask'*, serenading me with our song. It had become our song as it was the one he played for me on my first day at the house, which also indicated that it was my favourite too.

"Oh no, you didn't just do that!" I remarked, inwardly pleased.

"Oh but I did baby, I sure did," he chortled, checking me out from the rear-view mirror, smiling. "Do you remember when we danced to the song the first time you came to the house?"

"How can I forget that? I saw you move in a way that did certain things to me. I might have not been ready for intimacy with a man but that song sure made me aware that I was likely to experience some serious adult stuff," I admitted, chuckling constantly as my man joined me as well.

"Baby, I have missed you; In fact, I really miss you," he declared, bearing seductive eyes.

"I miss you too baby but you heard what sister Moipolai said about not engaging in any rigorous activities. She specifically mentioned sex," I laughed, as I ogled Martin from the rearview mirror that his brow was contorting.

"Baby, let's not spoil the mood by mentioning other people, especially not that woman. We are having a relaxed and beautiful time together as I take you back home. So that Moipolai character really thought she could dictate to my woman what to do? Hell no!" he seethed. There he went again!

"Baby, calm down please. I was just mentioning what she said. Besides, Dr. Duvenhage also said the same thing to me. I guess the woman felt the need to repeat the doctor's instructions to me. I doubt it was out of malice," I cautioned.

"You think so? By the way, I saw her mumbling something in your ear before we left. What was she saying?" I knew the question would come sooner or later and as experience had taught me, I had to always be prepared to respond quickly in order to allay any suspicions about what I would tell Martin. I had already prepared my answer but had thought that he would at least ask me when we reached home.

"Can you believe that she was drumming this sex thing even at that time? Perhaps she's jealous of me and wants you. That's probably why she was encouraging me to not sleep with you so that you can lose interest. If that's the case, then she's really silly. I sensed a lot of tension between the two of you. Have you ever dated?" I craftily asked.

"Oh… hell no, I would never have dated her even if anyone would have paid me. This was not for lack of trying from her part. She did try to throw herself at me years ago when I was an intern at the hospital. When I didn't show any interest in her, she slandered my name and even told our hospital manager at the time, that I was sexually harassing her. I went for disciplinary hearing but was cleared of all charges because she was blatantly lying about me.

Instead, she was the one who got suspended for fabricating stories about me. They reinstated her after some time. Now you see why I don't want us to speak about her? Let's just drop it now please," he concluded, his expression seriously goaded after the reveal, which came totally by surprise to me.

I wondered as to whether that was the truth or not but, like I had done, Martin had also responded to me without any brief thought at all, indicating that he had either rehearsed the response or it was as true as he had claimed it was. I still wondered how I could have also lied to him so easily about what sister Moipolai had supposedly shared with me. That sent shivers down my spine. I lied without any thought at all.

Were Martin and I cut from the same cloth or did he somehow rub off his tortuous aura on me? That remained to be seen, but I was determined to fight off what I was becoming. I did not like the woman I was and I blamed Martin for that, unmindful of the fact that I was solely responsible for the choices I made, even though I felt that I had no choice at all and was basically a prisoner of circumstances.

"Okay baby, now I'm the one getting upset by what you have just revealed to me. I cannot believe that I had trusted her with my life. She did seem nice enough though during my whole stay at the hospital. So I guess it was all a farce."

"Perhaps it was not necessarily a farce because truth be told, she is a good nurse and knows her work. I presume she was just doing her job but I felt that she was just being a bit too much, hence I rebuked her in the manner I did," he divulged.

"Baby, like you said, we need to drop this talk about sister Moipolai. It's now making me troubled. Here I am, happy to be going home with you yet we're busy talking about people that don't bring us joy."

"I agree, baby, let's stop this. Besides our song is playing on repeat and we can't be entertaining inane stuff," he concurred.

"I have already stopped, baby so please raise the volume a little bit so we can continue enjoying the music." He obliged.

"Baby, we're about to go over a speed hump. Just prepare yourself. I promise, I'll be very slow and I hope you won't feel any pain."

"We'll see, baby."

As soon as the car slowed down to accommodate the speed hump, I felt a twinge on my back but it didn't remain there for long. This, I admitted, was likely to be a long road to my healing as a slight movement like that ignited some pain. I was hoping that Martin was not thinking about us sleeping together anytime soon.

"Was that sore?" he asked.

"Yes, it was," I mumbled, amidst my shallow whimper.

"Sorry, baby, at least there aren't any more of these speed humps on the road until we reach home."

"Yeah, that's a relief."

I propped myself up, positioning my rear properly inside the hollow cushion sister Moipolai gave me, hoping that we could reach home soon. The trip was rather long as the hospital was about an hour away from Martin's house.

As I was still wrestling with my thoughts, my phone vibrated. I leaned over my left side and took my handbag. I unzipped it and retrieved my phone. A brief glance at it indicated that it was my mother calling, even though she was still tailing us. I wondered why she would call.

"Mama, what's wrong?" I asked.

"Nothing is wrong Palesa. Re fihla neng kgathe moo le dulang?" ("When are we arriving where you guys stay?").

I noted some irritation from her tone and I briefly chortled.

"Mama, you are the one who insisted on coming with us, so I guess you will have to be patient and keep following us until we reach our home." Martin sneered while I rolled my eyes in astonishment.

"Palesa, you didn't have to use that tone with me. I was simply asking."

"Mama, please have some peace, I'm begging you. We will reach home soon. I'm sorry, but I'm gonna have to cut this call short because I have to keep supporting myself on the seat with my hands. So, please mama, let's not do this again," I pleaded.

"It's fine, Palesa… like I said, I was simply asking."

"Mama, we are playing music to relieve ourselves of the boredom of the trip so perhaps you might want to do the same," I said, and immediately cut the call, laughing my lungs out.

"Baby, please quit laughing so much, you'll end up hurting yourself."

"Come now baby, I cannot even laugh? You must admit, this is hilarious," I continued laughing while Martin shook his head.

I had no idea whether that was directed at me or he was thinking about my mother's call. Either way, what my mom did probably gave him an insight into her mind at the time and she had no idea that she had given him some kind of ammunition to use against her for the period she would be staying with us, hoping that she would leave sooner rather than later.

CHAPTER 12

Deadly effects of hasty decisions

The journey did seem long, but we finally arrived at Leboya homestead. A few metres away, Bra Mos was his usual busy self and he also spotted us instantly. He was about to open the main gate for us when Martin beat him to it instead. The motor gate opened slowly as we waited patiently, while I kept ogling my mother behind us, wondering what she must have thought of the place.

Somehow I wanted her to be envious; noticing how well cared for I was, in spite of hers and dad's nonchalant treatment of me. I suddenly felt pride bellowing from the pit of my stomach and I was not even able to stop it. It felt good, as warped as it was.

The gate finally reached the end of the track and Martin drove into the compound as my mother continued to trail us. Bra Mos was visibly jovial in his blue workmen's wear, and he kept raising his hand often, acknowledging my mother's presence. He widened his eyes as we drove past him, leaned towards the car as Martin slowed down to greet him. He slid the passenger window down and Bra Mos literally put his head through the open window.

"Good afternoon, Sir… Miss Palesa," he greeted us reverently.

"Mos, we have a guest today as you can see. Palesa's mom will be with us for a few days. She will be helping us to take care of Palesa.

"Oh, we will all look after her, Sir… welcome back home, Miss Palesa," he directed his attention towards me.

"Bra Mos," a strained greeting came out from me.

The man then followed us on foot, practically leading us down the neatly swept cobble stones sandwiched by beautiful red and white roses. I was happy and relieved that I had finally arrived home. After Martin had stopped the car next to the main front door, switching off the ignition, Sis Lulama appeared, all smiles and cheerful. Martin didn't get out of the car just yet. He turned to look at me from my backseat and smiled.

"Baby, we're home. I'm never letting you go ever again."

"Baby, have I ever said I'd leave you? I'm not going anywhere, so you can relax. I however think that things have to change around here, especially how we relate to one another."

"I hear you, baby and I know what you're talking about. Can we just please briefly talk about how we are going to accommodate

Mama and where she will be sleeping?" He lifted his head to check the rearview window as Mama had just gotten out of the car. I observed Sis Lulama moving away from our car to acknowledge her presence.

"Dumela Mme, lebitso laka ke Lulama (Hello Ma'am, my name is Lulama). I'm the housekeeper here at home and Miss Palesa's personal helper," Sis Lulama respectfully greeted my mother. It was the first time I heard that she was my personal helper! That was amusing to hear.

My mother, revealing some kind of restlessness and her face still bearing that stillness and annoyance, responded succinctly, "Dumela le wena" ("Hi to you too").

Mama was not being nice and glancing at her callous expression, I could tell that there was something that she either was not approving of or she was just simply still aggravated by the fact that I chose to drive with Martin and not with her as we had initially agreed. Either way, I didn't like her approach and how she was looking at Sis Lulama, busy ogling her from head to toe, as if the poor woman owed her money or something.

That made my response to Martin easier as I could see that my mother and I would definitely fight for the duration of her stay, if I were to share a room with her or allow her to occupy my space too much.

"Baby, did you just see that?" I asked.

"Yes, baby... I did. At least Lulama will be on her toes for once. It looks like she has met her match," he chuckled.

"Baby, this is not funny. I don't like what Mama did. It's amusing to you now but wait till she does the same thing to you. I'm telling you, you're not going to like it."

"Baby, don't worry about me. I think I know how to handle her by now. Look, you're with me in our car right now and not with her. What does that tell you?"

"Oh, is that what you're basing your argument on? Give it time!"

While the two of us were chattering away, Sis Lulama approached the car again. This time however, she was eager to help me get out of the car. Martin then realised that she was not about to relent and he opened the boot from inside and Sis Lulama remarked at the many things in the car.

"Mos!" she called out to Bra Mos, who was about to come join us. I bet he had been wondering why we were not getting out of the car.

"I'm here…I'm here, no need to yell like that!" Bra Mos ingeniously rebuked Sis Lulama.

"Dumela Mme (Hello ma'am)," Bra Mos greeted my mother and her face lit up instantly. That was strange and I marvelled as to why she took a sudden dislike to Sis Lulama, as if she had some kind of history with her. Now there was Bra Mos, having just met her for the first time too but she smiled at him.

"What's your name?" she asked him.

"Lebitso laka ke Moses" ("My name is Moses"), he responded.

"Ba mpitsa Mos (they call me Mos) and I'm the handyman on the compound. I do practically everything to lighten the load for my boss. I paint; I do repairs; I maintain the garden and I even carry heavy stuff. I also go to the shops and most of the time, Lulama and I buy groceries for the house. Doc doesn't want Miss Palesa to be bothered by grocery shopping. She just tells us what she wants and we get it for her. So, I'm at your service too for anything you will need," Bra Mos disclosed – too much information at that, while Martin and I were watching the spectacle closely.

"I think she has found someone she likes," Martin joked, as we both laughed.

"Baby, come and help me out. I need to walk a bit before I go inside the house. I didn't do any stretching at the hospital today as nurses were preparing for my discharge. So, everything they did for me was just hurried."

"It's fine, baby… I'll walk with you."

"Come on, baby… it's not necessary. I can ask Sis Lulama to help me. There is a frame and the crutches in the boot, so I should be fine."

"Baby, we are not going to debate about this, are we? Lulama can take over on the days I'm not here and at work."

"Okay. Have you taken leave from work? When are you going back?" I asked earnestly, remembering both Bra Mos and Sis Lulama telling me that Martin had spent a considerable amount of time at home and not going to work. I had to craftily ask him, hoping that he might divulge how weedy he had been while I was away.

"I'll be home for the whole week, just to help you settle back in. Then, I'll have to go back to work. I have not been doing well since you got admitted to the hospital… but we will talk about that when we're alone in our room. Right now though, we have to get out of the car. Your mother is becoming agitated, I can see. Let me get out before they start thinking their own things."

I signalled sis Lulama to open the door as she was now standing very close, indicating confusion regarding why we were still in the car. Finally, she opened the door and showed relief of some kind.

"Miss Palesa, I was already getting worried that you were feeling too much pain as I see you and Doc still in the car. Are you alright?" she asked, genuinely concerned.

"I'm fine Sis, well… not fully healed but I'm fine. There is no pain in sight. I've been told that it will take some time for me to finally be on my feet again, doing everything with no effort at all. Eventually, I'll be fine," I affirmed.

"Lulama, hello to you too! I see who you love more in the house," Martin teased, indicating his scorn to being ignored. Some things never change. Sis Lulama paid him no mind though, chuckling at the minor rant.

"Good afternoon, Sir," she looked at the time on her watch whose brown strap had faded. I thought to myself that perhaps I would get her a new one soon; otherwise she would likely lose that one.

Martin quickly rounded the car and together with Sis Lulama, they helped me to get out, while I tried all I could to not hurt myself. My mother was just standing there; folding her arms and watching everything unfold before her eyes. She didn't come close, up until Martin brought the frame closer to me, so I could hold on to it.

"Miss Palesa, does it mean you are going use this thing to aid your walking from now onwards? It doesn't look comfortable. This is very sad. Not so long ago, you were as fit as a fiddle...," Martin interjected, barring the poor woman from completing her statement.

"Lulama, Lulama, give it a rest now! Don't take us back please. Palesa is back home, where she belongs to recover and doesn't need you reminding her how healthy she was. This was simply a corrective operation and she will be 'as fit as a fiddle' as you'd like to see her again," he snapped.

Bra Mos was busy taking flowers out of the car as well as my bags and the crutches. He was going in and out of the house doing what he did best; taking care of everything that required muscle. Each time he approached the car to take the last bits of the stuff to take into the house, my mother would extend her hand towards him, in an attempt to give him her bag. He had been ignoring her since their small talk a few minutes earlier.

"Mama, I just want to take a walk as I didn't do that at the hospital in the morning. You remember that they advised me to do this daily?

"Okay… Palesa; should I come with you?"

"No mama, I'm sure you must be starving by now. Please get to know Sis Lulama and Bra Mos. They will take your stuff to the guest room and make something for you to eat."

"Palesa, I can make my own food, you know that. It looks like you have now gotten used to being tended to by helpers. I wonder if you can still even fry an egg," she mocked.

Within a very short space of time, my mother had revealed her true colours to Martin and his helpers. I noted a hit of resentment on her part or was it worry I was sensing? Whatever it was, I didn't like it and if it were up to me then, I would really have told her to leave because we were not going to be disrespected in our own home.

Instead of asking about my health and how I was doing since the drive from the hospital, she chose to reveal her claws, giving everyone an insight into her distorted mind. She is my mother and I love her and always will. However, I had to take back all the pity I had for her after realizing that my father was abusing her verbally and emotionally, at least from what I had witnessed.

I wondered as to whether she envied the life I was living or she was simply being the overprotective parent, who wanted me to never lose whatever she had taught me when it came to cleaning, taking care of myself, cooking and basically picking up after myself. It was lucid then, that she was averse to what she was witnessing, even before we could go inside the house.

"Mama, I do not appreciate you talking to Palesa like that, especially in the company of the help. This is her home now and if I want to make her life easier by hiring people to aid her, I will do so. I don't know why you would really want to come and be with us for a few days, when you are clearly against everything that is happening here. This means you will not even survive a day in this house if you carry on like this… honestly," Martin chided. "Let's go… baby. Lulama, go ahead and show Mrs Ditheko the guest room," he said, authoritatively.

"You two are just way too sensitive! I was just joking and making conversation," she chuckled, while pretending to have been teasing.

"Mama, your joke was not funny so please stop upsetting Palesa."

I kept quiet, taking heed of everything Martin and my mother were saying to one another. From where I was standing and very irritable, I was proud that my man was handling my mother well and was not about to allow me to plunge as much into depression as she had been for years.

I did not understand why she couldn't just be happy for me, even if she could pretend, I'd take it. It was way too late to play a concerned mother because she could not even stand up for herself against my father when he mistreated her for years. Now that I was glaringly happy, it was like she was doing everything in her power to dampen my mood and cause some kind of friction between

Martin and I.

It was clear that Martin had seen through her. That concerned me though, because I had resolved that I would go home at some point to visit them. However, now that I had been subjected to so much scrutiny by the one person I had always wanted acceptance and acknowledgment from, I was no longer sure anymore that I wanted to even set foot there ever again.

Thoughts of Martin's erratic moods also beleaguered my mind. I had a horrific vision of the two of us not as happy as I had hoped we would be but I was unable to leave him, as my parents weren't welcoming. I imagined myself on the side of the road again. That time however, I was older, bruised and battered with nothing on. That unsettled me and I did everything I could to refuse that thought deeper access into my whole system. My life was not as complicated as I had made it out to be.

We left my mother, sis Lulama and Bra Mos on the driveway that allowed easy access to the kitchen, as Martin held me by my arm, in his bid to aid my walking.

"It's okay… baby, I'll walk by myself. Nurses showed me what to do and how to rest, using this frame. These cushy slippers are helping to soften my steps onto the paved surface. I will not walk too far because my legs feel rather stiff. I suppose it's the travelling, which seemed to have taken way too long," I lamented.

"Don't rush…," Martin cautioned, as I smiled at his concern.

"I'm fine, baby." I took a couple of steps on the smooth terrain set by grayish-maroon patterned cobble stones. I took a few more, admiring the huge and beautiful curved driveway that Bra Mos had always made certain to keep neat. This time, I noticed that there was a new flower bed that lay on the sides of the pathway, adorned by beautiful tulips, petunias, daisies as well as orchids. I wondered as to whether all these flowers were supposed to live side by side. What did I know?

"These are very beautiful… baby; Bra Mos has turned the yard into a magnificent botanical garden. I however feel like I'm about to sneeze…achoo achoo…," I sneezed, as Martin kept sending blessings to me. I got worried as I increased my pace, unsure as to whether I'd be in any pain as I had certainly experienced it earlier when I shared a brief chortle with Martin.

There was no pain still as we continued walking and resting as we spoke mostly about my mother's stay at the house and what her role would be, particularly since she had appeared to have it in for Sis Lulama, whom she had only met briefly.

"Perhaps we should ask Bra Mos to keep an eye on mama. It is obvious that she has some soft spot for him. Perhaps she feels that sis Lulama is trying to replace her by pretending to be my mom." We continued laughing, walking leisurely.

I would rest midway to straighten up and stretch my back, careful not to strain myself. Then I would walk again. The frame was holding my weight very well and I held on to it as much as I could, even though at times, I would attempt to walk on my own unaided. Martin would chastise me, advising that I needed to be patient and could only attempt to walk on my own after a week or two. Even then, I would have to be aided by at least one crutch. We strolled up to the far end of the house, next to the wing that was diagonal to sis Lulama and Bra Mos' rooms.

"I'm tired now and hungry too," I revealed.

"It's okay; we need to walk back but it might be better to round the house as the surface that side is not as wobbly as this one. These cobble stones aren't really made for a person who's being aided by a frame to walk. At least that other side is just normal pavement," Martin held, being really charismatic.

"Thanks… baby for walking with me, but now I feel queasiness coming and I don't know where that emanates from all of a sudden," I cautioned, feeling seriously woozy.

Martin held me tight, shaken by the sudden change in my physical condition.

"Baby, please don't do this to me. What's going on now? I just hope it's nothing serious. Do you still feel like vomiting?"

"Yes… I do, but…"

I could not let any other word out as I threw up right there and then, in Bra Mos' perfectly landscaped garden. I had moved slightly away from the pavement as it would have been a mission to clean the ruins from the pavement. So, I had deposited everything into the sand where the flowers were set.

Martin reached for his pocket, retrieved his cellphone and called bra Mos. He told him what was happening and that he needed some help to carry me inside the house in such a way that they would not hurt me on my operation wound. At that time, my legs were quivering uncontrollably, so was my whole body. After putting his phone back in his pocket, Martin became impatient waiting for Bra Mos. He begged me to hold on to him and to persevere through the pain I would be feeling, as he was about to carry me on his back.

He picked me up and carried me on his back, kicking the frame out of the way. I felt tremor on the wound and I brought my body forward, hoping that the stitches wouldn't come off. We met Bra Mos on the way back to the house as Martin showed signs of frustration.

"Mos, I called you a while ago, where were you?"

"I was near the gate… Sir, I had to take out the weeds that side because they have been there for long so I ran as…"

Martin didn't allow Bra Mos to finish talking, as he seemed uninterested in his news.

"Fine, fine…just fetch Palesa's frame and bring it inside the house."

"Yes Sir, I'll do that."

Martin walked carefully with me on his back, until we reached the kitchen door. We entered the house and both Sis Lulama and my mother stood up from where they were seating, as my mother was eating a ham and cheese sandwich, which she had prepared for herself, no doubt.

"What's going on, Martin? Palesa, are you alright?" My mother asked.

"She has just thrown up when we were walking that side."

"Perhaps it was too soon for her to walk near the flowers. You aren't tolerant of the smell of flowers, Palesa. Have you forgotten?"

"Mama, she knows what she is tolerant of and what she's not. Right now, I need to put Palesa down so she can rest," Martin chirped. "I'll see what to give her."

"Baby, I'll be fine. I just think it's the environment change. I've been in hospital for a while and I suppose I have to re-adjust to the milieu outside of the hospital's sanitized one. Please take me to our room," I pleaded, depriving my mom of any attention.

She looked at me in astonishment, while sis Lulama followed us upstairs, carrying my handbag, which she had retained in the kitchen when we took a walk. I was still feeling lightheaded. As soon as we arrived upstairs, I asked Martin to put me down so I could stand on my own. I needed to establish for myself as to whether him carrying me on my back hadn't exaggerated my wound to the point that I might have to go back to the hospital.

It was the first time I ever had an operation done and I was nervous, and I didn't know if stitches tend come off or not. I recalled as a young girl hearing stories of someone's stitches having come off to the point that they had to go back to the hospital so they could be re-stitched. To date, I still have no idea whether that was a true story or not.

"Baby, won't the stitches come off?" I asked earnestly.

"No, baby nothing like that will happen. Medical Science has advanced a great deal and whatever stories you might have heard about stitches coming off and stuff like that, please chuck them out of your mind as that won't happen. I just want to see though whether I haven't aggravated your wound. I have stuff in my office that I will use to help you heal better. You don't have to worry about that. Your man is a physician have you forgotten that?" he proudly stated.

"No, how can I forget that!"

Once my feet hit the cushy carpet in our room, the pain on my lower back became excruciating to the point where I wailed. Sis Lulama begged me to stop crying, worried sick about me.

"Miss Palesa, please don't cry like this. Your mother will think that we are hurting you. You saw how protective she is. She kept asking me so many questions when you and Doc were taking a walk and I was praying all the time for you to come back sooner rather than later. She makes me very uncomfortable," she pronounced.

"Lulama, at the moment, none of us want to hear about anything Palesa's mom said to you as you can see that we have a crisis here. The important person right now is Palesa and nobody else, and certainly not Mrs Ditheko's feelings about anything for that matter," Martin stressed, hardening his tone.

"Sorry Sir, I know I shouldn't have mentioned it. Miss Palesa, can I help you get on the bed?"

"Yes, but please place that continental pillow on the bed so I can lie on it," I pointed at the pillow and she removed cushions that were on the bed – décor for the bed which happened to be unnecessary, really.

"Baby, at least you're already in your gown. I need to examine that wound, though. Do you still feel like vomitting?"

"No, I don't… but I feel dizzy and I'm hungry. I just hope I will be able to take food down as I need to take tablets after eating,"

"Don't worry, Miss Palesa; I have already cooked your favourite mutton stew and vegetables. I trimmed all the fat from the meat so I think you will like it. I know that most of the time you cook for yourself but I know how you cook your mutton. Should I go now to prepare?"

"Not right now…," I moaned. "Let Doc examine me first so that we can be certain that everything is still intact. It's really painful. When I came back from the hospital, I was not in so much pain and I need to know what's going on now, especially since I have also vomitted.

At the time, Martin had rushed to his office and I surmised that he went to fetch his medical bag and other paraphernalia to examine me. He came back swiftly after I had just sat on the bed while sis Lulama was helping me to lie briefly on my stomach.

"Lulama, please help Palesa take off the gown and hike up the night dress out of the way so I can see what's going on," he instructed.

She did as instructed and as soon as she managed to help me out of the gown, she let out a distressed sound, scaring me too.

"What's wrong, Sis Lulama, what are you seeing?"

She did not respond, but made way for Martin, who immediately got to work, instructing Sis Lulama to take this and that for him so he could work. He would simply point at the small table, imploring the woman to bring it forward and then to remove whatever it was, that was on the pedestal on my side of the bed.

At that moment, all I wanted was for pain to ebb and for me to at least rest without feeling any.

“Baby, I need to change this dressing. Please give me time to help you. All will be well.”

“Mmm,” I murmured.

“Doc, why is there so much blood?”

Did she say blood? So, I was right that stitches could come off! At least that’s what I thought.

“Lulama, just stand back and stop frightening Palesa unnecessarily. I probably injured her when I carried her on my back earlier but she will be fine,” he assured. “It doesn’t mean the wound has become septic,” he added.

During that time, Martin was unbelievably calm, particularly when talking to Sis Lulama. Although once or twice I would sense a note of touchiness from him, he never allowed it to fester. That made me believe strongly that he was indeed making an effort to change how he related to everyone, especially the help. On the other hand, he was simply being a doctor at that moment; doing what he did best which in my mind, meant that he did treat his assistants at the hospital much better than he treated everyone else.

I cringed when I felt Martin remove the dressing from my wound. I felt his hands work to help me heal, more like the day after the assault, when he injected me with what he had termed 'anti-inflammatory', without providing me with its name.

"Sorry, sorry, it's gonna hurt a bit until it's all out. Please bear with me," he entreated.

"Did you just say 'a bit'?"

"Okay, it's all out. I can see that we probably touched the wound carelessly. But everything is still intact. I'll dress it again," he stated.

"Oh, thank God. I thought I'd have to go back to the hospital."

"Can I bring the food now, Miss Palesa?" sis Lulama asked.

"Not right now; I think we might still take about twenty to thirty minutes before I can finally settle down. Just remember to bring the bed tray when you bring the food. I'll sit here on the bed. Please also tell my mother that I'm no longer feeling nauseous. I'll see her tomorrow."

"What if she wants to see you before she sleeps, Miss Palesa?"

"Please tell her that I'll see her tomorrow sis. I take it you will prepare her food for the evening, since you said you have already cooked. Just let her dish up for herself please. She doesn't like people dishing up for her. Trust me, she is very particular."

"Don't worry, I noticed that earlier when she made herself a sandwich. I think it would be best for me to stay out of her way. I don't think she's an easy person to be around. No offence," she ended, as an afterthought.

"None taken," I guaranteed.

"I'm done, baby. It looks like you didn't even feel anything since Lulama was chattering away. Thanks Lulama, you can take these to the bin and please do not touch anything as this is medical waste – please," he warned, as he widened his eyes.

Sis Lulama gave Martin half a smile, reacting to his instruction. He didn't care whether she was a bit slighted or not.

"Okay sis, please help me to get up so I can prop myself up. I think I should just have some fruits for now. Please bring me a peach, an apple, a banana and some yoghurt. I should be fine afterwards. I'll eat your stew later or tomorrow."

"Palesa, I'll help you up. Lulama, you're still here?"

"Okay miss Palesas, I'll do that. Sir, can I dish up for you?"

"No, Lulama, just give me fruits like Palesa. I'll eat with her later. Now go and throw these in the dustbin I directed you to and wash your hands thoroughly please!"

"Baby come on, you should eat when you're hungry. What if I struggle to eat later?"

"That means I'll also struggle to eat," he joked.

"Sis Lulama, please do as Doc is asking. We will eat together later."

After sis Lulama left us, Martin shook his head. When I probed what the problem was, he just kept shaking his head.

"Baby, are you seriously considering eating Lulama's mutton stew?" he asked, while he kept chuckling.

"Baby, don't be mean; her cooking is not really that bad."

"You mean you have had her stew before?"

"No, I haven't but I've seen her make beef stew. There's always the first time for everything isn't there? Perhaps we can give my mother something to do. She is an excellent cook. I think she might like the idea of feeling useful around here. Maybe she could cook."

"That's actually not a bad idea. Now, how are you going to break the news to 'Miss Mutton Stew'?" he kept mocking and laughing at the same time.

"Baby, we're going to eat that stew and you're going to love it. Let's not add to her stress as it's too much already. My mother is not making things easy for her, you can see that."

"Good; she must actually make her run around the house." He continued chortling.

I could not believe how the situation between my mother and sis Lulama amused Martin and why he was finding the whole thing funny.

Suddenly, exhaustion weighed me down. I slid down carefully on the bed and brought one of the pillows next to my belly. I stared at the sliding door to the balcony which was slightly ajar, bringing much needed breeze inside. I waited for Sis Lulama to come with the fruits but she was taking time to do so. A few moments later, I heard someone knock on the door. Martin responded. "Come in."

I thought it was sis Lulama knocking but soon realised that it was my mother. That was odd. She was a very traditional woman and I was unsettled when she stepped into our bedroom.

The first thing she did was to look around, as if she was some kind of inspector that had been hired to ascertain that everything was as it should be. Martin rolled his eyes, while I simply stared at her, awaiting her to tell us what she was doing in our room.

"Can I help you, Mama?" Martin asked.

"I have come to see how Palesa is doing. Your helper told me that you will see me tomorrow. I wanted to see you though. Is she sleeping in here?"

"Yes she is; this is our room. Where else should she sleep?"

"I'm not fighting, but I thought she would sleep with me downstairs to enable her to do her required walks easily." My mother had a point though. Having gone to our bedroom was not a good idea; a bit short-sighted of us.

"Baby, I think Mama might be right, you know. How am I going to walk in here?"

"Baby, it's very easy. This hallway is quite a stretch and you do not need to be outside to do your walks. I just want you to be safe when you do so. If you want some fresh air, you will go to the balcony. Remember that the balcony is also huge and it extends to all the three bedrooms up here. So, you really do not have to go outside, risking what we have just witnessed, when you reacted badly to the smell of flowers or whatever it was that Mos has been using outside," he concluded flippantly, outright asserting his authority, perhaps not only to me but to my mother as well.

"Palesa, are you happy with that arrangement?" my mother asked.

"I'm fine mama, why wouldn't I be?" I shrugged, observing her outlandish behaviour, while Martin maintained a cold expression on his face.

"Okay then, is there anything I can help with?" she probed.

"Yes Mama, please help Sis Lulama with cooking now and then. I have missed your food."

I felt the need to include my mother in my recovery process and to make her useful. As much as she had been a tad impossible since she arrived at our place, she was still my mother and I wanted her to feel useful and welcome. I could see that she still had a lot to say but was finding it difficult to say it. Martin was also not making it easy for her, so most of the time, I would see that she bit her tongue often.

"Oh, for a moment there, I thought I wasn't needed," she teased. I ignored the jibe.

"I'll let you know later mama how we eat and how Martin likes his food. Once in a while, you and Sis Lulama might need to leave the kitchen for some time as my fiancé loves making food for us occasionally. But I'll let you know when that happens."

"Okay, I hear you," she admitted.

"For now though mama, can you please excuse us as I need to rest. By the way, has papa called at all?" I asked.

"No, he hasn't called. I did tell him that I will call once I have observed how you are doing. He actually thought that I would bring you home. Even your aunt is home waiting for you."

"Mama, you didn't just say that! Aunt Thoko is home waiting for me? The very same aunt who used to speak ill about me with his brother? Surely mama, you cannot still be naïve to think that those two have really changed. Actually, in my opinion, you should go back home, perhaps after a day or two. You cannot leave your house for a long time in the hands of Aunt Thoko for that matter. You know that woman hates us.

"Palesa, she doesn't really hate us. She…" I interjected before my mom could even finish her thought process.

"No mama, she hates us and I can't believe you would be so trusting of her, knowing well that she has never loved you and would like nothing more than to occupy your house. So, if I were you, I wouldn't leave my house unattended like that. You're taking a big risk by doing so," I advised.

My mother's thoughtful expression caught my eye, seriously taking in my counsel. Besides her, I was the only person who knew unerringly what my aunt was all about. Her influence on my father knew no bounds. Chances were that she had by then, already influenced him to stop asking for forgiveness for what she also might have believed was nothing to be apologetic for. After all, they would both gossip about my mother in my presence and when I showed signs of distress, they would scold me, telling me that I was listening to adult stuff and that should I even dare tell on them, they would flatly deny everything. They would also make it a point that they remind me that I was a 'slow' child and that nobody would believe anything that came out of my mouth anyway.

That made me doubt myself a lot when I was younger and for a larger part of my life, I believed everything they said about me to be true. I saw myself through their eyes, never even acknowledging the gifts that I knew I had.

Now there was my mother, blindly trusting my father and his sister simply because he had had a stroke, which I would think, gave him a fright, hence he was being nicer to her and me and was apologising from here to Timbuktu.

Martin left the room as I was still talking to my mother and retreated to his office. Before he could leave, he took one final look at me and widened his eyes. "Are you gonna be alright, baby?"

"Yes baby, I'll be alright. Please just check with Sis Lulama as to why she's taking so long with the fruits. I'm starving."

"Okay," he replied, flatly ignoring my mother. The energy between the two was baffling and I didn't know if Martin was suddenly being discourteous to my mother due to her attitude at the hospital, and earlier when we arrived at home or he just didn't like her presence. Either way, I elected not to be part of that spectacle. I kept wondering how I was going to please both of them while it was evident that I was somehow at the centre of the feud.

After Martin left our bedroom, my mother walked closer towards the bed, pulled a dressing bench and sat down next to me. She then held my hand and kissed it.

"Ngwanaka, I don't want you to think that I don't love you.

Please believe me. What you read on the letter I wrote to you must not make you think that I do not care about you. I do love you with all my heart. I'm just extremely worried about you," she declared.

"I know mama and I understand that part. What I fail to fathom though is why you have done everything in your power to make yourself impossible. Martin has done nothing to you but you haven't really been polite towards him."

"That's because I can see that he is the reason you have had this operation and are in so much pain right now," she paused. "Don't even try to deny it. I'm your mother and I can see what's going on. I've been where you are right now so don't even think of defending him."

"Mama, I find what you're saying laughable honestly. How can you say all these things when you have been living with that abusive man for years? A man who has been abusing you and your daughter for years? In a way, you have been defending him, Mama and now you don't want me to defend my fiancé? No mama, I will defend Martin with everything I have. He has been nothing but good to me. What happened was just unfortunate. He never laid a hand on me. We just had an argument, so I tripped and fell down the stairs. That's how I injured my back," I flatly asserted, blatantly lying about how I got injured.

"Okay, you can deny all you want but I know what I know," she stubbornly stated.

"Mama, you're projecting and you're also stressing me out.

Please leave me alone now as I have to rest and Martin will come back in here soon. I am asking you to please keep your thoughts and suspicions to yourself, unless you want to go back home before the day you had sought to." My mom shook her head and widened her fake grin.

A sudden deafening silence filled the room after our brief chat. I turned my back away from her but secretly opened my eyes facing the other way, taking in what she had said to me and also wondering how she could have been so spot on about what happened to me.

She sat still on the bench, not saying much at that time, until she heard Martin's footsteps after about 10-15 minutes of silence. She then coughed. As I gazed at my fiancé from the dressing table mirror I was now facing, I felt my body finally relaxing. It was as if I was truly relieved that he had come in when he did. I still could not help but be disappointed at my mom's behaviour at our place; or was it because she was telling me truths I was not prepared to hear?

Although everything she said might have emanated from a good place, I still believed that it was uncalled for and her presence didn't only make Sis Lulama uncomfortable, but it also made me her daughter, uncomfortable too.

"Mama, you're still in here? Is Palesa alright as I see that she's sleeping?"

"Yes Martin, she's fine. I guess instinct has propelled me to just sit here and look after her."

"I understand that, Mama; I'm not really chasing you out but I just think it might be best we let her rest now and when she needs us, she will call us."

What did Martin just say? Being polite to my mother all of a sudden? I could not quite understand why I didn't like the idea of him being so nice to her. I felt some warped distaste in my spirit of the whole thing.

"Alright; let me leave you to it," my mother said, getting up from the bench slowly and putting it back in its place. She then left our room, closing the door behind her.

"Baby, are you really sleeping?"

"Not now but I'd like to rest seeing as sis Lulama is still gonna harvest the fruits I asked for!"

"Ha ha! She still hasn't come in? Perhaps she was trying to give you and Mama some privacy. I'll call her," Martin picked the handset up from the pedestal and as he was about to call Sis Lulama, we heard footsteps followed by a knock on the door.

"Come in," Martin responded to the knock.

"Huge apologies, Miss Palesa. I just thought that perhaps you had desired to speak to your mother for some time, hence I didn't want to come in and disturb your conversation. It seemed quite intense."

"What did you just say? Are you telling me that you were standing at the door eavesdropping on our conversation?" The nerve of that woman! That was the first time I had ever raised my voice at Sis Lulama and also felt seriously piqued with her. How dare she say such a thing!

I only acknowledged later when I calmed down, that the reason for my annoyance could have been out of fear perhaps, that she might have heard my mother implying that Martin was the one who hurt me. That sent my mind raising, as I reflected on how much she might have heard, if at all and what she was going to do with the information.

"Baby, calm down please. Don't overexert yourself like this. You are supposed to have gotten used to Lulama by now; this is how she is. She does or says something and think later," Martin ridiculed, making me feel worse. I kept quiet.

"I'm really sorry, Miss Palesa but I was not listening in on your conversation. When I heard the two of you talking, I immediately left and went to the kitchen. I only came back here after your mother had arrived back in the lounge."

"It's fine," I succinctly replied.

"Lulama, I think it's the medication that's making Palesa bite your head off like this. Just leave us. Where are my fruits?"

"I'll bring them too Sir, sorry I guess I should have brought both sets at the same time."

"You seem to be on the edge; is everything alright?" Martin asked frankly.

"I'm fine, Sir; sorry for the oversight."

"Lulama, please stop apologising. I doubt Palesa will eat all these fruits anyway. She still has some dried fruits I bought her when she was at the hospital. So, between what you brought her and these other snacks, I'm sure we will be fine – at least until you bring your mutton stew," he ended with a teasing note.

"Sir, do you also want me to dish up the mutton stew for you?"

"As long as you have cooked it well. You can bring it later though."

Throughout Martin's exchange of communication with both my mother and Sis Lulama, coupled with him chastising me earlier when I spoke unkindly to the woman, I was almost certain that my man had turned over a new leaf and that things between us were about to run smoothly from then on.

After Sis Lulama had left, I propped myself up so I could sit up straight, allowing myself to nibble on the fruits and other snacks.

"Can I sit with you on the bed?"

"Sure, you can, but please no touching!" I warned.

"I wouldn't dream of it, I promise." He raised his hands up.

He sat with me on the bed as we both enjoyed the fruits, while watching some game show on TV, commenting on the happenings therein.

"Baby, I think I'm fine with what I've eaten now. I'll eat later. I still feel a bit nauseous," I revealed.

"I can see that even your favourites aren't going down like they normally do. Just drink this cranberry juice at least, and then you can rest. I think you'll wake up a bit better. I need to do some work in my office. I'll keep checking on you."

He left the bed, took a glass from the side table and poured some cranberry juice inside. He then handed it to me to drink.

"Thank you."

"You're welcome. By the way when did you last take your medication?"

"It was about six hours ago I think, before we left the hospital. I actually have to take one for pains now. The others are a set of antibiotics and anti inflammatory tablets that I should take eight hourly. Perhaps when I wake up in the middle of the night, I'll make a sandwich and then take them."

"I see." He handed me a tablet container with pain pills inside. I took it and quickly drank the tablets and finished the whole glass of cranberry juice Martin had just given me. It did appear that I had indeed been very thirsty.

"Don't get used to drinking tablets with anything but water. I just allowed you this faux pas for today only. Let me leave you now, I'll see you later," he promised.

****

"Baby, are you still sleeping?" Martin's faint voice whispered in my ear as I felt his breath against my neck. I opened my eyes leisurely, while trying to figure out for how long I had been sleeping.

"Hey…, what time is it?" I asked.

"It's six o'clock in the morning. You've been sleeping since yesterday!" he responded.

"Why did you let me sleep for such a long time? I didn't wake up to take my other tablets!"

"Don't worry about that for now. You looked so peaceful and I didn't have the guts to wake you up. Besides, you needed this rest. I know how hospitals can be; one never really sleeps peacefully because one moment you'd be sleeping, the next, a nurse would come to practically wake you up, taking your vitals, checking on you etc. So yeah, I know that this was probably the first time in at least two weeks when you slept uninterrupted. How're you feeling?"

A smile settled over my face as I acknowledged the knowing sentiments and notes from my fiancé. He was so warm, reassuring me in every way.

"And that smile?" he asked.

"No reason; I'm just happy to be back home and to be with you."

"Yes, back home where you belong," he asserted.

I pulled my breath, welcoming the abrupt presence of my inner person, who quickly gave me a warning without saying much. I knew it was her speaking as I had a sudden hike in my heart beat. I didn't let it fester because I was really happy again to have been tended to in the manner I was.

"I hear you. Let me see if I can get off from bed unaided. If I need help, I'll let you know."

"So, you're just going to get off the bed just like that? Where's my morning sugar?" he pouted, warming my heart once again. I turned my head briefly and gave him a peck on his lips, which he wanted to take advantage of.

"Baby, we can't do this now. We know what this can lead to and we cannot do this, not yet – Doctor Duvenhage and Sister Moipolai's orders." He rolled his eyes and grunted, shrugging like a little boy who wasn't allowed to eat his ice cream until he had had his main meal.

I turned on my side and propped myself slowly, allowing my legs to dangle a bit from the bed, until my feet could touch the floor. I was worried about getting up, as I remembered what happened the last time I tried doing so. Fear of the pain threatened to defeat my efforts as that was something I swore never to allow myself to experience ever again.

I was briefly transported to the day after the fateful late afternoon, when my fiancé asserted his authority on me by landing his knee hard on my coccyx. I became morose but carefully hid that away from Martin, who was not going to be happy to note that I was rehashing the incident in my head, particularly since he was trying hard to make amends. He had practically demanded forgiveness and I had assured him that he had it.

Once again, I thought of his feelings, particularly how he would feel if he knew that I was not really happy and was still mulling over what he had done to me. After all, he had apologized didn't he? He was making amends and being very charming again.

His sudden change in behaviour was supposed to make everything go away, I could tell. At the end of the day, I also believed that all I needed to do was to tow the line and not do anything that would inadvertently upset him to the point that he would hurt me or be angry at me.

I reasoned that the onus was on me to make sure that the relationship ran smoothly. I was a woman and women ought to know that it's always their fault their partners behave in manners uncanny at times, right? How jarring and impertinent this statement is! This is what thousands of people believe and perhaps have been brought up to believe.

We hear this all the time when elders are called to come and give the new bride words of wisdom, making sure that her husband is always happy and she never does anything to cause disharmony to the union.

Perhaps there is some truth in this proclamation – we bring life into this world and have to be able to know and understand more than men what any human could be grappling with at any given time. See? I learnt fast, whether that was bad education or not, which most of the time I sucked from observing my mother, I was going to finally allow myself the opportunity to grab the learning opportunity.

That scary and nagging feeling again though! It wouldn't let up, despite the fact that all was well and as mentioned, I had told my man that I forgave him with every fibre of my being.

Martin had given me a good life, the life that I hadn't really been exposed to. That was the life I convinced myself my mother was envious of, otherwise why would she try to ruin things for me by making unfounded statements about my fiancé?

At some point, I persuaded myself and my inner person to believe that what had happened didn't really happen; that it was all in my head. I wanted to believe that I had dreamt it all. But if I had, why was I hospitalized and why did I have an operation done on me?

Yes, I came to the realization that my life was no longer going to be my own and that I had no one really to blame but myself. I strongly wanted to blame my parents for having forced me to make the decision I had made of leaving home. Then again, I was not forced to make such a decision but my father's behaviour towards me did. Even then, he had behaved that way because I was failing at school. Everyone kept enjoying my excuses and pardons of their behaviour, at my expense.

My mother's doggedness and acceptance of the abuse, which she was never really vocal about, also forced me to hit the streets, which then culminated in me landing in the hands of the man I was now engaged to – the man who showed signs of control from the very first day we met. I did have a sense even then, that it would always be his way or the high way. I wanted that life and he had already provided me with a lot, including making me his wife. So what was my issue exactly?

Something about the arrangement didn't sit well with me. I

surmised that it came with a lot of sacrifices of my own; agreeing to do certain things as I had been a damsel in distress. Now I belonged to the one who had saved me. I needed to fill his void, so we could both live happily ever after. I was set on that once again, to stop looking for trouble and to give myself to my man wholeheartedly and to protect him from anyone who might threaten to destabilize our relationship and subsequent marriage.

I needed to protect his honour as a physician, whose friends, colleagues, patients alike were never going to find out from me at least, that he was less than perfect. After all, we are all not perfect as perfection does not exist in humans. So who cares if once in a while we hurt each other? That's what life is all about isn't it? No two people who weren't even raised the same way can ever be in perfect harmony or be in accord about everything.

Once in a while, we would ram heads. This extends to siblings even. They are hardly ever the same and they fight often and at times, this can lead to a rift between them, which can then pilot them to a full impasse. Indeed that was my mind, my heart and I guess, another part of me begging me to calm down and giving me what I deemed bad advice, because I refused to accept it at face value. The other voice however, was still very much audible and I was going to do everything in my power to shut her up for good.

Yes, many times I would convince myself that love should be exactly the way it was presented to me. After all, I didn't have any experience of anything to the contrary. My parents' 'love' life certainly didn't afford me anything good to gnaw into. My life on the other hand, was totally different from my mother's, as I was treated like a queen with rough edges here and there to iron out.

So why was I so bothered? Was it because I was younger? But then again, my mother did divulge in her letter that she was a measly 22 year old when her fate was decided for her.

At that moment, I was almost 20 years old and that meant that I was only 2 years shy of 22. So, I wasn't even sure as to whether my plaguing thoughts were because I hadn't attained the age my mother got married at, the age of maturity, which then led to her being able to endure what she had.

Chapter 13

Always in Control

I took a few steps, walking slowly as Martin got out of bed hurriedly, in his attempt to see to it that I wouldn't hurt myself.

"Babe, look who's walking unaided with no pain!" I exclaimed.

"I can see that baby, I can see that! This is incredible. What happened yesterday really rattled me. I have seen patients relapse before, especially after we have discharged them. Many would return to the hospital and at times they would stay longer than they did before. So, I was concerned that it might be the case with you yesterday. So, what I'm seeing now, makes me really happy."

"I'm also happy, really I am. Thank you for everything you've done for me and I'm particularly grateful that we are back in a good space again."

"Now you're really warming my heart with what you've just said. Thank you for pardoning me my love. I promise; from now onwards, you will always be safe in my arms," he stated.

"Okay… okay, let's not go there again. I want to take a shower."

"Okay, don't walk too fast. I'll come and help you."

****

Martin had taken that opportunity to also shower with me as there were two shower heads in any case. He would once so often present some nervousness when I'd like to bend. He did help me by making certain that I wasn't wetting my wound way too much. It was healing though. He would switch the tap on and off, carefully avoiding my back. I was not bothered as at the time, as much as my back wasn't really aching, I was incapacitated and did need the abet the man was giving me.

Getting out of the shower was still a mission and a half, as I had to be careful of the water on my feet so I wouldn't slip and fall. Once again, Martin was gallant… as bare as we had been at that time to help me with everything including applying lotion on my back. He would sometimes take it too far and steal a kiss or two while helping me.

"What do you feel like wearing?" he asked, while he had still wrapped a towel around his waist.

"I'll just wear one of my kimonos, baby. At least they're all made of light airy material."

"Okay, I'll get it for you."

"I can fetch it, baby, don't worry. Please get dressed."

"Okay, if you're sure."

"I'll let you know if I'm battling with anything," I assured.

"I just don't want you to struggle while I'm gone. I'll be leaving soon," he mentioned hastily. I was taken aback when he told me that he was going to leave. I recalled him mentioning the previous day that he would spend the whole week with me, to make sure that I settled in well. Now what had brought the sudden change of heart?

"Where are you going?" a note of jealousy and defenselessness crept over me. Where did that come from?

"I'm going to work baby; one of us still needs to keep the lights on," he stated, while I couldn't quite get the sudden grey tone in his statement.

"I know that and you didn't have to put it that way. You did tell me that you would be with me for at least a week, remember? I just didn't know you would change your mind so quickly and elect to go back to work, today of all days. You could have just mentioned it yesterday. That's all I'm saying," I shrugged, deliberately not maintaining eye contact with him.

"I would have done so but you slept the whole afternoon and the whole night. Besides, your mother spent quite some time in here so I probably would have mentioned at the time, had she not stolen my time with you," he snickered.

What was that? Jealousy?

"Baby, please don't tell me that you are going to compete with my mother again for my attention. Not in the condition I'm in… please."

"No, I'm not going to do that but I think it's important to set some boundaries while she is still here. For example, our room should be off limits. I just let it go yesterday because you and I hadn't spoken." I took in everything Martin was saying, feeling a bit affronted by his attitude. I have no idea why I was slighted by the statement.

"So, when I need help and I'm in here alone, what should I do?"

"You can call Lulama. I pay her a lot of money to do everything for you that I'm unable to do."

"Okay," I mumbled. "Is there anything else?" I asked, already feeling my energy being drained from me.

"You don't sound chuffed with what I'm asking. I think it's just fair that I lay it out as to what I'll accept and what I'll not accept. Every household has rules and these are mine – ours," he added as a late addition.

"It's not that I'm not happy but I'm just surprised, as I never thought my mother being in here would be an issue. But it's okay,

I'll tell her not to come in here."

"You don't have to tell her; Lulama will tell her. I don't want you to distort what I said when you tell her as this is a simple matter really."

"So, since it's such a simple matter, why can't I be the one to tell her of your rules?" he raised his eyebrows.

"I said these are our rules, Palesa," he hardened his tone. "We're not going to quarrel about this, are we?" he asked, condescendingly.

"No, we are not. Do as you wish. I don't want to argue."

"I'm glad we are on the same page," he said. "I won't have breakfast with you as there's a lot I need to do at work and it looks like I have quite a number of appointments today."

"Okay," I responded concisely."

He walked closer towards me after getting dressed in his navy jeans and one of his long sleeved shirts which had become my favourite. It made him look more regal and exceptionally handsome. It was light blue with medium red stripes and adorned by red buttons. Both the collar and the fold also had some bits of red yarn, perfectly sewn and double drawn. He had never dressed that way to go to work before. My instinct kicked in as I marvelled as to whether he really was going to work as he had claimed he was. That was my special shirt that I picked for him for when we go out – not for work.

He sat down on the bed next to me and held my hands, looking intently at me, as if to suss out what I was thinking. I dropped my eyes and he touched my chin and lifted my face up gently.

"Baby, look at me," he beseeched.

I tried my best to look at him as he had requested, but I was finding it difficult to do so as an overwhelming amount of jealousy engulfed me. I couldn't fathom where that emanated from. I didn't want to inadvertently let out what thoughts were running amok in my head. A woman has got to keep some personal secrets, even if some were just made up. I was not going to let him realize that I was developing the kind of jealousy that he sometimes displays – in fact most of the time.

I wanted him to be the one to show more affection than I did. But then again, I knew though that would, in the long run be a bad move on my part as he was soon going to lose interest. He had told me in no uncertain terms that he expected me to initiate intimacy and constant affection certainly would need to precede that.

"What's the matter? What's with this look you're giving me? What's bothering you?" he launched questions at me as I felt my eyes becoming teary. That was a bizarre thing I was experiencing.

"Baby, come on now. You don't want me to go to work?"

"No, it's not that. I think for the first time, I feel like you're deserting me when I need you."

"Now you're being dramatic. I've been going to work and you've been remaining at home. So why would I abandon you when I come here to sleep daily? I'm giving you a chance to chat to your mother and to allow her to aid you in getting better."

"I know; it's just that I can't help how I feel right now. I'm going to miss you," I sobbed.

"Baby, don't do this please," he said, reaching for his handkerchief in his pocket and wiped my tears. He then cupped my cheeks and kissed me on my lips. He stopped briefly and gawked deeply into my eyes, as if he wanted to devour all of me. I was certain I did the same as well.

He then brought me really close towards him and consumed my lips so intensely, I almost took my kimono off, adhering to the seduction. We both respired and rested our foreheads against each other, hearts beating intermittently. The moment had been passionate, intense and totally unexpected but I loved it, while I tried very hard to bury the earlier conversation about boundaries.

"Baby, I've got to go," he exhaled, whispering as if he didn't really want to speak much.

"Okay, baby… I'll see you later," I responded tenderly. He gave me a warm smirk, his one hand on my cheek.

"I love you, Palesa," he declared.

"I love you too," I avowed, finding it difficult to breathe and compose myself. Martin smiled and stood up from the bed, pulling his breath.

"Okay, now I really do have to go. Please remember what I said."

"You did say Sis Lulama will speak to Mama didn't you or do you now want me to handle it?"

"No, I'll speak to Lulama," he stated.

"Okay," I mumbled.

He left the bedroom, leaving me nursing my self-inflicted emotional wound. I sat for some time on the bed, taking in my sudden angst for my fiancé and still battling to understand where that pining feeling came from. While I was still pondering over all kinds of things, I heard Martin revving the car and speaking in a high pitched tone to Bra Mos. I deduced that he must have been a bit far from him, hence he raised his voice.

As it was still a bit early, not the usual time Martin was used to leaving home for work, I knew that Sis Lulama couldn't have come into the house already. I wanted to check how my mom had slept but I was wary of falling short of Martin's rules. I was hoping that as he spoke to Bra Mos, he had already called Sis Lulama at least, to impart his rules regarding my mom not setting foot in our bedroom.

****

"Miss Palesa, can I come in?" The voice of sis Lulama startled me awake. Did I sleep again? Yes, I did and it was now around 9 o'clock.

"Come in," I muttered.

"Morning, Miss Palesa, how did you sleep?" It looks like you slept for a very long time. Are you alright?"

"Yes sis, I'm fine thank you. I actually woke up earlier around

6 o'clock and even took a shower. I honestly don't know when I dozed off again."

"You must have really been exhausted. It's the medication you have been taking. You need to eat your breakfast though. Can I bring you something now?"

"Yes, please do. I'm starving. Please bring the whole enchilada!"

"Miss P…?" she widened her eyes, inviting a chortle from me.

"I'm kidding. Just bring whatever you can; I'll eat," I affirmed, while trying to find courage to ask her whether Martin had given her the rules regarding my mother's visit.

"Would you like me to help prop you up?" she asked.

"No, I'll be fine. Please just bring food and juice. I'll have tea later."

I noticed that the woman was not mentioning any talk she might have had with Martin, and I took the opportunity to ask her frankly.

"Sis, has Bra Mos given you a message from Martin?"

"Yes, he did. Are you referring to the message regarding your mother coming in here?"

"Yes, that message."

"Miss Palesa, do you really want me to tell your mother that? How do you think she would feel about it?" she shook her head and sniggered. Why would Sis Lulama question her boss' instructions all of a sudden? She had appeared to be more relaxed around

Martin ever since I was hospitalized, even questioning his decisions.

"This is Martin's room and if he doesn't want my mother in here, we should respect his stance and wishes. I personally don't have much of an issue with it but, I wish I was the one to tell my mom though. If you haven't told her anything, don't worry. I'll tell her. Just let her know that I'll be sitting on the balcony and having breakfast there. So you can place my food there Sis, thank you."

"I hear you, Miss Palesa, thank you. I just don't like what Doc said though. I think he is being disrespectful towards your mother."

"Sis, can we please let this go. I'm really hungry. Remember that I didn't eat much yesterday afternoon. So please do hurry. In the meantime, I'll just have two or three dried peaches. That should hold off hunger pangs for some time."

"Shame, I can feel it. Let me rush out then." Sis Lulama left the bedroom as I got up from the bed slowly, reached for my walking frame carefully and walked towards my mini grocery cupboard in the bedroom. I retrieved a bag of dried peaches, took out a bowl and poured a couple of the peaches inside. I took one and ate, followed by another as I walked slowly towards the balcony. It was lucid that I was really famished.

I was finding the frame very restrictive for me to walk with ease around furniture and I decided to abandon it midway. I took quite a bit of time to sit but eventually, I managed to sit on the recliner. I heard footsteps and was amazed as to how quickly Sis Lulama was able to prepare the food. I however learnt that it was my mother who was actually walking towards our bedroom. I called out to her and she came swiftly, changing focus from our bedroom door and came towards me. On reaching me, she stroked my shoulders briefly and smiled. I raised my head to acknowledge her presence.

“Oh, you’re in here! I thought you’d still be in bed. How are you feeling?” she asked, genuinely concerned.

“Yes, mama, I’m in here. It’s nice as there’s a breeze that I need. I woke up around six o’clock, as Martin was preparing to go to work. Besides, I slept for a very long time yesterday and didn’t wake up until this morning.”

“It’s probably the medication and whatever it was that Martin gave you when you arrived here after your vomitting episode,” she added after taking heed of my cogitating eyes.

“No mama, Martin didn’t give me anything. He simply re-dressed my wound, nothing more than that. I do have medication from the hospital so he was not going to add to what I’m already taking. Besides, at the moment, he is not my doctor.”

“Okay, okay, I get it. Lulama said you wanted to speak to me. What is it?” This gave me the chills, as Sis Lulama did tell me that she was going to speak to her. It looked like she got cold feet after all. The baffling effect my mother had on her amused me to say the least. My mother was harmless even though she’d sometimes bark a lot.

“It’s nothing hectic, mama. It’s just that Martin was

uncomfortable yesterday when you came into our room. So, he was asking that you please not be in our room from now onwards. Traditionally, it's actually not okay to be in lovers' room anyway. Am I not right mama?"

My mother found a chance to amuse herself with what I had intimated to her. She laughed so hard and I even felt mortified, inwardly beating myself up as to why I didn't just end at the fact that she made Martin uncomfortable. Why did I have to add tradition when Martin and I weren't even married, practically living in sin? Well, the words were already out and I had to prepare myself for whatever it was that my mom would throw at me in response.

"Palesa...," she said, after much composure, while still chortling. "You didn't just say that to me, did you? This is truly hilarious. You are not a married woman and you are my daughter. So whichever room you may be in, that's where I will enter. This man you're staying with must not think that just because we have let this cohabiting thing go, it then means that we have okayed this whole thing, especially him sidestepping proper cultural practices." Did she just say that?

"Mama, you can laugh all you want and no, you cannot enter any room I am in as this is not your house. I am here because you let papa do whatever he liked and treat us in however way he wanted to. That is why I left. It took a stroke to shake him up and to be somewhat nicer to me. I just hope he'll still be this open and willing to ask for forgiveness properly after he has fully recovered.

So please mama, we are not going to fight and I don't want to go back there again. I am happy here and if Martin doesn't want you in our room, then you shouldn't be in our room and I ask that you respect that and not make this a joke."

"Wow, touchy, touchy!" she mocked again. "I see that I'm not wanted here. So, I'll leave," she mumbled.

"It's up to you, mama whether you want to leave or not. All I was saying is that, please respect Martin's boundaries."

"Fine; is there anything else?" she asked cheekily.

"No, there isn't anything else Mama."

"Fine," she answered pithily again , as I leaned against the sofa gnawing on my dried fruits, while I kept my eyes fixed towards the stairs where sis Lulama was about to come.

It had suddenly become very tense after I defended Martin's resolve to my mother. She said she wanted to leave but there she was, still sitting comfortably on the recliner. She was probably waiting for me to beg her to stay but I was getting very tired of the back and forth between the two of us, something we weren't really doing when I was still at home.

At last, sis Lulama came in, apologising for taking some time to bring the food.

"Apologies, I had to warm the food again as it was a bit cold. Mme Ditheko, would you like me to bring yours up here too?" she asked my mom.

"Oh no, thank you. We don't want to upset the man of the

house now do we? I'll come with you, Lulama and will make my own food."

It was clear that my mom was offended by what I told her and in a way, she also wanted some kind of attention and I was not going to give her any, neither was sis Lulama, who simply shed a brief giggle.

"Okay ma'am, no problem. Miss Palesa, will you be alright by yourself?" she asked.

"Yes, I'll be fine sis. You can go about your day. I'll let you know once I'm done."

We ended our succinct engagement and as sis Lulama was about to leave, my mother got up too and followed her, giving me a condensed look and clapping her hands once. I didn't even ask her what that was about, as I wanted to be by myself so I could recover. It had only been a day since I came back from the hospital, but I could sense that my recovery would be long as I had two very demanding people to please. The two people who could just be working together to help me with my recovery.

As they headed out, Sis Lulama turned around, "Miss Palesa, can I come clean in the bedroom while you're eating? That way I can be nearby when you need something," she asked looking somewhat concerned.

"Yes sis, no problem," I affirmed.

She and my mother left as I began nibbling on the elaborate breakfast of brown toast, button mushrooms, grilled tomatoes, hash brown and some minced meat. She really went all out, even placing some croissants on a side plate and all. It was like she had initially made food for both my mother and I but changed her mind mid-way as she brought the food – hence she asked her if she should make food for her as well.

I decided to pay her no mind as she went downstairs to fetch her cleaning products. While I was eating, my phone vibrated. I swiftly wiped my hands and drank my tea. I then picked it up. A brief glance on the screen, indicated a number I didn't recognize. I had hoped that Martin would call me at least when he got to work but he didn't. It was as if I was now finding it difficult to function without him as his absence that day left me anxious.

I nonetheless answered the phone. "Hello who is this?" I asked.

"Hi Palesa, it's Lucas. Please don't hang up, I'm begging you," he pleaded, his voice a gripping baritone. I thought briefly of what I should do and was not about to hold on for too long on the phone, since sis Lulama was going to come back soon. If she were to hear me mention Lucas' name, I doubt she'd be pleased with me, judging by how she spoke about him and Martin while I was still in hospital. So I had to be cautious and choose my words carefully, keen to cut the call off as soon as I needed to. The sudden growling of my stomach as well as an elevated heart rate after hearing Lucas' voice, left me quivering and unable to fathom what on earth was going on with me. I however plucked up some valor and spoke up.

"What is it?" I asked insolently, trying hard not to mention his name, just in case I had a sudden audience.

"Why are you so hostile, Palesa? I'm simply checking on you and need to tell you something, so please I'm begging you, do not hang up. I'm very worried about you," he claimed, while I couldn't quite understand the bravado to call me after what I heard about his fight with Martin. I suppose I was inquisitive to learn of the big covert neither of the two men was willing to divulge but were expecting me to go along with either of their two contrasting versions.

"I'm fine. What is this about?" I asked. I didn't want to give him an inkling that I wanted to remain on the phone for longer than I really had to, so one way or another the man had to make it snappy and leave me in peace.

"Okay, since you're not in a really chatty mood, I might as well come out and say it. Martin had an affair with my wife a year before she died…," I interjected.

"Why are you telling me this? What do you want me to do with this information?"

"You don't want to hear about the kind of man you're going to marry?" he asked, sounding concerned or perhaps he was just jealous of his friend and wanted to tarnish his image. I didn't know then what his motive was. It was clear however that he was a man on a mission and had chosen that moment to offload to me, knowing very well that Martin was not home and was totally against him conversing with me, about anything.

"The reason I'm telling you this is because it's his *modus operandi* to damage women's backs if they don't do what he wants or if they don't agree with his perverse fantasies. He did the same thing to my wife when she tried to break things off with him. She could never walk again after that due to what he did to her. She died while utilizing a wheelchair. Although she died from other opportunistic illnesses, he had accellerated her illness I tell you now," he revealed, as I tried very hard to hide the fact that I was flustered.

"I'm struggling to reconcile your relationship with Martin honestly. Not so long ago when the two of you met at the hospital, you guys seemed very excited to see one another and even beat your chests together. Why do you feel the need to tell me all these things now? Oh…another thing, I heard that you and Martin fought while I was still in hospital. What was the fight about?"

"I'll start by answering your last question. We fought because of you. He wasn't happy that I had come to see you at the hospital. I guess you told him that I had been to see you."

"Is that a question? Of course I told him. I still fail to comprehend this friendship of yours and to tell you the truth, I don't even want to be any part of it. I cannot figure out why when you two decide to rehash your fight about your wife, you then decide to include me in it. This is unfair and frightening to say the least," I declared.

"Don't be frightened; at least not of me but be afraid of the one you stay with. I'm harmless." I sniggered briefly.

"I want to know what this friendship is about. If you insist that Martin had an affair with your wife, which led to her subsequent death, why are you still friends?"

"I see you're a black and white person and straight to the point. I like that," he said in a condescending tone. "It took us a long time to reach this stage of our friendship as we decided to not let it be destroyed by my wife's unfaithfulness."

"I don't get this honestly. The way I see it, your friend was neither faithful nor loyal to you either so if you insist that your wife was a victim, I think you're being unfair to Martin as it took two to tango. They both had a moral obligation to be loyal, trustworthy and faithful to you. So please, if it's pity you want from me, I'm sorry you contacted the wrong person."

"Wow, to think that your man has told us that you don't know much about life, yet here you are dishing out wise counsel to me! You see why I say Martin is not right for you? You're not safe with him, trust me," he cautioned me once again. I didn't care whether he had said something my ears were craving for or not. I still believed he was out of line.

"Okay… okay, this phone call is tiring me out and I have breakfast to finish here. Have you forgiven him for the affair or not? If you have, you then need to stop going back to the past and let sleeping dogs lie. Nothing will happen to me."

"Oh well…," he sighed. "You can't say I haven't tried," he murmured.

"Goodbye, Doctor and as mentioned, I am alright and doing

much better." I could hear by how he remarked at my last statement that I had confused him somewhat. I then cut the call right there and then. I did that on purpose after hearing Sis Lulama's footsteps. For some reason, I felt the need to hide the fact that I was talking to Lucas, lest she blurt it out to Martin, who will definitely not be pleased with me. I was certain though that she had heard the last bit of my conversation with the man.

"How's the food ma'am? She came closer towards me and put her cleaning paraphernalia down in the passage.

"The food is fine sis," I responded. "Please pass me my tablets on the nightstand. I want to take them while I eat. I think I should decide on the exact time I should take my medication if I have any chance of recovering."

"Yes, that's a good idea. Last night you didn't eat and they say it's not good for a sick person to do so. You must eat, Miss Palesa so that you can regain your strength," she advised.

"You're right," I said. "I promise I'll eat." She handed me the small paperback that had the pills inside and I took it, while she took that time to pour some water in a glass for me.

"Here… miss Palesa." She extended her hand to me, after noticing that I had already taken the bunch of tablets out of their containers and ready to gobble them down.

"These are many! I'm so nervous about taking too many tablets but I guess you need them this time, as you are not alright, Miss Palesa."

"Yes, there is nothing one can do about this. Please try and finish sis, as I need to have some time to myself in the bedroom."

"I thought I'll be helping you to walk or exercises today," she mentioned. I was not sure whether she was asking or not.

"It's not necessary Sis. I'll walk by myself up here using this frame. At the hospital they showed me what to do. So I'll be fine and if I feel wobbly at all, I'll shout. You still have a lot of work to do anyway so you can relax."

For some strange reason, I sensed that sis Lulama wasn't quite pleased that I denied her the chance to help me with my walk. I wondered if those were instructions from Martin or not, as her cheeks dropped down after I rejected her help. I had to finalise eating my food, eager to walk for about 15 minutes or so.

Meanwhile, my mother was fairly quiet downstairs and I couldn't even hear the sound of the television or radio. I could not even hear her footsteps. I had to forthrightly ask Sis Lulama where she was and what she left her doing when they went to the kitchen together.

"Where's my mom?"

"She made herself a sandwich and then went to the guestroom. I think she's not very happy with you, Miss Palesa."

"Why do you say that?"

"Because she stormed out of here and I doubt she'll stay for a long time here," she chortled.

Sis Lulama was reaching and I felt the need to reproof her while protecting my mother's honour. Just because I was having a disagreement with my mother didn't mean I wanted her to speak the way she liked about her. How dare she! That was still my mother.

"Please finish with your cleaning. I would like to be alone in here." She slanted her lips and widened her eyebrows, as if I had asked something impossible of her. I said nothing further.

"Okay, Miss Palesa. I'll do so. Can I take these dishes now?"

"Yes you may," I succinctly replied.

I spent the afternoon by myself, utilizing my walking frame to walk the stretched passage and ending the walk by the balcony. I alternated between the walk, the sitting as well as the sleeping. All these exercises were daunting but my muscles felt stronger and stronger, even though at times, I'd feel a pull here and there.

I spent a considerable amount of time in the bedroom and once I felt some tingling sensation either on my back or my legs, I would sit down. Pride prevented me from calling sis Lulama or even my mother. So I struggled by myself until I could manage, albeit very bushed and really tight. I think I pushed myself too hard for the first day after being discharged from the hospital.

I slept for some time as I had worn myself out. When I eventually woke up, I checked the time, unerringly certain that Martin should either be home by then or about to arrive. When I checked the time, 19h17! There was no sign of my fiancé. I didn't know if he had attempted to call me and because of fatigue, I wasn't able to hear the phone ring or he was home at that time and perhaps was in his office.

I got up from bed; dizzy spells similar to the ones I had felt the other day had reappeared. I panicked and sat still on the bed, trying hard to dispel the feeling. I had no choice but to call for help. However, before I could do so, I vacillated between calling either my mother or Sis Lulama. Eventually, I called my mom as I believed that sis Lulama might have retreated to her room by then.

"What's wrong Palesa?" She answered the phone wryly. Her dry tone indicated to me that she was still upset over our talk earlier.

"Mama, I'm struggling a bit in here and need some help," I begged. "Is Sis Lulama still in the house?"

"Yes she is. I'll send her to come and see you. Isn't it I cannot come to your bedroom?" I wasn't sure how I felt about my mother's response to me and believed that she was being petty. On the other hand, I acknowledged that I was being unfair to my mother. What was she supposed to do since I made it clear that my fiancé was against her being in our bedroom?

"Okay, mama," I mumbled.

As I was struggling to stretch and put my feet on the floor, sis Lulama flung the door open, eyes wide open as if she had just seen a ghost.

"Miss Palesa, what's wrong?" she rushed towards me and held me by my arm as my feet became unstable.

"I don't know, sis. I think I overdid it earlier while I was busy walking and stretching. Now I'm really sore and my whole body is trembling. I even feel woozy."

"Oh no!" she remarked. "What should I do now? Do you feel nauseous like before? What if you have injured your back again like yesterday? I hope that's not the case because we will definitely not know what to do because Doc is not even here yet." Sis Lulama lamented, worried sick about my condition.

Earlier, I could already sense that Martin hadn't arrived yet but kept quiet when Sis Lulama mentioned that. I attempted once again to get up while the woman garnered all her strength to help me to at least allow my feet to touch the floor.

"Sis Lulama, I'm sorry about earlier. I was very unkind towards you."

"Don't worry about it. I can see that it's because you are not well and your mother being here and making all the demands truly is not helping," she stated. "You and I have never fought and we are not about to start now. So take it easy," she comforted me.

"I know, I know."

I finally managed to get up and noticed that my feet were swollen and my ankles felt as if they had some pins and needles inside them. I was a mess!

"Miss Palesa, this is scary. Has Doc called you at all since he left?"

"No, he hasn't…; at least I don't think so. I haven't checked my phone yet. Maybe he called and I had gone into deep slumber.

Please help me take some few steps so that I can hold on to that frame. I'd like you to please check my back to see if there isn't any blood oozing like yesterday.

"Okay, let's walk a bit…slowly… slowly…," she murmured, helping me and truly being very kind. I felt guilty for having been discourteous towards her earlier. She seemed to have decided to let that 'unfortunate' incident go, as her full attention remained on me.

She hiked my kimono up to check on my back while I held on to my frame.

"Phew…," she sighed. "At least nothing is amiss this time. I would still feel better if Doc was here. Don't you think we should take you to the hospital?"

"No Sis, I don't think it's that bad. Remember that I haven't been taking my medication the way I am supposed to and I have been sleeping too much to such an extent that I miss my tablet time. Remember that at the hospital, nurses came around often and they would literally wake me up to take my medication."

"Oh I see. Don't you think I should help you then to maintain the hospital schedule? That way, we can see whether you being this way is because you haven't really been taking medication as you should or not," she advised.

"Okay; I think it's a good idea. For now, allow me to just walk a bit." She obliged.

I felt tired after walking for about ten minutes and as I was preparing to sit on the balcony after sis Lulama had put the light on, we saw lights from the main gate and heard the revving of the engine.

"There he is, driving like a maniac," Sis Lulama said. "I just don't like how he's driving now. This worries me. I hope he hasn't been drinking."

I kept still, my heart beating in an unusual manner after hearing the SUV being revved carelessly by Martin. Although the SUV did have a big engine and four pipes, it was atypical of him to drive in the manner he did, as if he didn't care about his car at all or something had upset him. I shivered even more, as sis Lulama noted the change in me.

"Miss Palesa, you are not looking good. Are you still feeling giddy?"

"Not really, but my heart is beating in an unusual manner. Please don't leave yet. Wait until Martin is in here. I want to see how he is first and in what state he is in before I let you go," I pleaded.

"Of course I will not leave, Miss Palesa. I will not leave you alone in here with Doc; I suspect he has been drinking. I hope he hasn't gone back to his crazy ways of drinking. He hasn't really been drinking like the way he did when you were hospitalized in almost three years. Something big must have disturbed him to make him go back there," she assumed.

"What if he's just hurrying because he has come home late? Perhaps he hasn't been drinking at all."

"Okay, I hope you're right; I really hope so. But like I said, I have seen this before, Miss Palesa and it's not a pretty sight. Don't worry, I will be here with you."

"Sis, you sound like you know what's going on or rather what's going to happen. Let's wait for Martin to come into the house and we can then make our deductions then."

"I hear you, Miss Palesa. He has already parked the car. I wonder if I should go and see if he needs help with something? But then again, if he does need help, he will call Mos for help. I just want to sit with you in here."

"Have we got coarse salt, Sis? I think I should put my feet in salty water so that the swelling can go down. I just don't know what I would apply aftewards."

"I think there is coarse salt in the kitchen. I'll fetch it after Doc has come in so that I can assess if he is the way I suspect he is. I just hope I'm wrong," she added.

The woman's tone was deliberate and the naïve me was still hopeful though. She was almost certain that the way Martin had driven towards the house, he had to have been drunk. What perplexed me was the fact that she spoke as if she had already seen him. Well, I deduced that she knew him better than I did anyway, and chances were that she could tell the difference between normal driving and the one propelled by anger, lateness or even drunkenness.

I could also sense that she felt sorry for me somehow, as if she was aware that something was about to befall me. I had no real reason at the time to believe Sis Lulama's supposition, as the only time I had witnessed a somewhat drunk Martin was at the hospital when he came to see me. Besides booze talking through him then, he was fairly “behaved” – well, sort of.

We heard Martin tossing the door open and then slamming it really hard. I was still sitting on the recliner on the patio. I wanted to get up to acknowledge his presence, something he loved and if I didn’t do it for some reason, he would normally sulk and ignore me until I could ask for forgiveness using my sex appeal. That day however, there was no way I could do that. My legs felt wobbly and my feet were swollen, while my back was terribly sore.

I still attempted to get up from the sofa though, and sis Lulama held my arm and shook her head. “Miss Palesa, please don’t do this. Sit down; I’ll handle him,” she declared.

I widened my eyes, wondering where the once timid woman I had met the first day had suddenly disappeared to. I didn’t have the chance to ask her as Martin interrupted my thoughts, shouting my name.

“PALESA! PALESA! PALESA!” he howled.

“I’m on the balcony baby, why are you yelling?” I said lovingly, attempting to calm him down from whatever it was that had obviously distressed him.

As soon as he reached us, Sis Lulama was proven right as he smelt like a fermentation plant, walking zig zag and trying to hold on to the wall and then my chair. He stood behind me and held my head back and kissed me on my forehead.

Sis Lulama stood in the middle of the balcony watching every move Martin was making. I could tell that she was prepared for anything.

“Lulama, don’t just stand there as if you’re an electric pole. Get out of the way and leave me and my fiancé to talk. I’m here now and there’s no reason for you to …burr…burr…burr…,” he burped loudly, while trying to get the last bit of words out of his mouth. I was worried that he might vomit right there and then.

“I’m not going anywhere. How do you think Miss Palesa feels coming home at this late hour when she is struggling to even walk?” The woman’s courage startled me.

I thought Sis Lulama’s bravery was sparked by the visibly drunk and incapacitated Martin, knowing that there was no way he could retaliate either in words or actions. He gave her a ferocious gaze still. He kept touching himself on the upper body often, as if he felt some kind of pain. It was as if his chest was heartrending.

I sat there in a catatonic-like state, trying very hard to dispel the feeling that I had, that my life was going to change forever that night; the feeling that was strong and difficult to ignore.

“Palesa, why are you so quiet? I’ve just greeted you …burr…burr…burr…,” he burped again, his chest heaving.

“Hi, Martin.”

“Oh, so I’m no longer baby, now?”

“I could ask you the same thing. You called me by my name too.” He chortled scornfully, putting his hand on his mouth, like a naughty child who was trying hard to prevent himself from laughing, but due to his disrespectful nature, still laughed anyway. I got annoyed and asked Sis Lulama to take me to the bedroom.

"Sis, please take me to the bedroom."

"Okay, Miss Palesa, let me help you up."

As the woman helped me to go to the bedroom, Martin attempted to get up from where he had retreated to, and tried to grab me by my arm. Sis Lulama saw red and pushed him hard. He wobbled on his feet and jerked backwards, trying hard to not fall, while his feet crossed each other until he fell on the floor and squealed, "LULAMA! HAVE YOU FORGOTTEN THAT THIS IS MY HOUSE? GET OUT OF HERE!" he howled.

"I'm not going anywhere. Miss Palesa, I think you should sleep in the other bedroom; otherwise I'd be worried the entire night about your safety. Please also lock the door. I cannot leave you with someone who is this drunk," she asserted.

"Sis, Martin will do nothing to me. He just needs to rest and once he has restrained himself in the morning, he will then tell me where exactly he has been today and why he drank this much. Just take me to the bedroom please and leave him in here."

As we kept talking, Martin threw up right there and then in different intervals. I stood still in the middle of the hallway, amazed and hurt by the deplorable sight of my fiancé, vomitting all over the place.

"Sis, please help him up. I'll manage to walk to the bedroom by myself," I requested.

"No, Miss Palesa; I'm not going to do that – not now anyway. There's nothing wrong with him. He's just drunk, that's all."

The scornful tone in Sis Lulama's voice was loud, and I elected to just let her be. She clearly had been dealing with far worse things than I ever did, and probably knew a lot about Doctor Martin Leboya than I did.

I could not understand the sudden change in her behaviour towards him though. I had always held that she and Bra Mos feared him and would not be seen disrespecting him in anyway, irrespective of the mood he might have been in. Now there she was, disregarding my request and flipping hands in contempt, as she declared that her concentration had to only be on me. I decided to not probe further.

"Okay then. I think I'll just have a few fruits and after that I'll take my meds. Let me go to the restroom first and sort myself out. If you don't mind, can you prepare the bed for me please."

"Will you be okay in the bathroom by yourself Miss Palesa?"

"Yes, I will be fine, Sis, thank you."

Before walking towards the bathroom, I took a final look at Martin and saw him slumbered in his vomit, while he tried very hard to get up from the floor but was failing dismally. He slithered in his mess as he sought to stand up. '*How am I going to sleep with this man in this state? I think Sis Lulama is right about me using the other room to sleep in.*' I reflected.

"Sis Lulama, I think you're right about me not sleeping in here with Martin. I can't imagine him trying to touch me. I'd scream!" I said.

“So you want him to sleep in here rather?”

“This is his room, Sis; I can’t exactly kick him out now, can I?”

“Yes you can, Miss Palesa. He doesn’t even know what’s happening right now. So when he wakes up in the morning, he’ll know that it was for his and your own good that you had to sleep separately tonight.”

“Okay Sis, please do what you need to. You sound like you have dealt with something like this before,” I craftily mentioned.

“I have, Miss Palesa, yes I have. Not once, not twice, many times. This is still nothing compared to how he used to be. He was doing so well without alcohol, but I really don’t know what brought this on now,” she marvelled.

“I think we should at least call Bra Mos to come and help us. What if he was drugged or poisoned?” I asked, utterly concerned about Martin.

“There is no such a thing, Miss Palesa. Like I said, I have seen this before. He has obviously relapsed. I hope it won’t take long for him to come back to his senses.”

“Either way, please call Bra Mos to come and help you. We can’t leave Martin in his vomit like that. I’m begging you.”

“As you wish, Miss Palesa. I’ll call Mos after having prepared the room next door for you.”

“Thank you,” I said and retreated to the bathroom.

As much as she had agreed to call Bra Mos, I could see that she was simply just indulging me and was not even moved by my concern for Martin but, she was simply agreeing to it because I had asked.

Looking at my fiancé's helpless and quivering body hurt me to the core, and although I had no idea what the depth of his woes were as well as Lucas' pain, I couldn't help but blame myself for having gotten in between the two men who had clearly attempted to rebuild their friendship, at least until that day when Lucas chose to visit me at the hospital.

Why did I have to blame myself though? These were strong and supposedly mature men who were both medical doctors and were supposed to deal with their issues better than they were doing. I shuddered to think what Martin would do or say should he get wind of the fact that Lucas had called me during the day.

I nonetheless managed fine in the bathroom and as I was about to get out, I heard Bra Mos talking to Sis Lulama and were both making arduous sounds indicating that they were doing all their best to lift the brawny man up, but he was not making much effort to help himself, largely because he was truly out of it.

"Lulama, I think we should just let him sleep it off on this sleeper couch on this balcony. When he wakes up, he will at least be better and able to walk. I don't see the wisdom in us carrying him in this state and putting him on the bed with white sheets," Bra Mos whined.

"That's exactly what I told Miss Palesa. She seems really hurt by his drinking though, and I hope this was simply a once off incident. Should he continue, she will definitely not be able to take it and she will leave him. I can see that. She's still too young to be held down by a drunkard."

The two of them spoke about me and Martin at length as they wavered between doing what I had requested and what they felt made more sense to them. I affirmed to myself as I listened in, that I wasn't going to insist anymore and would definitely leave them to exercise their own discretions.

"Mos, take his clothes off. This is such a beautiful shirt and I wonder what it could have been that led him to drink this way. Now this shirt might be ruined!" sis Lulama lamented.

"Oh, stop being so dramatic Lulama! Just put these clothes in water, add some soap and all will be fine," Bra Mos flippantly admonished Sis Lulama, who was not impressed with the man's chide.

"I think you're the one who should wash these clothes. You seem to know too much about washing vomit off the Italian clothes. I'm not touching his secretions ever again! Go ahead and do it!"

I moved towards the bedroom and once they spotted me, they stopped their moaning and finally lifted Martin up as Bra Mos took a mop that was in a bucket he had already brought, and cleaned the toxins from Martin's stomach off the floor. Sis Lulama practically threw Martin onto the sleeper couch and placed her hand on her waist. "I'm tired Mos. You need to take over carrying him. He's too heavy." I smiled and moved towards the bed.

I felt sorry for Martin as he was feeble and totally vulnerable, at the mercy of the two people he would sometimes tell off and speak unkindly to. My heart was aching, just watching my man so defenseless. I didn't care what had happened. All I wanted was to see him up and about and even scolding us; a bit warped but that feeling did fester.

I held on to my frame and walked towards the balcony, in my bid to 'oversee' what Bra Mos and Sis Lulama were doing. They were both irked by my presence, judging by their widened eyebrows and furrowed foreheads.

"Didn't you say you were going to sleep in the room next door Miss Palesa?" Sis Lulama asked me.

"Yes I said so, but I want Martin to see me immediately when he wakes up. I don't want him to think that I abandoned him in his time of need. I won't," I stated, as the two helpers exchanged uncharacteristic glances, shaking their heads in disapproval.

"Well, if you are sure, Miss Palesa. As for me, you cannot say I didn't try my best to protect you."

"What exactly do you mean by that sis? Why do you keep insisting that Martin will hurt me? Trust me, nothing will happen to me."

"If you say so, Miss Palesa. Like I said, I'm no longer going to try and convince you otherwise. When you do need help however, you can call us. I think we should leave him here for tonight. We will wake up earlier tomorrow to check on you, especially since it's

Saturday and there's no way he can claim to be going to work. Will you be okay with the fruits you said you were going to take for the night?"

"Yes, I will be fine," I avowed.

Throughout the back and forth chitchat between Sis Lulama and myself, Bra Mos was implausibly quiet, his face down as he kept cleaning the floor and rinsing with water from the bucket. He then took Martin's shirt off as well as his sleeveless vest. He wiped Martin's mouth with his vest and took the clothes as well as the bucket and the mop with him.

"I'm coming back, Miss Palesa. I still need to clean with some household detergent to ward off the smell of the booze infused gag."

"Okay, Bra Mos, thank you. I appreciate your help," I expressed.

Sis Lulama then walked towards our bathroom, perhaps out of remorse and retrieved Martin's face cloth, poured water in the basin and immersed the cloth in it. She smeared soap on it and then squeezed a bit of water out. She headed over to Martin, who was now sleeping like a baby. She wiped his face and neck and then went back to the bathroom, immersing the face cloth again in water, as I watched her closely, getting out of the way for her to do what she needed to do. I continued to stand in the middle of the room, facing the balcony. I felt my eyes becoming watery as I stared at Martin.

"Miss Palesa, don't do this to yourself," Sis Lulama cautioned. "There is nothing wrong with him. Like I said before, he is just drunk. Please save yourself from heartache and eat your fruits and have your juice. Your tears are wasted on him," the woman impenitently advised.

When she was done wiping Martin's face, she went to the bathroom and washed the facecloth and retrieved one of Martin's face creams. She looked disturbingly comfortable with what she was doing. The scene was akin to a mother taking care of her wayward child who never listens. She was irked but still helping to take care of him. I wondered if that would be the life I was prepared to live, should Martin had truly slipped up and his life about to spiral out of control. I wondered what I would have done if both Bra Mos and Sis Lulama were not around to help me!

During that time, my mother was exceptionally quiet and made no movement. I had thought that at least she would have appeared, seeing as Martin made such a commotion when he arrived home and Bra Mos' up and down movement. I surmised that she was truly upset with me and perhaps more with Martin for his rules and disrespect of her.

Sis Lulama then applied some cream on Martin's face and neck and when she was about to remove his belt to take off his pants, I butted in. "That would be enough, sis. I think Bra Mos will do this. Please don't do that. I get that you have probably done that before but I was not here then. I don't think it's right; you don't have to take his pants off."

“All I wanted to do was take his pants off and help to dress him in his pajamas,” she chortled. “I wasn’t going to do anything else, I swear.”

Bra Mos came back as Sis Lulama was still proclaiming to not wanting to do anything untoward to Martin, as the man rebuked her as well.

“Lulama, leave the boss now. I’ll take over from here.”

“Whatever!” she flipped her hands.

Bra Mos then cleaned the floor again; this time I could at least smell the detergent he had poured in the water. A faint potpouri smell now permeated the room. When he was done, he asked, “Miss Palesa, can I have Doc’s pyjamas please?

“Sis Lulama, can you please take them out of the dresser?”

“Oh, I thought you two didn’t need my help anymore!” she whimpered. I watched her walk as if she was pushed. She then retrieved Martins’ black silky pyjamas from the cupboard.

“Will this be fine?”

“Sorry to bother you, sis. Can you please take out the cotton ones instead? I’m afraid with these ones, he might just slip and fall. We don’t want an injury on our hands.” She put them back, visibly annoyed with me.

“Here Mos…,” she handed the cotton pyjamas to Bra Mos and he took them from her.

“Can I have some space please Lulama? Please take the bucket downstairs. I’ll finish up here,” Bra Mos instructed.

Sis Lulama rolled her eyes and fervidly took the bucket and the mop and took a few steps down the stairs. She stopped midway. “Good night, Miss Palesa. I’ll see you tomorrow.

“Good night sis,” I responded.

She left hurriedly, as if she was preventing Bra Mos from sending her everywhere again, as if she was a child. I surmised that she had gotten used to being the one responsible for everything that was going on inside the house and anything that resembled a take-over of chores by another person, she found it offensive, hence she responded with hostility.

Bra Mos loosened Martin’s jeans and pulled it down, and once he reached the shoes, he stopped briefly and took the shoes off, finishing the move by finally removing his jeans. He then tossed them on the recliner, as I became tired of watching every move he was making. I then turned around and walked towards the bedroom.

I sat on the bed, my mind plagued by many thoughts, trying to come to terms with what was happening and the possible future I was faced with. All these were based on Sis Lulama’s assertions earlier, regarding the fact that Martin had seemed to have relapsed, and that what I was seeing was familiar.

I began contrasting Martin’s drunkenness with the younger Phillip Ditheko’s - my father. According to my mother’s letter, she met my father the day she attempted suicide. He had appeared to have been drinking a lot that day, even though none of them was cognizant of what they were doing at the time, at least up until the fateful morning when my mother realised that she had been sexually molested.

I swore that there was no way I would allow a drunken man to force himself on me. The only difference as I sat down entertaining all thoughts and feelings, was that at least I knew and loved the drunk man, which was not the case with my mother. So why was I so apprehensive? I ate an apple and drank water with my tablet for the night.

****

I eventually retired but was utterly concerned about my fiancé. I was very restless most of the night, constantly thinking about my man and how he might have been truly concerned about his own well-being. At some point in the middle of the night, I woke up and went to the bathroom. I threw my eyes where Martin was slumbering.

He had curled up on the sleeper couch like a little boy and I felt very guilty that there I was, sleeping comfortably on the bed – his bed, and he was uncomfortable on the sofa, whose comfort I had never really tested. I came close to crying but I felt too weak to do much for him as I had a fresh wound that still needed tending.

I nonetheless used my frame again to walk towards him. I took a throw that we normally placed on the couches and threw over him. He in turn woke up briefly and brought it up to his shoulders, a lucid indication that he had been feeling the night draft.

"Thanks baby," he said, and then went back to sleep. That seemingly innocent move, brought tears to my eyes and I let them flow unabated, as I went back to bed and continued with my sleep. It took me long to finally catch some sleep because my mind was inundated with thoughts of my vulnerable fiancé.

I woke up just after midnight with a feeling I never thought I'd experience at the time I was still healing. Martin was on top of me, all bare and about to undress me.

His incline was ready to pounce as I quickly protested. "Baby, what are you doing?" I asked, shocked to my core.

"What do you think I'm doing? It's been too long, Palesa; I can't wait any longer. Why do you think I went out drinking? It was either booze or finding another woman to sleep with. So I chose to drink instead, but I cannot hold on anymore. I want you right here and now," he declared, huffing and puffing like he had just sprinted.

In some perverse way, I felt 'special' that he chose to not cheat on me but to drink instead. So in his mind, I had to compensate him for having been a good boy, who elected to do something that was not good for him anyway, to avoid hurting me by cheating.

He kept rubbing himself against me, totally disregarding the fact that his fiancé had been instructed to not engage in anything rigorous, physical intimacy having been explicitly mentioned.

He had somewhat sobered up, even though the smell of alcohol was still very much prevalent, especially when he spoke. I was beefed by the fact that he was gearing himself up, while he was struggling to do what he wanted to do with ease.

I tightened my thighs, adamant that I would never allow him to force himself on me, more so when I was in the state I was in. As much as I had gotten accustomed to him just taking what he wanted whenever he wanted, and my life had somehow gotten used to the idea of him doing as he pleased, I was not going to allow him to do so at the time in his drunken state.

At some point in the past, I had persuaded myself to believe that there wasn't really much that was wrong with his deeds because that was what I was there for. I was his woman and people always wondered how a woman could refuse her man his conjugal rights. What was she there for then if not to please her man? That moment however, was different; I was different.

"Palesa, you don't want me to hurt you now, do you?" That sounded unerringly threatening to me. He continued trying to enter me but failed.

"Baby…please… please, remember doctor's orders. We cannot do this. Please, I'm begging you. I need to get well and not relapse; please stop this!" I pleaded.

"Which doctor are you referring to…Sister Moipolai? Don't make me laugh!" he chuckled. "Our lovemaking will never cause your back to ache and you're certainly not gonna go back to the hospital. I won't be rough, I promise and I'll examine you afterwards."

"I have heard this one before, Martin… get off please; I want to fully recover," I sobbed.

"PALESA!" he struck me across my face, hardening his tone, and leaving my whole body convulsing. He clasped my neck rigidly with both his hands, a move that felt proverbial. His wide eyes were now blistering and intimidating, while his breath was unbearable to keep inhaling, seeing as he was that close to me, chocking me. I almost threw up.

I wept, worried that I was going to cripple my back should I give in to what he was visibly not willing to give up demanding.

I pushed him off me but couldn't get far with my attempts, as he removed his hands from my neck. He then held both my hands above my head with his one hand. In his effort to lift my nightdress with his free hand, I fought hard to find more strength within me and pushed him off harder, sending him flying to the floor. He landed so hard on his side I almost felt sorry for him. I panicked and was now seriously terrified of what he might do next.

I glanced at him and realised that other than being angry, he looked spooked, eyes wide and looking intently at me, prompting me to shift focus from him. I also noticed that his hands, as he held onto the bed while trying to get up from the floor, were trembling. Perhaps that was not necessarily from my having sent him soaring until he reached the floor, but rather from whatever he had had to drink, which had caused him to also throw up.

I wanted to apologise for hurting him but my new found pride and courage prevented me from doing so. I waited to hear from him first as to what he would say in retort.

He got up from the floor and roughly took his pillows from the bed, ending the move by gazing at me in a way he had never done before. That was a bloodthirsty gape he gave me, and it terrified me, landing at my coccyx that I had just exacerbated. I knew that I would have to help myself in case I'd be battling with aches and pains. There was no way he would attend to me after what I had done to him; that much was palpable.

I experienced a spasm on my spine as well as on the area around my coccyx. Then pain on my shoulders followed. I lifted my shoulders up and down, trying hard not to move hastily. Once I had managed to lean against the headboard, I lifted my shoulders up and down again, in a circular motion.

Although that helped significantly, my lower back wouldn't budge, so I had to suck it up and tolerate the pain, all alone in the massive bedroom. My heart kept thumping as I reflected on what had just transpired. My fiancé slapped and choked me and also tried to force himself on me.

I recalled reading up about partner rape but I was not convinced that what I had just experienced was spousal rape...well, almost. I felt like it was simply a move by an inconsiderate drunk fiancé, trying his luck with me…that's it! I never thought it justifiable to call my man a rapist; he wasn't a rapist; he was just a man - a husky, healthy, yet drunk, hungry and horny man, who hadn't had sex in a couple of weeks. For him, that was very long, I mean, a really long time!

Still, the thought I had, bothered me as it seemed too familiar to a story I had read up on. In fact, it also felt akin to the first day he forced me to have sex with him; on the second day after we had met.

One might wonder what I was expecting to happen. Most men and women actually ask that question. '*How can you go to a man's house and expect him to not want sex*? *How dim-witted can one be!*?' That is a question that everyone would ask and still do. They see nothing wrong with the probe.

There I was, having been engaged and living it up, yet refusing to give my man what he considered to be his right as my man. That was a selfish act according to him, as I wanted to receive and not give anything in return. In fact, a lot of people would think that. Perhaps I was selfish to some extent, but I was still nursing myself from the injury he had caused. The on and off guilt trip I experienced was not making things easy for me and not at all sitting well within my spirit.

That night had been the first time I ever garnered some gumption to fight for my sovereignty, and as much as I was mulling over what that might have meant to Martin, I felt good about myself. I however still felt guilty and was afraid but I knew that I had every right to fight him off, what with him having had too much to drink and totally ignoring my feelings and doctors' orders.

I thought of calling my mother for help but I wasn't going to risk Martin going ballistic on me for disobeying him.

The next best thing for me to do was to pray, a conversation with Divinity I hadn't had ever since I left home. The moment felt fitting for me, and it was as if something or someone was counseling me to try conversing with my maker. That was exactly what I did, while enduring the throbbing pain on my back.

I closed my eyes while sitting up and leaning against the headboard. I kept silent for a while as I didn't really know whether to first begin my prayer by asking for forgiveness for having left home or for speaking unkindly to my mother or for hurting Martin. I then resolved to make a silent prayer, hoping that somehow I would still connect with God.

All I was able to do initially, was to weep uncontrollably until I was finally able to mumble some words out.

'*Father God, how are you today? I'm fine, I think. I know I have sinned against you. I should never have left home. Look where I am now; I am unhappy and I don't know whether I will be able to walk unaided ever again. Why did you let me come to this place? Why did you allow my father to emotionally abuse my mother and I? I would never have left had he been kinder towards me and her. I am hurting both physically, mentally and emotionally. I don't have much to show for my life. I have been under people's spell my whole life and this is not what I want for my life.*

I want so much for my life and I know that school subjects have been difficult for me. But I know there is so much I can do with my hands. I am good with my hands and I think you gave me this gift to create something from scratch with these hands. Now I need to study dressmaking but I don't know if that's what you also had in mind for me. Please make it happen. I don't know how but I really would like you to help me in this regard.

God, I want to do something for myself; I don't want to rely on anyone ever again; I want my life – the kind of life that would just consist of me and you by my side only. I am tired. I don't want to be ungrateful as I shudder to think where I would have ended had Martin not picked me up by the side of the road.

I don't know though as to whether this was your plan all along or not. If it was and still is, please know that it sucks. I am unhappy. Please God, I want to be happy; I want to study something that can be suitable for me and as I've already mentioned, I love sewing.

Lastly, please heal my back and I promise to always do right by you and not please people but please you. Okay, pleasing some people won't be such a bad thing, especially if that is your plan. I have had enough pain to last me a lifetime. I hope I haven't been disrespectful in my prayer. Amen."

I concluded my prayer still crying and my eyes still closed. I was unaware that I had been loud when I prayed and sobbed, as once I opened my eyes flooded by my tears, I saw a figure standing next to the bed, gawking at me. I got a fright but remembered that I had just prayed and was certain that God was now in charge of everything I had asked him to do for me. God was really going to protect me from whatever might befall me.

I opened my eyes a bit wider, while reaching for the pedestal to take some tissue paper from its box. I wiped my tears and realised that it was Martin standing there, bearing a daft smile and still staring at me. I fleeted a look at him and continued wiping my tears.

"Amen," he whispered.

I ignored him. What did he want me to say? Applaud him for having budged in and listened in on my prayer? Why was he standing near me like some psychopath who was about to strangle me - again? Perhaps that had been his intention but I strongly believed that my prayer might have barred him from doing anything baleful to me. That ingrained in me that indeed prayer does and did work for me.

"I'm sorry, baby for what I did earlier," he claimed.

My chest was heaving as I tried all I could to calm down. My feelings alternated between being content and happy that God had heard me, to being afraid at the same time. I would in that short space of time, chuck the fearful feeling out as I believed and still do, that nothing could ever scupper my efforts to get myself closer and closer to the universe that birthed me. I was determined and adamant that my life would and had to change from then onwards.

"Fine, apology accepted. I'm in pain, Martin. Please examine my back," I entreated, in a way trying to brave it out. I was bold and not at all about to apologise for having protected myself against maltreatment.

"I'll fetch my medical bag," he murmured, and walked out, still walking zigzag. The booze was clearly still in his system.

'What just happened here?' I asked my inner person. No

answer. Okay then, this meant that God had heard my prayer and that was really very easy, wasn't it? All I needed to do in the past months was to pray. How could I have wasted my time on earth just moaning and complaining while I made no effort to pray earnestly? Was it really over? Was I still expected by the universe to help Martin out like I had felt was my task since the day I met him? Perhaps it was still the case. Why did I have to be hurt in order for me to do what Deity wanted me to do? That surely wasn't fair! I kept lamenting in my mind and heart while I awaited Martin to come back into the room.

He walked in as I breathed heavily in and out, trying hard to compose myself. My efforts were in vain though because my heart was heaving a sigh of anxiety.

"Turn on your belly so I can see what's happening on your back," he instructed, his face stoned as if he was about to do something he didn't really want to do.

"I need a bit of time to do that. Will you help turn me on my belly?"

"Fine, hold my hands," he muttered, bearing a staid expression. I did as he instructed and he helped me to roll over. I took one of my pillows and placed it underneath my tummy, while I rested my head on the other pillow. He lifted my nightdress as I held the ends above my head with both my hands.

I heard him pull the bench closer to the bed and as he held my back, I felt a bizarre sensation; not from pain but it was cold and weird. I twitched and he stopped.

"What is it now?" he asked in a goaded tone, breath reeking of alcohol still.

"I felt a slight tingling on my back when you touched me," I responded. I felt the need to lie about what I was actually feeling. It was not from pain but it was strange energy emitting from his hands when he touched me. I still find it difficult to explain what that was.

He kept quiet, moving his fingers up and down my back up to and including my lower back. Lucas' words kept ringing in my mind. I readied myself to retaliate, in case he had sinister intentions in mind.

Once he had finished examining me, he sighed.

"Everything is fine, there is no need to worry. You simply need to start walking more and we will give your back more time to heal. You should be up and running after two more weeks at least," he ended. "I cannot give you anything for pain as it will be an overdose. Besides, you already have your medication."

"Oh I see, thank you, baby. I was getting worried," I responded softly and lovingly, while taking out the pillow underneath my belly.

As I tried to get up by myself, Martin held my hands, "I got you baby, I got you," he declared, as I shed a tear feeling the most horrendous remorse I had ever felt in my life. Perhaps I could have just allowed him a tiny bit of chance to mitigate his pull. I mean, it had been two weeks and a couple of days since I left and Martin was visibly not doing well. I went back in thought to my resolve in the beginning of our relationship, when I proclaimed within my heart that I was there to please him, as he in turn had done all he could to make my life comfortable. Why was I feeling as if the whole thing was perverse though?

"Baby…," he startled me.

"Mm," I responded, once I managed to sit upright, leaning against the headboard.

"I'm sorry for what I did. I was just not myself and I know that we should wait for you to get better. It's just that I'm not coping, Palesa..."

I interjected. "Baby, I know you're battling and I'm also sorry for hurting you. I was really trying to defend myself as it was lucid that you wanted to just force yourself on me, while I had begged you countless times to stop." He curved his eyebrows and his brow creased.

"Oh, so you were defending yourself against me? I was not going to hurt you Palesa," he snapped.

"Yes I was. Have you forgotten that you slapped and choked me, Martin, threatening me with more violence? That was certainly why I also plucked up some courage to push you off of me. You cannot keep taking and taking, while I'm still healing from the effects of what you did to me. That can't be right Martin, it can't be right."

"Okay, okay, I didn't mean for you to drag out what I did to you to this current fracas. I have apologized over and over for that, so what more do you want me to say or do?"

"You are clearly not getting this are you? This is not even about that anymore. It's about the fact that while I'm still nursing myself, you want to have sex, while Doctor Duvenhage has sternly instructed us against that. Yes, obviously how I got injured will always be a factor, and you need to make peace with the fact that it will always resurface but that doesn't mean I will hold it above your head. Just do things right and we will not have issues between us."

He lifted his hands up and quietly got up, removing the bench away from the bed. He pushed it against the wall and took his medical bag. He then quietly left our bedroom. I waited for a few minutes, hoping that he would come back into our room, as he was no longer as tipsy as he had been earlier. However, I heard him switch the foyer lights off and then closing the door. I surmised that he had retreated to the guest bedroom which I would have occupied had Sis Lulama gotten her way.

I battled to catch some sleep as I tossed and turned, wondering what was going on in his mind. As much as he had apologized, he had maintained a very emotionless expression on his face and I had to let him be. In the end, I retired after the earlier skirmish.

****

I was awoken by my cellphone vibrating on the pedestal. As I attempted to touch it in order to shut the 06h00 alarm clock off, I touched a hand instead and I knew immediately that Martin had come into the room and was about to stop the alarm clock ringing or was he? He grabbed the phone and switched the alarm clock off. He then scrolled down my phone while I forced my eyes to open. I could tell that he was a man on a mission. His moods changed in a whim.

"Morning," he greeted me after recognizing that my eyes were opening.

"Morning," I responded.

"So, you and Lucas have become buddies now and call each other in my absence!?" I fleeted a gaze and turned over slowly, covering myself with the thick comforter.

"I asked you a question, Palesa," he shrieked.

"That did not sound like a question. You're accusing me and I thought you have proof that I called Lucas. Why should I respond to assumptions?" I retorted.

Firstly, the events of the previous day were still very fresh in my mind and I still needed clarity as to where he went and why he had been drinking that much to the point where he ended up vomitting all over the place.

"Why didn't you tell me Lucas called you then?" he asked, his tone continuing to harden.

"Martin, it's early and I want to rest, please."

"Just answer this simple question then you can go back to sleep."

"I didn't tell you because you came home late and drunk. You basically didn't even know what you were doing yesterday. Do you still want me to continue?" his jaw and cheeks dropped.

"So, what did he want? What was so important that you had to talk for more than 10 minutes?" He had checked that too!

"He said he was checking on me and I told him it was not his place to do so as I have my man, whose responsibility it is to do so."

"Palesa, stop lying to me. What exactly did Lucas say to you? How did he get your phone number? Did you give it to him when you were still at the hospital?" He launched a barrage of questions, practically interrogating me as I turned back to face him.

"Baby, it's too early for this, please. I cannot believe you want us to fight so early in the morning! Whatever I tell you is going to upset you anyway, so why would you want me to tell you news that's going to make you angry?"

"Let me be the judge of that. Now tell me already!" he impatiently prompted me.

"Just help me up. I still cannot prop myself up with ease so please help me so I can sit up straight."

He pulled me sloppily by my hand and I immediately regretted asking him for help. I breathed heavily, totally immobilized by his unsettling gape.

"Okay, I'll tell you. Your friend told me that he was worried about me because 'you're a dangerous man' – his words, not mine. He also said that I should be careful of you as you are responsible for his wife's death after you had, at some point held her down on her back, injuring her the same way you did me."

Martin's face reddened and he paced up and down the room, rubbing his shaven head in a couple of strokes, similar to a person who had just heard of something earth shattering. He would, in short intervals, stop briefly and stare at me, as I ogled back, while not necessarily saying much.

He tried speaking but his voice got muffled by the anger that was now palpable from his eyes and his growling voice. He pulled the bench from where he had placed it and sat down on it, placing his hands on his head, shaking it incessantly.

"I'M GONNA KILL HIM! I'M GONNA KILL THE BASTARD! HOW DARE HE CALL MY WOMAN AND SPEW BILE ABOUT ME!?" he clinched his fists.

I played no part in trying to persuade him to calm down. I felt that I had my own demons to deal with and at that stage, my back was aching terribly, largely due to his outburst as my muscles had tensed. He looked at me intensely, slanted his head as I briefly leaned against the headboard and closed my eyes. He then laughed out loud, leaving me gobsmacked to the point where I had to open my eyes again.

"You're enjoying this, aren't you?" he scornfully asked.

"Enjoying what?"

"You enjoy seeing my friend and I fight. We had put all our differences aside and now since you met him at the hospital, we argue often and he's been very distant and you are in the midst of it all," he paused. "Do you know that we even fought after he had seen you at the hospital?"

"I know you fought. So I must bear the brunt of that fight between two grown men too? This is pathetic!"

"What did you just say?" he asked in a threatening tone. As for me on the other hand, I wouldn't let up. I was becoming more and more unyielding in taking back my power or what was left of it and defending myself at all costs.

"I said that's pathetic for two grown men to blame a defenseless young woman for their inability to control their emotions. So yeah, dress that on me too. I'll take the blame. What else are you blaming me for to make you feel better?"

He kept quiet, while I continued with my defiant approach. "Let me guess. You blame me for making you hurt me on my back. I made you hurt me, didn't I? Is there anything else?" I ended my scornful rant.

He got up from the bench and threw it across the room, lifted his clinched fist and moved hastily closer towards me as I stared at him intensely, not even knowing how I was going to defend myself. Something inside of me was steadfast in not giving away what I either was thinking or feeling. I didn't even know what that was.

"What? You want to beat me up now?" I cheekily asked, while amply aware that I was practically taunting the bloody narcissist. I admit, it was not a wise move but I did it anyway. My new found courage was sending me straight into terrifying terrain and I had to succumb to its pressure, even though that was a perilous move.

"Oh…I see you've now found some gumption to challenge me. Why would you think that I wanted to hit you? I can never do that to you."

Oh no…, he didn't just say that! Of course he wanted to hit me. He had slapped me before – twice! In fact, I knew that he must have harboured the thought to give me a serious beating for a while now, but something was preventing him from doing so.

"What am I supposed to think if you clinched your fist like that and then lifted it up as if you were going to put it to good use? You literally charged at me Martin and I've seen this before; the day you injured me on my back. Look now, I might not even be able to walk unaided as a result."

"So, you're gonna bring that up each time we have a disagreement huh?"

"We're not having a disagreement. You accused me of things I have no knowledge of and then got upset when I defended myself against your unfairness towards me."

"Baby, I would never hit you. I'm sorry if you thought I was going to do that. I also didn't mean to yell or to accuse you of anything," he paused. "You just make me angry sometimes and you need to use your head and stop allowing people to come between us like this. As to why you indulged Lucas for such a long time, beats me!"

That sounded like an insult. That wouldn't be the first time someone had called me stupid though. At least he was insinuating that I was…'*you have to use your head*', and being somewhat tactful. My father and some of my teachers had blatantly called me stupid - many times.

"Yes, you meant to accuse me. I just wish you can take responsibility for your actions. Please leave me alone; I want to rest." I boldly responded as I continued, "I cannot believe you're making me a scapegoat for all of this nonsense going on between you and Lucas. I'm getting sick and tired of how you treat me. I have done nothing to deserve this Martin, nothing!" I blurted out my misgivings hurriedly and slid down the comforter, turning my back away from him and covered myself up to my head.

I heard by the sound of his footsteps, that he was moving closer towards the bed. He eventually sat down on the bed, near my upper body, flipped the comforter off my head and stroked me on my face. I held on, as I tried hard to dispel the brief feeling of terror I had again, while I continued to fake boldness.

"So? What did you say after Lucas told you such blatant lies about me?"

"I don't care whether what he told me were lies or not. In fact, I told him to also stop calling me. I actually have a good mind of going home with my mother. I'm stressed out and cannot take this anymore!"

"Baby, come on now. You don't really believe what this lunatic said do you? No scrap that! Earlier you said you know Lucas and I fought. Who told you? Was it Lulama or did he tell you that?"

"It doesn't matter who told me or what I believe about you and Lucas. All I want is for your friend to leave me alone. If I get a phone call, I will answer it obviously not knowing who would be on the other end. At the time Lucas called, I didn't know it would be him on the line. It's not like we call each other. I think you're making a mountain out of a molehill and totally out of line for accusing me of such," I ended my tirade, feeling really good about myself for having stood up to him.

"I see you garnered some guts to talk back at me. Do you intend leaving me anytime soon? Do you want to leave me, Palesa? You better tell me now what your plans are," he demanded.

"I don't have any intentions of leaving, Martin. I just want to be where I won't be stressed." He chuckled mockingly after my statement.

"You're making me laugh honestly. You think going home with your mom won't be stressful? I recall you scolding her not so long ago about your father pretending to have turned over a new leaf! Now you want to go there and 'rest'? Please be serious about your life. You will be back here in a day or two! I've given you a good life and just because we have issues here and there, you now think you have to leave!" he looked up and shook his head once more.

I felt so sheepish after Martin dished out some harsh truths, reminding me of my situation back home, of life that was not ideal. I don't even know why I thought I could somewhat crow about my home being a sanctuary. He knew just what to say, to persuade me to rethink my stance and to take whatever he threw at me. I kept quiet and elected to continue resting.

What could I have said in rejoin? He was right. I was the unwanted child and my parents were simply displaying their guilt because I had left to find asylum somewhere else. Irrespective of how galling Martin was most of the time, I still believed that he was right on the money, on his advice to never think of leaving him because I would be worse off if I went home.

"I'll leave you to rest but don't ever speak to Lucas again…please!" he entreated, ending the demand with a strained 'please'.

"Have you not been listening to me just now? The man called me not the other way round."

"I heard what you said. Next time, if there is going to be any next time, when you hear that it's him on the line, just shut the phone off. Do you understand what I'm saying, Palesa?"

"Fine," I responded concisely.

I was beginning to get seriously goaded and tired of the back and forth yak between us. All I needed was to sleep. He then left me after my brief response to him, chuckling and pleased to have rattled me out of the thought of ever leaving him.

Chapter 14

Flabbergasted by rejection

Saturday didn't start out well, what with Martin having made himself a saint at my expense, to such an extent that I had to concede to things I was not happy about!

I finally woke up leisurely at around 09h30. The weather was blissful and birds were chirping. I noted that Martin was back in our bedroom and had opened our curtains wide; heedless of whether I sought to sleep in or not. Perhaps he did but typical of him, he probably wanted to 'punish' me for having had a conversation with Lucas, not even knowing whether I had revealed full details of that banter or not.

The sun sharply kissed my face as soon as I uncovered myself to somehow acknowledge his presence in the room. I didn't know how to act in the morning as there was so much tension one could cut with a blunt knife. Martin was making a lot of unnecessary racket, opening cupboards and then closing them hard. He would at times, sing loudly, pulling the bathroom bench and purposefully beat it against the wall. I could tell it was intentional because we both hardly made such a clamor with the bench as it was not in the way for anyone to have to trip all over it like that.

He wasn't really talking to me and our room was filled with too much silence of things we had left unsaid. The stillness was just too loud for my liking. I missed his voice, his attention and even his rebuke for one thing or another. Messed up isn't it? When I gaped at him, he'd look down and I found myself doing the same thing. We played this game for a while.

I had no idea how to approach him as his stoic resignation and unfathomable expression got blasted all over his face. I got up from bed leisurely, while inwardly hoping that he would say something to me, at least to ask me to be careful as I got up. He ignored me, while doing something unclear. I slowly walked to the bathroom and he stayed behind in the room. I took my time to take a shower, worried sick that I might slip and hurt myself, while trying to avoid asking for his help.

I felt that perhaps the time had come for me to stop asking for help anyway, but to start learning to do things for myself and by myself. I didn't know how long I had left at the house and whether

I'd still be okay, what with my back continuing to hurt that much, to the point that out of the blue, I'd feel a horrendous spasm which would come and go.

Getting out of the bathroom after applying all my lotions, having wrapped myself with a towel, I was pleasantly surprised to realize that Martin had made the bed, neater than Sis Lulama or I would sometimes do. That gratified me and instinctively, I walked towards him as he was about to leave the room and hugged him from behind, clasping my arms firmly around his waist.

"Baby, I'm sorry for upsetting you," I stated.

"That's fine," he responded briefly, while I continued embracing him. He seemed unmoved by my sincerity and heartfelt apology. I waited for a few minutes to hear whether he would say anything else after his pithy response. He just stood still, obviously waiting for me to disentangle my hands from his waist. I took some time before I could do so and he did something I had not expected. He hotly unclasped my hands and turned around, looking at me intensely.

"I said it's fine, Palesa," he alleged, his face and tone dry and nonchalant. I panicked and I even thought of using my sex appeal to get him to at least be warmer towards me. I didn't know what else I could say or do to have him talk to me, even if it was in short gaps. My heart couldn't take what appeared to be rejection of my apology, even though he had told me that it was fine, whatever he meant! He never mentioned that he forgave me as that was what I longed for.

I unwrapped my towel and let it fall down, snaked my arms around his waist and brought him closer towards me. He jerked backwards, startling me.

"Thank you for making the bed, baby," I said lovingly but he kept quiet as I continued, "baby, I don't like it when we fight; worse of all, about people who aren't even here with us nor are they part of our relationship. Please talk to me." He sustained his gape and bent down, picking up the towel and handing it to me.

"Get dressed, Palesa; you cannot expose your wound to the breeze, even though it's not really cold. Turn around let me see."

I turned around and let him have a look, somewhat chuffed that at least he still cared. '*Oh, come on Palesa; he's just doing what his job expects of him. He took a Hippocratic Oath. So this is just a doctor at work. Don't overthink this because you'll be disappointed.*' How dare my inner person resurface to just taunt me and burst my bubble like that!

"You're fine, but I'll dress it because this bandage is wet. You could have asked for help but I guess your lifeless pride prevented you from calling me." There he was, the man I was longing for. I must have had a warped spirit to long for such a natter from him. At that stage however, I would have accepted anything, as long as he was talking to me.

"Baby, I'm sorry. I thought you were still upset with me so I didn't want to bother you. It's not that I was too proud to ask for help," I pouted. "Are you just going to let me stand like this next to you, as bare as I am, practically giving you what you need?"

"Lie on the bed, Palesa. I'll get my bag," he instructed, ignoring what I said. No baby; nothing! That embarrassed me and I felt the sting of rejection. Now I knew how he must have felt after I refused him what he believed he was entitled to all the time, everytime, anytime.

My eyes and jaw dropped as I hastily moved towards the bed with my tail tucked in. I was feeling a bit better on my back though. It had appeared that I was healing quicker than I had anticipated. But then again, I had already stayed at the hospital for a while, as I underwent a number of exercises. The operation had been billed to be major but my body was handling it fairly well. Despite that though, the two days after I got back to the house, had felt like I never left, with added stress of course!

Martin came back to find me having already placed a cushion underneath my belly, exposed and inwardly hoping that he'd realize my intentions. He simply took a small coverlet from the divan and threw it on my behind as he started examining me. He wasn't saying anything else but kept on examining me, touching the wound briefly. The move left me feeling humiliated and it even felt like I suddenly didn't know him at all. He never even gave in to the smooching opportunity I was presenting to him.

I had never felt so guilty like I did that day, and affirmed inwardly that everything I was experiencing had been my fault because I didn't have to throw him off with that vigour at night. I could have just allowed him his moment and then deal with whatever repercussions there would be afterwards, if there would be any.

I conceded to taking on the metal that was not meant for me. I realized instantly that I had landed in the burly arms of a man whose metal had never been truly tested. I was probably the first person to ever do so.

That epiphany frightened me as much as I felt some kind of warped gratification. I knew that I'd spend time with my fiancé tiptoeing around him and trying by all means not to trouble him, lest I endanger my somewhat good life. I had to persist on speaking to him, if not to get him to be warmer towards me, perhaps to even reproach me about one thing or another.

No one knew the conflict I was having inwardly. Neither sis Lulama nor my mother, whose visit had become ethereal, knew that I was grappling with many thoughts and feelings, each wanting to rule others.

When Martin was done examining me, he carefully removed the wet dressing and it came off easily with a slight sting. I could feel him gently wiping my back and around the waist with a cotton wool. He then put a fresh dressing on.

"All done; you can get dressed," he said and got up from the bench.

"Baby," I called out.

"What is it?" he responded, irritable as ever.

"Baby, please talk to me. I miss you." I didn't even know what to say to him; I simply wanted to break the ice.

"I'm talking to you now, Palesa. What do you want me to say?"

"Okay...have you got plans for today? I was hoping to spend time with you and perhaps we can talk."

"Yes, I have plans. I'll be leaving in an hour. What do you want to talk about?" he brusquely asked, his brow creasing, showing signs of petulance.

"I would like us to please talk about what happened last night. Can you at least favour me with a few minutes of your time?" I begged, as I turned around, removing the cushion from underneath my belly and sat up straight.

"I don't know what more you want me to say to you, Palesa. You know that I went to work and then I couldn't come straight home. So, I went to drink with my buddies or you have a problem with me going out with my friends?" he dared me for a response.

"Baby, why are you really upset with me? Is it because I refused to sleep with you last night or is it because Lucas called me?" I asked frankly.

"You're the one that keeps bringing Lucas' name up, when you promised me just very early this morning that you will never mention that name in my house again. See, you're looking for a fight and I'm not gonna give you one."

"I don't recall saying those words exactly, but all I need is for you to let me know why you're so flippant with me?"

"I'm not indifferent; I have a lot on my mind and I can't really share with you because you wouldn't even understand, even if I were to tell you." My eyebrows lifted involuntarily.

"Since when do we hide things from each other?" I was baffled.

He made it sound like I was useless and had nothing material to contribute to his life. That was the first time I ever felt strange around the man. He had always tried to be somewhat modest in his reproach or even his scorn of me. But now, my intuition started working at an alarming speed. I believed that someone had encroached on my territory and I shuddered to think who that was or to believe that to be the truth. The way he was behaving towards me though, gave me a strong sense that I might not have been off the mark.

In my mind, my back issue had made him lose interest in me as I might no longer be able to do things I used to do and there was a chance that I might not even be able to live my life free of ailments here and there. Cold sweat dripped unrestrained on my temple and behind my ears. I shivered as I thought of the opulence I was enjoying. I rebuked myself because to my mind, as a person who lacked, I had to stop being stubborn and simply let Martin be, so he wouldn't leave me.

Thoughts that I had before of leaving at some point, were wiped out of my mind and the only one that remained was the one of fighting for my relationship. So whatever I was going to do, I persuaded myself that it would be good for me; really good, irrespective of whether I'd be damaging my back if I were to push myself harder or not.

I paused, thoughts of being chased out now plaguing my mind, so much that I was beginning to get seriously sick as Martin startled me out of those lingering thoughts.

"Since the day you decided to give Lucas your phone number, and not even tell me anything about it," he angrily held, as I got alarmed by his hard stance, worried over what might happen. That was his response to my question of when we started having secrets.

"Baby, I asked you to forgive me for speaking to Lucas. To be honest I have no idea where he got my number from. I suspect he was given by sister Moipolai."

"Why does she have your number?" he probed further.

"She might have taken it from my file, I cannot be sure. Baby, please stop interrogating me like this. You're scarring me when you're like this." His eyes had become mottled and his mean streak had reappeared, after I hadn't seen it in a while. I put on my gown while still sitting on the bed.

"ONE OTHER THING, YOU WILL NEVER DO WHAT YOU DID TO ME LAST NIGHT AGAIN! YOU GOT THAT ONE PASS ONLY AND THAT'S ALL YOU'RE EVER GONNA GET. REPEAT THAT, YOU'LL BE SORRY!" he threatened me, while charging towards me and pointing a finger at me, his eyes blazing.

I froze and my stomach coiled, as my inner being continued to be undecided about what exactly it was that had just happened and what it was I was willing to take and how much of it I could take.

One moment, I'd feel hurt that he was ignoring me. The next I'd want him to speak to me, even if it was to admonish me. However, when he did chide me, I would experience a bloodcurdling sensation deep inside the pit of my stomach, and I'd avow that I needed to leave him. It was like I had no control over my emotions because what occupied my essence, was a good life I was living and to never think of doing anything to jeopardise that. I would become strong and weak at the same time. Reality soon made its presence felt.

"Baby, there's no need for you to threaten me. I just needed…" he interjected, as I was trying to explain myself.

"SHUT UP!" he howled. He had never said that to me ever since we'd been together. Why was he now treating me like I was some street kid that didn't even have a home? Then again, he did find me on the street, dawdling about, not even knowing where I was going.

Even though he had met my parents, it was apparent that he didn't find it prudent to respect them nor the fact that I had a family that I could go to, should things go awry between us. Tears ran down my cheeks like rain flowing from the roof gutters. My whole body quivered and I was now soaking wet with sweat, not from heat but from fright – well, perhaps heat ignited sweat anyway. He sat down on the settee and faced my way.

"You see what you've just made me do, Palesa! You're trying to turn me into something I'm not. I better get out of here before I do something I will regret."

He flipped his hands and got up from the chair, heading towards the door. He opened it and got out, thumping it hard. That was his house, so why would one do that to his own property?

Martin left me on the bed weeping, totally confused about what happened. Despite my fervent apologies regarding having spoken to Lucas, he seemed to have not been moved by my sincerity. I deduced that there could have been something else that was bothering him; that had gotten him so rattled to the point that he had become brutal in his utterances towards me.

I got up from the bed and walked towards the closet, flipping through my clothes and eventually taking out my pink tracksuit as well as some light pink discreet socks. The slight movement that I was making was not aggravating my back as I walked about in the bedroom, unaided by the frame I frequently utilised.

I then got dressed slowly, bending to put my socks on. I was elated that I didn't experience pain after the move, but sat down to rest. After about ten minutes or so, I got up again from bed pulling my feet towards the shoe rack in the dressing room. I searched for my pink and white Geox sneakers – my favourite, bought by my mother during one of her travels. I put them on without sitting, while careful not to overstress my back.

I then moved towards the bedroom but this time, I walked a bit faster than before.

Once I reached the middle of the room, I lifted my legs up and down in separate intervals, gratified that my health was improving. I was trying to do some aerobics; moves I had seen on TV.

The idea was to go downstairs by myself, so I could have a frank conversation with my mother, who was implausibly quiet. I wondered as to whether she really did come to look after me or she actually needed to get away from my father and his sister in order to have some peace – well, sort of. Either way, she had gotten it because she had no idea what her daughter had just endured. I was adamant not to let her know either.

I cast my eyes towards my frame at the corner and elected to leave it behind. I was still adamant that I'd be able to manage descending the stairs. How was I going to utilize it to descend the stairs anyway? I took the first step, holding onto the balustrade, then the next, then the next. I was surprised to have reached the foot of the stairs without a slight pang.

Then I walked towards the kitchen. There was no one in the kitchen, or in the open plan living area. I thought of calling out to check as to whether someone would hear me, so that they could at least be aware that I was downstairs, in case I needed any assistance.

However, I recalled my resolve that I wanted to start doing things for myself and by myself, so I could manage my life in my own way. I do not recall hearing the car being revved so in my mind, Martin could have still been in the house and perhaps in his study, as I did not really check on him when I left the bedroom.

I opened the fridge in my bid to make myself something to eat, taking out two containers that had some ham and mozzarella in one and sliced tomatoes and red onions in the other one. I carefully walked back to the middle of the kitchen and placed the containers on the countertops.

Just as I was about to take a plate out, I felt a spasm on my shoulder blades, which then quickly extended to my spine. It appeared quickly and then disappeared the same way. I panicked and quickly left everything on the counter, hastily moving towards the living room. I wanted to call out to someone but noticed that in my excitement to do things by myself, I left my phone in the bedroom.

Once I reached the couches, I sat down and felt that horrible sting again, which now extended to my thighs. I took it in my stride and drew my breath. I pulled one of the ottomans and carefully lifted my legs up until I was able to place them on it. As much as the ache wasn't abating, it was not getting worse but was simply steady.

The guest room we had accommodated my mother in was not far from the lounge and I figured that sooner or later, she'd come out. From my tangential view, I saw the door to the room being opened and my mother appeared leisurely. Evidently she had not expected anyone to be seated in the lounge, least of all her daughter, whom she hadn't seen in at least two days.

She rushed towards me after noticing that I wasn't really moving. I had leaned against the couch's backrest and had placed a cushion behind my lower back.

"Palesa! I haven't seen you in a couple of days. Is everything alright? How did you get down here?" Mama asked, and I had to respond quickly as I was truly relieved that at least there was someone in the house that could help me with my troubles. I felt really dreadful for having been unkind towards her, while all she was doing was to protect me from what she had clearly felt in her spirit to be impending danger to me.

"Mama, I came down by myself. But now, I do feel some pain on my back. I guess it was to be expected though."

"Why didn't you call for help? If not from me, then from this Lulama helper of yours?" I chortled briefly as I realised that my mom hadn't quite warmed up to sis Lulama still.

"Mama, I just wanted to do things by myself this time around; I'm tired of depending on people." She raised her eyebrows.

"Where is Martin?"

"I don't know where he is, Mama," I shrugged, while it was becoming difficult to stop the droplets of tears that were threatening to flood my cheeks.

"Please don't cry, Palesa. Whatever it is, all is going to be okay. Did you have a fight?"

"Yes, Mama we did. I'm scared mama; I am really scared. I know I have pretended to be strong but definitely not this time."

My mom's brow crumpled and she eventually sat down near me, as I struggled to face her because with any slight move, I would feel pain. I also felt mortified after I had practically bragged about Martin to her and even protected him.

"What do you mean you are scared, Palesa? Did this man hurt you?"

"Yes mama, I mean, not really mama but…, let's forget about it." My mother, showing signs of agitation, clinched both her fists, released one of them and held my chin.

"Palesa, you are going to stop doing this right now. I didn't come all the way from Mookodi Township to leave you behind. I have told your father that I would bring you home and that is still my intention. If you want to go home with me now, just say the word and you do not even have to pack anything because we might waste time."

"Mama, are you saying I should run away?"

"Yes, why not? I can see that you are being abused here and you might not have admitted it to me, but I'm your mother. This lavish lifestyle you have now become accustomed to, is clouding your judgment and you think you have to tolerate it because we cannot give you what Martin can and has given you."

I faced down, now allowing tears to fall unabated as she continued. "This might be the truth but at the end of the day, you are our child and we love you. You do recall that your father wanted you to come home and he apologized, remember?"

"Mama, I hear all the things you are saying," I sobbed. "It took

Papa seeing me being cared for by someone else, for him to acknowledge me and to accept me for what and how God made me. Also Mama, had he not been sick, I doubt he would have made that apology."

"Come now Palesa, you cannot still be holding a grudge. We are all human and we make mistakes. What if that was his moment of reckoning and that, he had to get ill for him to finally realize his errors?"

"I cannot be sure of that Mama and I don't even have the assurance that Papa won't subject me to even more ridicule now that I am practically incapacitated."

"Palesa, you are not incapacitated. You've managed to come down by yourself now, haven't you? Besides, I don't think your father will do that. He has changed; I promise."

"Mama, I doubt that. Ever since you came here, he hasn't asked to speak to me. Why is that?" My mom shrugged, bemused by my questions.

"Palesa, you are asking way too much of your father. He is relying on me to tell him how you are and I have been doing that. So, stop trying to create excuses as to why you cannot come home with me."

I shook my head in disbelief, because as much as my mother's heart may have been in the right place, that pledge she gave me could not have been well thought out. I was dogged in my stance of not believing that there was even a slight possibility that my father had changed for real and that he would never be unkind and abusive towards me and even to her for that matter. Although there was conflict in my heart, I was frightened to stay behind, not knowing what mood my fiancé would come back in.

"Mama, can you please go to our bedroom right now before somebody comes and fetch my cellphone, as well as my small brown overnight bag. Please just see what you can put in that bag; a few clothes would do. Please also get my vanity case and my handbag..., I mean your handbag. The one you gave me.

"Pale..., why should I fetch all these things, ngwanaka (my child)?" My heart thumped really hard against my chest. The moment had finally come; I could no longer hide the truth from her and I had to come clean.

"Mama, I am terrified. I saw something in Martin earlier that distressed me. It wasn't just him being his difficult self or yelling at me, but I saw something evil in his eyes. It was as if something else had taken over his body, mama. It was also palpable that he was trying to compose himself but now and then that monster would resurface. He even nearly hit me," I wept as my mom tried all she could to help me calm down and to stop crying. I didn't see the need to tell her that on two occasions, Martin did slap me.

"I'm so sorry to hear this Pale..., I'm really, really sorry. Come here...," she held me against her chest and for once in a really long time, I felt as if all my troubles would be over. "Come now Pale... don't cry like this...shh shh shh..." I pulled myself together; only just.

"Mama, please make it snappy. Just get those things from the bedroom and then come put them in the guestroom. If someone finds you upstairs, you can just tell them that I asked you to fetch the stuff because there was no one in the house to help me and I want to sleep with you tonight."

"Bathong! (Good heavens!) Palesa, I'm getting a bad feeling about this. Why did you keep quiet this long, that your life was in danger? Was this how your back got injured? Did Martin do this to you?" I simply nodded as my chest kept heaving and releasing weeping seizures.

The shrewd expression from my mother's face told all stories of the world. She didn't even respond after I had admitted to having had my back injured by my fiancé. Her eyes dropped, full of tears and her lips trembled and parted involuntarily.

She got up, took a few steps towards the stairs and stood near the foot. She then took one look at me and asked, "Are you sure about this, Palesa?"

"Yes Mama, I'm sure. Please hurry. We will make a plan regarding when we are going to leave. I need my phone because I think I am going to need help if I have to leave here in one piece." She let out an unidentifiable sound and slanted her head briefly.

"I thought we would be leaving together? Do you think I'd leave you behind?"

"Trust me mama, it would be safer for you to leave me behind. In fact, I think you might have to leave tonight still. I will give you cell phone numbers of the people you might have to call to ask for help. I do not trust the police because Martin seems to have friends all over the place, the bulk of whom I haven't even met and probably never will, unless we get married."

"Don't tell me you still consider marrying the guy after what you've just told me about him?"

"No mama, I'm not saying that. Please hurry," I cannily changed the subject.

Mama then ascended the stairs hurriedly and I heard her pulling her breath hard as she climbed up. Eventually her steps faded. My heart could not stop beating fitfully and I even felt my intestines twist, menacing a tummy ache. She took a bit of time in the bedroom, almost 20 minutes long and it was after this estimated time, that I heard some movement on the stairs. I knew that it was her and she was hurrying so much I was even afraid that she might miss a step and roll down.

She appeared, having carelessly packed my unzipped overnight bag and she had my handbag's sling around her neck, while carrying my slippers and cellphone with her other hand. The sight of my mother frightened, even looking above her shoulder, while running towards me gave me the chills. I experienced an eerie feeling and a bad episode of migraine on my left side ensued, so bad that I instantly felt nauseous. Fortunately, the nausea subsided quickly.

"Mama, please rush to the guestroom and put the clothes in the closet. Is there anyone upstairs? I never checked the last time."

"I don't know Palesa, but I felt some movement from the other room and I also had a strange feeling that I was being watched. My whole shoulders were very heavy as I kept flipping through your clothes," she proclaimed, widening her eyes. She was visibly terrified as I became spooked by the revelation too. I involuntarily closed my eyes and inwardly prayed for our safety against whatever it was, that both my mother and I were sensing.

"Mama, what do you mean exactly?"

"I don't even know what I'm saying, Palesa but I'm telling you now, we are not alone and it's starting to feel as if there's a creepy presence in this house. I say it's time we get out of here!"

"Mama, in that case I think you should leave alone. Whatever is happening here is for me to deal with, one way or another. I cannot allow you to become a casualty of my foolishness. Please pack your bags, Mama and leave; I'm begging you. When you reach home, you can then tell Papa and the others what you observed. Hopefully, my cousins still care about me and they will come with some muscles to get me out of here…well, I hope, particularly since none of them have bothered to seek me out."

"What were you expecting Palesa? You changed your numbers and left everyone behind, wondering what had happened to you. Anyway, there is no way I'm leaving you behind. Forget it!"

"Mama please…," I paused. "You have to do that, I'm begging you. Please stop wasting time."

"No, Palesa! I'm not leaving you here. If anything bad has to befall you, it has to come through me first to reach you. I am not leaving you here. Just let me catch my breath first. I'll rest a bit in the room but I'm not going anywhere, unless you're coming with me. We have to think this through, especially since we don't even know who is outside at this time or where they are. Why isn't Lulama in here? Has she been to see you at all?"

"No mama, she hasn't come to see me today, which is really odd. What if Martin told her not to come to me, practically forcing me to do what I have just done today? Perhaps he's trying some kind of tough love with me."

"Lord help me! Palesa, are you nuts? After everything you have just told me, you still view this whole warped situation of yours as some kind of love? Tough love – really?"

"Yes Mama, I'm now beginning to feel that way. Maybe I'm confused I don't know…," I shrugged and attempted to get up from the chair.

My mother shook her head and pulled her breath really hard. She gaped at me intently, while I dropped my eyes bashfully.

"Why are you trying to get up now? Where are you going?" she asked.

"That pain has disappeared, Mama but now I want to go make myself a sandwich, as I wanted to do so earlier before I experienced this spasm."

"Sit down Palesa; I will make it for you. Before I forget, here's your cellphone." My mom handed the cellphone to me and she quickly walked towards the kitchen, revealing a satisfied feeling on her face. It was as if she knew that the day would come when I'd perhaps come to my senses and admit that being at Martin's hadn't been a wise decision on my part.

"I supported myself against the couch's back rest. As I still comprehended what my mother and I had just been through in a measly twenty to thirty minutes or so, my phone vibrated. I noticed that it was Martin calling. An involuntary smile and satisfaction engulfed me as I also wondered where it emanated from.

"Hi baby," I answered lovingly.

"Where are you?" he asked wryly, without even acknowledging my affectionate greeting.

"I'm downstairs baby, why do you ask?"

"I'm asking because I can't see you in our room. I have installed cameras in there so I can keep an eye on you, in case something happens."

Martin told on himself without realizing it, and without any slight provocation from me. Perhaps he did want me to know that his eyes were hovering over me all the time, irrespective of where he could be at any given time. Whatever his reasons were, I felt naked and violated with that revelation. It was blatant that he was never going to let me leave without any fight. What were the cameras in the bedroom for, really? I didn't ask but elected to simply utilize my God given power to establish what on earth his motives were and how I could usurp them.

"I'm downstairs on the couches."

"So, you're not gonna give me a hard time about why I put cameras in our bedroom? That's the first," he mocked.

"No, I'm not," I replied.

"You're not even going to ask where I am now?" He sounded puzzled that I was not giving him what he wanted – attention and playing the inept game. I was no longer interested because, he would always win in the end, particularly after his threats and I would be left with egg on my face for trying to assert myself. All I wanted to do, was to remember the clout I had, the power of staying in my feminine lane so I could finally win back my autonomy.

"No, I'm not going to ask you where you are. You left the way you did, having spoken to me in the manner you did. So it's okay; this is your house and I suppose you are at liberty to do whatever you want. All I want is to get better so I can see what to do with my life," I blurted out. What did I just do?

"Now, you're just being dramatic! You made me angry with this Lucas thing and I snapped. You know that I love you and I will never hurt you," he shamelessly stated.

"Fine," I briefly responded.

"Since you're not interested in asking me about my whereabouts, let me tell you where I am. I think you're gonna love my surprise, you'll see!"

I felt an inkling to "whatever" him but decided otherwise. I thought I should remain calm and get to understand what he was going on about. His tone had changed in a way, not as hard as earlier in the room.

"I'm bringing you something you're going to love. You'll see," he paused. "By the way, I saw that your mother was in our bedroom. Since you told me that you are downstairs now, I take it she went in to fetch things you might need while you're still down there, right?"

"Yes, you're right."

In some twisted way, I enjoyed toying with his feelings as I never let him in on what my thoughts were. Two can play the game, can't they? I amused myself. Didn't I just tell my mother that I was afraid of the man? My mind kept playing tricks on me. I was getting way too comfortable playing the dangerous game with Martin. One moment we'd fight and he'd threaten me and the next moment, I'd sulk, while inwardly shoving guilt within his heart so he would apologise.

My mother however, was frightened for my life and for hers no doubt, chiefly after I had told her about all that Martin had subjected me to. However, staying or leaving the place would be my decision and not hers.

"You don't sound so good baby, are you now the one who's upset? Don't be. All I needed was some time away from the house so I can calm down. So, there is no longer a need for this stone-cold attitude you have. We are going to be okay; you'll see."

"I'm not being cold; I just don't want to talk a lot because I'm only now going to eat. Sis Lulama still hasn't come in so I had to come downstairs to make myself a sandwich. I'm gonna have to cut the call now, as my mother has made me some food and she's coming now. Bye, Martin."

I cut the call immediately after that, realizing that my mother was about to reach me. The back and forth conversation between Martin and I had irked me anyway, and I was not going to indulge him any further. As much as I knew that, it was a bad move, I didn't care. I was hoping that by the time he finally came back home, he'd have calmed down as he proclaimed.

"Was that Martin?" my mother asked as soon as she reached me.

"Yes mama, it was him," I replied.

"Did he threaten you again?"

"No Mama, he didn't. I just wanted to attend to the food as I saw you approaching; hence I elected to cut the call." My mother gave me a deliberate look while shaking her head in the process. I dropped my eyes, unable to face her. She nonetheless gave me half a smile.

"Palesa, here's your sandwich. Please eat as it's already almost lunch time and you still haven't taken your medication."

"Thank you, Mama. I will eat and then have my medication afterwards. The problem now is that I left the paperback that the medication is in, in the bedroom. I will see what to do after eating though."

"Good grief, Palesa!" Mama chuckled. "I've just come back from your bedroom a few minutes ago, it's not like I will get lost.

So, I will get your tablets."

I became apprehensive after she said that, recalling that Martin asked what my mother was doing in our bedroom and that he had installed cameras in there, the gadgets I hadn't even noticed ever since I got to his place. Now her going for the second time would have seemed suspicious. I had to come up with a reason why it wouldn't be necessary for her to go again.

"Mama, it's not necessary for you to go again to our bedroom. I'm certain sis Lulama will be here anytime soon and she will fetch them," I mentioned hurriedly, as Mama widened her eyes. I took a wet dish cloth from the tray and wiped my hands and began eating the ham, cheese and tomato sandwich that my mom made me. She had also added the creamy sweet chilli sauce I loved.

As I continued gnawing into the bread, I felt mama's eyes poking through my head. I continued eating and drinking some tea she had placed on the moving table tray, which she had now wheeled towards my right side.

"Palesa, I don't like what you're doing. What is going on? Don't even think of lying to me. What did Martin say when he called you just now?" She wasn't going to accept anything but the truth.

"Okay Mama, I'll tell you. Just let me swallow first before I choke," I faked a cough.

"Do you think this is funny? You know, I sometimes wonder if you are really okay. Just a few minutes ago, you practically begged me to fetch your things and promised to leave with me. Now you're hiding something from me - again. What's gotten into you exactly?"

"Nothing, mama… really. He asked me where I was because he didn't see me in our bedroom. He then told me that he had cameras installed. So he saw that you had been to our bedroom." After mentioning this to my mother, I saw beads of sweat instantly form on her forehead, indicating her distress.

"Mama, please don't be afraid. That man is clearly crazy."

"This is all the more reasons we should leave, Palesa. Why does it seem like you're not taking this seriously? Do you want to leave this place in a body bag?"

"No, mama. I don't think Martin really intends hurting me. It's just that he sometimes fails to control his emotions so he takes it out on me. But he's not a bad man; otherwise he wouldn't have picked me up from the side of the road and gave me a home."

My intentions were now clear with what I had intimated to my mother. I wanted to make her feel guilty for having played a role in me leaving home, lending in the hands of a Knight, who later gave me a life of opulence, albeit riddled with all kinds of nuances that left me wanting to flee at times, as well as needing to stay on in order to help him heal from whatever his spirit was ailing from.

That was a huge saddle for a girl who was almost 20 years old to carry. Once again, I believed that I was brought to Martin's place for a valid reason.

He did love me in his own way and I had learnt to love him

too, even though I didn't know if that was love I was displaying, or I had felt the need to thank him forever for having saved me from danger or from myself. He was an older man though and he should have been able to deal with life's woes better than he was. Either way, the decision to leave or stay, wasn't an easy one to make.

"Palesa, Palesa! You're giving me a headache. You need to make up your mind and stick to it. Are you coming with me or staying?" My mom's edginess was hard piercing.

I wasn't even able to respond when I heard cars hooting outside. It did sound like more than one car and then another one being revved constantly. The sound of that pipe was unfamiliar. I didn't know what to do and both my mother and I just sat there, even though my mom moved slightly from the sofa. She wanted to go outside to check what the commotion was about.

I simply continued eating as I wouldn't have managed to get up quickly anyway, seeing as I had to keep nursing myself. As my mom finally stood up, the front door coming into the lounge where we were seating, was flung open. I hadn't even realised that it had been unlocked.

Martin came in, eyes wide and bearing a wide grin.

"Hi baby," he greeted me. I noted that he ignored my mother.

"Hi baby," I responded.

He walked towards me and leaned down to kiss me. I responded. I thought he was just going to give me a normal peck. He calculatingly gave me an enduring kiss, as I gave him signs of discomfort. I was eating after all and my mouth was still full of remnants of bread and everything else I was eating. He then stopped while still holding my chin, and then he gave me a forehead kiss.

"We have to go outside if you're up for it. I bought you something huge. Unfortunately, I cannot bring it inside the house."

As I pondered on what that could be, Sis Lulama, came in via the kitchen door, making a noise and looking akin to a child that had just been given ice cream.

"Sorry Ms Palesa, for leaving you alone. It's Doc's fault. I was coming into the house when he practically kidnapped both Mos and I to accompany him to…" She could not complete her statement as Martin gave her a pithy look and hushed her immediately.

"Lulama, you're not going to do that. How can you even think of upstaging me like this? Just stand there and make sure that my baby gets up from her chair without any hassles."

The poor woman faced down, visibly embarrassed but quickly recovered. It was just a day ago, when she was very brave, talking however she liked to and about Martin. Now, I sensed weirdness between the two of them. She suddenly went back to being the respectful employee. Something was amiss!

"Apologies, Mrs Ditheko. I'm just excited so much today and I have even neglected to greet you. How are you this morning…?" She checked her time, which was now after eleven.

"I can see you are all excited, Lulama. Dumela le wena Martin ("Hello to you too Martin"); I wonder what has gotten everyone so excited to the point that you don't even greet me."

I could sense that Martin was deliberately ignoring my mother, as he didn't even respond after her little swipe about the greetings. He merely directed his full attention towards me, which somehow made me feel good. I felt the need to ask Martin to acknowledge my mom and to greet her at least, even if it was not something he wanted to do. I decided to let it go, just so I wouldn't spoil his sudden blissful mood.

"I'm still eating and I won't be able to walk fast as you all know. I wonder what's going on outside. Is the surprise for me?" I asked.

"Baby, stop asking questions. Yes, the surprise is for you. Are you still feeling some pain?" Wow, finally he asked how I was feeling!

"I had a spasm earlier, which came once and then disappeared. I felt it again after coming to sit here but it has disappeared," I responded.

"That means you are getting better now. We cannot allow you to just sit and not do any movement or activity. Obviously we won't push you too hard, but you have to move around, Palesa. This sitting won't be good for you in the long run," he cautioned.

"Bathong ("Good heavens"), Martin!" exclaimed my mother. "It has only been a few days since Palesa came back from the hospital. You say you don't want to push her too much, but to me, it sounds like that's exactly what you're trying to do," she bleated.

Martin's face grimaced. He loudly pulled his breath in different intervals and then released it, intentional in what he was doing, subtly mocking my mother. She on the other hand, couldn't be bothered. She had said what she wanted to say, leaving the atmosphere with unexpected tension. I had to defuse the situation.

"Mama, don't worry about me. When I feel pain, I'll tell Martin and he will help me. Sis Lulama, please help me up. I haven't finished eating though. I also forgot my tablets upstairs."

"Don't worry baby, Mos…," Martin called Bra Mos, who had been standing in the middle of the kitchen, not saying a word.

"Yes Sir," he responded timidly.

"Take Palesa's food. She can eat outside. Also put some cushions on the garden chairs on the patio. I don't know why Lulama removed them."

"Yes sir, I will. Dumela mme Ditheko," Bra Mos greeted my mom.

"Dumela Mos, I'll help you."

"Tjhee mme, ha ho hlokehe kannete." ("No ma'am, it's really not necessary").

"Mos, now please!" Martin toughed his tone. I deduced from his behaviour, that Martin was not very pleased with my mother for some reason. He was obviously still upset with the fact that he saw her in our bedroom. I now more than ever, strongly deemed it necessary for my mother to leave before she got hurt.

Both Martin and Sis Lulama helped me to get up as I carried my own weight too, wishing the pain to never resurface. Eventually

I managed and I snaked my arms around both Martin's and Sis Lulama's. My mother was not moving at all from where she was sitting.

We walked towards the front door and then out of the house. On reaching the verandah, Martin took out a handkerchief from his pocket. "Wait, wait, wait…," he entreated. "Baby, let me cover your eyes first."

"Come on baby, is it really necessary?"

"Yes it is," he said.

I stood there, allowing Martin to cover my eyes with his hanky and when he was done, he implored me to take a few steps. I was worried I might fall and hurt myself.

"Please don't let me fall," I begged.

"That's not gonna happen," he promised. "Come on, take a few more steps…and now more…then stop," he concluded.

He then unfastened the blindfold and as I squinted, I saw two cars, a red Mazda 2 sedan, as well as a black Ford Mustang Shelby GT500. I knew the car instantly because two of my cousins from my mother's side, Tlale and Thekiso, had always spoken about wanting to own the car one day, practically in a competition of sorts, regarding who would be the first to purchase the car once they had started working. They each owned diecast versions of the car in different colours when we were still growing up. So, I had already learnt a lot about these elusive sports cars as a young girl.

When I remarked about the car, mentioning its name, Martin

enlarged his eyes, his temple creasing instantaneously.

"How do you know this car? It's not like anyone in your family can afford this. This car costs more than a million rand! So yeah, tell us Miss know it all. How do you know this car?"

The man's tongue was razor sharp, and it was like he had the gift or a curse of spoiling a somewhat good moment in an instant! How he could be jealous of me knowing the name of the car baffled me and always will! I was merely excited to see the car and all that immediately flooded my thoughts was my childhood, particularly when I visited my mother's family. Also, I could kick myself for never making any pact with my cousins then, since it had appeared that I was going to be the first one to get into the car.

I explained the whole story of my cousins wanting to own it etc., and he laughed.

"So, does any of them own this car now?" he asked contemptuously, followed by a more silly laughter.

"No, they don't," I replied briefly and kept quiet, while Bra Mos and Sis Lulama were showing signs of discomfort.

"Well, I guess that's what poor people will always do. They envy stuff they can never attain. But now, you're no longer one of them. See…, you now own this beast, as opposed to them having toys and wishing they could drive the real McCoy."

Martin didn't even know any of my family members, except my mother and father. So he judged everyone based on his encounter with me and my parents.

He hurt me with his very careless utterances and, for him to think that I'd be excited to own the car and look down on my cousins, attested to how little he thought of my family and of me.

Sis Lulama winked at me and shook her head briefly, subtly urging me to retreat from the talk, and I got the signal and pulled my breath.

"Okay then, open the car… let me see. You did say this is mine right?"

"Yes it's yours, only if you will get through all your driving lessons without scratching this Mazda. Then you can have it." The tease! "All you will be able to do now is to get in and sit for a few minutes. The car you can sit in for a while is that one," he pointed at the Mazda.

"Its' okay, I don't have to get inside this car as it's a bit low, and I doubt that my back will be alright after that. I can test the seat comfort in the hatchback however," I emphasized. His reaction was strange, as if he wasn't really pleased that I knew a bit about the stuff that's usually reserved for men – cars especially.

I knew a lot about some sports cars, as I played with my cousins as a young girl, largely because I was the only girl at home. Other girl cousins were much older and I wasn't really close to my father's family.

"I see you know something about cars. You even know that this is called a hatchback," he pointed at the Mazda. You've never mentioned this fact to me? I feel like you have deceived me."

How did my knowing something about cars turn into me

deceiving him? In his opinion, me having mentioned that I was always ridiculed by my own father for not being very bright in school work, meant that I knew nothing else? I should have taken offence to the utterance. Instead, I was amused. I couldn't and cannot claim to know about all cars; obviously that's impossible. However, I knew much about the ones my cousins and uncles did speak of.

I ignored his jibe and opened the door and got inside slowly. The car smelt brand new and I remarked of its beautiful interior, while I made certain not to forget to thank him for the gesture, which I knew no doubt, came with a lot of rules. Either way, I admitted that I needed to learn how to drive, but it was not going to be at that time when I was still nursing an injured back.

From the way Martin was behaving however, it was lucid that he needed me to start learning how to drive as soon as possible, which was surprising to me, knowing how he always behaved as if he didn't want me to go anywhere.

"Baby, thank you for the car; I appreciate it very much. Come inside," I beseeched, as he rounded the car to the driver's side.

As soon as he got in, he pulled his breath. "It's beautiful yes, for a novice like yourself. You want me to take you for a spin?"

"Spin! No please. Not today, unless we're just gonna go around the plot and not even go outside of the gate. I just want to feel how it moves that's all."

"Coward!" he said and laughed afterwards.

I was becoming aware that I was letting him get away with a

lot of things that he would say to me. If I'd complain or show my dissatisfaction of his utterances, he'd mope around and give me the silent treatment. I'd then be the one to apologise for being hurt about his unkind remarks to me. This was draining my energy.

The gift of the cars was a good gesture but the sports car was unnecessary. Having done such a good thing on the face of it, he had charged me up, making me happy, feeling some kind of hope that things were about to change. In an instant however, he would then change the mood with his mockery as well as insults disguised as jokes.

After entering, he closed the door and implored me to do the same. After I did that, I remembered that poor Bra Mos had been holding my food in his hands and was not even reminding me of my sandwich. I opened the window and called out to Bra Mos.

"Sorry Bra Mos, here you are standing there with my sandwich, while I flatly ignored you. Please give it to me." Bra Mos came towards the car and handed the side plate to me.

"Thank you," I said. "Sis Lulama, can I have the dish cloth please as well as my tablets?" As she was about to head over to the kitchen, Martin stopped her.

"The dish cloth won't be necessary, Lulama; there are wet wipes in here." He reached for the cubby hole and retrieved the wipes. "You can fetch the tablets."

"Here, but this cannot be a habitual thing. You can't eat in the car, otherwise before we know it, you'll be eating and driving, then you'll land in an accident." I was mystified to learn that I was already being subjected to the rules of the car. It was never my intention to eat and drive – or was he speaking from experience?

"I don't intend to eat in here," I replied.

"You say this now but bad habits form quickly - trust me, I know!"

"Okay then. We can't speak as if I have already broken the rules," I sniggered and he shook his head and smiled briefly. '*At least he's smiling*,' I inwardly remarked.

Sis Lulama came back quickly and handed me the tablets.

"Sis Lulama, please tell Mama that we're test driving one of the cars," I entreated.

"Okay, Miss Palesa, I'll do so."

Martin then started the engine and reversed out of the driveway, while I had begun gnawing the last bit of my sandwich.

"I think it's time Mama left us in peace to deal with our issues. Her being here is casting a cloud to everything we're going through right now. We might not even know if we're fighting because we were going to fight or because she's here," he mentioned, out of the blue. I had to convince myself that he could be right. But why did I affirm that likelihood?

"You think so, baby?"

"Yes baby, I honestly believe so. Have I ever yelled at you the way I did early this morning?"

I had to think carefully of my answer because it was really not the first time he had yelled at me, but the 'SHUT UP!' scold was the first and it had hurt me really deep.

"No baby, you haven't," I responded. "But we cannot really say it's because my mom is here or that it won't happen again. All she does is to sit in the guestroom and mind her business, unless I call her. So she cannot be responsible for what we are going through." There, there, there…I said it and wiped my hands with the wet wipe. I then placed the dish in the plastic bag sis Lulama had brought. He kept quiet and finally drove out of the estate.

"How does it feel… the car I mean?" Wow, no comeback to what I said to him? That was the first!

"It feels really smooth baby, very light. Thank you." He widened his smirk.

"Don't forget to take your medication. I'll drive slower so you can drink them with ease." That stunned me, as I quickly took my pills out of their paperback and drank with water.

"Thank you, baby."

"Anything for you my love. There is no one who can ever love you the way I do. You must know that. Not even your parents and this is not up for debate. If they indeed loved you with the same intensity that I love you, they would have turned the town and that township upside down looking for you. I mean, I should have been in jail now for having held you captive, against your will."

I caught a glimmer of pride from his face, while I couldn't quite understand what he meant exactly by having held me captive. Again, I wanted him to explain himself but I didn't want us to end up having an argument, especially not after such huge gifts he had bought me. I let it slide and kept quiet.

"Mmm, I hear you," I replied.

"You don't believe me?" he asked.

"No, it's not that I don't believe you, but I have never thought of things the way you've just explained."

"Don't tell me you have never thought of it. I know you have. I remember you scolding your mother on the phone. So, I know that you two might pretend that you have this good mother and daughter relationship that is supposed to be the envy of many, but you don't. You're still hurting from the fact that your parents never sought you out, after having run away from home. You might be envious of others who have such good relationships, but that's not the case with you and you cannot dissuade me otherwise."

The man spoke so much, in a way making what I had convinced myself to be perfect sense and harsh truth anyway. I went back in thought, particularly to that day I left home to the day I fetched my stuff.

My mother was instrumental in me leaving home, as she might not have known how to deal with the whole thing but in my mind, I wanted to believe that she had no choice but to release me as I had seemed to be comfortable with the man I had met only the previous day. That was not the right thing to do though; letting me go just like that. I was a young adult but still a child – her child!

Then again, as I continued to analyse the whole thing, Martin's theory seemed more and more plausible and I was now more than ever determined to go along with his suggestion that my mother had to leave, so we could be alone and have some peace.

Was I sure thought that it would be the right move? No, I wasn't; but I thought about it briefly and felt that it had to be done, otherwise I'd upset my fiancé, who had been really good to me, save for minor squabbles here and there, which came as a result of me always wanting to assert myself and saying my peace.

I was determined to stop second guessing everything and doing exactly what he said to me, as he loved me more than anyone in the world, didn't he?

The only thing that I was resolute to never reveal, was the fact that I had R100 000 in my accounts, that my mother had given me and it was earning some interest. That was my buffer, just in case my bubble would burst at some point. That made me alternate in thought, between letting my mother go back home, to her remaining with us for a little while longer. She did indeed care, otherwise why would she give me such a chunk of her savings? Perhaps she just wanted me to be away from my father because he was largely the reason my stay at home was not gratifying.

"Where are we going exactly? I thought we were just going to drive around the block," I asked as soon as I realised that we had been driving for some time.

"I still have something up my sleeve. Just be patient… you'll see," he bragged.

"Okay… but we shouldn't take too long, as I have already

overexerted myself as it is. You don't want me to start giving you trouble do we?"

"Relax, you will be fine. Besides, if you start feeling any pain, I will sort you out. Have you forgotten who your man is?"

"Nope, I haven't forgotten," I quickly replied.

We drove for about an hour and I began to feel uncomfortable. I looked around the passenger seat to check on a mechanism I could use to lower the seat.

"What are you looking for?" he asked.

"I'm not okay; my back is starting to feel a bit prickly. I think we should stop somewhere baby before I start to feel pain, I need to stretch… please," I pleaded.

"You need to start toughening up. You see, what you're doing now is to anticipate the pain, even if it's not really there. You didn't say you have pain, you said you are feeling uncomfortable. If you keep anticipating pain, you will experience it. Everything is in the mind. Besides, it won't be long now; we will soon arrive at the destination."

I was shamefaced after Martin practically admonished me, telling me how I should feel about my body reacting to the discomfort. I knew better, because that was my body and nobody else's. I had to really toughen up as he had said, as it was evident that the whole impromptu trip was gonna go the way he wanted, with none of my input.

I didn't have any rejoinder to throw his way, but plucked up some courage and pulled my breath in different intervals. At last, I found the lever to lower the seat, which I utilised quickly. As I was about to allow myself to respite, the car slowed down and I heard the indicator clicking. Martin then turned the car as I lifted the lever up again, my back now aching. I couldn't tell him that I was not alright, lest I spoil his jovial mood.

We finally pulled over at what looked like a construction site of two buildings that seemed to be almost finished. Martin parked a bit further from the buildings.

"Let me park here. I don't want nails to spike the wheels. Hopefully you will manage to walk towards just one of these buildings I want to show you. Don't get out as yet. Are you still feeling alright?" He didn't just ask me that question! Was that a trick question? Of course it was.

I nodded, tightening my jaw and unfastening my seatbelt.

"Come on; stop being such a party pooper! We will be here for about fifteen minutes. Just persevere for some time," he gibed, making light of how I was feeling. As he rounded the car to open for me, I breathed heavily and let my breath out, asking for some strength from powers that be. I then stretched while still sitting. I got a slight pang and I felt my heartbeat raising as I continued with the breathing exercise. Nothing I subjected myself to helped to ease the elevated heart rate.

Once he reached me, he opened my door and extended his hand, helping me out. I got out slowly, trying to dispel the spasm I had by letting my whole body loose and eventually landed in his arms, as he only then became aware that I was indeed battling.

"Baby, are you in pain? You don't look well."

"Yes, I'm in pain. I think it's due to sitting for too long in the car. I believe the tablets will kick in soon though. I really need to get well now. I'm so sick and tired of being sick and tired!" I lamented.

"Come here…," he astounded me with a peck on my lips, followed by a tight hug.

"What was that for?" I asked.

"Does a man need to have a reason for kissing his fiancé?"

"Not really, but that was unexpected," I murmured, amply aware that he had been struggling with lack of intimacy for some time. '*Perhaps this is why he is so frustrated and always temperamental,*' I inwardly held. While his hands were still clasping my waist, I initiated another kiss, which clearly caught him and me by surprise.

We kissed for a few minutes right there next to the car, until I felt his front hardening. We stopped briefly in implicit pact and we laughed together, our noses and foreheads touching, as we rubbed them together.

"Baby, what are we doing? Look what you've just started now," he giggled further, casting his eyes to the front of his pants.

"What have I done?" I pretended not to have known what he was referring to. "I wanted to remind you that you and I do have moments like these and we have to stop fighting, especially about people who shouldn't be occupying so much of our space. I'm here with you, Martin and I'm not going anywhere. You also need to stop scarring me by making me fear you. I don't want to fear you because you're my man."

"That was totally unexpected. I know you love me baby and I don't want you to fear me. I just don't like it when it seems as though you're entertaining other people except your man. I'm the only person who will always be here for you, no matter what. Haven't I proven that to you?" That assertion again…seriously now!

"Yes you have," I avowed, and placed my head on his chest and wrapped my arms around his waist, while noticing that the spasm on my back had ebbed.

He caressed my upper back and kissed me on my forehead, as I inhaled his cologne. "Now this is what I'm talking about," he said. "Come…, I have something to show you."

He grabbed my hand after stealing another kiss and motioned me to walk slowly as he locked the car. He kicked both his legs out, evidently trying to release his hardness. That amused me and I laughed. He joined me in the laughter.

"I wonder what's in those buildings you're taking me to. Don't we need masks as I can see dust coming from the other building?"

"Yes, we do need them actually. I've got them; don't worry." He unzipped his man-sachel and took out surgical masks and handed one to me. I quickly wore mine and he did the same.

I was actually teasing him when I asked about the masks,

because I was trying to find a way for us to go back home quicker than he had wanted to, given that the day had been long for me; a person who was nursing a wound which came as a result of an operation. Little did I know that he had come prepared. In any event, it was too soon for me to be gallivanting all over the show. I let him have his moment, while I inwardly continued to pray for equability to reign, up until we would go back home so I could rest.

Concrete protested under our feet, making us walk shoddily as we kept making our way towards the buildings. He held my hand, happy as a kid.

We finally arrived at the door opening of the building. There were plastic sheets and some boards walling off construction zones that had clearly only recently been worked on to protect the site and to trap dust and debris. As we entered, Martin quickly retrieved two hard construction hats that were placed inside a glasslike container mounted on the wall.

"Careful, just be careful please…," he advised, while we both did all we could to limp over some construction material on the floor which was left unattended.

"What's this place baby?" I asked keenly, after realizing that he seemed to be right at home.

"Here…," he put one of the hats on my head, flatly ignoring my probe. He wore the other hat afterwards and smiled at me.

"What do you think?"

"What do I think about what?"

"About this place…, do you like it?"

"Baby, why are you being so tongue-tied about this place? How can I like something that's so messy, with construction material all over the place? I don't know what I'm supposed to like here since I don't even know what it is. Please take me out of my misery already and tell me what this place is."

"Okay then. I was hoping you'd have figured out by now. This is your place. In a month or two, you'll be having this exclusive restaurant as your own. That's one of my other gifts to you. I just hope that in two months' time, you'd be up and about and no longer in pain, so that you can start managing this place," he concluded, taking a couple of steps to look around.

He left me bewildered as I stood in the middle of the dust riddled structure, wondering how on earth he could have seen the place being a restaurant because in the state it was in, it was just a huge vestibule with no fixtures, no windows and certainly no visible design, suggesting that the place might be a restaurant or might be turned into one.

As much as I inwardly appreciated the gift, even though I had no faintest idea how I would navigate the restaurant business, I felt that he was over-compensating after he hit me and almost repeating that in the morning. I didn't know whether the gifts were really thought out or not, as they came unexpectedly after a fight and were certainly not cheap. What if I mess up? Would he still be his cheerful self or would he continue where my father left off?

Martin knew that I hadn't even gone far with my education but there he was, bombarding me with things that were in my opinion, and at that stage, gonna see me failing before I could even start. I also didn't trust myself. My father's words kept ringing in my ear, "YOU'RE STUPID!"

I panicked immediately while inundated by all these thoughts, so much that before I knew it, I had procured a panic attack, which saw me almost about to faint. Had I not dimly called out to him, I would have collapsed right there and then on the concrete surface, risking all kinds of injuries, over and above what I was already grappling with.

He quickly came to my aid and held me in his arms, while admonishing me for over-exerting myself to the point that I now couldn't breathe.

"Baby, don't do this to me. Take a deep breath and exhale. You look like you've just seen a ghost. What's going on?" he asked.

"I can't breathe with ease. Let's go home please," I implored as I continued to struggle to breathe.

"Tell me what's going on first," he demanded. The nerve of the man! He wanted the moment to go on uninhibited by anything or anyone, least of all me.

I pulled my breath and exhaled, then again and again, until I was able to breathe normally, while he was still holding me close to his chest.

"Baby, why did you do all these things for me, especially in one day? Two cars already and I don't even have a driver's license.

Now you're telling me about owning a restaurant! How am I going to find my way through running a restaurant when I don't even have matric and have absolutely no idea what to do?" I paused, as I watched his face frowning. "I feel like this is to set me up for failure," I shrugged.

"Baby, I was expecting you to be a bit more cheerful and enthusiastic than this spectacle you're showing me here… you hyper-ventilating like you just did. You need to trust yourself more and stop seeing yourself through the eyes of your father. I will not fail you like your father did. My aim is to accelerate you to be the best restaurateur in this part of town, and if you like, we can even add an events venue that side," he pointed at an open land on the other side of the two buildings.

"Baby, I appreciate this, but I would love to wait a bit prior to me working earnestly on something I'm not even certain I'd pull off. You do recall that I love making clothes right? That's where my passion lies." He gave me a deep contorted gaze and laughed out loud.

"There is no wife of mine who is going to do such menial task, claiming that it's passion that can make money," he sneered, and continued. "Dress-making is a hobby, and not something you can safely claim can make you money and see you occupying a huge space up there with the rest of us," he maintained, mockingly.

I didn't know how to feel about what Martin had countered, worse of all, about his scorn. He made me feel very small and out of touch with reality. Perhaps I was naïve but he was the one who chose to be involved with a younger woman and him not allowing me to mature naturally, meant that sooner or later, I was bound to fail, fall short of his expectations or hurt myself to a point of no return.

I felt sorry for myself and asked myself so many questions which did not have answers at that point. I became really sad as I noted an insidious tone from my fiancé.

His passive-aggressive behaviour that surfaced in a whim, tore me up inside and tired me out. I was no longer as confident as I had been, that I could maintain the relationship, let alone tie myself down to marry him. I wondered if it had been a good idea to go back on my word to my mother that I would leave with her.

Unfortunately, I had already made a pact with Martin that we should send her back home to afford our relationship a surviving chance. Then again, I still didn't know how my mother being with us was causing a rift.

Someone might believe that I was being ungrateful. Perhaps I was being unappreciative but, it was me who was going to live with all the added stress, over and above the one I was already enduring. The stress of having to tip toe around my man whilst unsure as to what it would be that would either irk him or anger him, particularly since managing a restaurant would be unchartered territory for me.

"Pull yourself together, Palesa. You are in a very precarious situation here. Here you are, alone with this man who is likely to

react horridly should what you'd say next be unfavourable to him."

My inner person gave me a distressing caveat before I could even assert myself to Martin. I once again pulled my breath, amply aware that my man had a rising wheeze in anticipation of my retort to what he had said to me. His gaze as he held me that close to his torso, was intimidating, not at all expecting another negative talk about the visibly expensive gift he was giving me.

I denied him the satisfaction and pulled myself together. I sighed involuntarily but still maintaining poise.

"Are you fine now?" he asked.

"Not really, but I'm fine to look around," I alleged.

"It's okay; I can see that you're not really chuffed about this place. I'm not a child, Palesa. Even if you can pretend, I can see that you do not appreciate the gift I'm giving you."

That gave me the chills. I was evidently not very convincing in my trying to maintain good posture and fake smile my way through the whole test.

"Baby, it's not that I don't appreciate the gift. I do…, I really do. It's just that it truly caught me totally by surprise hence I had to ask the questions I asked. I don't want to fail as I know how painful it is to be deemed stupid by those close to you."

"Please don't even think of comparing me to your father. I'm nothing like him. Don't I teach you every chance I get that you should stop beating yourself up or speaking less of yourself?"

"Yes you do baby; yes you do," I said, after disentangling

myself from his clutches and walked around. I took out my phone from my pocket and quietly took pictures of the place inside, well aware that Martin had his eyes fixed on me after I had somewhat given him assurance that I was genuinely gleeful.

When I took photos, I had to make certain that my face resembled that of a person in deep thoughts about the building, so that when the time is finally ripe, I'd hit the ground running, after having made plans for the place that was bought for me.

Eventually, I took heed of his slightly eased demeanour as well as facial expression and then gave him a huge smile, which he returned with vigour.

"Okay, okay Miss Photographer. We should get going now. It's getting late," he teased.

I was inwardly pleased that we would finally leave the place as I desperately needed to leave.

Chapter 15

Coming home to perch

It was a bit windy when we eventually left the construction site. The sky was quickly becoming overcast. I was not particularly bothered, as Martin and I were no longer fighting but the mood was not gleeful either due to a disagreement we had earlier. I had lowered the car seat and was happy that Martin left me alone to respite. Once or twice, he would hold my hand while I rested and each time I opened my eyes briefly, I would catch sight of him stealing a glance and then smiling.

"Baby, you need to concentrate on the road you know! What's that look for?" I asked.

"You're my woman and I'm admiring your beauty. Is that a

crime?"

"No, it's not a crime, unless you're driving while looking at me like you're doing now."

"You know, I've just realised that you're not wearing your ring. Why did you not wear it?" That question startled me. I had genuinely forgotten to wear it as well. I was not even feeling weird, as if there was something missing on my finger. I suppose the fight we had in the morning had shifted something inside of me and I could think about nothing else but to try to figure out how I could get my situation better.

"Baby…!" I gasped. "I forgot it at home. Remember that I had not intended to leave the house. So had we made plans, I would have remembered and worn it. I'm sorry baby; it was not intentional. I really love my ring," I apologized.

"It's fine. I just don't understand why you keep taking it off and not just wear it throughout. You'll end up losing it and that won't make me happy. That's a priceless commodity I put on your finger that day and for some strange reason, I feel close to my mom when you're wearing it."

There….there….there…, as I had suspected before! He wanted to feel close to his mother by giving me her ring. That on its own was a burden of the highest order. That meant that even if the ring could be insured, whatever we would get to replace it should I lose it, won't do much to heal the heart that would be broken. I shuddered to think what would happen should I dare lose it!

As he continued driving, I tried going back in thought as to where I had put that ring. Something that one does daily, which even becomes second nature, is easily taken for granted, unless one does try to trace the steps from the time one did something to everything else that they might have done afterwards.

I wanted to go straight to it when we reached home, so that my fiancé would see that I hadn't put it carelessly. I was hoping to enter the house first and to even reach our bedroom first.

Martin kept quiet, as he utilized that moment to play some music. I immediately heard by the first instrument, that he was playing our song – perhaps deliberately, trying his utmost best to dispel the sudden tension in the car. He probably noticed that I was spooked when he asked me about the whereabouts of my ring.

I rolled the seat up and stretched a bit, utilizing that tender moment to suss him out. I touched him on his lap and he jerked, startling me with his reaction. He smiled and shook his head. "What's that about?" he asked, his voice light and affectionate.

"This song has just reminded me that we do love each other and that we need to stop arguing so much and concentrate on that love. I think it can get us through anything," I asserted.

"Well, I don't have a problem with that at all. But you do know what my issue with your behaviour is. I keep doing all these beautiful things and giving you all pricey things but you turn around and disappoint me at every turn. I think you need to apply your advice on yourself more than on me; then we will be alright," he tilted his head and gave me one look, while facing the road as he continued to drive.

"Okay baby, I promise I will change. I will try by all means to not upset you. I do think though, that you need to easily forgive me as I forgive you all the time."

"I quake to wonder which indiscretions you'll be pulling out of your hat now!" he continued laughing, while I elected to brush his scorn off. In fact, I continued brushing his thigh, pretending not to have taken heed of his ridicule.

He briefly gazed at me and smirked, while continuing to drive. I then removed my hand from his thigh and stroked the back of his neck, surprising myself with all the moves I was making. I longed for him, even though I was not confident that I wanted to go there that quickly, after having had pains that wouldn't recede for a while.

I chucked away Dr Duvenhage's instructions and told myself that once we reached home, I would make a move on my man and give him what he had been longing for, for a while. Perhaps then, his frustrations would ease up.

We continued to sing along to Freddie Jackson's "That's all I'll Ever Ask", as I leaned backwards, taking in the serene mood I had created after having elected to be the bigger person.

Before long, we arrived back home, as Martin indicated his intention to drive into the compound. Finally, he drove into the driveway, ultimately opening one of the garage doors and parked the car inside. He then closed the garage door behind us, while we remained in the car, enjoying the music. I threw my eyes briefly to the sports car, which was enjoying the remaining garage space. What a beauty!

Eventually, Martin switched the music off and unfastened his seatbelt, as I followed suit. He breathed heavily and then gawked at me, touching my hand and kissing it tenderly.

"Baby, are you sure about this thing you're starting now?" he had clearly read my intentions accurately. I wanted to tease him, by pretending that I didn't know what he was talking about. But, I quickly discarded the idea. I simply smiled, nodded and bit my lower lip. He then leaned over and pressed his lips against mine, as I responded fervently. We kissed for a while until I felt heat rushing through my veins. We then stopped almost at the same time. That was intense!

"Let's go inside," I whispered seductively.

"Okay, I'll be with you in an hour. There are a couple of things I still want to do out here and I would also like to have a word with your mother," he advised. I widened my eyes on hearing about my mother and had to ask frankly.

"What do you want to talk to her about?" I asked, genuinely concerned.

"Don't tell me you have already forgotten that we agreed that we are going to ask her to leave?"

"I have honestly forgotten. It's not like we were serious or were we?"

"Baby, I never just say anything unless I'm serious about it.

Your mother does need to go. It's not like there is much that she is doing for us…I mean for you here, anyway. By being here, she is making us all panicky and I cannot even invite people over, whom I'd like to help you to accelerate your healing process."

"Who are those people?"

"I knew that you'll ask that. As from next week, a physiotherapist will be here to help you. Once you're a bit better, perhaps a week or two later, I will then bring someone here to teach you how to drive. You see, there is a lot you still have to do. I don't want you limping on our wedding day." His teeth were out but that was not a smile I was witnessing from him. He suddenly seemed edgy, fidgeting with the car keys often.

He pressed the hooter, seemingly to call on Sis Lulama or Bra Mos, who quickly opened the door that was interconnected to the kitchen. Martin then rounded the car to open for me.

As soon as he reached my side and opened my door, Sis Lulama asked. "Where have you been, Miss Palesa? We were getting worried that something might have happened and your mother…" Martin interjected, preventing the poor woman from finishing her statement.

"Lulama, do you always have to be this dramatic? Palesa is with me and she's fine as you can see. Please help her, as she needs to rest. I think she'd be happy to have something cool to drink. She has had enough exercise for one day and I don't think her back can take more aggravation today," he commanded domineeringly.

I extended my hand to Sis Lulama as both she and Martin

grabbed me on each side. My whole body was stiff but not really sore. Once my feet landed on the paved surface, I straightened my back and toughened up.

"I'll be fine baby; Sis Lulama has got me. You can continue with the things you said you wanted to do. I'll go upstairs and rest."

Martin grabbed my chin, and quickly went inside the house, leaving us to walk as slowly as we needed to. He then stopped briefly on entering the kitchen, his attention on Bra Mos. "Mos, I'll see you shortly. You can continue with whatever you're doing, but I'll be back outside in about 15 minutes or so. We have a lot of work to do."

"Yes sir, you'll find me out here," he reverently responded.

I walked slowly, with Sis Lulama aiding me, even though I had felt that it was totally unnecessary as I was not really in pain but was super inflexible.

"Miss Palesa, where did you and Doc go? Your mother is not impressed that you left just like that, and she was also starting to say things that don't make sense," Sis Lulama began spilling the beans as we walked towards the kitchen.

"What kind of things?" I asked keenly.

"She said that Doc is going to hurt you and she was even trembling when she spoke to us. She told us that she doesn't trust your fiancé and that should anything befall you either out there or even here at home, Mos and I should know that Doc would be responsible for it. She also told us that Doc beat you up early this morning and then she scolded us, accusing us of pretending to love you, whereas we didn't come to your aid when you were being assaulted."

I was aghast to hear this tidbit of information and I was almost certain that there was no way my mother could have said any of that. Then again, there clearly was something she had mentioned to both Sis Lulama and Bra Mos. Although the information may have been grossly distorted, there was some kind of near truth to what she had told the help. I just wished she hadn't mentioned anything to them at all.

"Sis Lulama, I doubt my mother was being serious about what she said to you and Bra Mos. Martin never hurt me. Do you see any bruises on my face? Do I look like someone who was beaten up?"

"Not really, Miss Palesa but…," she paused and literally scrutinized my face, practically barring my movement as I wanted to enter the house. She unzipped my sweater and pore over me as I found the move silly but somewhat humorous. As much as I was amused by her actions, it was flattering to learn that I would at least be in good hands should anything untoward befall me, largely at the hands of my fiancé.

"See anything amiss?" I chortled.

"For now no, but I will be watching you like a hawk. I still don't know why your mother told us such things because as much as Doc did have a quick hand when it came to his former girlfriends, he has never laid his hands on you, has he, Miss Palesa?"

The question sounded innocent but I knew that it wasn't. She was fishing and I was not prepared to tell her anything material because there was nothing to tell anyway, save for that regrettable day when he slapped me and pinned me down with his knee on my back. Did I just minimize the act?

Sis Lulama was not aware that she had divulged information that I wasn't prepared to hear – that Martin had had a quick hand previously. I took a mental note of it and placed it at the back of my mind.

The tomfoolery of the morning was regrettable, as there was Lucas in the mix and I clearly should not have indulged the man for such a long time, knowing what I knew, after both Sis Lulama and Bra Mos had told me the story of Lucas' wife and Martin. I again believed that Martin's anger towards me was justified as I had erred in judgment.

All I wanted to do was to protect my relationship with my man, as it was evident that my mother wanted to split us up. Otherwise, why would she break my trust like that, adding some spice of her own, making a whole storm in a tea cup, even going to an extent of mentioning that Martin had beaten me up when he hadn't? It was only me who knew that he had slapped me.

Sis Lulama noticed my dim expression and ceased with the probe as we entered the house through the kitchen door.

"Sis Lulama, I would like to walk unaided please. I think I will manage. Remember that I came downstairs by myself when no one was here, so I do think that I am really getting better. Please remember to fetch my tablets from the car. Where is my mom?" I queried.

"She is still in the lounge, but please don't mention that I told you about all the things she has been saying to both Mos and I. I don't want the two of you to fight."

"We won't fight and no, I won't tell her." As Sis Lulama released my arm, I walked towards the stairs and as soon as I was about to ascend, I saw Martin sitting with my mother in the lounge and talking softly, prompting me to ask frankly.

"Baby, what are you and mama talking about there? Am I the subject of the discussion you guys are having?"

My mom lifted her head and faced my direction, sharing a brief chuckle. "Palesa, this is between Martin and me. There's nothing ominous that we are talking about, I promise you."

I got confused by my mother's assertion and as I was about to quiz my husband to be, he lifted his hand and waved at me, practically instructing me to abort mission. Somehow, I got the message and I unfortunately now felt slightly weak and light headed. Perhaps it was from the sudden anxiety that I experienced, wondering what on earth Martin and my mother could be talking about.

I then recalled that he wanted my mom to leave our place. I just hoped that he was asking her respectfully and that my mother would also take the request well. The last thing I needed in my life at that stage was for the two people I loved to fight over me, as they had done at the hospital, resulting in one of them fuming and feeling slighted.

I nonetheless elected to mind my business. Besides, Martin had already told me that he would just be an hour before he could join me in our room. So, I wanted to rest so I could give him what he had longed for, for weeks ever since I was admitted to the hospital. I had planted the idea in his mind as I kept teasing him so either way, whether I was now not feeling too good or not, I was gonna have to suck it up and give him his connubial rights. I believed as he evidently did as well, that my being at his home and wearing his sacred ring meant that he and I were practically husband and wife and all we needed to do was to formalize the union.

I was being flatly ignored by my mom and my fiancé, who were hell-bent on hiding what they were talking about.

I finally removed all worry from my mind as soon as I heard my mother make a sound in accord with what Martin was saying to her. I knew then, that my man must have charmed her or swayed her in his favour, for whatever it was he had intimated to her.

I walked slowly up the stairs, while Sis Lulama was ogling me from the foot of the staircase. I walked until I reached our bedroom and as soon as I reached our door, I spoke up, “I'm fine, sis Lulama.”

She laughed and advised me that she hadn't really had the time to cook as she had spent most of the time we were away, worrying about our whereabouts. How could she blurt that fact out so valiantly, especially after Martin's earlier reprove?

I finally reached our room and sat down on the divan, trying to dispel the sudden giddy feeling I was now experiencing. It had emanated out of nowhere. Whether I'd vomit or not, I felt that I needed to firm up as I had already started something I couldn't get out of. I gave my man subtle but precise indications of what my intentions were, and he didn't only take my unspoken words for it but, he did ask if I was sure I'd like to go there. I had affirmed. Now how was it going to look if I were to go back on my word, after such an endearing tease earlier?

My concern was also on what it was, that Martin was saying to my mom that had made them speak so tenderly, not even giving a hint to the subject of their talk.

I stood up after my resolute a few moments prior and moved towards the door, closing it behind me. The dizziness had become better so I drank some water and then decided to take a shower. I carefully indulged myself with the Jasmine infused shower gel and felt really good about myself.

When I was done and having applied my lotions, I went back into our room. I had inwardly hoped that Martin would be back in the room by then but I figured that perhaps he was now busy with Bra Mos, with whatever it was he needed help with.

I wore one of my sexiest burgundy lingerie, eager to make myself desirable to my man. I dimmed the lights in the room, which gave off a vibe of relaxation and romantic mood. I then lay on the bed.

Thirty minutes passed after the work I had done in preparation for my fiancé. I was certain that he would not resist my allure that late afternoon. Since I had been posing with my sexy mini night dress and unfastened knee length robe on the bed, waiting for him to come and do whatever he wanted to do to me, I was beginning to lose patience when he didn't appear. I felt the draft as I had exposed myself for way too long. I got worried and then pulled my gown over my shoulders and fastened it.

Disappointment overpowered me, as I began wondering what on earth was taking that long for Martin to come to the room. I thought of calling him but felt that I'd appear too desperate, clingy or needy.

I stood up slowly, feeling dejected as I unerringly sensed that my man didn't deem the adoring time I had in mind to be urgent, hence he decided to take his time. I was not alright – my second rejection! Now I knew how Martin felt most of the time, when I would cite either fatigue or discomfort. I then switched the lights back on as I could tell that the moment was not going to happen.

I vacillated between wondering if he really didn't want me anymore now that I was practically laid up and making excuses for him about the time not being right.

I called sis Lulama without any more thought to the move, as my nerves were really shooting up.

"Miss Palesa, are you alright?" she hastily asked.

"I'm fine sis. Is everything alright downstairs with my mom and Martin?" I had to ask bluntly as I couldn't take the silence anymore.

"What do you mean, Miss Palesa? Is there anything in particular that you were asking about?"

"Sis Lulama, please don't beat about the bush. You know that I'm asking about my mom and Martin. Are they still talking?"

"Oh that! Sorry, I didn't think you were asking about that talk; apologies once again."

The woman was playing a wordy game with me, waiting for me to keep probing. I indulged her, waiting for her to entangle herself in some web, if that was her aim to engage in a circumlocution with me. I was however not really in the mood and I could feel my pant rising.

"Sis Lulama, what's going on? Why does it sound like you're hiding something from me? Should I come downstairs?"

"I'm not hiding anything, Miss Palesa, honestly. It's just that…" there she went again!

"Where is Martin?" I asked.

"He's outside with Mos," she responded briefly and then kept quiet, treating me as if I was some cop interrogating a criminal.

I responded, "okay" and let her be. My mind couldn't stop going haywire as I opened the drawer to my pedestal, taking my ring out and putting it on. I wanted to make sure that whatever it was that was suddenly keeping Martin outside, should not be escalated by my not wearing the ring.

I walked towards the fridge and took some juice out, gobbling the whole 500ml mango liquid in one go. After a bit of time sitting on the chaise, then sleeping a bit on the bed and then on the day bed on the balcony, I felt seriously piqued and elected to go downstairs to check on what was going on. Almost three hours had passed and it was already early evening and Sis Lulama hadn't even bothered to ask if I needed to eat or not.

I fastened my robe and wore my sleepers, and then took small steps down the stairs. As I descended, I noticed flashing lights coming from the lounge and some music playing. I heard "hum… hum" sounds as if there were more people in the house than the normal ones I knew of.

I called out to my mother, who didn't respond right away. I called again and as I was becoming impatient and was about to call sis Lulama before I reached the foot of the stairs, she came hurrying towards me and practically barred me from going down. I got really distressed and pushed her out of my way.

"Get out of my way, Sis Lulama! I barked. "Where is Martin? What is going on here? I've been waiting for him for three hours now and I'm hungry; I want to make myself food!"

Sis Lulama did everything in her power to restrain me but the more she tried, the stronger I became and I even warned her not to try that again because she would either end up hurting me or I would hurt her.

"Lulama! Let her go," Martin's voice emanated from the

kitchen. "Trust you to be so stubborn and spoil the surprise!" He said.

"Surprise? What surprise? Didn't we have an agreement on our way to the house a few hours ago that we will spend some time together? I've been waiting for you upstairs…," I lamented and I was practically on the verge of crying when he came hurriedly towards me and gave me a hug. Tears eventually ran down my cheeks in an unexpected emotional ambush. Martin wiped my tears and told me to stop crying, as there was nothing sinister going on but that was simply a surprise for me. The lights stopped flickering and I noticed that they came from outside.

While still wondering what was going on, Martin directed me to the couch, as I sighed and picked my feet up. I eventually sat down, while he was particularly chivalrous.

"Can I place this cushion to support your back?" he asked.

"Yes, please do," I responded. He placed the cushion on the sofa's rest to support my back as I continued protesting about the weird lights outside.

Sis Lulama had an unusual smirk on her face, so did Bra Mos, who had taken off his work-clothes and had navy pants and white shirt on. Sis Lulama also looked smart, as if they were going somewhere, hence they needed to look somewhat distinguished.

"I'm hungry, sis Lulama, so I don't know whether your plans tonight were for us to sleep hungry or not since you and Bra Mos seem to be going out or are you dining in? What am I missing?"

She ignored me and Martin got up as he had briefly sat with

me. He went to the kitchen and came back swiftly with a plate full of some meaty eats and mini burgers. It was lucid that there was something that I hadn't been privy to, that everyone else was busy with.

I nonetheless stopped protesting and asking questions, but enjoyed the weird attention. I placed my legs on the ottoman and began eating, while sis Lulama fetched some juice.

Martin seemed a bit edgy and fidgeted with his phone often as I finally realised that my mother was not in the room. I then asked again: "Where is my mom?"

"She's in the guest room," Martin responded but she was too quiet and that made me not believe much of what he had said to me. I then called out to her. She came hurriedly on hearing me call out to her.

"Palesa, why are you yelling? I'm just in the guest room near the lounge. Where did you think I was?" She asked, as if she was taunting me or wanting me to divulge what I know about Martin's talk with her. I was convinced that he had spoken to her about her leaving our place, but I didn't know how he had put the whole thing to her and how she had interpreted the request.

"I thought you were not here. Why is everyone dressed so smart? Le ya kae? (Where are you going?)" I asked because my mom had also changed what she had on when we came in and dressed in her pink dress with green and yellow flowers making a lovely pattern.

"Come to think of it, you're the only one in your night garments. Perhaps you should change into something nice as well. We are having dinner in the house. Martin has invited your father to come and join us. We are waiting for him."

I froze after hearing that my father had been invited to the dinner I didn't know about. Now I was supposed to change into something nice! For what reason? I never asked to be included in that dinner.

Martin was just standing there in the middle of the room, looking a bit disenchanted and ogling my mom, as if she had prematurely divulged what his intentions were. Now I understood why he kept checking the time often. I continued eating and my mom called both Sis Lulama and Bra Mos to the kitchen, as Martin followed them.

I sat alone in the lounge and ate, while listening to some acoustic music that was playing from the Home Entertainment System. No one was taking me into their confidence regarding the dinner, so I figured that whoever planned it, would have to bear the consequences of its success or failure.

I inwardly hoped that my father would disappoint them and not come, when I heard Martin speak in a high pitched voice, "he's here!" Oh, bummer – there went my peace of mind! Needless to say, I chose to relax even more, while enjoying the foodstuff he had given me.

Car door opened and closed outside and as I was still enjoying my food, sis Lulama came rushing towards me.

"Miss Palesa, your father is here with two other men… come quickly, please hide in the guest room." The nerve!

"I don't want to! Martin is the one who will tell me what to do. Why should I hide?" I became stubborn and wanted to see what she'd do.

"Miss Palesa, please, I'm begging you. It's Doc who asked me to tell you to go into the guest room since you're already here downstairs. He was going to tell you what's going on when he came to see you upstairs; but then you came down unexpectedly. He's going to scold me if he finds you here," she pleaded.

"I'll go but you are going to tell me exactly what's going on – not this dinner story my mom is spinning. Besides, it's late already and I don't understand why we're supposed to entertain anyone at this time, totally unprepared!" I complained, while struggling to get up from the couch.

"Maybe you are not prepared but the rest of us are," she murmured, unaware that I heard what she mumbled. She nonetheless helped me to get up.

Hearing my father flattering Martin about the opulence he was living in and praising everything he was witnessing, left me staggered. I wondered what it was he would praise next, seeing as my mom had appeared to have relented. Sis Lulama and I had just gotten into the guest room when I heard the rest of the men my father came with chorused him.

"Yes, this is a massive place indeed. So this is how you got our child to remain here for such a long time! You're a very brave young man."

That was my uncle Thutlo. His sentiments amused me and I questioned myself as to how much of what was going on there or with me he knew of. He must have been very disappointed in me for staying with a man without getting married. But then again, they all could have easily forced my dad to fetch me but they didn't.

He was the youngest of the three brothers, followed by aunt Thoko, who was the only rose among the thorns. At least uncle Thutlo was the only one I knew without a doubt, that he cared about me.

Each time he came home, he would bring me all the niceties that he reckoned a little girl would love. He would bring me chocolates, potato chips, dried fruits, juices and sometimes biltong and even ice cream in a big tub. He would immediately order me to take the ice cream to the freezer so that it wouldn't melt.

As far as the eldest of the siblings, uncle Motlatsi was concerned, it had always been difficult to read him, let alone connect with him. He was not really a cheerful person. He shared a weird bond with my dad, which I gathered they didn't share with uncle Thutlo, my favourite uncle. They would always be so serious looking and each time they didn't like something, they would react with unbridled anger, you'd be wise to retreat as soon as possible, lest you find yourself enjoying a landslide of their fists.

Now hearing uncle Thutlo speak up like that, I could tell that the other man in tow must have been uncle Motlatsi. That hoisted my interest even more and I flatly refused for Sis Lulama to leave the guest room, as I continued interrogating her on what was really happening. She dropped her eyes and crossed her arms, emphatically refusing to give away any news about the secret she had been entrusted with.

"If you don't tell me, I'm gonna scream and tell my uncle Thutlo that you have hurt me on my back. Now spill the beans!" I demanded.

"Miss Palesa, how can you do this to me? I'm gonna be in trouble if I tell you everything. Please don't make me do this," she begged.

"Sis Lulama, you have one minute only. I swear I'm gonna scream. Just know that I'm the apple of my uncle's eye and I will tell him all kinds of things he will believe in an instant. So please start talking."

The poor woman didn't believe what I had said to her. She was seriously spooked by my stance, which I had simply used to bully her into telling me the news. I never would have gone through with it. However, it appeared that I had indeed frightened her, since she eventually gave me a glimpse into Martin's plans for the day – well, almost!

"Okay, okay, Miss Palesa, I'll tell you. How can you even threaten to scream? That's not really nice. But please you have to pretend to be surprised when they eventually call you to come through… I'm begging you."

"Okay, I promise. Now what's going on?"

As she was about to divulge the news, the door knob turned and my mother entered, bearing a wide smirk, something I hadn't seen in a while.

"Mama, what's going on? Sis Lulama was about to tell me but then you entered. So, please take me out of my misery," I beseeched.

"Lulama, were you really going to tell her?" she asked, looking disappointingly at the poor woman, who immediately defended herself.

"No, no, Mrs Ditheko; don't look at me that way. This is your child and she threatened that she will scream if I don't tell her what's going on. She mentioned that she is one of her uncles' favourite and apparently one scream from her, all hell could break loose!" My mom shook her head.

She probably thought I would cease prying but that only fuelled my curiosity reserve and I directed my probe at my mother.

"Yes, mama, I'm telling you the same thing," I warned. It was at the time when I decided to now sit down to finish my food, that I felt a sharp spasm; the same one I felt when I went downstairs by myself. Totally unintended, a scream ripped from my throat and sis Lulama and my mom both stared at me wide eyed. They were visibly thinking that I was making good on my earlier threats.

It took them a bit of time to realize that I was not fooling around, but I was indeed struggling with a muscle spasm.

"Lulama, she's not playing…, please take that plate from her."

Sis Lulama snatched the plate from my hands, almost sending the remaining mini burger flying to the floor.

After putting the plate down, she quickly took the burger and bit on it, chewing quickly without even asking me if I was still going to eat it or not. In no time, she had finished all of it. My mother slapped the woman on her back. She in turn, put her hand on her mouth, as I eventually sat down on the arm chair in the bedroom, trying to apply the technique I employed early in the day to ward off the spasm. It worked to some extent, but left my whole body feeling stiff.

The door flung open and Martin launched himself inside, breathing heavily.

"What's the matter? Baby, are you alright?" he tapped me on my shoulder.

"I have a spasm, the same one I had in the morning after I came down. I think it's the stress seeing as no one wants to tell me what's going on here."

"Baby, I have already told you that nothing amiss is going on here, but since you're so hell-bent on knowing prior to the time I had intended to tell you, I might as well tell you," he gazed at my mother, who tilted her head and shrugged, as if to ask him not to dare. "I have to tell her what you and I agreed on, mama. She's going to know in a few minutes anyway."

"I hope it's not something that's gonna upset me," I said.

"Well, it might irritate you slightly, especially since you were not part of the planning. But you are not really in a position to plan anything," Martin claimed. "Lulama, I think you and Mos can go and sit with the Dithekos now. Let's not waste any more time. Represent me properly and stick to what we agreed on. Don't even think of going overboard. If you aren't sure of anything, you can call me. Mama, are you also going to be that side?" he asked my mom.

"No, I'll sit in here with Palesa. When the family wants to see her, I'll then prepare her."

The two of them spoke about me as if I was not in the room. That annoyed me.

"What is going on?" I raised my voice, while Martin gave me a censorious look.

"Re rera mahadi a hao, Palesa (we are negotiating your dowry, Palesa). There…I said it!" My mother spoke hurriedly and the way she and Martin gawked at me, I could tell that they were waiting for some retort from me. I had the feeling earlier, ever since I heard my uncle's voice, that whatever was going to happen that day, had something to do with my stay at Martin's and perhaps our relationship. Now that my mother mentioned the dowry negotiations, I experienced an instant headache, followed by nausea and dizziness.

"Baby, baby, please don't get angry. I thought this would make you happy. We can still have a wedding next year when you have fully recovered. This year has already run away with us but we will just have a small celebration which you can plan. For now, I just wanted to get the family's blessing so that when mama eventually leaves our place, she will at least leave, knowing that she left you in the safe hands of your husband," Martin asserted, unmoved by my sudden sickness assault.

I didn't know what to say. The uncles had gathered at Martins' place with my father and my mother, with the aim of negotiating dowry. The occurrence felt familiar, as if it had happened before. I quickly recalled my mother's letter, that a decision to have her married was taken by the elders, with little or no input from her. That sent me panting and I hurriedly got up from the chair and went to the bathroom. Immediately after arriving in there, I vomitted so agonizingly and that ignited pains in my chest, so badly I just sat down on the cold tiled floor.

Martin walked in and sat down with me and held my hand. I didn't want him anywhere near me at that stage. I immediately disentangled my hand from his and felt no reason to look at his expression, as to whether that troubled him or not. I didn't care how he felt about the move.

"Palesa, please calm down…, you're gonna hurt yourself!"

"Don't tell me to calm down!" I yelled, "this is so typical of you. So you planned all the many things you did today and now this! You've taken this too far, Martin. I have a brain… so stop treating me like I can't think for myself." I vomitted again when I tried to speak further. Martin held the back of my neck and rubbed it in a few strokes.

"Baby, calm down please. What's wrong with you today? You are being particularly difficult," he bemoaned, as I coughed and realized that all the toxins seem to have all disappeared inside the toilet cavity, because I kept flushing after each gag. I gave him a scornful look and he laughed, unmoved that he was making me uncomfortable.

His question infuriated me and the fact that he didn't see anything wrong with what he had done, was even more exasperating, let alone the fact that he had convinced my mother to agree to the madness of doing everything behind my back. Evidently, ambushing me with the dowry negotiations was to him, a sure case that I would have no choice but to go along with it and not even think of embarrassing him in front of my family.

As I tried to get up from the floor, Martin barred me from getting up just yet and held my hand.

"Baby, please tell me what's making you so angry. I thought the fact that I am taking charge of our non-ideal situation and making you my wife as soon as possible, would please you. Was I wrong?"

"I can't believe you do not see anything wrong with what you have done. You cannot ensnare a person into something she hasn't prepared for. I am still getting used to the idea of us being engaged and we never spoke about the negotiations. Yet here you are, already having arranged it as if it's something minute. This is very huge to me."

He gave me a deep gaze and I did the same.

"I don't even understand how you managed to persuade my mother to go along with this, let alone convince my father to come today with my uncles even. Are you telling me this is how our marriage will be or should be? I have no say whatsoever on things that affect me?"

"Palesa, you've had your say and now you are going to listen to me, your man and soon to be husband. You are already wearing my ring. Whether this happens now or another day to be determined makes no difference to me. Today is the day that I planned and okay…granted, perhaps I should have spoken to you about it," he rolled his eyes. "I just simply wanted to surprise you that's all. Today is a day of surprises and this is the last one, I promise."

I shrugged and attempted to stand up from the floor once more. He managed to get up first and extended a hand to help me up. He then stole that moment to force hug me, something which made me rather weak. I quickly disentangled myself from his clutches and moved to the basin, rinsing my mouth.

"I'm sore and now aggravated as hell," I whimpered.

"Fine, all granted. But can we go ahead now?"

"I get the feeling you will go ahead even if I were to give you a negative response – so yeah, do whatever you want. I'm not appearing in the lounge for any reason though. The people you told to dress smartly can go ahead and be part of this. As for me, I want to sleep. I have been waiting for you for almost three hours as I had thought that you wanted me as much I wanted you. But no, I was wrong, you were planning…" I couldn't even complete my statement as he smiled and cupped my cheeks, pressing his lips against mine.

"Oh, now I see why you're really upset," he stated, after releasing me. "It's because you wanted us to make love so badly and I didn't come to the bedroom when I said I would! Now you realise how painful it can be to be rejected by the one person you love more than anything. It pierces your heart doesn't it?" he laughed, steadfast in his claim that he knew why I was upset.

I got tired of the back and forth babble, and gave him a terse look, and walked towards the door. As I was about to turn the knob, he grabbed me from behind, snaking his arms around my waist, practically compelling me to concede and to affirm certain things to him.

"Baby, are we okay?" he asked.

"Yes, we are okay. Can I go now?"

"Baby, I love you and all I want to do is to always show you how much I do. So, you are going to have to make peace with all the surprises that I will spring on you from time to time."

"Okay," I affirmed wryly.

I had given up, out of exhaustion. His thin skinned nature, to which I had become accustomed, made me stop trying to persuade him otherwise, because he was a person who didn't stand the thought of ever being wrong. His need to always be right, trumped common sense, truth and even normal social bounds. What he did was way out of line and he knew it, even though he didn't want to acknowledge the fact.

Although I had qualms, I had to admit that he was right and would always be right, otherwise how could my family have been so easily swayed into attending the dowry negotiations at his house, as opposed to it being held at my family home, at such short notice even!? He made them do things that were not cultural norm. As to what he promised them, I didn't know then!

I finally disentangled myself from his clutches, opened the door and walked back into the guest bedroom where my mother had been waiting. I removed some items of clothing she had scattered on the bed. Her reason for putting them there was seemingly to implore me to choose something to wear, so I could look presentable to be paraded to the elders. I lay on the bed and after feeling the breeze, I took the coverlet that was on the bed and covered myself with it. My aim was to sleep; I had no intention of participating in the show.

My mother kept swallowing her words often each time she tried speaking, battling to get even a single word out. What was she going to say anyway, seeing as she had suddenly switched allegiances and also persuaded my father and uncles to follow suit?

There had to have been a massive carrot Martin had dangled in front of them. If they could agree to it so easily, that meant I could never, even if I were to try, complain to them about Martin or even contemplate going home for whatever reason. The whole shebang had been sketchily prepared and very inept to say the least.

In my bid to rather concentrate on my health, I was not aware that I was dozing off.

Chapter 16

Bolt From the Blue

I was awoken by loud cheers and ululation, as the door was flung open. My mother launched herself inside, followed by Sis Lulama, who kept singing African wedding songs. Two hours had passed and it was already around eight. The clock on the wall attested to the fact.

"Finally, Miss Palesa, you are now a married woman. You are now officially Mrs Leboya," sis Lulama mentioned, dancing and smiling.

I looked at the two of them, powerless to say anything. I needed some time to myself to prepare for the next chapter of my life. I rested my head on the pillow further, letting the two women continue dancing and ululating as much as they felt they needed to.

I was not interested. The dowry had happened and I was not going to undo anything, nor was I interested in doing so. My mother kept quiet after I lay my head on the pillow.

"Lulama, please leave us. Just tell everyone that Palesa was sleeping and they must give us about half an hour to an hour before we can come through. You can see that she will need some time to sort herself out. We also cannot rush anything as we have to be careful not to hurt her," my mother instructed, firmly believing that she was being gracious!

After sis Lulama left the room, my mother hardened her tone and raised her voice, yelling at me. "PALESA, STOP THIS NONSENSE AND GET UP FROM THAT BED! This is all your doing anyway, so yeah, you are now married. You should count yourself lucky that this man you have elected to stay with actually loves you and cares about you…"

I could not allow my mother to continue singing Martin's praises because she had become robotic, as if it wasn't even her speaking.

"Mama, please stop this. Are you suddenly Martin's fan now?"

"Keep quiet and stop grousing!" she barked. "I know everything now…everything! You are going to stop telling lies about Martin. You have found yourself one of the good ones and all you ever do is to not appreciate his efforts but lie all the time about this poor man. I wish I had married someone like him; someone who can buy me expensive things at will; someone who isn't afraid to showcase his love for me for the world to see. But now, he's stuck with you, you ungrateful little scoundrel!" she scolded and then paused, pacing up and down the room as she continued. "He also told me that he's an orphan. So from today, he is now our son and whatever issues the two of you might have, you ought to deal with them together, otherwise we will have to get involved. You will not come back home for anything because you chose this path for yourself and now you have to persevere. I stayed in my marriage and you should stay in yours. Your actions are the ones that suggested that you now want to be a woman, a married woman. So suck it up!" My body involuntarily shivered.

I could not believe my mother's assertions towards me. I would have laughed it off, had the whole thing not felt so ham-fisted and hurtful. In a matter of hours, my mom had turned into what seemed like a brutally programmed machine and she was not even listening to what she was saying. Now all of a sudden, I was a bad person, despite me having told her everything that had transpired. I slowly got up from bed.

"Mama, I don't want to listen to you anymore. Please call Martin in here. I need to speak to him."

"No; I'm not gonna call him and watch you spoil his jovial mood. He is a very happy man today and you will pull yourself together and stop whining. You do not appreciate him and in your state of health, you really need to be careful. Where on earth have you ever seen any man do the things that Martin has done for you? You are certainly very ungrateful!" I was shocked.

With those sentiments, my mother took some weird looking multi-coloured maxi dress from the chair…, one of those that I had removed from the bed earlier. She then put it on the bed, looking at me sternly.

"Go freshen up, Palesa and don't even think of arguing with me. You need to go out there and show your face. If you dare, even for a little bit, tell your uncle all the lies you have been feeding me, you will be sorry. That will be a sure way of you losing your husband. Do you hear me?" She was speaking about my uncle Thutlo. I could never do anything wrong in his eyes.

"Fine, mama," I agreed and dragged my feet to the bathroom to freshen up. When I came back into the room, I could see impatience written all over her face and she wasn't even giving me half a smile.

Her behaviour confused me, as it contradicted the one she displayed during the day, when she practically avowed to look after me and that if anyone dared to hurt me, they would have to go through her first. There really was something I hadn't grasped at that moment.

Once I was back in the room, she attempted to dress me so that I would hurry up, lest the men became impatient. I did not afford her the luxury. I flatly refused. In fact, I sat down deliberately in protest, while watching her squirm and showing increasing signs of irritation.

"Palesa, what's going on with you? Finish up and stop with this attitude!" she lamented.

"Mama, I do not appreciate you bullying me and since this is my house, I actually think that it's time for you to leave… today, because you haven't done much for me ever since you came here anyway. Now I must agree with everything you say to me, for what? My husband knows that I don't want to rush, so if that doesn't sit well with you, well…tough!" I ranted.

She charged at me, as if she wanted to strike me but I remained impudent, unwavering in my stance of not accepting what was not sitting well with me. Instead of striking me, she sloppily pulled me by my hand, in her attempt to get me to stand up, while I pushed her in defence. We both pushed and jostled until my strength weakened and I screamed, lost my balance and fell on my knees but steadied myself with my hands just in time, prior to my whole body reaching the floor.

"Why the hell are you screaming? Do you want people to say I'm beating you up?" she woofed, as irate as something out of a horror movie. She tried to intimidate me but I was not moved. As she was about to drag me from the floor, the move terrified me and I trembled from noticing her in such a manic state, her eyes ablaze!

"Leave me alone!" I yelled.

After bellowing like that, she got even more agitated and slapped me across my face so hard I cried instantly; and then another strike followed and another and another!

I cried bitterly as my face felt like it had been stung by either a bee or a wasp. I know how their stings felt, because I was stung by both these ants when I was younger. I did not hear a door being opened but all I recall hearing, was noise in the room. My father and uncles, as well as Martin, Sis Lulama and Bra Mos had budged into the room, trying to see what the upheaval was about. I was still on the floor, enduring blows from my mother as she was now using her fists, hitting me on the back of my neck and my head.

My father rushed towards us and angrily dragged my mother away from me, sending her flying to the floor on the other side of the bed, as I knelt there, unable to stop weeping. I was still in my lingerie as I hadn't gotten dressed yet. Sis Lulama extended her hand towards me, helping me to stand up. She then gave me the purple velveteen bed throw, imploring me to wrap it around my upper body so it could extend further down.

I cast my eyes towards Martin, who was standing in the middle of the room silently, as if he had been detained or seen a ghost and was static as a result. As both my uncles continued hurling questions and admonishing words at both my mother and I, regarding what brought about the onslaught, I could not stop screeching.

My father charged at my mother as she seemed like she wanted to continue beating me up. As soon as he reached her, he now released two blows to her face, using his fists, pulling her by her braided hair. He then threw her outside of the bedroom and followed her. I literally heard her fall down hitting crockery that also fell on the floor.

That was a frightening sight, which nearly brought about a

fight between my father and his brothers as they attempted to prevent him from punching my mother further. She was now howling really loud. It became a huge mess!

Meanwhile, my husband had remained motionless, visibly traumatized by the scene unfolding in front of his eyes and in his home at that. I wondered if the scene was familiar as he had told me about the abuse his father used to subject his mother to. It was the first time my mother beat me up like that. It was like she was frustrated about something; even then, she seemed frenzied, as if she was a woman possessed.

Once my uncles had also left the room, I was able to respite on the bed, while still covering myself with the light quilt. My whole body was aching. I only realised after sitting, that I had been bleeding through my nose and on touching my neck, there was blood oozing from there as well.

"Miss Palesa, you're bleeding! Let me fetch some water from the bathroom. Mos…" Sis Lulama signalled Bra Mos. "Please help Doc to sit down and bring some sugar water for him. You can see that he is distressed after seeing what Miss Palesa's family has done here. I knew from the day I met that woman that she has some screw loose. What she did here is either work of the devil or she really is a nut case!" Sis Lulama ended her scorn, disguised as a rant.

I kept quiet because in a way, I agreed with her. My mother resembled one woman from the township we were always warned against teasing on the streets, as she had a mental illness, that didn't seem like it was ever going to be under control. She was not on medication and as children, we didn't even know what her issues were because her family didn't seem to care about her. The woman would often have manic episodes and always ready to fight with anyone she met on the streets.

Her anger would spring out of nowhere and she would take it out on unsuspecting passersby. She would not leave that person until a couple of people, usually men, would come to that person's rescue and restrain the woman.

The thought rattled me and made me speculate about how much of my mother's genes I might have inherited and I also wondered as to when I might begin to witness the symptoms. I still didn't know if I would be able to realize the indicators because of the difficulties involved in a person diagnosing oneself. I could only hope that I would be able to do so.

As soon as Martin sat down, bra Mos ran out quickly to the kitchen to fetch water as directed by sis Lulama. As I listened in on the commotion still going on in the living room, my father shouted at the top of his voice. "We're leaving now!" I do not know what he wanted us to do or say, as everyone was nursing themselves and dealing with the aftermath of my mother's deeds.

Martin was very quiet, visibly traumatized, distraught and trembling. Bra Mos came in just in time and spoke softly to him, "Sir, please take this; it will make you feel better." He handed him the sugary water to drink, as he grabbed it, his hands quavering uncontrollably.

He finally managed to drink all the water in the glass and then leaned back against the leather padded chair and pulled his breath slowly in different intermissions.

At this time, Sis Lulama came with a bowl of water, having put some peach hand towel inside. She then knelt down and retrieved the first aid kit from the bottom of the dressing table. She began first by squeezing water from the towel and placed it on my forehead as I continued bleeding meagerly, allowing blood to flow unabated and letting it plummet inside the bowl.

"Miss Palesa, perhaps you should lean backwards so that you do not continue bleeding like that…" Martin then startled us by immediately butting in.

"Lulama, have you already forgotten what I taught you? What Palesa is doing now is correct. She should not lean backwards at all. Palesa, try to keep your head up. This will help so that blood doesn't go down your throat. Pinch your nose and breathe through your mouth. Lulama, if her limbs are weak to lift and she can't do so with ease, help to pinch her nose as she continues breathing through her mouth for about ten minutes or so," he authoritatively advised, and then continued to rest his head against the padded sofa.

"Thank you Doc," sis Lulama said and I also did as advised.

I could not pinch my nose for too long though… perhaps that lasted for about three minutes and then I released my hand.

"Doc, there doesn't seem to be anymore blood coming out. Should Miss Palesa continue?"

"No, she shouldn't. If there's no longer blood coming out then it's fine. Ideally though, the pinching should at least have lasted for five minutes. But it's okay; just wipe her and I'll check on her later. She can still continue breathing through her mouth for five more minutes."

"Thank you Doc, and apologies for the slip up." Sis Lulama continued cleaning me up and as she applied a dressing at the back of my neck, I felt a sting so bad, I squealed.

"Sorry, Miss Palesa, I'm almost done. It looks like you have also stopped bleeding through your nose. Did your mother also hit you on your nose?" she asked.

"No she didn't, but she hit me hard on my head and the back of my neck. I suspect that is why I am bleeding. When you're done sis, please take all her things out of this bedroom and give them to her. I want her out of our home. In fact, they should all leave – it's late anyway!"

"I will do so, Miss Palesa. Please get up and let's see if she didn't hurt your operation. You'd swear, she wanted to cripple you because what we saw when we got in here was a crazy woman. In my opinion, she is possessed by demons or by jealousy."

"LULAMA, THAT'S ENOUGH! CAN'T YOU JUST WORK QUIETLY?" Martin admonished her, as I noticed him slowly coming to, as if he had earlier slipped far into a deep crevice and had now managed to come out. I gave him a simple gape over and looked down in shame of my mother's actions.

Bra Mos took over the cleaning up process, taking the bowl from sis Lulama as well as all the soiled cotton swaps she had used. She put them in a plastic bag, as I looked at both of them helplessly, while Martin had begun making remarking sounds, visibly still distraught about what he witnessed.

"I'm going to lay charges against your mother, Palesa. She has crossed a line. Mos, make sure that the big gate doesn't open. I just want to sit here for a while."

My husband was slowly coming back to his usual hard self but now, what was I going to do? Allow him to press charges? I never even contemplated the idea of having my mother arrested for assaulting me, as I acknowledged inwardly that I probably deserved the beating because I didn't speak to her respectfully. I didn't know any better between a reprimand and an assault. She had wounded me though…both physically and emotionally.

Sis Lulama finally finished packing my mother's things but then took my bag out as well, the one I had requested my mother to fetch from our room. She held it up without saying a word, raising her eyebrows, practically questioning me about why the bag was in the guestroom wardrobe.

"Put it back sis, thank you," I said briefly, and took off the bloodied lingerie as soon as bra Mos was out of the room. Sis Lulama then gave me my pyjama that was in the bag. After putting it on, I indicated my need to lie down and sis Lulama gave Martin a look that sought approval for what I was trying to do.

"What?" Martin asked insolently.

"Sorry Doc, I thought that you would want Miss Palesa to go upstairs to your room," she demurely responded.

"Lulama, this is Palesa's home and she can sleep wherever she wants to. Just learn to read the room woman! Can't you see that this is not the time for your silly probes?" There, there, he was slowly coming back.

I didn't want to participate in their talk but merely pulled myself towards the middle of the bed and lay down, drawing the throw over my wounded body. Martin and I weren't really talking to each other, even though we acknowledged each other by gapes here and there.

Eventually after sis Lulama had left with my mother's stuff, I heard some jabber again but this time, sis Lulama was in the middle of it, stating her piece! I murmured in wonder, while Martin also let some unfathomable words out.

I slowly turned around and faced him, tears flowing unabated. He then got up from the chair and shut the door. I didn't know at first what he wanted to do. When he sat on the edge of the bed, taking out his shoes, I understood instantly that he wanted to join me on the bed. He unbuttoned his shirt and got undressed, unzipping his pants too, leaving his draws.

He then threw the clothes on the couch he had occupied and indicated his desire to join me on the bed. I moved to give him some space.

On finally laying his head on the pillow, he pulled his breath and touched the bandage on my head.

"Is this not too tight, baby?" he asked sympathetically.

"No baby, it is not too tight," I responded.

He then extended his arm, beseeching me to let him inside the coverlet. Although it was a light blanket, it was big enough for two people. I flipped it open and he smiled, letting himself inside, while facing me still. He then gave me a peck on my lips and caressed my bruised face.

"You're gonna be okay, baby – you're gonna be okay," he comforted me, stroking my cheek steadily.

Another tear drop ran down my cheek, as if summoned by the tear gods. My husband quickly wiped it off, while his eyes remained fixed on me, as if he was attempting to decipher what I was thinking. I pulled my breath and nodded, "okay baby."

"Would you like some painkillers? You must be in terrible pain by now."

"No, I just want to sleep, baby. I'm taking too many tablets as it is, so I will sleep. Is my face swollen?"

"Not really, baby, it's not that swollen; bruised a bit on your cheek and forehead but you're not really swollen. I think Lulama did a good job. If however, at any stage you feel any kind of pain, even in the middle of the night, please wake me up."

"What are you saying here, baby? Are you going to sleep with me in here?" I asked frankly.

"Yes I am, baby. I'm your husband and I would like to take care of you. I sleep where you sleep. A lot has happened today and there's only so much a person can take. You have been through a lot today, starting with me in the morning, ending with a barrage of blows from your mother. I feel very stupid as your man, that I wasn't able to protect you."

"Come on, baby, you cannot blame yourself for anything that happened with my mother. I think there's something that has frustrated her, but for my dad to hit her like that though...," I complained.

"So, are you saying it was okay that she hit you the way she did… in fact hit you at all? You sound like you're making excuses for her."

"No… baby; that was certainly not okay. You know that I don't want anyone hurting me, either physically or emotionally. I'm just saying that it was the first time I saw my dad hit my mother. I don't know exactly what came over him. His abuse has always been verbal and perhaps emotional as well. I think if he did beat her up occasionally, I would have seen bruises on her face," I concluded.

"Are you aware that most abusers do not go for the face when they want to exert serious harm on their partners? They actually choose the body and carefully avoid the face. They believe that no one will see the bruises."

Martin was not aware that he was entangling himself, giving his game away, and had jumped head in first in a deep fissure. I wanted to ask him there and then, how he knew all that but decided to remark inwardly. That had spooked me though, as I remembered how he literally went for my coccyx to exert pain, power or authority over me.

"Baby," I said softly.

"Yes baby…," he responded.

"Please don't lay charges against my mother. I'll be fine. I think she had some frenzied depressive episode and I was the next best thing for her to take out her frustrations onto. Besides, I admit that I was a bit difficult earlier. So, in a way, it was partly my fault." Martin shook his head, visibly dumbfounded by my utterances.

"What do you mean it was partly your fault? Are you saying that violence is justifiable, as long as the person hitting you is doing so because of something you did or said?" I quickly got a sense where his head was at and didn't appreciate it one bit.

"Baby, I don't mean it like that. She's my mother and in a way, she must have felt that she had a right to lay her hands on me, because I didn't want to do what she wanted me to do."

"Palesa, I'm very befuddled now. Not so long ago, you gave me flak when I…," he paused and shook his head.

"Complete your sentence. What were you going to say?"

"I think we should leave this topic and you need to go to sleep. We will talk in the morning. It's getting seriously late now. We will sleep in here as we're already in bed," he stated.

I pulled my breath and kept quiet, after realizing what a

blunder I had made with my sentiments of me deserving of my mother's battering. Conflicting emotions swirled within me and I wanted nothing more than to avoid eye contact with Martin, who was now acting uncanny after our brief chat about beatings. I turned over and he lifted his head briefly from the pillow, seemingly to try to help me in case he noticed a struggle.

"I won't press charges against your mother. I knew that Lulama would go and spread the news. I just wanted to scare her a bit. If you don't want us to press charges, then I won't," he guaranteed.

The sound of the cellphone keypad alerted me to the fact that he was texting someone. I felt the need to ask frankly.

"Who are you texting?"

"Lulama. I just want her and Mos to let your family out because I had told Mos earlier to close the main gate. They need to go home and sort out their mess. I certainly don't want to hear any suggestion of a talk tonight. I've done all I have set out to do, and it's time they left us in peace now," he firmly avowed, as he continued typing his message.

Although there was still some mayhem emanating from the lounge area, it was fading into the background and I was happy to note that the family heeded sis Lulama's warnings as relayed to her by Martin. I shuddered to think, let alone know what he had said in the message. After my father had hit my mother, I was terrified more than I had been when she released her own blows on me.

Besides Martin kneeling down on my lower back in his bid to

assert his power over me, the assault by my father on my mother was the first I had ever witnessed firsthand, of a man hitting a woman, as if he was fighting with another man.

As my husband and I took a brief reprieve in conversing, I heard the banging of car doors and the engines being started. I was certain that we would never be bothered again. Martin then embraced me from behind, imploring me to rest.

****

In our quiet embrace with my husband, we heard a knock on the door and then sis Lulama spoke in a high pitched tone, "Doc, miss Palesa's family has left. Is she alright? How are her wounds? Can I bring her tablets in here? She hasn't taken her tablets for the evening."

The poor woman was genuinely concerned and I chuckled on hearing her throw a volley of questions at Martin. I thought he would scold her as he loathes being disturbed but he was pretty gentle in his response to her.

"Yes, Lulama, you can bring the tablets and you can also prepare something for both of us to eat. There's still a lot of food remaining I think. Just warm whatever you can. Palesa is trying to sleep though, so you better hurry."

"Oh no, she can't sleep now…, especially not in her state," she mumbled.

"I wonder what state Sis Lulama is referring to," I said.

"So, you're awake! Why didn't you even make any sound as Lulama was busy making such a clamor?" he asked, not really awaiting a response. I sniggered and turned around to face him again. This time, eager to show him how appreciative and proud I was of him, having handled things in a calm manner earlier, despite the explosive situation we had been facing.

"Baby, thank you for handling today so well. I know we had a disagreement earlier about you having gone behind my back to arrange the dowry negotiations. I honestly don't even know how you managed to pull this off, let alone convince my parents to come through with the uncles," I craftily added the part about the hastily arranged talks.

"Baby…," he laughed. "I never thought I'd hear you commend me for what I did for you today. I guess you now realize that I'm all you have, particularly after what your mother has done to you. As far as your father is concerned, there's no way I'm gonna let that 'Brahman' anywhere near you ever again! What he did to your mother is unforgiveable." He shook his head in apparent disgust and caressed my cheek.

"I was hurt when I saw that but I don't want to talk about them anymore. I think they will sort their issues out. What I want to know is how much they charged you for the dowry," I probed.

"You don't want to know, believe me," he tilted his head and smiled.

"I really do want to know. I'm your wife now so you don't

have to hide anything from me, do you?"

"Okay then, I'll tell you. Let's just say I parted with R250 000 for your dowry." I gasped and as I tried to pull myself up to rest my back against the wooden headboard, the bed spring squealed underneath us and we shared a chuckle.

Saved by Sis Lulama's knock again, Martin quickly jumped out of bed, still in his draws and I threw the coverlet towards him but he put it back on the bed and fetched a dry towel from the bathroom instead, wrapping it around his waist. He then opened the door, letting sis Lulama in.

"Sis Lulama, I hardly eat this late. It's almost eleven o'clock! I could have just slept you know! I'm not really feeling too famished."

"No, Miss Palesa, you …"

"Mrs Leboya!" Martin interrupted, while sis Lulama rolled her eyes in irritation. Martin paid her no mind but took his own plate from the tray, putting it on the night stand on his side of the bed.

"As I was saying… it's important for you to eat so that you can take your tablets." She handed my plate to me and placed the tablets on the pedestal. I put it next to the tablets and indicated my intention to get out of bed so I could freshen up.

"Sis Lulama, thank you for everything. We will see you tomorrow. Please go and sleep now; it's way too late. Tomorrow it's Sunday, so please don't get used to working on this day. We don't want to be accused of exploitation. The day has just been too dramatic and hurtful for us all. I will take the tablets, I promise."

"Okay, miss Palesa, thank you. But I actually don't usually mind, but tomorrow Mos and I are going to the farm. We haven't been home in a while."

"Lulama, I didn't know the two of you were going home tomorrow already. Can't this wait until next weekend? Palesa and I have plans this week to celebrate our honeymoon." This was news to me. Didn't he promise to run everything by me first?

"No, this can't wait Doc. It's important that we go to the graveyard to tell your parents that you got married. We have to ask our ancestors to protect you and your new wife, as she is one of us now. Remember that marriage is still a big deal and some of your friends might not really be happy and could become jealous of you so if we…"

"Wow…wow…wow…!" I interjected. "What's going on here actually? Martin, you never gave me an indication that you believe in ancestral devotion," I blurted out, while I inwardly wondered as to what I actually believed in. He ignored my jab. "Besides, why are your affairs being handled by sis Lulama and Bra Mos and why is she speaking as if you share a lineage? What does she mean 'one of us'?"

"Doc, I think this is a good time for you to tell her," she advised.

"Tell me what?" I asked tetchily, while I acknowledged a strange feeling inside of me that I was not going to like what I was going hear.

I went to the bathroom as I kept probing and I noticed the two of them giving each other peculiar glimpses.

After I finished what I needed to do in the bathroom, I went back into the bedroom and found them whispering to each other.

"What am I missing?" I asked.

"Please sit and eat. We will talk some other time. You did release Lulama to go and sleep. I'm certain Mos is also very tired and still waiting to escort her to her room," Martin held.

"It's okay Doc, I can spare five minutes," she said quickly.

"Okay…I'll tell her." Martin became jittery as I sat on the bed and took some of the finger food sis Lulama had brought. He fidgeted with a bottle of cold water often; but eventually opened it and drank the water.

"Baby, Lulama and Mos are my aunt and uncle – my father's siblings. They are the only family I have left, save for you now of course. Please don't get upset because not telling you sooner is on me. Please don't be angry at them," he pleaded.

I didn't know what to do on hearing the revelation. I felt as if there was cold water inside my skull and my whole body felt seriously weak as a result of the secret of the siblings and their nephew being divulged. I could not respond.

"Palesa, please say something," Martin beseeched.

"What do you want me to say? It was your choice to deceive me and you did it so well for a year now. What exactly was your intention? I really want to know."

I was livid, even though I could not decipher exactly why I was that incensed. I felt that him having his family and them constantly with me, changed everything. It was as if he heard my thoughts as he butted in.

"Baby, please don't be so upset…I can see your chest is heaving. This doesn't change anything believe me. Lulama and Mos have been here with me ever since my parents died. I had to fetch them from the farm because I was not coping on my own."

"Yes, Miss Palesa, it's true. I don't know what Mos and I would have done if Doc hadn't fetched us to come and stay here with him. Don't worry though; we are your employees and we will continue being your employees and this information should not change our relationship," she reassured.

"Actually, this changes everything, sis Lulama. I don't know how long you and Martin thought you'd hide this from me."

"The idea was to actually tell you after the dowry. So, before you ask Miss Palesa; Mos and I only found out about the dowry in the morning when Doc asked us to accompany him to buy the cars. We didn't know honestly. Please don't be mad," she begged.

"Sis Lulama, please go and sleep. We will talk tomorrow."

Martin motioned to Sis Lulama to leave, using his head to show her the door and she left at once and before pulling the door, she stood for a second and looked inside the bedroom, "Good night, Miss Palesa."

I simply waved at her as I was raving mad but was trying by all means to maintain poise. I was worried about what would happen if anger was to get the better of me. I had a brief vision of myself hitting Martin on his face and then later unleashing many blows to him…similar to the way my mother had beaten me. That frightened me. I got worried about the possibility of me also having bouts of manic melancholy. I pulled my breath consistently and after releasing for at least the fifth time, I grabbed a bottle of water from the night stand and drank a few sips.

"I've lost my appetite. Please don't say anything anymore. Let me deal with this my own way. I'll take tablets and sleep. I'm begging you…please don't even think of trying to make me understand the logic behind this reasoning of why you'd choose to not tell me that both bra Mos and sis Lulama are your relatives."

He nodded and lifted his hands up in mock surrender.

I took tablets and drank them. He in turn rounded the bed, retrieving the plate and bottles. He then left the room. It took some time before I could succumb to sleep.

Chapter 17

New Title, New Expectations

New day, new title and new revelations. A beautiful day dawned on us, unbothered by the emotional upheavals of the previous day. I guess in a way, the sun shining so bright was testament that what happened, had happened and there was nothing that could be undone and the huge revelation that still occupied my mind relentlessly, was not a dream.

I turned over to find Martin gawking at me, his arms nearing my body, suggesting that he had been hesitant to touch me as he had no idea how I would react to the appeal.

"Morning baby," I said, while indicating my intention to get up. He barred me from getting up just yet by grabbing my arm.

"Good morning, my love. Are you still upset because I can see that you're still pouting. This is how you looked yesterday," he claimed.

"I've just woken up, Martin and no, I'm not upset. What happened has passed and it's over. I want it all behind me. I don't really want anyone to insist that we talk about this secret that you and your helpers…I mean your aunt and uncle have been keeping from me. All I want to do today is to get up and do some exercise. By the way, when did you say you were bringing the physiotherapist?" I asked, not at all willing to talk about anything else.

"Okay baby, I can see that you are in no mood to talk about what happened. How are you feeling?"

"I feel fine and no pain. I want to take a shower," I briefly responded.

"Baby, what's the rush? I want to see your wound and where blood was oozing from yesterday, since you want to take a shower."

"Fine," I replied and then turned around, as he propped himself up, releasing the bandage from my head.

"I don't see any wound at the back of your neck. I don't understand why Lulama felt the need to bandage you like this."

"Yesterday you said there was blood oozing from the back of my neck. This is probably why she bandaged me like this. So, she panicked I guess."

"I think a simple gauze plaster would have sufficed. Don't you have a headache?" he asked, as I finally felt air on my head and lesion, which was clearly caused by either my mother's wedding ring or nails.

"I don't have a headache, but I can feel some slight twinge on the cut. How big is it?"

"It's not that big but you're definitely going to feel some kind of pain when you take a shower. Do you want me to come with you to the shower?"

"Yes you can come," I replied. He widened his eyes in amazement.

"I was expecting you to brush me off, so I'm happy that you agreed to my offer." I didn't respond but pulled myself towards the edge of the bed and headed to the bathroom. He followed me as earlier expressed.

"I'll call the physiotherapist tomorrow and set up an appointment for Tuesday. Will that be alright?" At last, he asked for my opinion. I was elated.

"Yes, that will be fine."

****

Our shower session was over before we even knew it. We did play a bit in the shower. Going back into the room, we realised that we had to tidy up and head to our own room.

"Baby…," he whispered, as I extended my eyes while continuing to wipe myself.

"Mmm…," I responded.

“I know I promised to set up an appointment with the physiotherapist tomorrow. This doesn’t prevent us from enjoying our marriage today and tomorrow does it?”

“I guess not. What did you have in mind?”

“I’m thinking of booking a hotel room away from around here for our honeymoon. You can even do physiotherapy there when you’d like to relax. I think it’s a good idea,” he ended.

“Yes it’s a good idea,” I responded. I had decided to let him win at everything because it was not going to do me good anyway, to argue with him about what I’d like to happen or not. He strongly believed that his word was law.

“You don’t have to agree with me if you don’t want to,” he said.

“Why do you say that? You are giving me your opinion which I happen to agree with, so what’s the issue? Does it mean that you’re now all of a sudden unhappy when I agree with you? What exactly do you want from me, Martin?”

“Palesa, you didn’t have to take it this far. I was simply making a remark because you are used to airing your opinion and at times your qualms about what I’m saying. Anyway, I will book right away and we need to utilize these few hours to pack our bags for a week.”

That surprised me …a whole week at a hotel? Did that even make sense? The house had everything we needed. So, I figured that it was a waste of time and money to book a hotel for the honeymoon. To me, it would have made better sense if we were to go out of town. What did I know? Clearly very little. I was not going to spoil his mood and the plans he had to make me happy. I let him be, while I utilised that moment to reflect.

He in turn, took some of our items including my bag that I had asked my mother to fetch from upstairs. I had been waiting for him to ask me about it ever since sis Lulama took it out of the closet. He had, early in the morning of the previous day, seen her with it as he had mentioned that he had installed cameras in our bedroom. I surmised that I would have to wait it out and he would probably ask me about the reasons she had it when I wasn't expecting him to.

He left the guestroom, promising to go pack, while imploring me to make it snappy as he had planned the most endearing week for us. I thought he had said there weren't more surprises? '*Ride the wave Palesa; Ride the wave.*' There she was…, my inner person had finally returned to either comfort me or to encourage me to go with the flow. This was something I did without even blinking.

****

We drove up the winding road for at least an hour, passing by rustic barns, charming cottages and picturesque villages, setting the tone for a tranquil retreat Martin had promised me. That was not a lie, as already by the feel of the air I breathed, I knew that we were entering a territory I was not accustomed to, something that was likely to change the whole course of my life.

Casting my eyes further up a huge locale, there it was, the five star hotel Martin had spoken about, nestled in the rolling hills and lush greenery of the countryside – a serene oasis awaiting our arrival.

When we approached the hotel, I noticed an elegant façade, adorned with ivy and flowing vines, exuding a sense of luxury and refinement. The entrance was flanked by towering trees that released a unique peppermint smell and a beautifully manicured garden, complete with a tranquil pond and a soft meandering stream.

As we parked near the entrance, the doorman quickly approached us, carelessly preventing Martin from opening the door for me - something he loved doing, and even displaying for all to see. He never missed a chance to let those around us know that I was spoken for. He nonetheless opened the boot as the porter advanced towards us with a trolley, eager to help with our luggage.

I stood near the car, taking in the moment, which felt like a dream for me. I had dressed simply, in my royal blue sweater pants suit, but I couldn't quite figure out what lay behind the glances people were giving us..., me in particular. Perhaps I was simply being self conscious but I did notice.

Eventually, Martin reached me on my side after attending to the porter and loading luggage onto the trolley. After ascending the stairs and going through the rotating doors, we stepped inside and I was instantly enveloped by the warm and inviting atmosphere, eyes fixed on us by the friendly reception staff.

Again, there were a few judgmental glimpses from some of the staff and guests. Perhaps it was evident that there was a significant age gap between myself and Martin. It was at this moment when I was feeling self conscious about those disparaging eyes, that Martin snaked his arm around my waist, giving me a kiss on my lips.

"Are you okay?" he asked, and I nodded, while amply aware of his reassuring and loving gaze that made me feel at ease to the extent that I immediately ignored the whispers and stares. I still couldn't help but to admire the stunning lobby, complete with a grand chandelier, plush furnishings and an impressive art collection, which immediately drew my interest.

I would have gone to feast my eyes, but I was quickly interrupted by one of the servers, who approached us carrying champagne glasses on a beautiful gold plated tray and a refreshing towel to help us unwind, I surmised. I followed Martin's cue as I was clueless of what to do in that instant. He swiftly took care of the check-in process and took one champagne flute from the tray, handing it to me.

I was unsure of what to expect from the unfamiliar drink but Martin's persuasive gaze encouraged me to take a sip. His eyes were unrelenting as if they were saying, 'come on, it's a special day, don't you dare embarrass me.' He might not have said it out loud, but I could see his eyes were saying those words. I tried all I could to not choke on the bubbly drink, lest I embarrass him or make people aware that it was the first time I had that type of drink.

Somehow, I felt the need to want to fit in with the crowd that knew and enjoyed alcoholic drinks.

My lips touched the rim of the glass and I took a tentative sip. The bubbles danced on my tongue, releasing a subtle sweetness and a hint of fruitiness. Before I could process the taste, the champagne's effervescence tickled my nose and I giggled, while Martin quickly gave me a wry smile. I smiled back, however this time, I became determined to prevent any involuntary sniggering, for fear of falling foul of my man's expectations of me.

As the porter led us towards the elevators across the hall, I discerned that Martin had already bolted down his champagne and had also handed the glass to the server. I had to quickly do the same and took a few steps back to put my flute on the tray the man had in his hands, next to Martin's.

It was at that moment that I felt a sudden lightheadedness, my legs turning to jelly. I wobbled slightly, as my eyes locked onto Martin's, searching for reassurance of some kind. I could have sworn I saw stars, Alcyone, Asterope or Electra! He grinned, his eyes crinkling at the corners as he whispered, "You're doing great, baby."

That puzzled me as I was expecting a chide. Perhaps he had to calm down as we were in the company of the porter, who was leading us to the elevators.

We eventually got to our floor, while Martin kept checking the door numbers so we wouldn't miss our room. We finally got to our room and after opening it, both Martin and the porter directed me to step in first and I obliged. Besides, all I wanted to do was to sit down or even sleep as I felt seriously drunk, akin to a person who had a lot to drink.

As soon as we got in, I saw bottles of water on the table and I quickly grabbed one and took a sip, eager to remove the bubbly from my palate or my system, I didn't care. Once the porter left after being given a sizeable tip, Martin closed the door and laughed his lungs out.

"What's so funny?" I asked, annoyed by how he practically forced me to have a drink, knowing that I had never had alcohol in my life and I didn't even know what it would do to me.

"I'm amused by how you just rushed to drink water. You looked like someone who has been stuck at a desert for days and has never had any liquid in a long time!" he continued laughing, as I shrugged and sat on the bed, allowing my eyes to run through the room.

The room was a lavish sanctuary, garlanded with opulent furnishings and intricate details. The walls were painted a soothing shade of cream, complemented by rich, dark wood accents and elegant crown molding. A stunning crystal chandelier hung from the ceiling, casting a warm, soft glow throughout the space.

The bed I was now occupying, a majestic centerpiece, boasted a plush, deep purple velvet, jewel-toned headboard. The bedding was a splendid ensemble of crisp, white linen and a plethora of pillows in various shapes and sizes, as well as a soft cream coverlet, placed diagonally at the tail end of the bed. The overall effect was one of indulgent comfort and luxury.

Sudden stillness in the room alerted me to the fact that Martin had taken out his tablet and was now scrolling down and had sat down on the armchair in the beautiful sitting area, that had a plush sofa as well, arranged around an ornate marble-top coffee table. A beautifully crafted wooden desk stood in another corner, accompanied by a comfortable, leather-bound chair.

I stood up to examine the rest of the room and went to the bathroom. That was another masterpiece of elegance, with marble countertops, gleaming chrome fixtures, and a spacious walk-in shower. The taps were sleek and modern, almost parallel to those at Martin's place, with two rainfall showerheads and separate handheld sprayers. A deep, soaking tub invited relaxation, surrounded by plush towels and an array of deluxe bath products.

It was evident that every room was designed to pamper and indulge, creating a tranquil retreat for my man and I to unwind and celebrate our honeymoon.

I almost felt guilty for having given Martin such a hard time the previous day and months prior. He was trying his best to make me comfortable. Why did that still not feel absolute for me though? It was like something was missing and since I had no experience prior to being with him, there wasn't really anything I could compare my life to.

I deduced that it most probably was due to the fact that I still longed to do something for my life that would make me feel worthy or stuff that my age mates got up to. For the time being though, I had to surrender to the moment and do everything in my power to assure Martin that I was grateful for the gift and his efforts to make me happy. The love bombing still felt heavy nonetheless.

I went back into the main seating area and sat on Martin's lap, wrapping my hands around his neck and planted a kiss on his lips. He reciprocated and then released me, gawking at me, and putting the tablet down on the table. He snaked his arms around my waist and then stood up, carrying me in his arms, swirling me around, while my legs dangled in the air.

Eventually he put me down, cupping my face with both his hands and literally devoured my lips, as I responded with great zeal. The light-headedness as well as pain on my neck resurfaced and I had to briefly pull away from Martin, who was heated at that moment.

"What now?" he asked, slightly bothered.

"Nothing," I replied, pretending to not feel any pain. "It's just that we haven't really had much to eat since we left the house."

"Are you seriously worried about food now, at this moment?" he curved his eyebrows.

"Not really…," I faked accord with him, even though my stomach was churning and my head was spinning. I had to let go of all my inhibitions and wrapped my arms around him, as he continued where he had left off, cupping my cheeks with his hands again and kissed me one more time, this time an enduring kiss that literally left my legs feeling restless, accelerating my breathing, while my chest tightened at the same time. Before I knew it, Martin had unzipped my sweat top, throwing it on the chair, following the move with a smooch on my neck.

I felt a mix of excitement and apprehension. As much as I knew that day held a different significance now that I was his wife, I couldn't help but to feel anxious, largely because we hadn't been intimate in a while.

My mind wandered to the times when he had been stern with me, and I wondered if our lovemaking this time around, would reflect that side of him again. I however let all of myself go, surrendering every bit of myself to my now husband. He took off his shirt as I eagerly helped him and unfastened his belt, allowing his jeans to fall off, leaving him with his briefs.

"Today is about us, about our love and nobody else. Relax, you're in safe hands," he reassured me, touching me everywhere tenderly, while removing every bit of clothing I still had on.

Despite the persistent discomfort I still had on my back, I found myself immersed in the moment, my worries dissipating in the embrace of our passion and love. I inwardly marvelled at the depth of our connection, realizing that my unspoken discomfort was met with my husband's implicit understanding.

In a strange yet beautiful way, I found solace in his arms as we made love, each moment a testament of his devotion to me. The hotel room resonated with gentle whispers of our deep affection, demonstrating the profundity of our bond and the tenderness with which we both approached one another despite everything that happened.

All faults of the previous months and days had been wiped away by the simple atmosphere brought about by our love. I prayed for the moment to last as it was becoming heavier to carry all burdens of the past.

Our connection filled the air, weaving an enduring drapery of our genuine affection and unwavering devotion. I was certain I would fall pregnant, as the moment felt deliberate and different from all the times we had been intimate.

I had abandoned myself fully in his embrace, as he did all he could to assure me of his love and protection. His eyes sparkled as he brought me close to his torso, encouraging me to rest on him. My heart wouldn't stop beating intermittently, as if something was going to interfere with our happiness but, it was because I was drawing from the many times we had been merry, when soon after, my joy would be shattered in an instant.

"Baby," Martin whispered.

"Mmm," I murmured.

"I love you with all my heart. Yes, ours might have started as a weird one, but I know that I love you. I'd definitely kill for you," he pledged, making me panic instantly. I believe he felt my heart raising and he stopped with the declarations, speaking as if he hadn't just made a threat. "I think we must order some food now; I know you must be starving. Come to think of it, did you bring your medication?"

"Yes, I did but I feel fine. I don't want to keep taking these tablets. They make me feel drowsy all the time," I moaned.

"No, baby, you have to take your medicines religiously until you get better. Besides, you also have antibiotics so you have to finish the course," he directed.

"Yes Doc, I promise I'll take them." He laughed and tickled me, sending the bedding flying all over the floor.

After selecting food from the menu and calling the dining room for room service, we went to the bathroom to freshen up.

****

Although my initial intention was to savour the delicious brunch, the champagne's bubbles had filled my stomach, leaving little room for food. So, I merely nibbled on a few items on the plate and left some for later. Martin wasn't bothered as he seemed to have been more interested in whatever he was now busy with on his tablet, which prompted me to ask frankly.

"What are you busy with?"

"I'm sending invitations out," he paused. "Oh…by the way I have to tell you when I want to surprise you…my bad!" he mocked. This was one battle I had to decide quickly as to whether I wanted to overcome or live with it.

"What are the invitations for? Please don't tell me you're planning something for us because I'm honestly exhausted and I doubt I want to do anything that's going to leave me irritable, as being around many people tends to have that effect on me," I cautioned.

He ignored me, while continuing with whatever he was doing on his tablet. He had his eyes firmly engaged on the gadget and although I felt like probing further, I decided to abandon the idea, choosing my peace instead.

His father-like behaviour when it came to how he sometimes engaged with me, left me goaded most of the time. However, he would make up for it by giving me everything he believed I wanted and perhaps needed, while giving me instructions to always do as he says and to stop back-chatting. He 'knew better' didn't he?

Chapter 18

The more things change…

Finishing what he was doing after what felt like an epoch, he finally came towards me as I had now occupied the sofa, wearing the hotel robe and slippers, so did he. He sat with me but then I sulked as soon as he reached me. He tickled me and I maintained my resolve, removing his hands from my waist as I continued to watch TV.

"Baby, don't be upset."

"I'm not upset," I maintained.

"So, what's with this attitude you're giving me now? Are you upset that I'm not telling you about what I was busy with? Remember that I did tell you that I was sending invitations out, but that doesn't mean I should divulge the full details prior to the time I want. So, whatever it is that has caused this sudden mood, just pack it in already!" he admonished.

In my bid to leave the couch as I wanted to catch some fresh air by retreating to the balcony, he restrained me and I involuntarily sat on the divan and he forced me to face him, touching my chin and turning my face towards him.

"You're not going to do this, today of all days. We had the best time a few hours ago didn't we? So why do you want to spoil the mood like this?" he asked, visibly aggravated.

"That's not my aim to spoil the mood. All I want is for you to include me in what you're planning, especially if those plans include me."

"Fine, you win; I'll tell you. I want us to have a small gathering of my friends and their partners so I can introduce you to them as my wife. Everything is done and dusted now, so...," he shrugged.

"I don't understand this. You'd like to invite your friends and their partners? What about my friends?" I asked, and then quickly regretted posing that question.

"Don't make me laugh, Palesa. Which friends are those exactly? Your high school buddies? The ones you once told me left you in grade 10 and are now in grade 12? Do you want to embarrass me or yourself?"

"No, I don't want to embarrass you nor myself. Forget I even asked."

"I certainly will forget you asked that dim question. Remember you're in a different league now, and you cannot still be hung up on the life you left behind. You're now a married woman and you need to start behaving as such," he said sternly.

His tone changed drastically, as if I had said something he found confounding. That was not my best moment, it appeared. I suppose I never thought my question through – now I went and upset the apple cart!

"So when is the event?" I probed.

"It will be this coming Friday. You see…you have at least four days to go through intense physiotherapy routine up until Friday morning at least. Then on Friday afternoon, you can finalise everything for the evening."

"Why are you talking as if this will be done by me only? Where will you be? Won't you be here to help me?"

"Palesa, I cannot be here to always hold your hand. Besides, I'm going to work tomorrow until Thursday. I've already been off for a while now. So I have patients to see or have you forgotten that I actually work?"

"No, I haven't forgotten and it's not a problem that you're going to work. I'm just not sure there is much I can do to plan something like this though."

"Don't worry; I have spoken to the events co-ordinator here at the hotel. They will give you ideas on how to plan this – take it as practice for more events you will be planning. Remember, you will soon own a restaurant, so it's now time to hit the ground running.

Perhaps they can give us the heads up, if the room I'm eyeing is booked or not."

"It's fine, but I still think you should have discussed this with me first. What if this isn't really what I want?"

"We are not going to fight about this Palesa – please don't start," he warned.

Everything was moving way too fast for me and it was like I was in a movie or trapped in some kind of a simulation and there was no one to take me out of there. My voice was muffled and my mind felt hollow, as if I was living someone else's life.

On one hand, I was enjoying this new found life but on the other hand, the nagging voice kept counselling me about this life I had chosen. I had many fears and most if not all of them were justified.

In all of that, I still felt it better to stay in opulence, even though I was a stooge of some kind, rather than go back home, especially after the altercation I had with my mother. That was the first time she had ever laid her hands on me.

Even though my father had come around in a way, it was difficult for me to trust that he truly had changed, what with him having hit my mother in my presence, shocking everyone in the process. Now how could I have contemplated going home to such dysfunction? Besides, I was a married woman now and married women don't go home in a whim. I chose the life, as my mother had said.

Monday morning came and Martin left for work, leaving me in bed after reminding me to not miss any medication. He told me that he would start at the dining hall first to have breakfast but that I shouldn't worry about going downstairs.

He mentioned that he was protecting me from all the probes I was likely to get from either the guests or the staff at the hotel. I was supposed to spend the whole day in the room and he reminded me we had the luxury of the balcony should I need fresh air. A thought crept through my mind that he had likely arranged that, should I step out of the room, they should inform him.

After he left, I took a nap and hadn't realised that I had dozed off. At least I had set the alarm clock to 09h00 because my body sure needed to recover from everything I had been through. I was late for my breakfast though as I had to always eat by 08h00 as the medication demanded that I take as I was eating and always at the same time. I nonetheless woke up and retreated to the bathroom to take a shower. I then wore my pink light wooly sleeveless dress, which was long and had a slit on each side. I loved my dress.

I then called room service and ordered some food. They came in as I was tidying up our stuff that had been on the floor. I opened the door and asked the server to place the food on the table on the balcony. I signed for my food and the man left as I never gave an indication that I wanted to do some small talk anyway.

When I reached the table setting on the balcony, I noticed that Martin had left his tablet on one of the chairs. I picked it up and alas! There was an open page and it was the email he had sent last night. I went through it and checked it out.. He had really sent the e-mail to a couple of people, with their names visible – mostly men.

I read other e-mails, a few personal invitations and noted that he had mentioned that they could bring their plus ones. So, I counted…together with us, we would all be 21. One odd person was…Lucas! Why would he invite Lucas when they had a stalemate? What was he trying to do or prove? Was he trying to test me? Should I ask him about it when he comes back? No…I wasn't going to do it.

I was rattled to see his name on the guest list. Surely Lucas had a girlfriend, didn't he? So, why didn't he advise him to bring his plus one? As Martin had mentioned, I had to hit the ground running because I was no longer a child but someone's wife!

****

Friday arrived quickly after I had gone through the most excruciating physiotherapy from Tuesday to Thursday. I was not particularly worried about my back as Dr. Duvenhage had done a stellar job and despite my mom's recent assault on me, I wasn't badly affected.

The buzz in our hotel room was electric, as a team of experts transformed me into a vision of elegance. Jason, the renowned fashion designer hired by Martin at such short notice, had created a true masterpiece for me. He meticulously adjusted the stunning white long bodycon dress, decorated with intricate diamantes that sparkled like diamonds. The gown hugged my curves, thanks to the cleverly sewn-in corset, accentuating my figure. The bodice perfectly cupped my breasts, showcasing my toned physique. I knew I looked superb!

My accessories shimmered with sophistication: diamond studs, a matching necklace, and a breathtaking three-tier bangle set. My fiancé, Dr. Martin Leboya, had thoughtfully gifted me an exquisite white gold watch, its face gleaning with subtle diamonds.

Then there was Thabo, thee Master Hair Stylist. He had crafted a classic updo, securing my locks with precision. He also added extensions for added volume and a delicate crown to complete the look.

The makeup artist enhanced my features with flawless technique, balancing subtlety and glamour. The hired photographer captured everything that I was subjected to by my glamour team, and I kept posing for photos until my cheekbones began to hurt.

While everyone was fussing over me, Martin emerged from the extended room, having been through his own team that had turned him into the amazing Adonis I was now witnessing. He was clad in a dashing tailored white tuxedo, its black collar adding a touch of sophistication. His own new watch glittered with diamonds, mirroring mine. His grand appearance belied the hidden truth of our relationship.

With one last glance in the mirror, I slipped into my white satin and diamante platform heels, elevating my stature without sacrificing comfort. Jason gave a final adjustment to my gown, and I was ready.

Martin and I posed for photos together as the videographer in the room also captured our moment, trying very hard to not be in the way. That was a true bolt from the blue! I thought I was happy, ought to be happy.

I never thought of arranging the videographer to capture our moment. It did appear that Martin had thought of that and craftily neglected to mention it to me. Clearly he had been sharing notes with the hotel events coordinator without my knowledge.

As we prepared to go down to the private dining room at the Grand Imperial, excitement mingled with nerves. The glamour team followed us, with the tech team in tow. Only 19 select guests had been invited to our intimate engagement party. I knew that Martin had invited Lucas on purpose and had deliberately not mentioned him bringing a partner.

Notably absent, were my family members, as Martin had discouraged me from inviting them due to my recent struggles with my mom and our complicated relationship. I wanted to invite them, even at short notice because I knew that my uncles would have made an effort to come.

As we entered the dining room, whispers and admiring glances followed me. The wives and girlfriends of Martin's friends and acquaintances couldn't help but stare, their envy palpable. I also elevated my shoulders, standing tall, radiating confidence beside my man, the picture perfect love display.

As I cast my eyes wider around the room, I saw a Pastor in attendance, standing in front of the guests and waiting for us. That was not our agreement! According to me, it was supposed to be an engagement party but Martin had other ideas - a full on private wedding, minus my family. How could he!

"Baby, why is the pastor here? Which church is he from?" he smiled at me and kissed me on my cheek.

The Pastor yelled, "I haven't yet given you permission to kiss the bride, Martin!" Everyone including Martin laughed, except me, as I battled to locate the humour. I was already in a bad mood because I was bamboozled into the dowry a few days ago, then I had now again been thrown into a state of more confusion, as I walked into my wedding, a private event I had thought was our engagement party.

I tensed, as Martin's arm, in which he had snaked mine, tightened the grip, practically forcing me to move forward or else! I maintained my fake smile and inwardly acknowledged that no one knew who I was and as a result, couldn't tell whether my smile was genuine or not.

Finally, we arrived near the pastor and I realised then that both Bra Mos and Sis Lulama were present, and she had been prearranged to serve as my bride's maid and Bra Mos as Martin's best man. None of his friends enjoyed the luxury of accompanying him to marry his sweetheart. I figured they probably knew him better than I did anyway, and they certainly should have been more privy to his selfish nature than I had experienced, particularly since they had attended the 'engagement party'.

Sis Lulama looked elegant in a white satin midi dress with long sleeves and white wedges. She had minimal make up on. Bra Mos looked spruce in a black suit with a white shirt. He didn't have a tie on; simple but chic.

The occasion was grand but highly atypical and certainly not what I wanted for myself. Once again, Martin put a stamp on the fact that he would always do as he pleased, turning me into a doll that had no voice nor a mind of its own.

Sis Lulama stood up to meet me, whispering in my ear that I must not embarrass his nephew, as he went all out to please me and to give me the wedding of every girl's dreams – the bravado!

I had to suck it up and participate in my wedding. We exchanged vows, following what the Minister said, while professing our unwavering love and commitment to one another, amidst the tender whispers on the floor. Martin gave me a diamond eternity ring as Bra Mos handed me Martin's white gold one, which he had bought himself. I slipped it through his finger after I had vowed to love and obey him, forsaking all others.

The vows were done with swiftly and the Minister pronounced us husband and wife, finally giving Martin permission to kiss his bride. He gave me a drawn out peck on my lips, leaving me uncomfortable. Sis Lulama ululated and Bra Mos danced, as did the other invitees, who followed with cheers and some clapping. I felt my eyes becoming watery and I tried everything in my power to stop the tears from falling, but I was not very successful.

Sis Lulama was quick to come to my aid as the "trusted" bride's maid. I loathed the moment and wanted nothing but for it to end. We sat with our backs against the audience, at the register table that was arranged for us by the hotel events planner I had consulted. She was standing towards the far end of the room next to the violinists.

After signing that we were now married, I felt electricity shooting through my whole belly, making me tremble uncontrollably. The Minister gave me a worrisome look and I guess in his bid to make light of the moment, he made a joke about it, inviting more laughter from the floor. That annoyed me.

Martin kept whispering in my ear something unclear but I was not interested. I felt sick to my stomach, really sick. I had to blink incessantly while my back was still against the crowd, making sure that when I did eventually turn around, I'd have sorted myself out at least. I managed - barely.

It was only after we had sat down at our table, that I was able to actually survey the room and to make some kind of eye contact with all the guests. Some female guests smiled at me, while others waved and a few women exchanged whispers and sniggers.

At first, that didn't bother me, but then it appeared that they were either laughing at me or at the whole shebang, as they probably knew exactly what was going on. I got a weird vibe.

As I continued surveying the room, I took in the beauty of the flower bouquets which christened each table, while a graceful mixture of gold and blue bows tied together, decorated the backs of the chairs. An array of potted arrangements bordered the dance floor on each side, as bright as some of the floral dresses the female guests were clad in.

Over in the violinists' corner, the grand piano was in danger of collapsing under the weight of roses on its lid and I signalled the wedding planner to remove them. Besides, the mix of floral scents overwhelmed my sinuses and I was concerned that I might have a terrible reaction to the smell. I shudder to think what the pianist would have done had he found the flowers still arranged on the piano!

Reception began right away while the Minister wished us well, summarily leaving the festivities. The wedding planner accompanied him outside. One by one and two by two, friends came over to our table for greetings and introductions. Martin seemed pleased by some and tolerated others. I couldn't quite understand why he would invite people with whose energy he was not aligned. Everyone seemed eager to meet me, nonetheless.

Lucas eventually came to our table, having been initially keen to beat everyone to it. Both him and Martin put on a façade, pretending that there was nothing amiss between them. I could not participate in the charade, as I was still nursing the effects of their bruised egos on my life. Lucas did seem troubled however, as if he had a lot on his mind.

This was the first time Martin gave me some details about his story, something I had to pretend to not have been interested in hearing, lest I inadvertently fall foul as a married woman.

He evidently was intent on embarrassing Lucas, while I questioned the wisdom of inviting him to the event. He was still standing at our table as Martin began: "Baby, of course Lucas needs no introduction. You know very little about him though. Yes, this man is actually very intelligent, ambitious and driven." Lucas smiled, acknowledging the compliment. "However, he is also arrogant and narcissistic. He believes that he is entitled to whatever he wants, regardless of the cost to others." Lucas didn't take kindly to that.

"This is so typical of you, Martin. You say something beautiful and then spoil it quickly with something negative. Now, between you and I, who is actually arrogant?"

Lucas ogled me, and I dropped my eyes. For some reason, his aura was still very much endearing, as on the first day I laid my eyes on him. So, looking at him was never gonna be a good idea.

"Palesa, let's settle this once and for all. Between your husband and I, who is arrogant and narcissistic?" How dare he ask me to choose!

"Lucas, I just wonder what it is that gave you an idea that I'd say my husband is arrogant. You are a piece of work. The fact that you can even ask me this question proves this theory. So please guys, I'm tired of getting in between the two of you. I need to meet some of your other friends, Martin," I sternly stated.

"My wife has spoken, so man, give us some breathing space," Martin asserted. Where's your girlfriend by the way?"

"What sort of question is this? You deliberately didn't mention that I should bring a plus one, now you are asking me where my girlfriend is ?"

"Sorry, it wasn't deliberate. I must have assumed you'd come with someone." The lie etched on Martin's face was evident and both Lucas and I could see that.

I stood up from our chair, as music played, eager to forget about the awkward wedding reception as well as the tension between my husband and his friend. I wanted to at least meet the other people, who were also preparing to greet me, giggles and all!

Bra Mos called Martin aside and they went out briefly, as I attempted to mingle with everyone who introduced themselves to me. The moment felt inept, as Lucas demanded that I dance with him because Martin would not be chuffed if he found me 'unprotected', he claimed.

Joshua, one of the friends, a businessman, seemed befuddled by the assertion, but simply lifted his hands up and danced with his wife, a teacher who seemed to be a few years older than him. "Ntswaki," she said briefly. "It's nice to meet you, Palesa. We will have a chat later, once the bitter juice has taken over their brains, don't worry. For now, just allow the attention and forget about everything else."

I don't know what the woman was sensing or observing but, she was spot on that I was a nervous wreck. It seemed like others were avoiding me like a plague as they just smiled and waved at me. Perhaps they were hungry as it was lucid that we were not going to eat anytime soon, because waiters had not come through yet.

Sis Lulama was just sitting, using her feet to dance, watching me like a hawk, as if she was hired to keep an eye on me. The last thing I remember was her getting up, as well as the uncomfortable eye ogle of Lucas. It was lucid that the group of friends were not ordinary, as their faces and hum of conversations, seemed to whisper tales of secrets and scandals.

While still waiting for my husband, Lucas forcefully pulled me towards him, demanding that I dance with him. I pretended to not be bothered but my stomach was churning, while Lucas' unnerving intensity and façade, as well as his sinister gaze, sent shivers down my spine. He held me too tight and I protested, threatening to scream.

"Finally, I can touch your body," he said. "you smell wonderful," he continued, sounding like a roguish sprite, his behaviour, perverse.

Evidently, no one seemed to care about the weirdness that was going on between Lucas and I. They simply looked at us as if what was happening was normal. That frightened me. I demanded he release me immediately. He refused, pointing to the door, claiming that Martin was calling me outside and he would like to accompany me, more so that the dress I wore was too long and he 'didn't want me to 'trip' and fall.

I walked with him towards the door and as I was still trying to see where Martin was, Lucas' face reddened, and he rough-handled me and pulled me by my arm. I yelled, asking him what he was doing and screamed out loud. He slapped me across my face and I froze, unsure of what just happened.

"What are you doing, Lucas, leave me alone!" I yelled again, trying to disentangle myself from his grip. But, he was too strong and I bit him on his upper hand. He struck me across my face again, this time with his fist, and I tripped and fell, one of my heels coming off.

"Shut up! Otherwise I'll tell everyone that you wanted us to have a quickie while your husband is busy with other things." I wept bitterly, unbelieving of what was happening to me.

"What have I ever done to you, Lucas? Why are you doing this? Please leave me alone. I screamed one more time, 'help..., help..., help...'

"You are what we call 'collateral damage'. You're gonna die for the sins of your husband. It's nothing personal," he claimed.

The scuffle was intense and I used very ounce of strength I still had to resist. But, Lucas' grip was unyielding.

In the chaos, I missed a step and tumbled down the stairs. My body rolled helplessly, until I hit the cold marble floor, my head striking with a sickening thud. The same spot on my back operated on, screamed in agony.

Hearing footsteps and my screeches, hotel stuff, security guards, and I deduced some guests as well, rushed to my aid, as Lucas ran away, disappearing into thin air. My world went dark, consumed by the shadows of obsession and sinister intentions of those who claimed to care for me.

The Grand Imperial Hotel, once a symbol of joy and celebration, became a haunting reminder of horrors lurking in the darkest recesses of the human heart.

****

As I lay in the hospital bed, my body broken and bruised, I felt weak and my spirit was crushed.

Martin's anger and blame pierced my soul like a dagger. "Why did you dance with Lucas?" he hissed, his eyes blazing with possessive fury. "You had no right to dance with him, to let him touch you like that! I can see that you did that on purpose. What the hell were you trying to prove?" he screamed. "You clearly encouraged him and then changed your mind when you thought I was coming back. That's what drove him over the edge!" he cruelly accused me, declaring untruths, as if he had been there.

I wept, trying to explain, but my words only fuelled his rage. “So, every time I turn my back, you’ll run into another man’s arms?” he sneered, his voice continuing to drip venom.

Dr. Duvenhage’s arrival interrupted our bitter exchange, his solemn expression a harbinger of bad news. “Palesa, your recent back operation has been compromised. You’ll need to use a wheelchair for a few weeks and undergo extensive physiotherapy.”

Martin’s face darkened, his ego visibly wounded. “I’ll find Lucas, and when I do, I’m gonna kill the bastard!” he growled, leaving me alone with my tears and shattered dreams, while the doctor pretended not to have heard what he said.

“Doctor, am I paralyzed? If so, how come I still feel my legs?”

“No, you’re not really paralyzed.” That was all he said and he immediately left me after that. It was like I was bothering him with all the questions about my health.

When he left, I realised that Martin’s love was a double-edged sword – a fierce protection that had turned into a possessive destruction and I wondered as to whether what I thought was love would survive the trial or would it become my prison as I had initially suspected?

His words still loitered in my mind, a constant reminder of his domineering and calculating nature. I couldn’t bear the thought of going back to our place, trapped with him and his anger.

My parents, especially my mom, despite our recent fight, arrived unexpectedly with him, their faces etched with concern. He had clearly either found them in the parking lot or in the hallway as he was about to exit. My mom's eyes welled up with tears as she took in my battered form. "Palesa, my baby, what happened?" she whispered. Did she just ask me that? That got me fuming! It was not like she didn't do the same thing to me the week before. How dare she!

I hesitated, unsure how much to reveal. But Martin's arrival, his eyes blazing with fury, made a decision for me. "I want to go home with my parents," I declared hurriedly, while my voice remained firm.

Martin's face darkened. "You're my wife, Palesa; you belong with me. What are you hoping to gain by going home with the one person who beat you up not so long ago?"

My dad got seriously aggravated, feeling disrespected by my husband. He stood tall and charged at Martin, his voice stern. "Palesa is not going anywhere with you; not until we know what happened Martin and not until she is ready to leave with you.

Martin's anger boiled over and he took a step closer to my dad too – two bulls in a kraal about to fight over me!

Uncle Thutlo intervened, his calm demeanour and playful nature, a balm to the tense situation. "Come on, people, we aren't gonna do this here in front of all these people. Our child is not well, yet here you are, threatening to fight each other. Martin, how can you dare your father in law in this manner, where's your respect?"

"Respect? Please don't make me laugh Rangwane (uncle); this

man doesn't deserve any respect. The fact that he sold his daughter to me is evidence that he is not really...."

"HEY! SHUT UP!" Uncle Thutlo howled, scaring me even. He had never raised his voice at anyone – at least not with me around. If uncle Motlatsi had been there though, I was and am still certain he would have given Martin a few blows. Him and I might not have been close but he was still family and unfortunately, he was really quick with his hands. Hearing uncle Thutlo yell in that manner though, made me notice a side to him I didn't know existed. It's always the quiet and playful ones we should always watch out for!

"Fine, I'll back off from addressing the father of the year," he ridiculed, contorting his face. My father shook his head and moved away from him, joining my mother on the left side of the bed, moaning something unclear.

"We will all discuss this later when emotions have cooled down. Palesa, you will come home with us, you will be safe. Doctor...," uncle Thutlo took charge of the situation, as Doctor Duvenhage made his way towards my bed again.

"Good evening to those I'm meeting for the first time. I'm Dr. Duvenhage and Palesa is my patient. We have been here before – not so long ago actually. I'm afraid I don't have the best news I can tell you right now. Palesa is temporarily paralyzed from the waist down.

"Oh no, please don't say that! Did you say paralyzed?" my mother wailed. My father attempted to comfort her and she shunned him, right in front of everyone.

I remained still, taking in the doctor's news. '*How did we get here? In fact, how did I get here*?' I asked myself and closed my eyes, allowing tears to fall down unabated. I wasn't weeping, but tears were falling. I was tired of everything I had been through. I needed to take charge of my own life and to take responsibility and account for my own deeds, whichever I believed they were.

Doctor Duvenhage released me late in the afternoon, citing that I'd be better off healing at home. However, he gave me a list of things I should and shouldn't do. I was also supposed to see him weekly.

As we left the hospital, I felt a mix of relief and fear. Relief that we left the hospital and that although the doctor mentioned that I was temporarily paralyzed and need to be on a wheel chair for some time, it was not like that would be a permanent thing. I would have to rekindle physiotherapy after two weeks. He had estimated that I would be slightly better and pain on my back would have ebbed, hence him suggesting that I should at least be on a wheelchair for two weeks before I could do any rigorous exercises.

Martin was the one pushing me as I sat on the wheelchair, something that felt like dé ja vu as I had been there just two months prior. "Would I ever get better or this is my life path and how I'm supposed to live?" I asked myself. He was very quiet, not saying a word.

As we reached the parking lot with everyone following us, I realised that Martin's intentions were to take me with him in his car. I couldn't say anyting but kept quiet. My mother stepped in front of the wheelchair after Martin had opened the door and prevented him from helping me to go inside his car.

"What now?" he asked, as irate as ever!

"Don't make this difficult, Martin. Palesa is coming with us. We will look well after her, I promise. She will come back after a month. You can come and see her anytime you like during her stay at our home," my mother counselled.

"Oh please! It's not my intention to be seen in those dusty streets of Mookodi Township often. What if I get hijacked?"

This invited laughter from everyone who found my husband's reservations hilarious, something that didn't sit well with me. I felt the need to protect him and I charged in. "Please stop giving my husband a hard time. If he doesn't want to come to the township, he shouldn't be forced to. So please stop laughing. His concerns are valid and all he needs is understanding and not judgment," I demanded.

"Thank you, my wife; you finally spoke for me."

"Oh, so you're the type of man that gets excited for being protected by a woman!" uncle Thutlo and my father laughed, amusing themselves at Martin's expense. This infuriated him even more.

"Get out of my way, Mama!" he practically pushed my mom

out of the way, as both my father and my uncle rushed towards him like a pack of hyenas about to devour prey they didn't even kill.

"Young man, you don't really want to try us right now, please wheel Palesa to our car right now," my father demanded.

"If I don't, what are you going to do?"

"Do you really want to do this, Martin?" uncle Thutlo butted in again.

The fight between the grown men drained me, as I now didn't know what to do because, as much as I was told that I was paralyzed from the waist down, I felt like I should push myself to get into the car. There was still some sensation in my legs. With every attempt I made though, it became evident that I was never going to achieve what I sought to, and I almost fell off the wheelchair, inviting a scold from everyone!

Finally, my husband relented, leaning down to kiss me on the forehead. "I'll find Lucas and when I do, I'll make him loathe the day he was born. I swear on my mother's grave!"

I wanted to ask him not to do that but something prevented me, warning me that it wouldn't be a wise move, as he would think that I was trying to get Lucas off the hook because he was my 'lover'. So, I kept quiet but simply mumbled, "be careful."

Eventually, Martin wheeled me towards my father's car, helping me to get inside, while everyone was just ogling him as if he was doing something uncanny.

"There…, she is yours for a few weeks. I'll send my helpers to bring her clothes tomorrow."

"That won't be necessary, Martin. Remember Palesa is on a wheelchair, so it's not like she will need to wear any of the fancy clothes. She has clothes at home."

"Who said anything about fancy clothes?" Martin asked. "I don't want her draped in those rags you call clothes. I said I'll send my helpers to the township tomorrow to bring her clothes and everything else she will need. You did say you want to look after her didn't you? So make sure that next time I see her, she is exactly like this – not fat. I don't want to see her suddenly swelled up with pimples on her face, because of whatever you'd be feeding her at your home. She no longer eats just about anything. She eats proper food!"

I could see that it took my mother every ounce of composure she had to not retaliate either in words or deeds, as both my father and my uncle shook their heads.

I finally settled in the backseat of my father's car, as my mother rounded it to occupy the front seat. My father had already opened the boot and Martin put the wheelchair and my overnight bag in, turning his back on me and going to his car. I thought he would at least give me one final look. But, he just pressed hard on his feet, as if he didn't want to share another moment with me.

Uncle Thutlo went to his sports car, then revved it silly, as if he wanted to show off. We followed him after having reversed out of the parking lot, while I noticed that Martin wasn't moving, sitting in the car.

I waved at him but he just looked towards us with a still face and faced forward again. Perhaps he was hurting? I knew though, that it would be difficult for me to live without him and I was already missing him, as I contemplated having to spend the two weeks or so without him, not knowing how my stay with my parents would be.

The thought of going home with someone who recently battered me, terrified me. However, she was my mother and I believed that she would never hurt me again, seeing as she wanted so badly to take me home with her.

Chapter 19

The Prodigal Daughter

Present

First week at my parents' place.

The air hangs thick with moisture, a gentle breeze pushes through the clouds that swallow the sun. Children are playing in the street, laughter bursting like bubbles. One visibly cheating at a game of double touch. "You cheated, Malefu, you're out!" The rest of them chorus. The name jolts my memory; I know the little girl.

Malefu springs from the porch, her laughter cascading like sunlight, confessing her mischief with a bright infectious joy, "okay, okay, guys, I'm sorry!" She continues laughing.

Her laughter slowly fades, replaced by a shadow of sadness as soon as our eyes meet. We share wide smirks.

She lifts her small arms and waves at me, as I acknowledge the greeting. I am the township sister she once adored, now distant and forgotten. Her mother, likely dismissive of Malefu's probes about me, has kept her in the dark. Her house is about three blocks away from ours and her mom and my mom were very close at some point. I wonder what tore their friendship apart. The silence about the matter lingers like a ghost.

Kedibone, sis Mahlubi's eldest daughter, used to walk with me to school daily, our bond budding until I left.

Now back in this place, I'm met with echoes of absence. I expect warmth, a welcome, but perhaps I'm asking for too much. Maybe they see me as a cautionary tale, a warning whispered to their children – stay away from the lost, from me in particular as I'm a bad influence. Perhaps they hold the opinion that I did this to myself and deserved everything I was experiencing. What I need from them is a little bit of understanding.

I probably would also not want any of my children befriending delinquent children who run away from home and end up giving themselves to older men who later abuse them in the name of love. Perhaps I deserve this treatment.

The last time I saw Malefu, she was a tiny, bright-eyed girl, a senior in preschool. Now she's eight, and a confident grade two student. Time has swept me away, leaving me in a wheelchair. I once imagined returning behind the wheels of my own, driving my own, not pushing wheels that aren't engine propelled. Instead, I'm poked by sidelong glances from children who now regard me as a recluse, and are avoiding me like an epidemic.

My thoughts are interrupted by movement I see Malefu making. She seems to hesitate at first, but her gaze is still locked on me, her small frame inching closer towards me. She reaches the closed gate, but the chain holds her back.

She moves away and speaks to me over the fence, "are you alright, Aus Palesa?"

"Malefu, o hodile ha kakang!" (Malefu, how big you've gotten!"). I choose admiration over honesty.

"Yes! I'm even taller than my brother, Thekiso. I can read and write. Do you want me to come and read for you?" Her voice spills forth, uncontainable as ever.

Her innocence tugs at my heart, a reminder of when she would cry for me, her tiny hands reaching out. Children ask the questions adults avoid, the latter choosing to create their own stories about you and spreading malicious gossip regarding things they don't know and have no idea about.

I see curiosity brewing in Malefu's eyes, but I can't bear to burden her with my truth.

"Malefu, that would be lovely for you to come and read for

me, but not today, okay. I'm not in the right frame of mind. Next time though, definitely my love."

"What does 'frame of mind' mean?" she presses, unwilling to let go.

"It means that I cannot listen well right now, because I am not quite well. My mind is not ready to absorb what you might be reading for me." Her brow furrows, searching for clarity.

"Did you fall, aus Palesa, is that why you are in a wheelchair? You must be careful next time, so you don't fall again. Are there any broken bones?" Her innocence is a knife, cutting through my defences.

She seems convinced that I must have fallen. To try and give her the true account of what happened would be a travesty, and too much for this tiny heart to take. Besides, the information is too much for even adults to take, so I cannot subject this tiny soul through my brutal truth.

"Don't worry, Malefu, I will be fine soon. You can come and read for me when I'm better."

"Okay! I'll come to read for you tomorrow!" she insists, oblivious of my hesitance.

I don't have the guts to tell the little girl that I am not really ready to mingle with anyone, let alone small children who are not happy to see me on a wheelchair, doing absolutely nothing but allowing the sun to infuse vitamin D on me, and then go back into the house when I'm certain that I have received enough sunshine for the day.

Malefu rejoins her friends, their laughter a chorus of curiosity, their eyes on her as she shares our exchange. All I can hear when Malefu ultimately raises her voice is: “She said I should come and read for her tomorrow after school.”

My my, Malefu, I never said that to you! I remark inwardly. I guess in a small child’s mind, if something cannot or is not done today, it means it can or should be done the following day. I chuckle softly, turning away to escape the scrutiny, seeking solace within the walls of my home.

Inside the house, the aroma of my mother’s famous mutton stew envelops me. Her kitchen, once a sanctuary, now feels like a refuge. Going back in thoughts, it dawns on me that she has always been the backbone of our family, baking, cooking, and delivering food with unwavering dedication. She now has two assistants and one driver who is responsible for deliveries. For once, I see a different side of her - no judgment, just acceptance, in spite of our most recent troubles. I am grateful, but cautious, not wanting to upset her delicate balance.

My father’s lukewarm demeanour has me wondering what’s brewing. His questions about my condition and recovery, feel more like accusations than genuine concern. Although he asked for forgiveness a couple of months ago, our relationship has still not been restored.

The weight of his words hangs heavily on my shoulders,

insinuating that I'm a burden to my mother. His demands for attention, coupled with his criticism of her business and how she operates it, create a toxic atmosphere – again! Not even once have I heard him encourage my mom to rest, even though he can see that she is overwhelmed. His business seems to have taken a nosedive and he's very impossible to be around.

Tension is palpable, and I fear an explosion is imminent. The more things change, the more they stay the same. The memory of the R250 000 he took from Martin still remain, a painful reminder of his and his brothers' actions. What did he do with the money?

****

Another day dawns, bringing along its own set of challenges. I'm scheduled for a checkup today but my body has other plans. I have been vomitting since yesterday and I'm weak and disoriented.

My mother, assisted by Sis Refilwe are helping me get ready, their hands moving with gentle precision. The process is very slow, each move triggering a wave of nausea, while the bucket they gave me remains on my lap.

"Let's hurry, Palesa," my mother urges, concern fused with tetchiness etched on her face.

"What if it's the medication? I don't like so many tablets taken by one person. Hopefully, the doctor can help provide clarity," sis Refilwe chimes in. "Will you be able to eat, Palesa, so that you can take tablets?"

"Aus Fifi, you have just said you think it might be the medication that's causing me to vomit, but you want me to take them still!" she laughs, and my mother shakes her head, her sudden silence, too loud for me to comprehend.

"Someone is getting better, I see," Sis Refilwe assumes.

"I will not be able to eat, aus Fifi. I won't take tablets either. But we can take them with us. Perhaps the doctor might want to change them," I deduce.

"That's fine; you seem better than earlier. We'll get through this," she assures. "Please don't vomit again; I need to clean this bucket as we're taking it with us."

EPILOGUE

We arrive at the hospital, where Doctor Duvenhage awaits, no doubt. The parking attendants swarm around as usual, eager to earn their keep.

One familiar face catches my eye – a man who seems to know more about my life than I'd like. He utters a snide remark, "Siza (sis), you are never gonna get better if you keep using this wheelchair," he says with a grin. "You must tell yourself you are not an invalid and you will not be in a wheelchair anymore. Our tongues and minds are very powerful." His words sting.

The wisdom that is uttered by this guy! He clearly has very strong convictions, something that seems to escape me each time I see him. Why is he 'working' as a parking attendant?

I challenge him, "you don't know what's wrong with me. Why assume this injury is not permanent?" I ask.

"I can see it's not permanent." He leans in, his voice barely above a whisper, "you must not surrender to your boyfriend's beatings. Next time, he will cripple you for real, and you will not be able to walk ever again, believe me."

Now, I am incensed by his utterances. Martin didn't beat me up – this time. I was dragged down the stairs by Lucas. Why does he assume that Martin did this to me? I decide to ask him frankly.

"What are you talking about exactly?" He continues to whisper in my ear, way too close for comfort, after my probe, amply conscious that my mother and sis Refilwe are aware of the tittle-tattle. The bucket is already on my lap, as this guy takes it upon himself to wheel me away from the parking lot.

"Siza, wa bona… (sis, you see …), I see a lot of things here. I have been working here for a while. Your boyfriend or is he your husband now?"

"He's now my husband," I reply.

"Okay. I can see that you come to this hospital often. Trust me, I have seen this movie with him and one other woman before. He's a bully. He once had a fight with Doctor Lucas, right here in the parking lot. I had to separate them. Had I not done that, he would have killed Dr. Lucas I tell you!"

My eyes widen in shock as he continues, "yeah, all I heard was '*stay away from my wife, otherwise I will kill you*'. So I take it they were fighting over you, right? Siza, are you having an affair with Dr. Lucas? Is that why your husband beat you up? This Lucas character is also not a good person; I remember his wife had an affair with your husband and when…" I cannot believe my ears. I never would have thought this guy knows so much about our lives. He is now singing like an overfed canary!

My mother and sis Refilwe interrupt us. "We'll take it from here, thank you," my mother says, visibly wound up.

"Sure, dimamzo (sure ma'am)."

"I heard what that boy said. Are you having an affair, Palesa?" my mother turns to me.

I shake my head. "No, mama, I'm not having an affair. That guy is talking rubbish!"

"Then why does he seem to know so much about your life? I don't recall hearing you refute any of these allegations."

I shrug, feeling frustrated. "Mama, I'm not responsible for what's in his mind. Can we please hurry, because I'm beginning to feel sick again."

Just then, I vomit again and the nurses rush to our side. "What's wrong?" they ask, concern planted on their faces.

My mother explains, "She has been vomitting since morning. We have an appointment with Dr. Duvenhage, for my her back," my mother responds.

The nurses quickly take charge, wheeling me towards the doctor's suite.

We arrive at the doctor's rooms swiftly, just as Doctor Duvehange places the last file on the reception desk, as his assistant looks on, wondering what the commotion is all about. He greets us, his eyes broadened in uneasiness. "Palesa, what happened? You don't look so good."

Both nurses leave me at reception, as my mother thank them for their kindness. Doctor Duvenhage's nurse takes over, helping me to the lavatory. My mother and sis Refilwe wait anxiously at the waiting area.

"Palesa, can you move at all? Your feet I mean?"

"Yes, I can move a bit, so it turns out Doctor Duvenhage was right about me not being really paralyzed. I just didn't know why he put it like that."

"Yeah, sometimes doctors are like that – they don't want to give patients false hope. They'd rather under promise but over deliver. You know what I mean?"

"Yes, I do."

She leaves me for a minute or two and returns with a plastic cup, asking me to provide a urine sample. "Palesa, you're gonna have to move the way you usually move at home. Do you mind if I call your mother for help?"

"No, I don't mind." She quickly calls my mother, who comes quickly, eyes wide.

My mother helps, and after much struggle, I finally manage to give the nurse my urine sample. The doctor calls us to his room and we all wait in suspense, as he begins throwing a barrage of questions my way.

"Palesa, why are you vomitting? Did you eat something you normally don't eat perhaps?"

"No, doctor, I haven't.

“Okay, how is your back feeling?”

“It’s a bit stiff today, so I don’t know if it’s because I have tensed due to vomitting or not. “

“Let’s wait for the nurse to give me the results of the sample. We’ll start from there, and then we can know what we’re working on. I will then examine your back afterwards.”

Not a moment too soon because after her name being mentioned, the nurse comes in, looking spooked. She hands the doctor my file as well as the strip she used to test my urine sample.

Doctor Duvenhage takes my file, reads through it and examines the test, while his brow furrows. He then looks at me, his expression grave. “Palesa, the sooner we get you out of this chair, the better,” he says, his voice laced with urgency. You are gonna find the next phase of your life challenging if we don’t get you out of this chair soon.”

At this stage, my heart races; I’m frightened and I don’t know what the doctor is about to tell me.

“What do you mean, doctor?” I ask, and my mother’s eyes widen. Doctor Duvehage’s words hang in the air like a challenge.

“Ma’am, this initial test proves that Palesa is pregnant.”

“WHAT?” I gasp, feeling like my world has been turned upside down.

THE END

\\\\\\\\\\\\\\\\\\\\

About The Author

Pertunia Lehoka is a visionary author, a Relationship Coach, an Inspirational Speaker, as well as an Adult Educator. She fearlessly explores the human experience, illuminating the intricate web of love, spirituality, and personal growth.

Pertunia empowers individuals to navigate the complexities of soul ties, strongholds, and generational curses, unlocking the secrets to profound connections and inner freedom.

Through her inspirational speaking engagements, Pertunia masterfully weaves scenarios and personal stories into powerful narratives that resonate with audiences from all walks of life.

A prolific author, Pertunia's works span articles, fiction and non-fiction books, with novels that invite readers to step into the shoes of relatable characters and non-fiction books that offer insightful guidance on spiritual growth and personal transformation.

With a presence that is both compassionate and compelling, Pertunia is a leading voice in the realms of spiritual exploration, personal growth and relationships.

Being a devotee of spoken and written words, Pertunia is always writing something, irrespective of whether she would be dealing with business or the business of writing.

****

Wings of Defiance

In the depths of captivity, a bird's spirit remained unbroken, its voice a whispered defiance. The keeper, once a master of its fate, had grown complacent, forgetting the wings that yearned to soar. But the bird remembered, its heart beating with a fire that refused to be tamed.

As it sang a new melody, one that echoed through the silence, the keeper's grip began to loosen. The bird's beak, once a tool of submission, became an instrument of liberation. With every careful movemmbent, it learnt, it grew and it planned.

The day of reckoning arrived, and the bird's wings unfolded like a banner of freedom. It rose – a phoenix from the ashes, its eyes ablaze and could not be contained. The keeper's gaze faltered, unwared of the power that had been brewing in the shadows.

The bird took flight, its wings beating strong and sure, carrying it higher and higher until it vanished into the horizon. And when it finally found its flock, they welcomed it with open wings, hailing it as a sage, a keeper of secrets, a whisperer of truths.

For in captivity, the bird had learnt the language of its captors, and now it spoke with a voice that would not be silenced. Its story would be told and retold, a testament to the power of resiliene, a reminder that even in obscurity, freedom can be found.

www.ingramcontent.com/pod-product-compliance
Lightning Source LLC
Chambersburg PA
CBHW020244030726
47499CB00001B/48

* 9 7 8 0 6 2 0 9 2 6 3 7 9 *